Her Unforgettable Laugh

A Pride and Prejudice Variation

The first book in the
Her Unforgettable Laugh Series

Linda Thompson

Her Unforgettable Laugh - A Pride and Prejudice Variation
Series: Her Unforgettable Laugh Book I
First Edition

Copyright © 2015 Linda Thompson
All Rights Reserved

This is a work of fiction. Names, characters, businesses, places, events and incidents are either the products of the author's imagination or used in a fictitious manner. Any resemblance to actual persons, living or dead, or actual events is purely coincidental.

For information, please contact:
1700 Lynhurst Lane
Denton, TX 76205

Cover Design and Graphic Flourishes: Lori Whitlock, MiStudio.com

ISBN-13: 978-1511996952
ISBN-10: 1511996951

DEDICATIONS

To Miss Jane Austen for creating the amazing characters, we can neither forget nor can we get enough of them.

To Bonnie Wood Mabe who shared my love of reading and for encouraging me to try writing the stories my reading inspired.

To Elizabeth Ann West for encouraging me to take the story I felt compelled to write and to share it with others that love Jane Austen Fan Fiction. She was a friend, teacher, and constant support during the process from early in my writing to published products.

ACKNOWLEDGMENTS

Many thanks to my betas, Ruth Morrel, and Kimberley Kay, for their outstanding work, thoughtful suggestions, and support.

Thanks to the ladies of the Denton 2nd Ward Relief Society Breakfast Club for acting as a sounding board.

Special thanks go to my final editor, my dear friend and book enthusiast, Julieanne Spoor.

Many thanks to my amazingly talented sister-in-law, Lori Whitlock, for her beautiful cover design and the graphic flourishes.

Lastly, thanks to the members of Author's Hub for their patience and support as I learned about the process of becoming a published author. They freely offered help as I asked questions about the process of becoming a published author or searched for bits of obscure information to make my story as authentic as possible.

Loving thanks to my family—Jim, Andrew, Megan, and Katie—for their patience and indulgence as I embarked upon this project. They stepped up to do what was needed when I became lost in my writing. They also listened patiently when I endlessly rambled about the thoughts in my head waiting their turn to be written. A special thank you to my daughter, Megan, for all the extra help she gave me.

Her laugh, like a bolt of lightning, struck my soul. It was a song of happiness and love that bubbled around me. It encompassed me in a joy and peace unknown. It was home, and I wished to pass the remainder of my days in its sweet embrace.

PROLOGUE

FITZWILLIAM DARCY OFFERED up a silent prayer of thanks for the lovely, late-spring morning as he watched his younger sister, Georgiana, and Nanny Marie set off down the street toward Hyde Park. Darcy knew Georgiana was old enough to need a governess now, but he did not feel this would be the best time to replace her. Nanny Marie had been with his sister since her birth. Georgiana was so heartbroken since their father's death that Darcy did not think she could withstand another loss. Finally, they turned in at the park entrance. Now that Georgiana was safely away, he returned to his study to prepare for his meeting with George Wickham.

It had only been a few weeks since his father's funeral and burial at Pemberley, and Darcy missed him very much. Even though he had observed his father's illness, his sudden passing had been a shock. His father was a generous master and devoted father. He had enjoyed all the time they spent together. He had been well-trained by his father to handle his duties as the Master of Pemberley. However, actually being responsible for the large estate and those who depended upon it was overwhelming Darcy at present. Additionally, he became the guardian of his eleven-year-old sister, though he shared the guardianship with his cousin, Colonel Fitzwilliam.

Darcy would have much preferred to seclude himself at Pemberley, but business necessitated a trip to town for a few weeks. Not wishing to leave Georgiana behind to wallow in her sadness, he brought her to London with him, as he was sure being together would be the best thing for both of them. Wanting Georgiana in London with him did not mean that he wished her to be exposed to George Wickham ever again.

It was difficult to think about the man that had been his childhood friend. George Wickham, the son of Pemberley's former steward, was a year older than Darcy. Mr. Wickham had been an excellent steward and a very good man. Upon Mr. Wickham's unexpected death, Darcy's father, who was George Wickham's godfather, watched over the young man. He also paid for his education at Cambridge sending the young Wickham up to school together with Darcy. To Darcy's father, George Wickham showed a charming smile and pleasant manners, always earning him Mr. Darcy's approbation. Unfortunately the true Wickham, the one Darcy saw at school, was nothing like that. Darcy was disgusted with Wickham's behavior, but he never had the heart to disillusion his father. So he never shared with him Wickham's exploits with women, drinking, gambling, and cheating.

Darcy was brought from his memories a short time later when Treywick, the Darcy House butler, announced the unwelcome visitor.

Sauntered into Darcy's study, Wickham smirked as he greeted Darcy with, "Good morning, Fitz." He knew that the name irritated Darcy and hoped to discompose him.

Darcy had his inscrutable mask firmly in place and ignored Wickham's attempt to irritate him. "I have agreed to this meeting, Wickham, so what is it you want?"

"Really, Fitz, such an inhospitable welcome for your childhood friend. Obviously the Darcy name is already losing consequence under its new master," Wickham taunted.

"If you have a purpose, please state it, as I have other business to which I must attend." Darcy seethed at the insult, but kept his temper in check. He focused on the fact that his father's death meant this would no longer have to deal with Wickham.

"I would have thought my reason obvious even to a dullard like you, Fitz. I came for my inheritance from my dear godfather," Wickham said with a smug smile.

Darcy wished there was no inheritance for the miscreant standing before him—he certainly deserved nothing more than he had already received. However, because Darcy had always protected his father from Wickham's true nature, he was left a gift in Mr. Darcy's will. Darcy almost laughed at the irony of his father's choice and looked forward to Wickham's reaction. "I will not keep you in suspense. My father left you one thousand pounds and the living at Kympton, once you take orders and the living becomes available."

"One thousand pounds and a living!" Wickham was clearly expecting a much greater prize. He started to pace, unable to hide his disbelief. His godfather had always treated him like a son, and Wickham expected to inherit Pemberley since he was older than Darcy. Wickham was in desperate need of funds. He would have and to leave his rightful claim to Pemberley until another day. Pulling himself together, he attempted to work on his old playmate.

"Darcy I think that we both know I am neither inclined nor suited for the church. I do, however, think I might be well suited for the law. Unfortunately, the interest on a one thousand pound legacy will be insufficient to support my endeavors in that area. I am sure you will agree that it is not unreasonable for me to expect to be paid the value of the living instead. I am sure the living must have been a very valuable one for my *dear godfather* to leave it to me. I imagine ten thousand pounds should be adequate to compensate me for giving up the living."

"I see your opinion of yourself is still highly over inflated. The living is worth no more than three thousand pounds."

"I am sure my *dear* godfather valued it more highly, at least seven thousand pounds," wheedled Wickham.

"The living is worth three thousand at best plus there is the original thousand pound bequest," Darcy stated calmly. "I am prepared to write you a draft for the total of four thousand pounds immediately with just one small condition. You must sign away all rights to the living in this statement that says you have been fairly compensated for it," he continued evenly. Darcy knew that Wickham would never accept the living, so he had prepared this contingency in order to end his dealings with Wickham forever.

Desperately needing the funds and knowing that he would not get more from Darcy today, Wickham grudgingly signed the statement and put his hand out for the draft. "If would advise you not to attempt to alter the draft, Wickham. I have already notified the bank of the amount as I had anticipated your reaction," said Darcy with satisfaction.

Wickham would bide his time and find a new angle, but he would get from Darcy what he rightfully deserved—no matter how long it took. Darcy handed him the draft and rang for the butler. "Wickham, I have no desire to ever see you again as all business between us is at an end. You are not welcome at any of my homes." Treywick entered at that moment, and Darcy requested his visitor be shown out. Fuming, Wickham followed the old butler to the door, which was quickly and firmly closed behind him, almost knocking him down the steps in the process.

Wickham turned and looked at the door all the time muttering to himself. "This is far from over Darcy. I am owed more, and I will get it before I am through with you."

Across town in one of the largest homes on Gracechurch Street in Cheapside, a carriage pulled to a stop at the door of No. Sixteen. The front door opened quickly, and an elegant lady watched as the attendant let down the steps, opened the door, and handed out two young ladies. The older one, Jane, was tall and stately with a serene countenance. Her blond hair shimmered in the sunshine, and her blue eyes were the color of a bright summer sky. The other one, Elizabeth, was in comparison quite petite. Her hair was dark chestnut, but the sun brought forth the sparkle of copper and gold. Her dark brown eyes were wide, and the twinkle in them was unmistakable. Whereas Jane's figure was willowy, Elizabeth's was surprisingly womanly for one so young. They quickly proceeded up the front steps to the door, where the fashionably dressed woman in her mid-thirties waited.

"Jane, Elizabeth," she cried. "I am so glad that you have arrived. Come in girls. I cannot wait to hear all the news from Longbourn."

As their aunt, Madeline Gardiner, led the girls into the parlor, servants retrieved their trunks from the carriage and carried them up to the rooms assigned to the visitors. The ladies were quickly settled and refreshments served, before their aunt began her questions. "Well, how was everyone at home when you left?"

"Things at Longbourn never change, Aunt, you know that," said Elizabeth with a smile. "Mama flutters about complaining of her nerves. Mary continues to quote Dr. Fordyce, who seems to have a sermon for every situation. Kitty and Lydia, argue, flirt, and giggle unendingly, and Papa hides from it all in his library. Nothing exciting ever happens there. I do hope that we will do something exciting while we are visiting you in town," Elizabeth ended with a sigh and a soft laugh.

Jane looked smilingly at her younger sister while shaking her head slightly. She knew she should remonstrate with her for the unkind words she had spoken, but she also knew it would do no good. Elizabeth always said what she thought.

"Well, we do have an outing or two planned for your visit. What would you think of a visit to Hyde Park and a concert?" asked Mrs. Gardiner. "However, I thought perhaps we could do a little shopping first to get you each a new gown or two."

"That sounds quite pleasant and very thoughtful of you Aunt," said Jane.

"Oh, I have always wanted to see Hyde Park!" Lizzy exclaimed, "and a concert, too! This will be the best visit yet!"

Since leaving the disappointing meeting with Darcy, Wickham had been holed up in a seedy inn by day drinking too much and scheming. By

night, he had frequented the gaming establishments trying to turn his pitiful four thousand into the kind of income he believed to be his due. Unfortunately for Wickham, Lady Luck had been against him in this endeavor. It had only been a couple of weeks, and he had gambled away almost half of his inheritance. He determined to visit Darcy again on the morrow to renegotiate.

Upon Wickham's unannounced arrival at Darcy House, he noticed Georgiana and her nanny coming down the stairs. He attempted to speak with her, but Darcy, who was standing in the door watching their departure, called out, "Nanny Marie, please continue on your way."

She understood, by the tone of her master's voice, that he did not wish this man to talk to her young charge. Nanny Marie tightened her grip on Georgiana's hand, and they moved around Wickham and continued on their way. Wickham sauntered up to the front door, only to be met by Darcy's cold glare and large frame blocking Wickham's entrance. "I say, Fitz, your manners do not seem to have improved since last we met. I only wished to renew my acquaintance with the sweet Georgiana."

"Wickham, when last we spoke, I told you I never wanted to see you again and that you were no longer welcome in my homes. Why have you returned?" Darcy asked coldly.

"Well," said Wickham with more confidence than he felt, "I believe that you cheated me on the value of the living. I have come to get the rest of what is due me."

"Are you forgetting, Wickham, you signed a form stating you received the full value and had no other claim on the bequest or this family?"

"You are just jealous that your father liked me better! I know you are cheating me regarding my inheritance. I demand what I am due!"

"You have received what you are due—more than you deserve in my opinion. Be grateful that I never told my father about the real George Wickham, or you would not have gotten that much," stated Darcy quietly.

"You owe me, Darcy, and I want it now!" Wickham grated through his teeth. In spite of his anger, he tried to maintain his demeanor. A confrontation on the steps of Darcy House would damage the gentlemanly image he was constantly trying to cultivate and maintain.

In answer to Wickham's demand, Darcy turned his back to him. He noticed that only Treywick remained in the foyer, and his stiff posture relaxed slightly. The butler and his wife, the Darcy House housekeeper, affectionately known as Mrs. Trey, had been with the Darcy family since before Darcy's birth. He knew he could trust Treywick with any information about the family and was grateful he had dismissed the other footmen usually on duty in the foyer. "Treywick," Darcy said quietly, "please ensure that all the footmen are aware of the fact that entrance is to be denied to Mr. Wickham should he ever again show his face." With that, Darcy turned and walked away towards his study.

"Certainly, sir," the butler replied with just the smallest trace of a smile. Treywick moved to close the door and saw the intense anger in Wickham's eyes. Before it had completely closed, he heard Wickham muttering about getting even with Darcy. Treywick returned to his duties thinking of what he had heard from Wickham. A quarter hour passed, before a startling thought occurred to him. Moving quickly towards the master's study, he knocked and waited. At Darcy's call, he entered the study and stopped in front of Mr. Darcy's desk.

"Sir, as Mr. Wickham was moving away from the door, he said something about getting even. I have no doubt you can take care of yourself, sir, but I recalled that he saw Miss Georgiana heading to the park."

Darcy, a look of alarm overtaking his face, started for the study door calling over his shoulder, "Thank you for the warning, Treywick." He rushed for his outerwear and headed for the park at a quick pace.

Wickham stormed away from the door, determined to find a way to hurt Darcy and extract more money from him. As he hurried back along the sidewalk in the same direction that Georgiana had taken, an idea formed in his mind. Wickham was devious, but often acted immediately on his thoughts not taking the time to plan as he should. He turned into the park thinking to grab Georgiana from her nanny and hold her for ransom. He knew many places he could hide, and perhaps if the ransom were large enough, he would leave the country to be completely out of Darcy's reach. Wickham continued down the path looking everywhere for a glimpse of Georgiana. He was pleased so see that the park was quite deserted at this time of the day. Hopefully this would allow him to get away unnoticed and quickly. Eventually, he saw his prey a short way up the path. The only others he noticed anywhere nearby was three ladies walking toward him but still a good distance away.

The three ladies had almost completed their circuit of the park and were returning to the entrance where their carriage was to meet them. Elizabeth was slightly ahead of her aunt and Jane. She had been enjoying the beauty of the park and the late spring morning immensely. She looked about, not wanting to miss of the glories of the park. Suddenly, she noticed a man sneaking up behind an elderly lady and a young girl. Elizabeth might not have noticed him, but for the angry, determined look on his face.

Suddenly, he reached out and shoved the elderly lady forcefully causing her to stumble and fall forward on to the hard gravel path. She nearly took the young girl with her, as she had a grip on her hand. However, the man grabbed at the girl's other arm and, with one strong yank, pulled her from the nanny's grip. He pulled her up into his arms, clapping a hand over her mouth. The frightened look on the young girl's face tugged at Elizabeth's heart. Taking a quick look around, Wickham still saw only the three ladies in the distance, so he took off the opposite way towards the park entrance. The girl struggled briefly but quickly quieted as Elizabeth saw him whisper something in her ear. However, as she looked back towards the woman lying still on the ground, Elizabeth could see the pitiful look of worry and fear on the young girl's face.

Elizabeth gave little thought to where she was as she called to Jane and her aunt to look after the elderly woman. Then she took off running after the young girl. Startled at Elizabeth's call, but unable to make out her words, her aunt looked up in time to see her run off down the path.

Mrs. Gardiner and Jane then noticed the elderly woman on the ground and stopped to assist her in rising. Jane remained with the woman retrieving her handkerchief to help clean the blood from her face, which had been cut during her fall by a stone on the path.

"Are you all right?" Jane asked.

"Oh, my dear girl! He took away my dear girl," the woman sobbed.

Commanding Jane to stay with the lady, Mrs. Gardiner hastened her pace continuing down the path after Elizabeth. She only hoped that she could reach her before she got into any trouble. Mrs. Gardiner had failed to see the man with the girl in his arms. She could not understand what

Elizabeth was doing running in such an unladylike fashion through the park.

As Elizabeth neared the entrance to the park, she saw the man attempting to enter a hackney carriage with the young girl still in his arms. Elizabeth ran straight up to him and began pulling on his arm so the girl could get away. She also began calling to the hackney driver for help.

Coming up the sidewalk, was Darcy. Nearing the park entrance, Darcy heard the cries for help and hurried his pace to see if he could be of assistance. At the noise the young woman was making, Wickham turned to push her away, delivering her a stinging slap to the face. Elizabeth's hand flew to her face briefly before she reached to delay the man once again. As he turned from striking the unknown person, Wickham noticed Darcy hurrying up the sidewalk. The hackney driver, not want to be involved in whatever trouble was occurring, began slowly moving away from the curb. Knowing he was defeated, Wickham tossed Georgiana at Elizabeth sending both girls to the ground and ran for the hackney. He managed to pull himself inside and close the door as it joined the other traffic on the busy thoroughfare.

Elizabeth quickly sat up and pulled the younger girl into her arms crooning soft words to her as she rubbed small circles on her back. Seeing that Georgiana was being comforted, Darcy was torn between following Wickham and going to his sister. He quickly decided that Georgiana must be his priority, but stared at the coach, horse, and driver looking for some identifying markings to help find it later. Arriving at the spot where the girls were, he reached down his hands to help both girls to their feet. The hand tugging at hers frightened Georgiana further until she realized it belonged to Darcy. Crying almost hysterically, Georgiana threw herself into her brother's arms. "You are safe now," he crooned, patting her back and murmuring softly just as the other young girl had done.

As he continued to calm and comfort Georgiana, he heard a voice call out. "Lizzy, what were you thinking behaving so wildly in the park?" When she managed to calm somewhat, he tried to find out what had happened. Unfortunately, Georgiana was still too shocked for coherent speech. He turned intending to ask the young woman what had happened, only to see her being herded in the opposite direction. Darcy then heard Nanny Marie call out to Georgiana, and she reached to take her from Darcy's embrace. Once Georgiana was safe in Nanny's arms, Darcy turned intending to thank the young lady who had come to his sister's aid. He could now see three ladies, a slight way off, entering a carriage. There were an older lady and two younger ones. He noted the blonde hair on one but thought he remembered tumbled dark curls when he had assisted the girls up from the ground. He noticed the young lady currently entering the carriage. Her long hair was in disarray, most of it having come loose from its pins, and curls cascaded down her back to her waist. He turned to make his way to the carriage only to be halted in his tracks by a melodic laugh. Then a sweet voice said, "But I had to run, Aunt

Madeline, it was the only way to help the little girl." By the time he recovered from the shock of the laugh that had struck straight to his heart, he looked up in time to see the carriage moving away from the curb. Too late to offer his thanks, he quickly shepherded his companions back to Darcy House.

Upon entering, he began issuing orders to his staff, calling for Mrs. Trey and her medicine bags, requested that someone be sent for the doctor and another for the Bow Street Runners. While awaiting the arrival of the runners, he quickly penned a note to his cousin, Richard Fitzwilliam. Darcy gave him the details of the event and requested that he keep an eye out for Wickham.

As he sat in his study later that afternoon, Darcy was still fighting the rage coursing through him at Wickham's infamy. He looked up at a knock on his door and called, "Enter." The door opened to admit his cousin, Richard, who was a colonel in the regulars. Richard wasted no time on pleasantries demanding a more detailed explanation of the events of the morning. He listened carefully only interrupting with questions to clarify a point to his satisfaction. By the end of the explanation, Richard's face and fury matched that of his cousin.

"What is being done to find the scoundrel?" Richard growled.

"I sent for the Bow Street Runners immediately after returning home with Georgie.

While awaiting their arrival, I had to help Nanny Marie to calm her. She was beside herself with fright. If I ever get my hands on Wickham, I will . . . " Darcy trailed off too angry to think of a just punishment.

"Not if I get my hands on him first," Richard grumbled. "There will not be anything left for you to worry over if that happens." The men shared a look across Darcy's desk each face equally grim. "Is Georgie recovered from the experience or do you think she needs a visit from her charming cousin?" Richard asked, concerned.

"The way she behaved when I first brought her home, I am not sure she will recover. She was . . . " Darcy was at a loss for words.

"I will go visit her and see if I cannot find a way to cheer her up a bit."

Darcy was at his wits' end. As the days had passed since her attempted kidnapping, Georgiana continued to be frightened and tremulous. She jumped at loud noises and ran to her room if a knock at the door was heard. In an effort to distract Georgiana from her continuing fears, Darcy asked over breakfast one morning, "Dear One, how would you like to attend a concert tomorrow? I believe they will be performing the works by Mozart, and I know you greatly enjoy his music."

"Would it be safe?" she questioned quietly.

"Certainly it would, but we could ask Richard to join us. Would that be pleasant?" Knowing she would be with both her guardians and thereby safe, Georgiana agreed.

As they settled into their box for the performance, Darcy gazed out at the crowds, and Richard entertained Georgiana with a story of his young troops. A melodious laugh caught his ear, and he noticed a lovely young woman with dark curls in a deep rose gown. She was taking in her surroundings with an enormous smile upon her pretty face. Darcy was startled to see anyone displaying so much emotion. None of the young ladies he met in the ton ever showed any emotion. As he watched her, she glanced up towards his box. Their eyes met for a moment, and Darcy felt a jolt as he took in her smile and the sparkle in her dark eyes. Richard had finished his story, and Georgiana began to look around the crowded theater as well.

She noticed that a young lady with dark, curly hair was looking up at their box. When she caught Georgiana's eye, she smiled and nodded. Georgiana was startled at first, but then recognized her as the young lady who had helped her in the park. Excitedly she turned to her brother. "Look, brother, there is the family that helped Nanny Marie and me in the park a few days ago!"

Darcy turned in the direction Georgiana was discreetly indicating and noticed she was referring to the young woman he had observed earlier. As he looked, he recognized the other two ladies from the park in company with a gentleman. He could only see the dark-haired young lady in profile and noticed the lovely color in her cheeks. He heard her musical laugh ring out again, and Darcy thought it was the most delightful, joyous sound he had ever heard. She turned back towards the Darcy box, and he caught another glimpse of her beautiful dark eyes sparkling with merriment for the briefest moment before the lights dimmed and the performance began. When the lights came back up at intermission, Darcy glanced toward the young woman again and saw her party moving towards the lobby. He quickly suggested they make their way out of the box to see if they could find the ladies to thank them for their assistance.

As they stood to leave the box, Charles Bingley was practically dragged through the door by his sister, Caroline. As much as Darcy preferred to avoid Miss Bingley, they could not leave their box while visitors were with them. Darcy tried to steer the conversation to a close several times so that they might exit, but Miss Bingley would not be deterred. She hoped if they stayed long enough they would be invited to join the Darcys in their box. Caroline was determined to win Mr. Darcy's attention and his name, and being seen in his box would make her the envy of all the other young ladies of the ton. Unfortunately for Caroline no invitation was extended, and they returned to their box just as the lights were again dimmed. Darcy leaned over and quietly whispered to the disappointed Georgiana that they would leave their box a little early in hopes of meeting them before departing.

Unfortunately for the Darcy party, they were again held up upon exiting their box. Elizabeth had glanced towards the box one last time as they stood to depart. The box was empty, and she felt unaccountably disappointed. She had noticed the handsome man with the dark curls and the telling eyes as he watched his young sister with concern. She hoped the young lady would be well and wondered if she would ever see him again. Darcy looked up quickly, as he again heard the musical laugh but caught only a glimpse of the young lady and her party as they exited the theater.

Upon returning home that evening, Darcy found a report from Bow Street had been delivered in his absence. The report indicated that the Runners had found the carriage in which Wickham escaped. The driver told him where Wickham was dropped off but also said that he crossed the street and got into another hackney. The driver could not provide them with any information about the second coach, so they were at a dead end. They had searched all of the public houses and shops in the vicinity where he disembarked, but there was no trace of Wickham.

Darcy mounted the stairs with a heavy feeling in his heart and an intense anger at Wickham. His valet, Chalmers, readied him for bed and poured him a brandy. Darcy settled into the wingback chair before the fire in his room. His ruminations over Georgiana's attempted kidnapping eventually lead his thoughts away from his anger with Wickham to wonder at the courageous young lady who had risked her safety to help his sister. Eventually, Darcy moved to his desk noting in his journal the disappointment he felt at being unable to meet and thank the young lady with the dancing, dark curls, sparkling eyes, and musical laugh.

CHAPTER 1

FIVE YEARS LATER

DARCY SAT BACK into the deep cushions of his carriage seat put his feet up on the opposite seat and heaved a sigh. Over the intervening years, Wickham had made Darcy's life uncomfortable on several occasions. He had spread a false tale about the bequest of the living, making himself the victim of Darcy's actions. He had used Darcy's name with several young ladies he had ruined, and Darcy had been left to clean up Wickham's messes and appease irate fathers. He had also opened charge accounts using Darcy's name, running up charges for the wardrobe and other niceties he felt his due and had the bills sent to Darcy when he left without paying them. Since Darcy had to protect his family name, he was forced to pay these bills, as well.

Then the events of the summer overwhelmed him. He had sent Georgiana to Ramsgate on a holiday after having taken her out of school. She had done well in her studies but was still quite timid. As he reflected upon that timidity, his rage at Wickham grew. Georgiana had always been a loving and happy child with a bright demeanor. However, after the first kidnapping attempt she had become timid and fearful around large groups of strangers—particularly gentlemen. She would only walk in the park when accompanied by her brother or cousin. He hoped the change of scene and new companion would help to bring her out of herself.

Wickham's situation must have been truly desperate for him to attempt another kidnapping of Georgiana. The guilt Darcy felt upon finding that her companion, Mrs. Younge, had been Wickham's accomplice, tore at his conscience. He had arrived at Ramsgate late in the evening to spend a few days with Georgiana. He had hoped surprise his sister by arriving in time to join her for dinner. Unfortunately, he had encountered a delay at the last minute. As his carriage rolled to a stop, he noticed the dilapidated carriage already parked in front of the door. The door was unlocked, and instinct told him caution was necessary. He removed one of the pistols he kept in the carriage and checked to be sure it was loaded properly. He told the two large footmen, Fields and Chaney, who accompanied him to follow him inside. He opened the door slowly noting only one lamp lit in the small parlor on the right. He glanced quickly around and moved forward cautiously. As he reached the foot of the stairs he saw Wickham carrying what appeared to be an unconscious Georgiana down the stairs. Mrs. Younge followed with a pair of valises. Darcy was exultant at the thought that George was trapped, but unprepared for Wickham to toss Georgiana down the stairs at him. Wickham turned and ran back up, knocking Mrs. Younge to the side and sending a valise bouncing down the stairs. He disappeared down a hallway, and Darcy heard a window break. Quickly passing Georgiana to one of the footmen, Darcy and the other footman raced up the stairs, pushing Mrs. Younge out of the way. Darcy ordered the footman to hold her until he returned and continued to follow Wickham's path. At the end of the hallway, he saw the broken window. Glancing out he noticed the roof of the back porch just below the window. Of Wickham, there was no sign. The alley gave way to one of the main thoroughfares of the town and people were milling about everywhere Darcy looked. He doubted he would be able to discover Wickham.

Pulling his head back in the window, he returned to check on Georgiana. The footman had laid her upon the sofa in the small parlor and placed Mrs. Younge in a nearby chair with a footman on either side. In spite of all that had happened Georgiana was still sleeping deeply. It dawned on him that she may have been drugged. He spun to look at Mrs. Younge his face not masking his concern. She saw his concern for his sister. Perhaps, she could help a little, and he would go easy on her. "What have you done to her?" Darcy asked intensely.

"I did not want to aid him, but I did not know what else to do. He threatened to hurt me if I did not help. I just put a little laudanum into her milk before she retired."

"How did he get in?"

"Georgiana had already retired and I was sitting in the parlor when the knock came. He forced his way in when the butler opened the door. He pulled a gun and forced the man back towards the kitchen. The housekeeper was just coming out with Georgiana's warm milk. After forcing them backward, he locked them in the kitchen. He had taken the milk from the housekeeper a pleased smile on his face before locking the door. He handed the glass to me and with the hand not holding his gun removed a little bottle from his pocket. I thought about throwing the warm liquid in his face but worried that it would not keep him from shooting me. I thought I could be more help to Georgiana by playing along. He told me he would not hurt either of us if I did what he said. He poured some of the liquid from the bottle into her glass of milk and forced me at gunpoint to take it up the stairs and get Georgiana to drink it. He stood out of sight of Georgiana but had his gun trained on me through the crack in the door. I encouraged her to drink it all, and she was asleep very quickly. Then he told me to pack a bag for her and follow him to the carriage outside. He said I was to go along, but he would let me down outside the city so that I could not send anyone after him quickly. I am sorry, but I have no idea where he planned to go."

Darcy listened quietly, but the same instinct that warned him of trouble, made him doubt her very rational explanation of the events. He reviewed what he had seen as he stared intently at Mrs. Younge. Then he remembered that she had carried two valises as she came down the stairs behind Wickham. One of the valises had tumbled down the stairs dumping its contents, including a dress he recognized as belonging to Georgiana. He nodded to Fields and stepped from the room. Mrs. Younge attempted to rise from her chair to leave the parlor as well, but Fields placed a hand on her shoulder to detain her. In the foyer, Darcy quickly picked up the other valise and opened it. It was obvious that the belongings were not Georgiana's except for a small black case. Removing the case, he marched down the hall and unlocked the kitchen door. He entered closing the door behind him and asked the elderly couple about the events of the evening. The accounts were similar, but it did not appear to the couple that Mrs. Younge had been very surprised or very afraid of the intruder. Darcy thanked them for their information and told them they could retire for the night but asked them not to speak of the matter to anyone. He also indicated he may wish to talk more about it on the morrow. Clutching the case behind his back, he returned to the sitting room and glared at Mrs. Younge. She shrank back into her chair a little unnerved by the expression on Darcy's face.

"Mrs. Younge, if you were told to pack things for Georgiana could you please explain to me why the second valise contained your things?" The woman stammered, but could not quickly think of a good excuse. Darcy continued, "I can only surmise that you packed for yourself because you were working with Wickham and planned to leave with him, as well." "Shoving the case forward, Darcy railed, "Did you plan to sell Georgiana's jewelry to finance your trip or did you plan to keep it for yourself?" Her startled expression gave Darcy his answer. "Mrs. Younge you will leave this house now. You will receive no further payment from me, and you shall certainly receive no recommendation from me. Give me an address and I will send your belongings to you, but you are to leave with only the valise you packed." She quickly handed him a card from her reticule. "Mrs. Young, if I hear one word of gossip about this evening, I will hunt you down and have you brought up on charges of attempted kidnapping and attempted robbery. You know that kidnapping is a hanging offense, do you not?" She nodded numbly. "Do not ever darken my door again." The frightened woman bolted from her chair, pausing in the foyer only long enough to grab her valise, and ran from the house into the darkness of the night.

After Mrs. Younge had left, Darcy sent one of the footmen for a doctor. He wanted to be sure that Georgiana was truly well. The doctor arrived quickly and assured Darcy that she was well but sleeping heavily. He informed him that she might be sleeping a long time depending on how much laudanum she had been given. Darcy carried her to her bed after the doctor departed. He pulled up a chair and sat at her bedside eventually falling asleep with his head on Georgiana's bed.

Darcy heard his sister begin to whimper and moan and was quickly awake. He was staring intently when Georgie's eyes fluttered open. Though she felt somewhat groggy from the after effects of the laudanum, she smiled to see her brother seated beside her.

"William, what are you doing here?" she asked huskily.

"I thought I would surprise you and visit for a few days," he replied.

"Well, it is a delightful surprise. I am so glad you've come. But why are you in my room so early in the morning. You look as if you have slept here."

Darcy looked sheepish and replied, "That is because I guess I did."

She looked at him quizzically, "You guess you did? Why would you do that?"

It appeared that Georgiana had no memory of the events of the night before. Rather than worry her, he quickly came up with an excuse. "I arrived later than intended, so rather than wake you, I just stopped in to check on you for a few moments as you slept. I guess I was more tired than I realized and fell asleep sitting by your bed."

"Do you know what time it is?" Georgiana asked. When William said it was nine o'clock, Georgiana was surprised. She had slept for a long time, yet she still felt so tired. "Well, I doubt you slept very well in a chair by my bed, and I am so very tired this morning. Perhaps we should both go back to sleep."

"Well then, you should certainly sleep until you feel like rising for the day. I will see you later, Little One." He kissed her on the forehead before departing and closed the door behind him. Darcy went to his room where his valet was waiting.

"Sir, your bath water will be delivered momentarily, would you care to begin preparations for your day?" As his valet shaved him, he pondered what to tell Georgie regarding Mrs. Younge's absence. While soaking in the tub, he realized the best course of action. He would tell Georgiana Mrs. Younge had received an urgent express regarding a family matter, and she had to leave immediately. Darcy decided they could stay for another day or two to enjoy the sights of the seaside town together. However, they would have to return to London on Saturday as he had a meeting on Monday and would need to be back to prepare. When he came downstairs, he related to the elderly couple his plans. He indicated they would each receive a bonus, but in exchange, they must never say anything about the events of the previous evening. As both had found the "young miss" to be delightful, sweet, and innocent, they said they would certainly say nothing that could cause harm to her sweet self or her reputation.

When Georgiana appeared for luncheon, Darcy told her the story he had prepared.

"I do hope all will be well for Mrs. Younge and her mother; and how could I be disappointed about leaving when it means I get to spend more time with you, dear brother."

They passed the next few days pleasantly with walks on the beach—even enjoying a picnic there once, a visit to a small museum, and attending a concert. Georgiana showed William many of her sketches of the area as well as the shells she had collected from the beach.

"Georgie, this sketch of the ocean is particularly well done. I think I will have it framed for my study." She blushed at the praise from her beloved brother and smiled brightly.

Upon their return to London, Darcy sent Richard a note telling him of the events in Ramsgate. He indicated that he would be looking for a new companion for Georgiana and would appreciate his input on the interviews. He also indicated that he wished to hire a special "footman" to attend Georgiana, one skilled in protection. The new footman's sole responsibility would be to accompany Georgiana and her companion wherever they went. He asked if Richard might know of anyone who would be suitable for the position.

Three days later, Richard strolled into his study, just before the interview with the most promising candidate he could find for Georgiana's new companion.

"Well, Cousin, how are you this fine day?" Richard asked as he dropped into the seat across from Darcy's desk.

"I am well, Richard. I am glad you arrived early. Here are the recommendation letters regarding Mrs. Annesley. I have contacted all of the previous employers and verified these recommendations. I do not want to make the same mistakes I made with Mrs. Younge. Are there any questions that you would like me to ask her?"

"I am sure you will be very thorough, but give me a nod before you extend the offer just to make certain," Richard replied.

"By the way, Darcy, I have a friend whose time in the service has just expired and he does not wish to reenlist. His father was injured recently and cannot work. He does not wish to put his life at risk any longer and needs a well-paying position so that he can help support his family. He was an excellent soldier and is very skilled with sword, knife, and pistol. He has also done some boxing in his day. I believe he will fit the bill very nicely. Would you like me to extend the offer, or would you prefer to have me invite him here so that we can meet with him together?"

Darcy breathed an audible sigh of relief. "He sounds ideal for our purposes, Richard. Thank you for your efforts with this. I need to be sure that she will be safe when she is not with me."

"You know that her safety is just as important to me."

A short time later, Treywick knocked at the study door. On hearing his master's call of "Enter," he opened the door and announced Mrs. Annesley. Both gentlemen stood eyeing the woman who entered. She was a small, neat-looking widow who appeared to be in her late forties. She was slightly plump with gray sprinkled throughout her brown hair and a warm smile on her open face.

"Good day, Mrs. Annesley, will you pleased be seated?" Darcy indicated the chair in front of his desk. "This is Georgiana's other guardian, Colonel Richard Fitzwilliam."

"Good day, Mr. Darcy, Colonel Fitzwilliam. Thank you for meeting with me today," she replied in a clear, precise voice.

"I have reviewed all of your recommendations and references, and they are very impressive. Could you please tell me what you think you can bring to the position as my sister's companion?"

"Mr. Darcy, I have spent many years raising other people's children. I love young people because of the joy they have for life and new experiences. My husband and I were never blessed with children, and I now find great pleasure in sharing time with those whom I am charged to direct."

"Based on the praises of your previous employers, I believe that you will be of benefit to my sister—at least that is my fervent hope. There is one thing that I require from all of my employees, Mrs. Annesley, and that is absolute loyalty. I do not expect to hear gossip about anything that happens in my home or about any of its occupants. Though, I know discussion of the family will occur when servants are gathered, I hope I can count on your discretion. Can you abide by this, Mrs. Annesley?"

"Certainly, Mr. Darcy," she replied seriously.

"Mrs. Annesley," Darcy began, "I must relate to you two incidents that are hard for me to revisit. I must also ask that you keep this information to yourself—particularly should you decide not to accept the position after hearing what I have to impart." Darcy then related to Mrs. Annesley the story of the two attempts to kidnap Georgiana.

"I can see how difficult this is for you, Mr. Darcy, but I do agree with your decision not to relate the details of the most recent event to her. It would only serve to further undermine her confidence. I believe that my experience will help her to overcome her fear and find the joy of this time in her life again."

"Well, Richard is there anything you wish to add?" Darcy asked.

"Only to tell you that Georgiana is one of the sweetest, most kind-hearted young women you will ever meet. We are trusting you with something most precious to both of us."

"I promise you will not be disappointed, sirs. I will care for her and guide her as if she were my own," replied Mrs. Annesley with another smile.

"Well then, I assume that all the details in my offer letter were acceptable?" Darcy asked.

"Everything was very generous, sir," she replied.

"When can you begin, Mrs. Annesley?"

"I believe I could start on Monday, sir if that would be acceptable?"

"That should be fine, ma'am. Oh by the way, I am hiring a new footman, whose main priority will be Georgiana's safety. He has a military background and is to accompany you and Georgiana whenever you are outside the house whether in town or at Pemberley. However, I do not wish Georgiana to know that he is there to protect her as it may make her more fearful rather than provide comfort. I think we should adjourn to the music room so that you can meet Georgiana." Darcy arose from his desk with Mrs. Annesley and Richard following.

The very next day, Richard brought his friend by to be interviewed for the position of footman. Robert Gregson was a large man, with hair the color of ripe wheat, bright blue eyes, and a pleasing smile. Richard explained Wickham's history with the Darcy family since any discussion of Wickham filled Darcy with a nearly uncontrollable rage. As Gregson had two younger sisters, he had a few choice words for scum like

Wickham. Darcy offered him the job with a generous salary and indicated he would alert his butler to Gregson's true position. Darcy wished Gregson's other responsibilities to be minimized, and to have him posted near wherever Georgiana was while in the house. Darcy rose from his desk and shook hands with Gregson sealing the deal.

"Gregson, remember that you have the safety of our dear girl in your hands. She is very important to the both of us," Richard added as he also shook hands with the man.

With these two tasks accomplished, Darcy was able to prepare for his visit to Bingley at the estate he was leasing with a lighter heart. He knew that both Gregson and Mrs. Annsey would watch over Georgiana's safety and well-being.

CHAPTER 2

UNEXPECTEDLY, THE COACH hit a bump in the road. Darcy was jolted from his thoughts and looked out the window to notice that the carriage was entering a small village. They must be nearing the estate that Bingley had leased. As Darcy watched the quaint village pass, he noted a bookshop and thought to visit it sometime during his stay. He also caught a glimpse of a young lady in profile with soft pink cheeks and dark chestnut curls. She appeared to be exiting the shop but had turned back to speak to someone as she left. There was something familiar about the profile, but as he could not see her face, he could not place the vague feeling of familiarity.

It was not long before they turned in at the gates of Netherfield Park. Darcy looked about at the condition of what he could see of the property as the carriage wandered up the drive. It appeared that the estate was well maintained. As they approached the entry, Darcy saw Bingley and Miss Bingley waiting for him on the steps. Noting the gleam in Miss Bingley's eyes Darcy took a deep breath as he prepared to exit the carriage. Bingley rushed forward calling out, "Darcy, welcome to

Netherfield Park. I am so glad you have arrived. What do you think of the estate?"

"From the little bit I have observed coming up the drive, it seems to be a nice property," Darcy answered. "I look forward to seeing more of it with you in the coming days."

Caroline was tired of being ignored and determined to take charge of the situation. She pushed forward and attached herself to Darcy's arm purring, "Mr. Darcy, we have so looked forward to having you join us. Please let me show you to your room. Then you can join us for refreshments in the large drawing room."

Disentangling her from his arm he stepped over to Bingley, a grimace on his face. "Caroline, I will show Darcy to his room, and we will join you in a little while." Darcy followed Bingley up the large staircase and down a hall to the right. Bingley opened the last door on the left, which led into a spacious corner bedroom decorated in shades of navy and silver, gray. Large windows on two walls filled the room with light. The windows on the back wall looked out over the manicured gardens, and those on the end of the room gave a view towards the stables and the fields beyond them. "There is a dressing room through the door in the corner there and a private sitting room through the door there to the left. I am sorry for the long walk, but you did want to be as far from Caroline as possible, did you not?" Bingley asked a large grin on his face.

"And you can be sure that I will be locking all my doors when I retire," Darcy said smiling back.

"I did speak to her before your arrival, Darcy. I do not know why she cannot seem to accept what she is told. She is just convinced that you will ask her to marry you," Bingley said with a rueful grin.

"I just want to be sure you understand there are absolutely no circumstances—and I do mean none—that could force me to marry her," Darcy stated firmly.

"I do understand and accept your position Darcy. I know if there is any compromising done, it will be because of Caroline, not you," he replied shaking his head.

The two friends visited for a short while longer before Bingley withdrew. Darcy's valet, Chalmers, came through the dressing room door as soon as the bedroom door closed. "Sir, would you care for a bath or prefer just to wash up before going down to tea?"

"The bath please, Chalmers, as it will keep me from Miss Bingley for a little while longer." The valet smiled conspiratorially as he turned back to the dressing room.

When Darcy entered the drawing room nearly an hour later, Miss Bingley bounced from her seat and rushed to his side. She pulled him towards the small sofa upon which she had been sitting. Darcy deftly extricated himself from her grasp and acknowledged the presence of Bingley's other sister, Louisa Hurst, and her husband Gilbert before taking the chair near Bingley. Miss Bingley poured the tea for everyone and launched into her current favorite topic.

"Charles, though Netherfield Park is a pleasant estate it is certainly not on the par of Pemberley which should be your example in finding an estate of your own. But the worst thing about bringing us here is the utter lack of refined society. There is no style, no manners, and no class in anyone we have yet met."

"How can you say that, Caroline? We have met several charming neighbors."

"You shall see for yourself tomorrow evening, Mr. Darcy, as Charles has accepted an invitation for our party to attend the local assembly. Of course, as you do not particularly care for such events, sir, I would be happy to remain behind to entertain you should you not wish to attend. I assure you, you will miss nothing by your absence."

Darcy thought an assembly—as much as he disliked them—would be preferable to an evening alone with Miss Bingley. "I would not dream of embarrassing my host by failing to attend since he has accepted the invitation for our whole party. Even were that not enough reason, you know that it would be most inappropriate for you and me to remain home unchaperoned, Miss Bingley," he said stiffly. Darcy and Bingley could not help a brief smile as they glanced at one another. Darcy also caught the anger and then determination that flickered across Caroline's face at his remarks. He sighed softly knowing this could be a long and potentially difficult visit.

The remainder of tea passed with polite conversation. However, Miss Bingley made several comments regarding the unsuitability of the neighborhood and made pointed attempts to draw Darcy into a private conversation with her. As soon as he had finished his tea, Darcy announced he would retire to rest from the trip until dinner.

Returning to his room Darcy moved to the desk situated under a window overlooking the garden and pulled out some writing paper. After preparing his pen, he began a letter to Georgiana.

Netherfield Park
Hertfordshire

Dearest Georgiana,

I have arrived safely at Bingley's estate, Netherfield Park. It is outside the small village of Meryton in Hertfordshire. The village appeared quite pleasant, and I will certainly find the time to scour it for a treasure to bring to you upon my return to London.

The room I have been assigned is quite handsome. There is a small balcony looking over the gardens at the back of the house. I also have a view in the direction of the stables. Fortunately, Bingley has several fine horses and the fall foliage around the countryside is quite appealing. I look forward to exploring the area on horseback while I am in residence.

Bingley has accepted an invitation for our party to attend the local assembly tomorrow evening. Normally, I would not wish to attend something like this, but as Miss Bingley offered to remain home to entertain me, it seemed the prudent choice.

I hope that you are well, Georgiana, and that you are enjoying your time with Mrs. Annesley. I will write again soon, dear sister, and look forward to your reply.

With love,

William

After preparing his letter for mailing, Darcy had Chalmers deliver it to one of his footmen to take into Meryton to be posted. Then he settled himself in a chair before the fire to read for a while. Before he knew it, Chalmers returned to help him dress for dinner.

Darcy precisely timed his entry into the parlor where the family was gathered. As soon as he entered the butler arrived to announce that dinner was served. Darcy was unfortunately seated to Miss Bingley's right and was forced to endure her constant chatter throughout the meal. She frequently reached out her hand attempting to lay it upon his arm, but he was able to move it out of her reach each time.

While the men lingered over their port, Caroline Bingley paced the drawing room floor complaining to her sister, Louisa. "What is wrong with that man? Why cannot he see that I am the perfect woman to be his wife and the mistress of his homes?"

With a resigned sigh, Louisa responded, "Perhaps he is looking for someone who cares more for him than for what he has?" she suggested softly.

"Caring for your spouse is not the way of the ton, Louisa. Mr. Darcy is far too important a man to believe such sentimental nonsense," Caroline huffed. "If he does not soon begin to recognize that I am the best choice for him, I may have to do something that will take the choice away from him."

"Whatever are you talking about, Caroline?"

"If he fails to come to his senses, I might just have to arrange a compromise during his stay." The devious smile on her face caused her sister concern.

"Caroline, you cannot be serious!" Louisa cried. "Suppose he refuses to marry you? You would be ruined."

"Of course, he would not refuse, he is too much of a gentleman. And, I am sure that if he tried to, Charles would force him to marry me. I am sure Mr. Darcy would not want to lose Charles's friendship by refusing," Caroline stated confidently.

"You know very well it is Charles who needs Mr. Darcy's friendship, not the other way around. You would be taking an incredible risk, Caroline. You should not attempt such a path," Louisa advised sternly.

The gentlemen entered following Louisa's comment, their laughter fortunately drowning out what the ladies had been discussing. Caroline quickly stopped her pacing and seated herself on a loveseat, inviting Darcy to join her. He ignored her less than subtle invitation instead requesting some music from Louisa. Before Mrs. Hurst could rise from her seat, Caroline rushed to the piano. After quickly selecting a piece of music, she began to play and sing an Italian love song, staring at Darcy all the while.

Darcy was deeply embarrassed by her display and turned his back as he walked to the window to look out. Miss Bingley's voice was a bit thin and breathy though she was able to stay on pitch, and her attempt at the Italian words was dreadful. To Darcy, the song seemed endless. When it was finally complete, there was a small amount of applause. Darcy continued looking out the window and did not join in. Before Caroline could play again, Hurst suggested a game of cards. Darcy said he would prefer to read and encouraged them to play so that Caroline would be kept busy and away from him.

He had barely begun to read when Caroline called out, "Mr. Darcy you must come and assist me. This is such a difficult hand I do not believe I shall be able to play it successfully." She batted her eyes at him as she made her request.

"Miss Bingley, I know you to be quite competent at Whist, I am sure you will be successful without my assistance." He make his reply without looking in her direction. Had he glanced at her he would have noticed her lift her chin and preen a little taking his words as a compliment.

After they had played several hands, a maid appeared with the tea tray. Darcy took one cup of tea, put up with a little more of Miss Bingley's chatter, and then retired for the night.

CHAPTER 3

THE NEXT MORNING Darcy and Bingley rode out to look over the estate. The steward, Mr. Moore, was in attendance, and Darcy asked several pointed questions while Bingley attempted to digest all the information that was being conveyed. Darcy noted the slight expression of panic that crossed Charles's face and gave him a reassuring smile. After luncheon Darcy kept to his room in order to avoid Miss Bingley as much as possible.

Following a pleasant dinner, they departed for the assembly. As usual Caroline and Mrs. Hurst were both overdressed and wore far too much jewelry and feathers. For all that, they aspired to be of the first circles neither seemed to have any fashion sense at all. Miss Bingley typically choose an unusual shade of orange for her dresses. Mrs. Hurst's gowns always overpowered her small frame with too many frills and flounces, and too much lace.

As their carriage pulled up in front of the assembly hall, they could hear the music; the dancing had already begun. Darcy was pleased with this fact and hoped it would allow them to enter with very little fanfare or attention. His hopes were dashed as the music ground to a halt when their party appeared. The addition of visitors to the local assembly was an unusual occurrence, and everyone was excited to get a look at the newcomers to the neighborhood. Sir William Lucas, who was hosting this assembly, rushed towards the doorway to welcome the guests, gathering his family as he went.

"Mr. Bingley, we are delighted to have you attend our little assembly tonight. You remember my son, John?" he asked. At Bingley's nod, he continued, "Allow me to introduce you to Lady Lucas, and my daughters, Charlotte, and Maria."

"It is very nice to see you again," Bingley replied. "Please allow me to introduce my eldest sister, Mrs. Louisa Hurst, her husband, Mr. Gilbert Hurst, my sister, Miss Caroline Bingley, and my good friend, Mr. Fitzwilliam Darcy of Pemberley in Derbyshire." After the introductions were completed the musicians picked up the tune they had left off, and the dancers again moved around the dance floor. Bingley asked Miss Lucas to stand up with him for the next set, and the others dispersed around the room. Louisa and Caroline moved to the side of the room and began criticizing the lack of fashion on the ladies. Hurst headed for the punch bowl, and Darcy looked for a quiet corner where he could observe and minimize the necessity for interaction. Despite his wealth and experience in the ton, Darcy was basically a shy man. The mundane small talk necessary in a ballroom was not something at which he excelled. He observed Bingley talking to another group of neighbors consisting of six females. He noticed the smile that lit Bingley's face as his gaze rested upon the lovely young lady with the delicate smile and blonde hair. At her side almost in profile was a petite young woman with dark chestnut curls, and, again, that feeling of familiarity washed over him. Darcy continued to watch as Bingley danced first with Miss Lucas and then with the young lady at whom he had been smiling. At the completion of their set, he watched them return to the young woman with the dark curls. Whatever Bingley was saying brought a wider smile from his partner and a laugh from the young woman with the dark curls. At that musical laugh, Darcy's mind was flooded with a memory from five years earlier. They had seen Georgiana's savior at the theater but had been unable to meet and thank her for her assistance. That laugh and the sparkling eyes that accompanied it had remained in Darcy's memory to be frequently recalled. He moved across the room to join Bingley hoping to gain an introduction to the lovely lady with the dark curls.

Elizabeth had noticed the dark, handsome man who entered with the Bingley party. His size alone made him hard to miss. He was a head taller than anyone in the room and broad through the shoulders. In fact, she laughingly wondered how he had ever gotten into his well-tailored evening jacket. She had watched as he drifted to a far corner of the room and stared rather unsmilingly about the event. He appeared to a member be of the first circles, so a small gathering like this should not be unusual. Did he think the neighborhood beneath him? And in spite of the feeling of familiarity, she felt her anger begin to stir. Quickly recognizing that feeling angry during a dance was a waste of energy, she returned her thoughts to her companions, laughing as she caught the end of Mr. Bingley's tale.

"There you are Darcy. Where have you been hiding so far this evening," he teased.

With a slight flush spreading up from his neck to his cheeks, he responded, "I have not been hiding Bingley, merely taking in the evening. Did you enjoy your dances? Perhaps while you have this opportunity, you might introduce me to your companions."

If Bingley was surprised at the unusual request, he did not show it and rapidly proceeded to comply. "Miss Jane Bennet and Miss Elizabeth Bennet may I introduce you to my dear friend, Mr. Fitzwilliam Darcy of Pemberley in Derbyshire."

Darcy bowed first to Jane in acknowledgement of her curtsey and then looked directly into Elizabeth's eyes as he bowed to her, as well. Elizabeth was surprised by the intense look from the handsome man before her. She felt there was something familiar about him but was sure they had not met before.

As Bingley looked on in surprise, Darcy spoke to Elizabeth, "Miss Elizabeth, if you are not engaged for the next set would you do me the honor of dancing with me?"

"As I am free for the next set, I would be delighted to accept, Mr. Darcy," Elizabeth replied with a smile. She hoped that while they danced she would be able to understand why he seemed familiar.

As they took the dance floor, two pairs of eyes observed them from the side of the room--one with a cold glare, the other with surprise. Caroline was shocked and angry. Mr. Darcy never danced outside of his party, and, in fact, he had not yet danced with either Louisa or herself. But, here he was lining up for the set that was to begin.

"Louisa, do you know who that is dancing with Mr. Darcy?" Caroline spit out through her false smile and clenched teeth.

"I have no idea," Louisa responded calmly.

"He is supposed to be interested in only me while he is staying with us. I will not have him distracted by some little country nobody with no style and little beauty. We must find out what we can about her; there must be something we can use to discredit her in Mr. Darcy's eyes."

"Caroline, I think you are over reacting. He could hardly avoid asking the young lady to dance after Charles had just introduced them."

Caroline ignored her sister's words and flounced away. Pasting on a superior smile, she began joining each group she came upon and asking questions about Mr. Darcy's dance partner. She was very unhappy with the information she was receiving. With increasing anger, Caroline returned to her sister and reported her information.

"Her name is Miss Elizabeth Bennet, and she is the second of five sisters. She seems to be universally well-liked, and the praise I was forced to listen to from her neighbors, for her beauty, kindness, and intellect was quite insupportable."

As Darcy danced, he made an effort to attempt conversation with his lovely partner each time the figures brought them together. He wanted to be sure that she was whom he thought her to be. Consequently, he questioned her about her home and her family. He gradually brought the subject to travel and asked, "Do you often come to London, Miss Elizabeth?"

"Not to participate in the season, Mr. Darcy, but I do try to visit my aunt and uncle at least once or twice each year. They live in Cheapside." She looked closely at her partner to see what his reaction would be to her relatives' address. She knew from the swirling gossip that Mr. Darcy was a member of the first circles of society and a very wealthy and eligible bachelor. She was surprised that Mr. Darcy showed no reaction, negative or otherwise.

"And while you are visiting with your family, are there any special places you particularly enjoy seeing?"

"I do love to attend the theater or a concert when I visit, but my favorite place to visit, if the opportunity presents, is Hyde Park. Here at home I love to walk about the countryside, and the beauties of Hyde Park are as close as I can come to that in the city. My walks are usually confined to the park close to my aunt and uncle's home, but we make an effort to visit Hyde Park at least once each trip."

Darcy was almost convinced this was the young woman who had helped Georgiana during Wickham's first kidnapping attempt. "You are right about the beauties of the park; my home is very nearby there. I hope that you are always well attended on your walks in the park as it can sometimes be a very dangerous place."

"You are certainly correct about that, Mr. Darcy. Several years ago I witnessed an attempted kidnapping."

"Miss Elizabeth, I believe you did more than witness the attempted kidnapping, did you not?"

Elizabeth was shocked, and her embarrassment showed on her flushed face. *How could he know this* she wondered? Her aunt had been quite upset at her behavior that day. At first she was surprised that she would exhibit such poor manners. They when she learned the reason why she had been running, she had turned quite pale as she pointed out the danger in which Elizabeth had put herself. Mrs. Gardiner had extracted a promise from Elizabeth not to act so recklessly again. The ladies also pledged to keep the event secret from Mrs. Bennet, as no one wished to hear her mother's comments on the subject.

Darcy was concerned for her as he watched the expressions that moved across her face and in her eyes. "Are you quite alright, Miss Elizabeth? Do you need to sit down?" he asked as he tightened his grip on her hand.

Elizabeth recovered quickly and replied, "I am quite well Mr. Darcy only very surprised. How could you know about the events of that day?" And then it dawned on her why he seemed familiar. She remembered the handsome man with the dark curly hair. "You were there, too!" she cried.

"Yes, I was. You see it was my dear sister, Georgiana, who you helped that day. Might we sit out the next set so that we can discuss this quietly?"

"I am not engaged for the next set and would be happy to continue speaking with you."

As the set ended, he led her to a pair of chairs in a far corner and began his tale. "As soon as I had her calm I turned to see about you, but you entered a carriage a short ways down the block and had pulled away before I could reach you. Georgiana was much too upset to tell me exactly what had happened. Even when she calmed she could not seem to remember much. She said 'It all happened so fast.' Before I continue could you please tell me what you witnessed and did?"

Elizabeth told of seeing the man knock the older woman down, grab the girl and run. She said she could see the look of terror on the young girl's face and felt compelled to help. Elizabeth said she quickly told her relatives to help the older woman—which her sister, Jane, had done—and just took off running after the man and girl. "I did not really know how I would stop them, but I hoped that perhaps I could slow him down enough for someone to come help. He struck me across the face, but I refused to stop. My constant hitting and pulling at him made it hard for him to get your sister in the carriage. The next thing I knew, the carriage began pulling away, and he tossed her at me as someone called out for him to stop. He grabbed the carriage door and was gone. Then a hand reached down to help us both up. Shortly after that my aunt appeared and dragged me towards her carriage. She was rather embarrassed by my behavior—at least until she heard why I had run in such an unladylike fashion."

From there Darcy continued his tale. "I was quite disappointed that I had not had the chance to thank you. Georgiana was deeply affected by the event and became somewhat withdrawn. In an attempt to cheer her, my cousin, Colonel Fitzwilliam—who shares in the guardianship of my sister—and I took her to a concert. She saw you from our box and pointed you out just as the performance began. We attempted to come out during intermission in hopes of bumping into you, but just as we were preparing to depart our box, Mr. and Miss Bingley arrived. They stayed until the intermission was over. We left our seats just before the final curtain hoping to place ourselves near the door to catch you as you exited. Unfortunately, we were again delayed by acquaintances, and I just caught a glimpse of you as you exited the theater. By the time we reached the doors, your party was nowhere in sight."

All the time they were talking Miss Bingley had been attempting to circumnavigate the room. She had to get Mr. Darcy away from that clinging nobody. Fortunately for Darcy and Elizabeth, Miss Bingley was frequently stopped in her progress, by those wishing to make her acquaintance or compliment her on her fine gown. By the time she reached the spot where they had been seated, the chairs were empty. Caroline looked around and discovered Miss Elizabeth dancing and Mr. Darcy nearby. He seemed to be watching that nobody closely.

"Mr. Darcy, how are you surviving this dreadful affair?" Caroline asked as she attached herself to his arm. "I saw that you were cornered and was trying to come to your aid, but I was delayed. Fortunately, you are now free of your companion." She said this in such a derogatory tone that Darcy looked at her sharply. He managed to disengage Miss Bingley from his arm and locked his hands behind his back to prevent her from taking them again. And, even though, he barely acknowledged her there by his side, she stayed close continuing to disparage everyone, particularly Miss Elizabeth. He was quite upset with her and her conversation. He knew it was quite rude of him, but he refused to ask her to dance despite the many hints she dropped. Finally, as he again saw Bingley with Jane and Elizabeth, he curtly excused himself and walked away. Caroline just stood there gaping. She had never seen him behave so in all the years they had known him. She was particularly upset to see him returned to Elizabeth Bennet's side.

She made her way back to where her sister was standing, her rage barely masked. When she reached Louisa, she fumed, "How could this happen. He was supposed to fall under the spell of my charms while I had him alone here at Netherfield. Why is he paying so much attention to that unattractive little country bumpkin? I will not have it! I will find a way to get him away from her no matter what!"

Louisa just looked at her sister a worried expression on her face.

With a sigh of relief to be free of Caroline, he stepped up to join the trio where they stood talking. Bingley was asking Miss Bennet if he might call at Longbourn tomorrow, and she shyly assented. Just then, the musicians indicated that the next set would be the last of the evening. Elizabeth was very surprised when Mr. Darcy asked to dance with her a second time.

As they took the floor, she teased, "You must like to live dangerously, Mr. Darcy? You have danced twice with me and no other young ladies. In a small town like this, people will talk," she said with a smile.

Deciding to tease in his turn he daringly replied, "Why should people be surprised that I would choose to dance with the prettiest girl in the room?"

Elizabeth blushed at the compliment and quickly changed the subject. For the remainder of the set, they spoke of the sights to be seen around Meryton and other commonplace subjects.

When they returned home, Elizabeth and Jane settled in to talk for a while despite the lateness of the hour.

"Oh, Lizzy, Mr. Bingley was so kind and pleasant. I cannot believe that he asked me to dance twice," said Jane with a dreamy look upon her face. "I cannot imagine ever meeting a better young man."

Elizabeth smilingly replied, "I think that asking you shows his good taste and intelligence for you are without question the loveliest and sweetest girl in all the world."

Blushing at her sister's praise, Jane changed the subject. "Did you have a pleasant evening, Lizzy?"

"I did indeed. I also learned something surprising about Mr. Darcy," Elizabeth answered. At Jane's questioning look she continued, "Mr. Darcy and I have met before."

"How is that possible, Lizzy?"

"Do you remember the time I took off running in Hyde Park?" As Jane nodded, she continued, "The young girl who I attempted to rescue was Mr. Darcy's younger sister, Georgiana! He was the gentleman who helped us up from the ground." Elizabeth then proceeded to tell Jane all that Mr. Darcy had said to her. Eventually, she reminded Jane that they should sleep as Mr. Bingley was planning to call tomorrow. Jane said goodnight and left for her room. As Elizabeth blew out her bedside candle, she wondered if Mr. Darcy would also visit.

The carriage had barely begun to move when Caroline Bingley started to speak. "I cannot imagine a more tedious evening. There was no one of fashion or breeding with whom to converse. The gentlemen were hardly deserving of the appellation, and I have never seen less fashionable clothing. The worst of all was the Bennet family. The youngest daughters' behavior was shameful. They were so brassy and loud. Mrs. Bennet talked of nothing but how much you and Mr. Darcy were worth, Charles, and how she hoped one of her daughters would catch you. While Miss Jane Bennet appears to be a sweet young lady—by far the only one with whom I should care to meet again—it was beyond belief that Miss Elizabeth Bennet is considered one of the jewels of the neighborhood. She has no style, no beauty, and no education. She would never be accepted in the ton, and the way she behaves—laughing out loud. No proper lady would behave in such a way.

Caroline continued her rant until the carriage arrived at Netherfield. She was oblivious to the fact that she was the only one talking. Charles did agree with her remarks about Jane, but otherwise was silent. Louisa tried to forestall her comments about Miss Elizabeth as she could see the anger building on Mr. Darcy's face. As the carriage pulled to a stop, Darcy swung open the door, stepped out, and announced that he was retiring for the evening. Caroline, her mouth hanging open, sat in shock, quiet for the first time since the carriage ride began, as she watched Darcy march up the stairs and into the house.

"Charles, I told you we should not have attended this evening. It has so distressed Mr. Darcy that he forgot his good manners!"

"I do not think that was what distressed him, Caroline," Charles said, irritation evident in his voice.

Caroline looked totally innocent when she asked, "Whatever do you mean, Charles?"

CHAPTER 4

As Darcy reached his room, he was fighting to regain control of his temper. Caroline Bingley was, without question, the most irritating female of his acquaintance. Her self-importance was intolerable. She was the daughter of a tradesman, yet constantly criticized her betters. Even if the Bennet family was not of the first circles they had been members of the landed gentry for several generations, which placed them above her in society's eyes.

Chalmers entered to help Darcy prepare for bed. Noting the dark look upon his master's face, he cautiously asked, "How was the assembly, sir?"

As Darcy thought about his evening, he let go of his anger with Miss Bingley. A small smile appeared on his face as he replied, "It was very pleasant, thank you, surprisingly so."

Years of experience allowed Chalmers to maintain a neutral expression in spite of the shock he felt at his master's expression. Mr. Darcy had many responsibilities on his young shoulders, and a smile was not often seen on his countenance.

Wondering at its cause, he continued to help ready him for the night.

"Do you require anything else, sir?"

"No thank you, Chalmers; you may retire. I expect to pay a call with Mr. Bingley tomorrow, so I will see you in the morning."

Darcy laid staring at the canopy unable to sleep; his thoughts kept drifting to the pleasures of the evening and Miss Elizabeth. He had long since given up hope of finding the woman who had saved Georgiana, so his shock at finding her at a country assembly was great. Darcy had never met anyone like Elizabeth Bennet. He marveled at the courage she exhibited when she chased after Georgiana and prevented Wickham from abducting her. He could not imagine any other young ladies of his acquaintance offering such assistance. Without a doubt, he knew that most of them would faint dead away or be so self-absorbed as to miss what was happening.

Miss Elizabeth held his attention throughout the assembly—and he was sure it was more than his gratitude to her. Darcy was drawn to her like no other he had ever met. He rarely danced at the events he attended yet he had danced twice with Miss Elizabeth and wished for more. He was surprised at how easily he was able to talk with her. The conversation as they danced displayed her sparkling wit. When they were not dancing his eyes followed her throughout the evening and his observations taught him much. Not only was Miss Elizabeth very lovely, she was also very kind. He had watched as she danced with all who asked—young, old, handsome or not-- and put each at ease no matter the quality of their performance. He had also observed her taking time to speak with all those who lacked partners—complimenting and encouraging. He often noticed her in conversation with Charlotte Lucas at which times her melodious laugh could be heard. The sweet sound of it had remained with him for the past five years. Darcy was left to marvel at what else he might discover about this unique young woman. He had never met anyone like Miss Elizabeth.

Darcy was very pleased that he would finally have the opportunity to thank Miss Elizabeth for her assistance to Georgiana. Words seemed inadequate to express the depth of his gratitude, but he knew he must make his best attempt. Horror struck, however, as he realized he should have expressed that gratitude as soon as he realized her identity. He immediately determined that he would accompany Bingley on the morrow when he visited Longbourn to correct this error. As he drifted off to sleep, his thoughts were filled with sparkling eyes, wayward curls, and a winsome smile.

Darcy was disappointed to see rain beating against the window as he awoke. He was frustrated to realize he and Bingley would be prevented from calling on the Misses Bennet. Sighing at the thought of spending the day listening to a repetition of Miss Bingley's complaints about the assembly, Darcy hurried down to break his fast. Fortunately, only Bingley was present when he entered the dining room, but he was clearly lamenting the fact the rain would prevent them from calling at Longbourn. Darcy suggested they use the day to go over the books with the steward, Mr. Moore, so that Bingley could learn more about the estate. Fortunately, they departed for the study before the others came down to breakfast.

When Caroline arrived in the dining room, she found only her sister and brother-in-law who informed her that her brother and Darcy had already dined and were working in the study with his steward. Her behavior was exactly as Hurst expected, repeatedly expressing her displeasure with Elizabeth Bennet and Mr. Darcy's attentions to her. When her fury was spent, she turned her efforts to finding a way to get Mr. Darcy's attention back on her where it belonged.

"It may be necessary to go ahead with the plan I previously mentioned," Caroline said to Louisa.

"Caroline, I really do not think you should attempt it. It has a far greater chance of failure than of success, and the consequences to you could be severe. I will not assist you in such a scheme."

"How dare you not support me," Caroline hissed. A wicked grin spreading over her face, she said, "Then perhaps it would be better to arrange for Miss Elizabeth's compromise so that he will be disgusted with her."

Caroline completely ignored Mr. Hurst, who appeared absorbed in his meal, but he listened and stored away the information for future use. If the truth were told, Mr. Hurst detested his sister-in-law, Caroline. Her selfishness and bad temper touched all of those around her. He particularly disliked that it had changed his wife from the sweet woman she had been when they were courting. Hearing Louisa disagree with her, gave Hurst hope that his wife might be returning to the woman he married. He was secretly delighted that Caroline was so frustrated. However, he knew her well enough to know she had very few scruples when it came to getting what she wanted. He determined to keep his eyes and ears open in hopes of thwarting any scheme of Caroline's.

All through the morning hours Bingley, Darcy, and Mr. Moore reviewed the estate's books. They had even requested lunch brought to the library. They stopped briefly to eat and discuss the things they had reviewed. As they enjoyed lunch, Bingley noticed that the rain had stopped and the skies were clearing. Unfortunately the heaviness of the morning's rain had left the roads impassable. Bingley noted that he hoped they would be much improved by the morrow. It was nearly time for tea before the men finished going over the books with the steward. Bingley had been a little overwhelmed with all that being a landowner entailed.

"I would never have guessed that so much time and work went into being a landowner. Most of the gentlemen we meet at the club only seem interested in drinking, gambling, and women. When do they have time for all of this estate business?" Bingley asked with a chuckle.

"Well there are many ways to be a landowner, Bingley," Darcy replied. "Many leave everything to their stewards and just reap the profit, sometimes squandering it in the process. Others at least know what is going on, but are not particularly involved in the day-to-day running of their estates. Still others have a good working knowledge of the day-to-day activities and oversee all that their stewards do. And, lastly, there are those like me, who feel a deep obligation to my ancestors for the estate that has been entrusted to me. It is my job to maintain it for future generations. I know all that goes on and make the majority of the decisions. I delegate to the capable men who work for me and make sure to express my gratitude to those who help to make my estate the great success that it is. You do not have to do things as I do; you must find what works best for you. But I would advise you to remember that without hard-working tenants, no estate can prosper. Respect their efforts and appreciate them."

As they approached the drawing room for tea, Miss Bingley again sprang from her chair and pounced on Darcy while chastising Charles.

"Charles, where are your manners? How can you keep our guest sequestered all day and make him work while he is here on holiday?"

"Miss Bingley, I do hope to relax and enjoy some shooting while I am here. However, my primary reason for this visit was to look over your brother's estate and help him to learn what goes into the running of one. Charles will need these skills if he is ever to fulfill your father's dreams of becoming a member of the landed gentry." Darcy, once again, detached her from his arm and sat down next to Bingley.

Miss Bingley poured tea for everyone and passed around a plate of small cakes. "Mr. Darcy," Caroline asked, "how is dear, Georgiana? It has been far too long since we have seen her, hasn't it, Louisa?" Mrs. Hurst nodded her agreement as Caroline continued, "Perhaps we should cut short our visit to Netherfield and all return to town so as to spend time with our sweet Georgiana. After all, there is nothing of significance to keep us buried here in the country any longer."

"I am sure that Georgiana would appreciate your kindly concern for her, but she is quite busy with her studies and her new companion at the moment. Also, I find the environs attractive and the atmosphere quite pleasant and relaxing here. Netherfield Park is an attractive and comfortable estate with an efficient and attentive staff. I also look forward to getting to know more of Bingley's new neighbors." *Particularly a pretty one with bright eyes and dark curls,* but he knew better than to voice this thought in front of Miss Bingley. "I will, of course, need to return before the holidays, but I am quite content at present." Darcy suppressed a smile at Miss Bingley's obvious annoyance with his reply.

"Excuse me, sir," said Dawson, Netherfield's butler, "but the post has just arrived and there are a number of letters for Mr. Darcy among them."

"Thank you, Dawson," said Bingley. "Please place them on the desk in the study. We will look at them as soon as we finish with tea," he said glancing to Darcy for his nod of agreement.

As he finished his tea listening to yet more of Miss Bingley's complaints—some directly referring to Miss Elizabeth—he was grateful for another excuse to avoid her. Replacing his cup on the table, Darcy arose and said, "If you will excuse me, I need to review the post and deal with any business that has arrived." He was barely out the door when he heard Miss Bingley's whine begin urging her brother to depart immediately. She did not even give her brother a chance to reply. Darcy closed the study door to block out her grating voice.

He separated his post from Bingley's then sorted his correspondence reviewing first his business mail and then going on to read his personal correspondence. He opened Richard's letter first.

Matlock House
London

Dear Darcy,

How are you finding the wilds of Hertfordshire? Did Bingley make a good choice when he leased his estate?

How is the sport? If it is good, I am sure I could get leave for a few days to join you for some shooting. Better yet, how are the ladies? A little flirtation would be an enjoyable change from the dull routine of continued training while we wait to hear if we will be sent back to the continent. Mother is in a constant tizzy worrying about just that.

I stopped in to check on Georgie the other day, and I think Mrs. Annesley is making progress with her. She seemed more like her old self, a little livelier. I hope that you are enjoying your visit with Bingley but know the presence of his sisters must temper your enjoyment.

Yours,

Richard

Darcy penned a quick reply to Richard and told him about meeting the girl who saved Georgiana from Wickham five years ago. He mentioned asking her how she would feel about meeting Georgiana and that if she were amenable, perhaps Richard could bring her to Hertfordshire. Darcy requested that Richard not say anything to Georgiana as of yet. Then Darcy opened Georgiana's letter.

Darcy House
London

Dear Brother,

How are you enjoying your visit with Mr. Bingley? Is his estate pleasant? Is it anything like Pemberley? Have you met any interesting people?

I am working very hard at my studies. Mrs. Annesley is an excellent teacher. We went to Montagu House earlier this week viewing several of the exhibits. Though they were all very interesting, my favorite was the musical instruments. I miss you, dear brother, but am doing very well with my new companion. Mrs. Annesley is a dear, sweet woman, and I like her even more than Mrs. Younge.

I hope you enjoy your visit and sport. Please give my best to Mr. Bingley. I look forward to your return in early December.

Much love,

Georgiana

Darcy wished to write immediately to Georgiana and tell her about meeting Elizabeth, but he did first want to ask Miss Elizabeth's opinion before assuming that she would wish to meet his sister. Perhaps the experience was an unpleasant memory for her. By the time he had completed his correspondence, it was time to dress for dinner. Now there remained only a few hours before retiring during which he must endure Miss Bingley's behavior.

As dinner progressed, it appeared to Darcy that Bingley must have spoken to his sister about her topics of conversation. When she started in her whining tone to again criticize the neighborhood and neighbors, Bingley looked at her pointedly and cleared his throat. He then turned back to his quiet conversation with Darcy. Nothing further was heard from Miss Bingley for the remainder of the meal. At the end of the meal, the men went to Bingley's study to enjoy their port.

"Bingley I would like to accompany you when you visit Longbourn tomorrow. Miss Elizabeth and I had an interesting discussion during our last dance, and I would enjoy having the opportunity to continue it with her."

At the mention of Miss Elizabeth, Hurst spoke up, "I say, Darcy, Caroline is particularly annoyed with your attentions to Miss Elizabeth. She has been grumbling and plotting about how to get your attention back on her. Louisa tried to discourage her but be careful, old man, and perhaps you should warn Miss Elizabeth as well."

Darcy and Charles were both aghast at Hurst's news. When would Miss Bingley let go of her preposterous delusions about being Mrs. Darcy? "I believe that I will retire now so as to avoid her. I will take an early morning ride weather permitting. I believe we should keep our destination to ourselves when we depart for

Longbourn on the morrow, Bingley. No sense in raising her ire further."

It was quite early to retire, so once he was prepared for bed, he settled in a large wing-back chair near the fire to read until he was sleepy. The book, The Vision of Don Roderick, by Walter Scott, held his interest for quite some time. When he gazed up from the page into the fire, what he saw was a pair of sparkling brown eyes and a warm smile. He wondered why he felt so drawn to Miss Elizabeth--was it the fact she had saved Georgiana or something more? She was certainly not like any young lady he had met in the ton. Her wit and joie de vivre set her apart. He put his confusing feelings for her aside and retired for the night only to find her invading his dreams.

After a restful night, Darcy was up very early and decided to take a ride before breakfast. Chalmers had already laid out Darcy's riding clothes and boots having anticipated his master's choice for the morning. Darcy downed a cup of coffee and grabbed a roll on his way to the stables. The stable hand on duty quickly saddled the stallion Darcy had been using during his stay, and he was off. Darcy kept a sedate pace until he reached the meadows around Netherfield when he gave the horse his head for a hard gallop. Darcy began to pull up when he came to the fence border between Netherfield and Longbourn. As the horse slowed, he saw a flash of color on the other side of the fence. He lifted his hand to shade his eyes and made out the pleasant figure and dark curls of

Miss Elizabeth Bennet. Darcy eased his mount closer to the fence and called out, "Good Morning, Miss Elizabeth! How are you this fine morning?"

Elizabeth looked up with a smile saying, "I am well, thank you, Mr. Darcy, and you? Are you enjoying your ride?"

"I am indeed. I try to ride every morning before breakfast when I am in the country. I particularly enjoy riding out over the grounds of Pemberley as there are beautiful views in every direction. Today, I am enjoying the Hertfordshire scenery on this lovely fall morning. However, I am surprised to find a young lady about so early in the day. Miss Bingley and Mrs. Hurst barely join us before eleven."

"I would be afraid I had missed the best part of the day were I to stay indoors until such a time. With four sisters and a rather excitable mother, my household can be very chaotic at times. I do not think that I would be able to survive if I did not start my day in the beauty and peace of nature," Elizabeth said with a smile and that familiar sparkle in her eye.

"Miss Elizabeth, I do not want to seem improper, but while we are here alone, might I have a moment of your time?" Darcy asked hesitantly. While they had been speaking, he had dismounted and tied his horse to the fence. His arms were folded along the top rail. Elizabeth stepped up close to the fence on her side and looked at him quizzically.

"Certainly, Mr. Darcy, is there something I can help you with?"

"No, but it dawned on me after reviewing our conversation about the events in Hyde Park that I failed to properly thank you. You can have no idea how precious my sister is to me, Miss Elizabeth. At the time of the attempted kidnapping, she was the only member of my immediate family remaining. My mother died shortly after Georgiana's birth, and my father had passed away a few weeks previous to our arrival in London. We had buried my father at our estate in Derbyshire and were in town only for a brief while to deal with some of the legalities related to his death. If Wickham had been successful in taking Georgiana, I would have been a devastated and very lonely man."

Elizabeth had tears shining in her eyes and apparent on her cheeks as she listened to Darcy. Unconsciously she reached up and placed her hand on his arm giving it a gentle squeeze. The feeling of warmth that spread up their arms from her gentle touch was a surprise to both. "I am so sorry for your losses, Mr. Darcy, and even more grateful that I was able to be of service to you. May I ask, how your sister is doing?"

"She is recovered, but the event has left her a bit shy. Originally, she was so upset by the incident that for quite some time she would not go back to the park. When we finally were able to convince her to return, she would not go without either the Colonel or myself. Thank goodness she does not know about the second attempt," Darcy muttered under his breath. "As you brought up my sister—"

Interrupting, Elizabeth exclaimed with horror, "Did you say a second attempt, Mr. Darcy!"

"I am sorry you heard that, Miss Elizabeth. I did not mean to distress you," Darcy apologized.

"I am not distressed, Mr. Darcy, just upset that your poor sister would have to suffer so. If it would relieve you to discuss it, I would be pleased to listen. Was it the same person? Who is he, and what makes him act so despicably toward your family?"

"Is there somewhere more private nearby, where we might sit, Miss Elizabeth. It is a long story, and it would not be good for your reputation, were we seen talking here for an extended period. I hope that it has not been too long already."

"Well if you were on my side of the fence," Elizabeth said with a disarming smile, "there is a place beside a stream among that stand of trees just over there." Elizabeth indicated a grove just a short distance behind her.

"Please move away from the fence, Miss Elizabeth and I will be on your side shortly." She watched him remount his horse and turn away from the fence for some distance. Then he raced toward the fence and, gathering speed, cleanly sailed over the top, landing just beside her. He slid down from his horse and indicated with his arm that she should lead the way. They walked a short distance into the trees where Darcy tied his horse to a low-hanging branch. He then continued to follow Elizabeth deeper into the copse. They took a seat up a large flat rock with a small stream rushing past, and Elizabeth looked to Darcy to continue his story.

After seating himself on the rock close to Elizabeth, he angled himself to face her. He then took a deep breath and began, "Most of what I am about to tell you, I would rather forget. Growing up at Pemberley one of my closest friends was the son of my father's steward. He went on to tell Elizabeth about his father and the elder Mr. Wickham. He told her how George Wickham had become almost a part of the family when he was orphaned. He also told her of their many escapades. "Looking back on it now, I can see that some of the dares he issued as we were growing up were designed to cause me serious harm."

Darcy continued his tale. "Where I was reserved and quiet, George had an easy way about him that was quite charming. By the time we were attending Cambridge together, I saw a side of George that I did not like at all. He lied, cheated, gambled and was a womanizer while we were at Cambridge." He told Elizabeth about all the trouble Wickham caused that he was left to clean up. "My father was never the same after my mother died. It was as if a part of him died as well. Wickham had always managed to cheer him, and I did not want to make things worse should he find out what a disappointment Wickham was." Darcy paused for breath, and Elizabeth nodded at him to continue.

"While in London after my father's death, George sent a note saying he wanted to meet with me to get his inheritance. I made sure that Georgiana was not in the house during Wickham's appointment. I told him my father had left him one thousand pounds and that, should he take orders, he would be given the living at Kympton when it became vacant. Wickham was extremely angry, but then a cunning look appeared in his eyes. He reminded me he was neither inclined nor suited for the church and requested that he be paid the value of the living, so he could study the law instead. After some negotiation, we settled on three thousand pounds, plus the one thousand that he was left outright. I wrote him a check and had him sign a document stating he relinquished his rights to the living having received compensation for it in cash. My only other comment to him indicated that he was not welcome on my property or near my family in the future. It was just two weeks later that he came back for more money, having gambled away almost half of it in just that short time." Elizabeth gasped wondering how anyone could go through so much money so quickly. It would have supported her large family for at least two years.

"He showed up unexpectedly just as Georgiana and Nanny were leaving for their morning walk. I reminded him he was not permitted in my home and stopped him at the front door. He accused me of cheating him out of his rightful inheritance and demanded more money. I refused his demands and reminded him of the form he signed, before closing the door in his face. Wickham often acts without thinking—particularly when angry. It must have been a spur of the moment decision for him to attempt to kidnap Georgie. You know what happened then. We called in the Bow Street Runners, but he was able to hide himself extremely well in the bowels of the city or to leave London undetected.

I did not see him again until this past summer. Not that he left me alone during the intervening years. Everywhere he went he spread a story of being cheated out of a living by me. He opened charge accounts with merchants in my name and ran out without paying his debts. He also occasionally used my name to seduce and ruin women. Three who were abandoned by their families are currently working at Pemberley. Then this past June, I removed my sister from school. Her companion suggested she might benefit from a month by the seashore, so I arranged for Georgiana and her companion to go to the seaside resort of Ramsgate. I arrived late one evening unexpectedly; as I entered the house, Wickham was descending the stairs with an unconscious Georgie in his arms. He was followed by her companion carrying two valises." He filled her in with the rest of the story about the companion's involvement and Wickham's escape. "Fortunately, Georgiana did not awaken during the event and does not know anything about it."

"If this was the reason for your aloof behavior at the assembly a few days ago, it is certainly understandable. I thought perhaps you felt we were beneath your notice," said Elizabeth with compassion.

"I am afraid that I have never been very comfortable in crowded situations, particularly when I do not know anyone. I am grateful I took the time to meet and talk with you," Darcy said with a considering look at Elizabeth whose face blushed becomingly. "Miss Elizabeth, I was wondering if I could ask a large favor of you. Would you permit me to introduce Georgiana to you? I think it might help her to recover still further to talk to you about the incident the two of you shared. Bingley indicated he would be happy to have her join us. If you would be willing to spend some time with her, I am quite sure she would enjoy it. I also need to keep her away from Miss Bingley as much as possible," Darcy said with a grimace.

"Mr. Darcy, I would be delighted to finally meet Miss Darcy and spend time with her. When might she arrive?"

"I will write to her and to my cousin, as well, to see how quickly she can make the trip."

"I will look forward to her arrival. I am afraid I should hurry back, I have been away longer than usual, and I do not wish to have my mother asking awkward questions. I should perhaps warn you, Mr. Darcy, that my mother's sole goal in life is to see each of her daughters married as soon as possible to the richest man she can find. She cares not for our feelings in the matter, and if you show too much attention to me, even if only as a friend, she will be pushing for an engagement. I do not mean to speak ill of my mother, but as we have no brother and our estate is entailed on a distant cousin of my father's, she worries about being left in the hedgerows should my father pass away suddenly. We have not even met the heir yet so cannot count on his kindness. Good day, Mr. Darcy. I look forward to meeting Miss Darcy soon."

"Good-bye, Miss Elizabeth."

He watched her walk towards Longbourn until he could no longer see her then mounted and set the horse in the direction of Netherfield. He was delighted that Bingley was the only one in the breakfast room upon his return. "Bingley, would you mind terribly if I invited Georgiana to Netherfield for a visit? I was hoping that Richard could bring her as he has some leave and might enjoy a day or two of shooting."

"I would be delighted to have the company of Miss Darcy and the Colonel. I will just let Caroline know to prepare the rooms."

"If you do not mind, Bingley, could you leave Caroline uninformed until the last minute? I do not wish to listen to her raptures about Georgiana for days on end. Granted I do believe my sister to be the sweetest, nearly-perfect creature, but Caroline has a way of making those traits sound like a bad thing." Both men chuckled. "Please place both of them in the wing near my room, and would it be acceptable if Georgiana's companion accompanies her? I believe she will be quite capable of protecting Georgie from your sisters' officiousness." Bingley agreed, and the gentlemen enjoyed their breakfast, just finishing as the others arrived in the dining room. Darcy acknowledged everyone and begged to be excused to attend to some business. Bingley also excused himself and went to speak to his housekeeper about the additional guests. He said he expected them within the week, but would let her know the exact date as soon as possible.

Upstairs, Darcy penned a second note to Richard asking if he could bring Georgiana to Netherfield Park in the next few days and stay for a day or two of sport. He mentioned Miss Elizabeth had been delighted at the prospect of meeting Georgiana. Then he began his letter to Georgiana.

Netherfield Park
Hertfordshire

Dearest Georgiana,

I was delighted to hear that you are doing so well with Mrs. Annesley. Netherfield is smaller then Pemberley, but it is a comfortable home, and the estate is well maintained. It would be a good investment should Bingley decide to purchase it.

We attended an assembly on my second day here. On the whole the attendees are not from the social circle to which we are accustomed; however, it appears that everyone speaks of the same inane topics in a ballroom. Bingley introduced me to the eldest sisters of his nearest neighbor. Their names are Misses Jane and Elizabeth Bennet. They were both very pleasant young ladies.

Now, I have the most startling news. Miss Elizabeth Bennet was your savior in the park from five years ago! Once I confirmed who she was, she asked after your health. Thinking you might enjoy her company I asked if I could present you to her, and she was delighted with the prospect.

I have written to Richard asking him to accompany you and Mrs. Annesley to Netherfield as soon as possible. I will send this by express and ask that the messenger wait for an answer. Please let him know when you think you can arrive. Mr. Bingley is happy to have you join us. As Miss Bingley has asked after you several times since my arrival, I am sure she will be delighted to see you as well. Do not worry, Dear One, we will visit Miss Elizabeth as often as possible, and you can study with Mrs. Annesley in your suite anytime you are uncomfortable with Mr. Bingley's sisters.

I look forward to seeing you soon, dear sister.

Your loving brother,

William

He had just finished sealing the letter when a knock was heard at the door. Upon Darcy's call to enter, Bingley stuck his head in asking if Darcy was ready to visit Longbourn.

"Your timing is perfect, my friend. I have just completed my letters and we can stop by the express office on our way to Longbourn to send them off."

As they crossed the foyer to the door, Caroline exited the drawing room and asked about their plans.

"We are riding into Meryton on business and then will be touring the area for a while, Caroline," Bingley answered with a studied air of nonchalance.

"Do try to return in time for luncheon. Charles, we have not had much opportunity to visit with Mr. Darcy." Darcy rolled his eyes at Bingley as they left without agreeing to her request.

CHAPTER 5

AFTER A BRIEF stop to send the letters, Darcy and Bingley continued through Meryton heading for Longbourn. Darcy noted that Meryton was much like the village of Lambton near Pemberley. Again, he passed the bookshop and reminded himself to see if it contained any hidden treasures. It was not long before the gates of Longbourn came into view. As they turned up the drive, Darcy noted the ancient trees that lined it on both sides. Then he looked towards the house. It was not as large as Netherfield but appeared well maintained. As they reached the door, a young man came around the side of the house to take their horses. Upon their entrance, Hill led the gentlemen to the parlor and solemnly announced them.

Upon entering the parlor, they noted all of the ladies of the house were present. Mrs. Bennet welcomed them effusively. "Oh, Mr. Bingley, Mr. Darcy, how very glad we are that you have come to visit," she said with a small wave of her handkerchief. The young ladies all rose to make their curtsey, and the gentlemen bowed.

"Thank you for receiving us, Mrs. Bennet," said Bingley in his usual happy manner. "We enjoyed meeting your family at the assembly and thought to call to further the acquaintance." Bingley spoke to Mrs. Bennet, but his eyes drifted to Jane.

Mrs. Bennet, noticing his look, said, "Why do not you take a seat here beside Jane, Mr. Bingley? My Jane is so lovely; is she not? None of the other girls quite compare except my dear Lydia." Jane blushed at the remark, but as her eyes were downcast, she did not notice the smile on Bingley's face as he happily took the seat indicated. Darcy, hoping not to have any attention drawn to himself, took a chair next to the end of the sofa on which Miss Elizabeth and Miss Mary sat. He could not help but notice the hurt and embarrassment her mother's words had caused. He noted that Kitty and Lydia were seated at a table near the window, but he was extremely uncomfortable with the flirtatious looks young Lydia cast at him.

With both Elizabeth and Bingley in the room, conversation flowed easily. Darcy sat quietly observing Elizabeth but managed an occasional contribution to the discussion. It was an unusual conversation, as Mrs. Bennet talked loudly, always bringing the conversation to a recitation of Miss Bennet's excellent qualities. She also seemed to make many comments to him about Miss Lydia's lively personality. Miss Mary seemed very stiff, as though she were uncomfortable, and seemed fond of quoting Dr. Fordyce. Lydia only paid attention to the group when she was being discussed; though Kitty attended to the conversation politely from their table across the room.

Elizabeth was a little surprised at his reticence, as he had not had any difficulty talking with her this morning. She wondered at his silence. Mrs. Bennet commented on the dress of both Bingley's sisters at the assembly the other evening and asked after them. She expressed the hope that they would meet again at the Lucas's in a few days. Mrs. Bennet then turned to Darcy and asked, "Do you have any siblings, Mr. Darcy?"

"Yes, Mrs. Bennet, I have one younger sister, she is but fifteen. She is my only family as both my parents have passed. I have written to ask her to join me in Hertfordshire, but I am not sure if or when she may be able to do so."

"You must bring her to visit, Mr. Darcy, I am sure that my Lydia would make her a wonderful friend." Darcy could barely hear her remark over the noise that Lydia and Kitty were making. They had returned to their task of trimming bonnets as nothing in the conversation was of interest to them. However, they were currently arguing over a piece of ribbon that both wanted.

Elizabeth, noting that Mr. Darcy seemed slightly uncomfortable around her sisters' unseemly behavior, quickly offered, "Mama, perhaps Jane and I could show our guests the gardens as some of the fall flowers are still in bloom."

"What a wonderful idea, Lizzy. You may not be my most beautiful daughter, but what a clever girl you are to think of a way to entertain our guests making for a longer visit. Perhaps you gentlemen might agree to take refreshments with us when you return from your walk," said Mrs. Bennet enthusiastically.

Bingley looked at Darcy, and at his nod replied, "We would be happy to accept your invitation, Mrs. Bennet."

The ladies took only a moment to get their outerwear, hats, and gloves and then led the gentlemen around the side of the house towards the garden. It seemed so natural that Bingley stepped up to walk with Jane as Darcy moved up beside Elizabeth. Shortly the couples were walking one in front of the other, and the distance between them grew. Elizabeth noticed Bingley and Jane seemed to be conversing quietly.

Then she looked at the stern features of her companion; and, with a slight blush on her cheeks, Elizabeth said, "Mr. Darcy, I do apologize for my mother's last remark, but I did caution you about her propensity towards matchmaking with any eligible gentlemen. I am also sure that you are not quite used to the confusion of a large family. I hope that it did not disturb you too greatly."

Darcy glanced towards Elizabeth and noted the blush of embarrassment upon her face. His features softening, he replied, "Do not be concerned, Miss Elizabeth. You are correct such exuberant behavior in company is not something I often see. However, I have been master of my estate from a young age, and I have certainly dealt with my share of matchmaking mothers." Seeing her face reddening even further, he haltingly continued. "Having only one much younger sister, I have never experienced what life in a large family might be. I imagine more noise would be normal with more people."

Elizabeth smiled at his stumbling attempt to soften the harsh words of his answer. He said he was awkward in crowds where he was not well acquainted with the people, and she had now seen that for herself. Her cheeks still pink she looked at the ground as she continued, "My younger sisters are quite silly. My parents have made no attempt to check their behavior, and they will not listen to Jane or me."

"Miss Elizabeth, please do not be concerned. I enjoy your company and that of Miss Bennet, so let us discuss this no further. I must disagree with your mother about one thing, though, Miss Elizabeth. I find you to be the loveliest of all your sisters." Darcy watched as a blush again spread across her cheeks; this time accompanied by a slight smile. She looked at him briefly as her blush deepened. "I sent my sister an express earlier today, I should know by tomorrow when she might arrive."

"I am so looking forward to finally getting to meet her. I wanted to speak to her that day in the park, but my aunt was in a hurry to get home. As I mentioned, she was a bit embarrassed by my behavior, and I did not get to explain until we were in the carriage."

"I hope that she has forgiven you for the lapse in manners, but if not, I would be happy to write thanking her for the thoughtful actions you took for my sister," he said with just the slightest of smiles.

Elizabeth laughed her musical laugh, and Darcy thought how pleasant it would be to hear that sound often. "I thank you for the kind offer, but she has quite forgiven me."

"Do you often visit your relatives in town?" Darcy asked.

"Not as often as I would wish," said Elizabeth with a sigh. "My Aunt and Uncle Gardiner are the most wonderful people. I am sure they are partly responsible for Jane and I being different from our younger sisters. They are a kind and loving couple and a joy to be around."

"You mentioned that you enjoy visiting the theater when you are in town. Do you have a favorite play?"

"I do not know if I could pick just one. I love seeing the stories I have read come to life. If I had to pick a favorite, it would be anything by Shakespeare. What I like most, however, is visiting the different parks to be found in the city. The day we almost met was my first trip to Hyde Park. It had been a glorious morning, and the flowers were lovely; I am glad I was there in Miss Darcy's time of need."

"Have you ever been to The British Museum?" Darcy asked as he watched the play of emotion over her face at her memories of happy times.

"Not as of yet, but I do hope to visit it sometime. I would be most interested in seeing some of the many things about which I have read," Elizabeth remarked with a twinkle in her eye.

"Do you enjoy reading, Miss Elizabeth?"

"Indeed I do! My father has always allowed me to read anything in his library. I am particularly fond of Cowper's poetry and Shakespeare's works. I also enjoy histories and the occasional novel. I frequently take a book with me when I go off on my morning walk. I love to sit on the rock we visited and read, sometimes dangling my feet in the water," she glanced at him to see his reaction.

"Miss Elizabeth, what a scandalous confession," said Darcy with a broad smile that reached even to his eyes. They looked at each other a moment longer, and both laughed. Elizabeth felt a tingle up her spine at his deep resonant chuckle.

"I do much the same thing with my morning ride. When I am pondering the issues of the estate or a problem with the tenants, I find that a good gallop across the fields helps to clear my mind so that I may logically arrive at a solution."

By now they had completed their circuit of the park, and Bingley and Jane were waiting at the corner so they could return indoors together. Mrs. Bennet did indeed have refreshments waiting when they returned, and after another thirty minutes of visiting the gentlemen took their leave.

Upon their return to Netherfield, Miss Bingley was awaiting them in the foyer. "Charles, where have you been?" she asked shrilly. Then noticing Darcy slightly behind her brother, she moderated her tone and continued, "I thought you intended to be home for luncheon. We have been waiting for you for more than an hour. I hope that the meal will still be tolerable."

"I am sorry that we kept you waiting, but you could have proceeded without us, Caroline. We were enjoying refreshments during our visit with the Bennets. We plan to grab a quick bite and return to our tour of the estates. There is much for me to show Darcy and for him to teach me if I am to purchase an estate of my own and establish our family as father wished."

At that moment, the housekeeper announced that luncheon was served. Darcy and Bingley were quietly engaged in a discussion of matters related to the running of an estate. Caroline could stand to be ignored no longer, and with a sharp tone asked, "Charles why on earth would you ever want to visit the Bennet family? They are so unsophisticated, and most of them are totally lacking in any of the social graces—particularly Miss Eliza. She is reputed to be a local beauty. I see no beauty in her at all just a conceited impertinence. And her conversation, she would be laughed out of the ballrooms in London; that is if anyone deigned to speak to her at all." Caroline cackled with laughter at her pronouncements, and Mrs. Hurst gave a small titter. Hurst gave his wife a stern look, and she abruptly stopped laughing. At her silence, Caroline looked first at Louisa and then at the others at the table. Both Charles and Mr. Darcy were looking at her with cold disdain, and Hurst's smirk was hard to understand.

As they arose from the table, Charles spoke harshly to Caroline. "I believe, Caroline, that if you cannot say anything pleasant about our neighbors, I would prefer that you not speak at all." With those parting words, both Darcy and Bingley left the dining room for the stables.

Hurst gave a soft chuckle and excused himself from the table. He had not gone far when he heard Caroline's voice raised in outrage. "How dare Charles speak to me in such a way. What has become of him that he would not accede to my wishes? He has never behaved so in the past." Hurst could hear the anger in her voice. "What could they possibly see in these chits?" Caroline asked.

"Well, Jane Bennet is quite lovely and a sweet young woman. What man would not find her attractive? And you know how easily Charles falls in love," Louisa offered.

"Really, Louisa, do you want Charles to fall in love with a girl from the country? How will we ever advance in society if he does such a thing? We have got to get him to leave Netherfield and the Bennets; and, if we cannot, we shall have to find a way to discourage Charles and Mr. Darcy in their current infatuations. What could he possibly see in that Eliza Bennet?" Caroline fumed. "I must get his attention back on me. Why cannot he see that I am the perfect choice for Mrs. Darcy? It seems I will have to compromise him; then he would have to marry me. I must think of a plan." Hurst had heard enough; he sauntered off to the library for a drink to help with his thinking.

Darcy and Bingley barely returned to the house in time to change for dinner. They were in good spirits having had a pleasant afternoon riding about the estate. Caroline maintained a polite and restrained attitude throughout dinner. When the sexes separated after dinner, Hurst gave a humorous account of the conversation he had heard after luncheon. "You had best watch yourself, Darcy. I have never seen anyone as determined as Caroline is to marry you, and she can be quite devious when trying to get what she wants," Hurst said with a chortle.

As the men were returning to the parlor, the butler came towards them. "This express just arrived for you, Mr. Darcy."

"Thank you, Dawson," Darcy said as he took the letter from the salver the butler extended to him. Opening the note, Darcy said, "Hurst why do you not go on ahead. We will be along directly." As Hurst moved on to the parlor, Darcy said, "Bingley, it appears that Georgiana and the Colonel will arrive in three days. Do you think we can withhold the information from Caroline until the day before they arrive?"

"Certainly, Darcy, will luncheon do or would you prefer it be at the evening meal?"

"The evening meal would be fine with me, but we do not want to raise Miss Bingley's ire too much by waiting too long." They both chuckled and headed into the parlor.

"Tell me, Mr. Darcy, would you prefer music or cards this evening?" purred Miss Bingley.

"Your playing is always a pleasure, Miss Bingley, but please suit yourself as I believe that I will entertain myself with a book again this evening."

Taking Darcy's words as a compliment, Caroline settled herself at the piano and began playing another love song, this one in French. Darcy grimaced as he took his book to a seat by the fire. Miss Bingley might not have felt quite so complimented had she realized that Darcy knew she could not converse if she were playing.

CHAPTER 6

As was usual, Darcy awoke early the next morning. He was anxious for a ride and hoped to see Elizabeth as he wished to tell her about Georgiana's arrival. He paused only long enough for coffee and a muffin and was cheerfully smiling as he made his way to the stables. Today he had no intention of looking over the estate as he rode; he headed directly for the fence that separated Longbourn from Netherfield. He did not have to wait long before a flash of color alerted him to Elizabeth's arrival.

"Good morning, Miss Elizabeth," Darcy called, a look of welcome spreading across his face.

"Mr. Darcy, how are you this bright fall morning?" Elizabeth replied her face lighting with a slight blush and her smile.

"I am very well, thank you. I hoped that I would meet you this morning as I have some news I wish to share."

"I think you were doing more than hoping, Mr. Darcy. It appears as if you have been waiting for me," Elizabeth smiled with a twinkle in her eyes.

Embarrassed about being seen through so easily, Darcy flushed. "I know it is inappropriate for me to meet you in such a manner, Miss Elizabeth, but I do have some news I am eager to share. I received an express from my sister last evening, and she will be arriving on Friday."

"Oh, that is wonderful," Elizabeth cried. "I do look forward to knowing her."

"I am very anxious for her to meet you, Miss Elizabeth. I hope that she will arrive early enough that we might be able to call on you in the afternoon. Would that be convenient? I am certain that she will enjoy your company; and, if I may speak honestly," he paused waiting for Elizabeth's approval before continuing. "I am hoping that she will become more confident around strangers, with you as her example."

Elizabeth blushed at his compliment, and Darcy thought how lovely she looked and what a pleasure it was to make her blush. He wondered what it would be like to make her blush like that each morning for the rest of his life. Darcy was startled by the sudden thought. He barely noticed the endless stream of young ladies presented to him among the ton. Why had this young lady so caught his eye and interest? He knew the disadvantages that would come with a connection to her. Could he possibly put aside the expectations of his family and society in order to have a relationship with Elizabeth? Until he was certain, he would have to be somewhat circumspect in his behavior—or at least try to be, as that would not be his inclination. Conscious of the amount of time they had been alone, Darcy expressed his wishes for a good day and turned his mount towards Netherfield.

Elizabeth watched him ride away thinking how pleasant she found being in his company. He was easy to talk to and so intelligent that conversation with him was a true pleasure. She found it something of a puzzle that he found conversation in a group of people to be so difficult when he did not seem to find it difficult to talk with her. She hoped she would make a good impression on Miss Darcy and perhaps help her, as well. Elizabeth eagerly looked forward to her coming. Mr. Darcy had finally crested the hill, and she could no longer see him, so she moved on briskly to continue her walk.

Darcy returned to Netherfield as Charles was coming down the stairs to break his fast. He saw Darcy entering and greeted him cheerfully, "How are you this morning, Darcy? Did you enjoy your ride?"

"It was very pleasant," Darcy said with a smile. "Please excuse me, Bingley, while I change. I will join you shortly." Darcy took the stairs two at a time and turned down the hallway towards his room. He was surprised to see Miss Bingley with her ear to his door and her hand on the knob as though about to enter. Clearing his throat, he saw her straighten with a start and turn in his direction her face flushing in embarrassment. "May I help you, Miss Bingley?" he asked coldly, noting her hand being removed from the knob as though burned.

"No, no, I . . . I . . . I just wanted to see if there was anything that you needed."

"I am sure that you would be able to hear my reply without having your ear to the door. Were you trying to determine my presence within the room without benefit of knocking?"

"I do not know what you could mean, Mr. Darcy," she said stiffly. "I was merely attempting to be a good hostess and inquire about your needs. If there is nothing I may get for you, I will leave and see you at breakfast."

Darcy entered his room, and Chalmers immediately emerged from the dressing room. "Chalmers, it is vital during this visit that we are cautious where Miss Bingley is concerned. She was outside my door just now with her ear pressed against it. I am sorry to inconvenience you so, but I would prefer that you sleep in the dressing room during our stay. Also, please keep all the doors to my suite locked at all times. Perhaps if you can determine what time the maids clean, you can find some reason to be here with the doors unlocked so as not to arouse suspicion."

"It is no inconvenience, sir. The talk in the kitchen is that Miss Bingley makes it quite plain that she intends to be Mrs. Darcy no matter how long it takes or what she must do. As I should hate to see you settled with someone who would make your life unpleasant, I will do whatever I can to be of assistance during this visit," Chalmers replied firmly.

Chalmers had been with Darcy since he was six and ten years old. He accompanied him to University, on his tour, and supported him during the loss of his father. He was a pleasant fellow, with a sharp mind, and his loyalty to Darcy was unequaled. There were few secrets between master and servant. And there was nothing he would not do to protect Darcy and ensure his happiness.

Darcy was quickly bathed and changed. As he descended the stairs to join the others at breakfast, he heard Miss Bingley's voice. It was cloyingly sweet as she said, "Charles, since you seem to find the Bennets such good company, perhaps we should invite Miss Bennet and Miss Elizabeth to tea to get better acquainted. I thought perhaps tomorrow afternoon."

Charles, not noticing the false sweetness in her voice, replied, "That is a wonderful idea. I am sure they will be delighted to attend, and I know that you will enjoy their company," was his enthusiastic reply.

Darcy entered the room, bidding everyone good morning. "I say, Darcy, how about a spot of shooting this morning? We have not had a chance for any sport since you arrived. You will join us, of course, Hurst?" Charles asked, turning to his brother-in-law.

"I thought the sport was the reason we made this trip into the country," Hurst replied. "Let us not waste anymore time here, then."

The gentlemen were gone until luncheon and quite pleased with the success of the morning. Bingley and Hurst were exuberantly recounting the hunt during the meal, and even Darcy, a smile upon his face, had a contribution to make. After luncheon they adjourned to the billiards room for some sport of a different kind. They rejoined the ladies in time for tea.

Miss Bingley, her voice again suspiciously sweet, said, "Charles, I received a reply to my invitation to tea. Miss Bennet and Miss Eliza will be arriving at four o'clock. Do you know anything of which they are particularly fond? I would be happy to be sure it is served."

"I do not know of any favorites. I am sure they will be pleased with anything you serve, Caroline." Darcy was watching her closely during their conversation. He did not trust the tone of her voice and found the look on her face disturbing. He would have Chalmers keep his ears open when in the servants' hall.

After tea, Darcy retired to the study to attend to the day's post. There was a great deal of correspondence that required his attention, and he continued working after dinner, not joining the family that evening.

Darcy rode out again the next morning, but this time he chose a gallop across the meadows, which enabled him to observe some of the tenants at work in their fields. After breakfast, he told Bingley that he wanted to make a trip into Meryton to visit the bookshop. As Bingley had scheduled a meeting with the estate's steward to discuss what went into planning for spring planting and what the harvest entailed, he wished Darcy a good day and turned towards the study.

Darcy mounted his horse and set off towards Meryton. The streets of the village were bustling with people going about their business. He tied his horse to the post in front of the bookshop and made his way inside.

When he opened the door, a small bell sounded, and a voice called from the back of the store, "Please look around, I will be with you in just a moment."

Darcy began to peruse the shelves, noting the efficient way in which the shop was organized. He was excited to discover a section labeled "First Editions" and glanced through the titles looking for something to add to the Pemberley library. His effort was interrupted suddenly by a familiar laugh coming from the back of the store. Delighted by the prospect of seeing Elizabeth, Darcy followed the sound. Looking around the last shelf at the end of the row, he saw her seated on the floor with a book in her hands and a smile on her face. She did not notice him, and when she laughed again, he asked, "What is it that so tickles you in the pages of your book, Miss Elizabeth?"

Elizabeth started and turned quickly to see Mr. Darcy peering at her from around the corner. Embarrassed at being found in such an unladylike position she hurried to stand, only to pause as she noticed his hand outstretched to assist her. Shyly placing her hand in his, she felt his warm fingers encase her cold ones as he assisted her to rise. She was startled to feel the tingling begin again at his touch. With color still upon her cheeks she said, "Good morning, Mr. Darcy. You caught me unawares."

He watched as a blush, again, brightened her face. It gave him a warm feeling when his words affected her. "I am sorry if I disturbed you, but I heard a delightful laugh and simply had to find its source." He paused for a moment deliberating, then spoke. "Miss Bennet, I have a confession to make," he said seriously. Elizabeth looked at him anxiously and waited for him to continue. "Actually, I knew to whom that charming laugh belonged. I first heard it as you were departing the park after the encounter with Wickham and then again at the theater in London five years ago." Elizabeth's face expressed the surprise that she felt. "I have always hoped to find Georgiana's savior so that I could thank you properly. You can imagine my surprise when I heard you laugh at the assembly the other evening. I was drawn to you, but it had been so long that I doubted my memory. I had to be sure that you were the same young lady for whom I was searching. That is why I asked you about London while we danced."

Elizabeth was stunned. How was it possible that he had remembered the sound of her laugh for so long?

"Your musical laugh has often been in my thoughts; I have never heard another so warm and sweet."

Elizabeth blushed yet again, but her heart fluttered at his words and the warm smile that accompanied them. Fighting her nervousness in the usual way, Elizabeth wittily replied, "I shall do my best then to laugh as often as possible whenever you are near." Her saucy reply was accompanied by a twinkle in her eyes, and it brought to his face the largest smile she had ever seen, including the appearance of two remarkable dimples. She was momentarily dazzled and knew not what to say.

Darcy was delighted at leaving her tongue-tied, as that was a position in which he often found himself when in her company. Offering her the opportunity to recover, he asked, "What brought you to the bookstore this morning?"

"Mr. Stevens always allows me to go through his new shipments before placing them on the shelves. He had not quite finished his inventory of the new items when I arrived, so I was visiting with some old favorites from the shelves as I waited."

Just at that moment, Mr. Stevens came through from the back of the shop. "Miss Lizzy, you can go and check the books now. They are all logged in and separated for the shelves. Go and have a look while I help this gentleman," said Mr. Stevens as he turned to Darcy with a smile. "How can I help you this morning, sir?" he asked.

Darcy watched as Elizabeth headed through the curtain to the back of the shop before turning to look at the proprietor. Mr. Stevens was tall and thin with glasses perched upon the end of his nose. He was balding but had a gray fringe and side-whiskers on his lined face. "Good morning. I noticed your shop as I came into town and felt compelled to visit. I have found many treasures in small bookshops during past travels. I was hoping to find one in your shop during my stay in the area."

"Is there anything in which you were particularly interested?" the shopkeeper asked.

"I was reviewing your first editions before bumping into Miss Elizabeth, but, unfortunately, did not see anything I did not already have."

"Well, I did receive a few additional ones in this most recent shipment. Would you like me to bring them out for you to peruse?"

"Please, do not bother," said Darcy. "I will be happy to follow Miss Elizabeth if that is acceptable?"

Mr. Stevens nodded and led the way to the workroom at the back of the shop. Elizabeth was bent over a table looking through the new titles with one book already in her hands. She glanced up at the sound of the curtain fabric rustling as the men entered. Mr. Stevens directed Darcy to the area where the first editions were stacked waiting to be shelved. Darcy gave them his attention as he listened to their conversation.

"Well, Miss Lizzy, what have you found?"

"I believe this book will make a wonderful gift for my father for Christmas," said Elizabeth showing him the book in her hand. "I would love to purchase this one for myself," she added indicating a book of poetry by Donne she held in her other hand. "Unfortunately, I will have to wait until I receive my next allowance. I loaned a portion of my funds to Lydia, and she has yet to repay me. I shall hope it is still here next week," she said with a rueful smile.

"Well, good day to you, Mr. Stevens, and thank you for allowing me to see the new books first. Mr. Darcy, my sister and I have been invited to tea at three this afternoon. Will I see you then?" she asked hopefully.

"At three?" Darcy asked confused, "I thought Miss Bingley said you were to arrive at four. Well, no matter. Whatever the time, I will be very much looking forward to it, Miss Elizabeth," he replied with a smile of his own. Darcy made a mental note to confirm the time when he returned to Netherfield, and he again wondered what Miss Bingley was planning.

As soon as she exited the store, Darcy turned to the shopkeeper. "I would like to purchase the book Miss Elizabeth wished for," he said. "She has done a great service for my family, and as my sister will be arriving shortly she can present it to her as a gift of appreciation."

"I am sure she will be delighted to receive it, Mr. Darcy," he replied with a smile. "It does not surprise me to hear that she has been of assistance to your family. Miss Elizabeth is one of the kindest young women you will ever meet. There are many who can tell you tales of having had help from her in time of need. I am glad to see that she will be the recipient of some kindness herself," said the gentleman with a knowing smile.

Elizabeth waved as she left the store and headed off down the street for the lane that would take her to Longbourn. Her thoughts were all of Mr. Darcy. He was very handsome, and so pleasant whenever they were together. She knew he was just the sort of man she had dreamed about marrying, but she warned herself to keep in mind their very different situations in life. She knew she would like the opportunity to know him better and wondered if she would get the chance to do so if she began a friendship with Miss Darcy. Elizabeth thought about all the things Mr. Darcy had said about his sister and hoped that she could be of assistance to her and help her overcome her shyness. Perhaps she could begin by encouraging Miss Darcy to walk with her while staying in the area.

Elizabeth arrived home in time for luncheon. Her mother dominated the conversation, discussing their invitation to Netherfield Park for tea. She told Jane that she was beautiful and that Mr. Bingley was certain to fall in love with her.

"You must remember that you need to let him know of your interest. You must catch him, Jane. It is the only thing that will save us from the hedgerows when your father is gone, and the heir makes us leave our home," whined Mrs. Bennet with her handkerchief fluttering. Then she turned to Elizabeth, "And you must mind your tongue, Lizzy. We cannot have you being impertinent and scaring Mr. Bingley away," she admonished.

"Yes, Mama," Elizabeth replied as she glanced at Jane and rolled her eyes.

Smiling sympathetically at Elizabeth, Mr. Bennet joined the conversation. "Mrs. Bennet, you have no cause for concern as both Jane and Elizabeth are pleasant, well-mannered girls. However, as you are the one who brought up the heir, I have just received a letter from him. He has recently been ordained and was granted a living in Kent. He would like to come for a visit to heal the breach that has kept our branches of the family estranged for the last generation. He writes that he has received the permission of his patroness to visit us for a fortnight and plans to arrive next Saturday. He says he is particularly looking forward to making the acquaintance of all his dear cousins," said Mr. Bennet with a sardonic grin on his face. Elizabeth could tell by her father's expression that Mr. Bennet anticipated the visit of the heir as an opportunity to be highly entertained. Mr. Bennet dearly loved to laugh at the follies and foibles of others. Like her father, she had learned to laugh at the antics of others rather than being bothered by them. However, she dearly wished that her father would take his role as a parent more seriously at least where his family was concerned. Rather than correct them, he just laughed at the antics of his younger daughters.

The girls carefully readied themselves for tea at Netherfield, and, with their mother's admonitions still ringing in their ears, they boarded the carriage for the short journey. Each was anticipating the afternoon with mixed feelings. Jane was looking forward to seeing Mr. Bingley again but was concerned that she would do something wrong and fail her family. Elizabeth had enjoyed all of her encounters with Mr. Darcy, but she did not want to lose her heart to him and have it broken when he returned to his life in town and a social circle in which she had no part.

Miss Bingley watched as the ladies entered. She had her questions planned; the answers to which she was sure would show Darcy and Charles how totally unsuitable these country chits were. She was very relieved tea had been planned for today as she had just learned from her brother that Miss Darcy and Mr. Darcy's cousin, Colonel Fitzwilliam, would be arriving tomorrow. It would have been difficult to carry out her plan had Miss Darcy been present. Miss Bingley rose and walked towards Elizabeth and Jane. "Miss Bennet, Miss Eliza, how delightful to see you again. Please, will you be seated?" She steered Elizabeth to a seat on the sofa next to Mrs. Hurst and indicated Jane should take the seat next to her.

"Good afternoon, ladies. How delightful you could join us for tea today." Caroline Bingley started at the sound of here brother's voice and looked up to see he and Mr. Darcy entering the drawing room, followed by Mr. Hurst. Neither gentleman missed the angry look that crossed her face at their arrival. She had deliberately given them the wrong time for the ladies arrival. Darcy could only wonder what mischief she had planned.

Bingley quickly took the chair at the end of the sofa near where Jane sat. Darcy remained standing, but took up a place near the fireplace where he could watch Elizabeth unobserved. Miss Bingley poured and prepared the tea for everyone—seeming to take an unusually long time to prepare Miss Elizabeth's cup, which aroused Darcy's suspicions. As she passed around a plate of biscuits, Miss Bingley turned to Jane and asked, "Miss Bennet, how is all your family today?"

"They are very well thank you," Jane replied.

"Do you have other family nearby?" she asked.

"Yes, my mother's sister and her husband live in Meryton. Mr. Phillips is a solicitor."

"A solicitor? Is not that interesting, Louisa?" she asked.

"Oh, really?"

Miss Bingley was looking at her sister, so Jane could not see the smirk on her face, but the derision she exhibited was apparent to Elizabeth. Caroline turned back to Jane with a look of interest and asked,

"Do you have a large extended family?"

"No, it is only the aunt and uncle I mentioned, and my mother's brother and his family who live in London."

Caroline's interest increased. "You have family in London?"

"Yes, my uncle is a successful importer/exporter. They reside in Cheapside so he can be near his work and his family."

"Cheapside," Caroline repeated, her smirk again in evidence, "I do not think I have ever been in that part of town before, have you, Louisa?"

"No, I am afraid I do not have an acquaintances in that part of town," she replied with quietly.

Elizabeth realized that Bingley's sisters—well at least Miss Bingley—were looking down their noses and laughing at them. Elizabeth remarked, "I am surprised that would be the case as so many families who have roots in trade get their start there. I understood your family got its start in trade, am I mistaken?" she asked with a confused expression on her face. Elizabeth caught the gleam in Darcy's eye and had to look down, so she did not give herself away.

"You are quite correct, Miss Elizabeth. Our family was very successful in trade. However, it was in textiles. We have several mills in the north that are still in operation," said Bingley pleasantly.

Darcy was pleased to see how skillfully Miss Elizabeth handled Bingley's sisters. He noted the angry look on Miss Bingley's face as she listened to Charles' explanation and watched as it changed to one of determination.

As Bingley turned the conversation to upcoming events in the area, Darcy noticed that when Elizabeth took a small sip of her tea, her face reflected something unpleasant. He watched her set the cup on the table beside her, as Bingley asked the ladies if they would be attending the dinner at Lucas Lodge next week.

Jane smiled shyly as she replied, "Yes, our family was invited to the dinner, as well. The friendship between our families is of long standing. Charlotte Lucas has been a very dear friend to Lizzy and me all of our lives."

"I am delighted to hear it," said Mr. Bingley.

Elizabeth had been wondering at Darcy's silence throughout the visit. He had maintained his pose by the fireplace, but she knew he had been closely following the conversation. He now moved from his position and took the chair nearest to where Elizabeth was seated, placing his cup on the table very near hers.

"Miss Elizabeth, my sister and cousin will be arriving tomorrow for a visit. I do hope there will be an opportunity for me to introduce her to you."

Miss Bingley, livid at Darcy's request, snidely commented, "You must be sure to introduce her to Miss Eliza's younger sisters as well. I am sure she could learn so much from them." Darcy glared coldly, but Caroline continued, "Certainly Miss Darcy will be able to talk about the many common interests they share. Tell me, Miss Eliza, do your sisters play the pianoforte, draw, sing, paint tables? Can they speak French? Did they attend the finest seminaries as Miss Darcy, Mrs. Hurst, and I did? I am sure they will have so much to discuss." Her voice was laden with sarcasm.

"Yes, Miss Bingley, each of my sisters has her own individual talents, just as we all do. However, I have never known a young lady in whom all of these talents you listed reside. She would be quite a sight to behold."

"Well, you will meet her soon for they all reside in the person of Miss Darcy."

"I am sorry to disappoint you, Miss Bingley, but my sister does not sing. I would also have to add something to your list. No lady can be considered truly accomplished if she is not well read and aware of the world around her," Darcy added with a warm look towards Elizabeth.

She smiled shyly in return, but her eyes were shimmering as she acknowledged his compliment. Elizabeth looked to where Jane sat and realizing she was uncomfortable with the turn the conversation had taken, sought to put her at ease again. "I am sure we shall enjoy meeting Miss Darcy no matter the talents she possesses, shall we not Jane?" Elizabeth said encouragingly.

"I am sure you will enjoy her company, Miss Bennet," Bingley added. "She is a delightful young woman if a bit shy."

Caroline sat and fumed as the conversation continued around her. She had to get rid of Eliza Bennet. How did her plan go so awry? Caroline had been certain when she pointed out her lowly connections and lack of talents to Mr. Darcy, he would lose interest. However, not only was Mr. Darcy still showing interest in Eliza Bennet, but he even wanted to introduce her to the sister he protected so carefully. She would have to find another way to discourage his interest. And Charles seemed to be more infatuated with Miss Bennet than ever. Perhaps she could find a way to encourage him toward Miss Darcy, or orchestrate a double compromise if necessary? She would have to give the matter serious thought in the coming days. Perhaps she could turn Miss Darcy against Eliza Bennet, telling her that she was a fortune hunter after her brother. She had so much to consider before Miss Darcy's arrival tomorrow.

As all of her plans for the afternoon had failed, Miss Bingley had a difficult time remaining polite through the balance of the visit. Her face hurt from the false smile she held in place, and her remarks were clipped, when she deigned to speak at all.

The conversation flowed smoothly, and the others continued to enjoy the afternoon. Mrs. Hurst participated more and more in the discussion as the visit continued. Hurst relished watching Caroline be thwarted by Miss Elizabeth; and, while Caroline's attacks had been obvious and rude, Miss Elizabeth's responses had been like iron in a velvet glove. They were masterfully done and had been a pleasure to witness.

Noticing that Elizabeth had not drunk her tea, Miss Bingley commented, "Miss Eliza, you have not finished your tea. Please do drink it, it is a favorite blend of mine."

Elizabeth was somewhat embarrassed; the tea had an unpleasant taste, but she did not know how to politely tell her hostess. "Perhaps I may try it another time," said Elizabeth. "I find that I am not particularly thirsty at the present. Darcy's suspicions of Miss Bingley increased, so he casually reached for his tea, taking Elizabeth's cup rather than his own.

Noticing what had occurred, Miss Bingley said, "Mr. Darcy, I believe that you picked up Miss Eliza's cup by mistake."

"No, I am quite sure this is my cup," he replied calmly.

Before she could move to stop him, Darcy lifted the cup to his lips but was assailed by the smell of sour milk. He moved the cup downward and noticed white lumps floating on the surface. "I believe you could be correct, Miss Bingley, this is Miss Elizabeth's cup. I understand why she is not thirsty, as the milk in her tea appears to be sour. That is quite odd since I have milk in my tea as well, and it is not spoiled. I wonder how that could have happened."

Embarrassed to have been caught, Miss Bingley rose hurriedly with her hand extended, "Please let me prepare you a new cup then, Miss Eliza." She took the cup from Darcy's hand and prepared another cup. However, as she crossed the room to return it to Elizabeth, Miss Bingley pretended to stumble spilling the cup of hot tea in Elizabeth's lap. "Oh, I am sorry." In spite of her words, Caroline made no effort to help her guest. It was Mrs. Hurst who quickly offered Elizabeth several serviettes to wipe up the liquid. Miss Bingley sat with her teacup in hand her head down. It did not disguise her smile of satisfaction from Darcy, however.

"Miss Elizabeth, are you quite alright? I pray you did not get burned," said Bingley worriedly.

"If you wish to step upstairs, Miss Elizabeth. I will have a maid attend to your dress.

It would not take long for her to clean the spot and return it to you," offered Mrs. Hurst.

Fortunately, the hour for tea had passed so Elizabeth said, "That is very kind of you, Mrs. Hurst, but perhaps it would be best if Jane and I depart. It has been an interesting afternoon. We shall have to return the invitation soon."

"We shall look forward to it," replied Mrs. Hurst in a sincere voice. The gentlemen rose and bowed as the ladies made their curtseys. The insincerity in Miss Bingley's words was obvious, but Mrs. Hurst thanked them for their visit and expressed her pleasure in getting to know them better. Bingley showed the ladies to their carriage.

Bingley watched as the carriage went down the drive and out the gates. He acknowledged that he was, indeed, more attracted to Miss Bennet with each passing moment. He began to wonder what it would be like to have a life with her. She was so beautiful, but also sweet, kind, and serene. Bingley, for all of his enthusiasm, just wanted a happy home and a peaceful life.

Darcy had excused himself to attend to his correspondence. He did not think he could tolerate Caroline Bingley's presence for a moment longer. Though his eyes were on the letter in front of him, Darcy's thoughts were only of Elizabeth. She captivated him in a way no other young woman ever had. He dreamed of her nightly and relived their conversations during his waking hours. She could converse intelligently on many subjects and was, indeed, well read. However, her family and connections would be a disadvantage to her acceptance by the ton. Miss Elizabeth showed how capable she was in dealing with the sharp tongues of the ton by the graceful way she had handled Miss Bingley's attack. Maybe it would not be a problem, particularly if his aunt, Lady Matlock, would help her? But would she? What would his family think of her? If Miss Elizabeth could come to town to visit with her aunt and uncle, he could see more of her and see how she handled the society to which he was accustomed. But what of her family in town, would they be like Mrs. Bennet since they were related? He remembered the people he saw with her at the theater. They had appeared very refined, so it would hopefully not be an issue. He would ask her when she next expected to visit.

In the drawing room, Hurst headed for the liquor and waited for Caroline's explosion. He did not have long to wait.

"Louisa, how could you turn on me like that?" she shrieked. "You promised to aid me in my plans. How dare you not support me?"

Mrs. Hurst stared at her sister. Initially, she had been prepared to help Caroline in her plan to gain embarrassing information about the Bennet sisters. Caroline planned to use it to discourage her brother and Mr. Darcy's interest in them. *Agreeing with her sister was so much easier than arguing with her.* However, she could not continue helping Caroline anymore. Miss Bennet was a lovely girl and very much like Charles. Louisa felt certain they might be happy together. Miss Elizabeth was a kind and pleasant your lady as well. To Louisa, it was also more obvious than it had ever been that Mr. Darcy would not offer for Caroline.

Finally, she spoke. "Caroline, I did promise to assist you, and up to this point, I have. However, I do not believe there is anything you can do that will make Mr. Darcy marry you. He is clearly not interested. Stop wasting your time and turn you attention elsewhere. As for Miss Bennet, she is the perfect woman for Charles. I would rather see him happy that worry about advancing in society."

Miss Bingley looked at her sister with mounting fury. "I will be Mrs. Darcy; you will see. I am the perfect choice. When I succeed, I will not forget your betrayal. You will never be invited to our events in town or to Pemberley."

"Caroline, if you continue in this way, it is you who will no longer be received at Darcy House or Pemberley. Be realistic. Look for your husband and future elsewhere, before it is too late."

Feeling quite proud of his wife, Mr. Hurst offered his arm and asked if she would care to stroll in the gardens with him until time to dress for dinner. With a surprised look on her face she accepted his arm and they left Caroline alone in the drawing room.

Caroline was pacing in her fury. She would never forgive Louisa for this. She looked down at the figurine on the table beside which she had paused. The figure was a petite girl with dark curls; incensed with the resemblance to Eliza Bennet, she picked up the figurine and hurled it at the fireplace. It hit the marble and crashed to the floor in a thousand pieces.

"Please remember that the items in this house do not belong to our family and kindly leave them alone," Bingley said firmly, a frown on his face. Caroline jumped at the sound of his voice. She had thought herself alone. "I did not appreciate your rather impolite questions, Caroline. In the future, please treat guests in my home more appropriately or you will no longer be the hostess here. And, this is the last time I intend to tell you, leave Darcy alone. He has no interest in marrying you and has stated that he will not do so under any circumstances. He has been kind enough to include you in invitations because you are my sister but please remember that he does not have to do so. If you continue in your obvious attempts to entrap him, you may find yourself no longer included in the invitations you so covet." Preparing to leave, Bingley stopped and again looked at his sister, "After your display this afternoon, I know why you misinformed Darcy and me of the time the ladies were to visit. Fortunately, Darcy saw Miss Elizabeth while he was in Meryton this morning, and we learned the correct time." So saying, Bingley turned on his heels and headed for the billiard room to relax before dinner.

Caroline stood staring after her brother. How had this happened? She had always been able to manipulate her siblings into doing whatever she wished. It all began when they entered this horrid county, and the Bennet family entered her well-ordered world. Miss Eliza's impertinent behavior was setting a decidedly bad example for her brother. How she hated the little country nobody. She would put her in her place if it were the last thing she did. Though not ready to give up on Darcy, she was determined that Eliza Bennet would certainly never have him.

CHAPTER 7

GEORGIANA WAS PRACTICALLY bouncing in her seat as the carriage got closer to its destination. Both Richard and Mrs. Annesley were delighted to see her spirits so high. The change had occurred upon her reading Darcy's letter. She had been enjoying her time with Mrs. Annesley, but she always missed her brother when he was traveling. It was not often that she was included when William visited friends. Mr. Bingley's company was always pleasant though she was not particularly comfortable around Miss Bingley and Mrs. Hurst. Perhaps Miss Elizabeth would want to be her friend, and she could spend time with her.

Smiling knowingly at Mrs. Annesley, Richard asked, "Georgie, are you anxious to see Miss Bingley? You seem unable to remain still."

Georgiana turned to Richard, her face aghast, only to see him regarding her with a big grin.

"Oh, Richard, you know I want to see William, I miss him so when he is away. I am also excited to meet Miss Bennet. I never had the chance to thank her for helping me escape my kidnapper. I hope she will enjoy meeting me, too," she remarked, doubt clouding her face.

"It sounds like she is looking forward to meeting you, from Darcy's letter. I have no doubt she will enjoy your company, Little One," Richard responded reassuringly.

"I agree with your cousin, Miss Darcy. I am sure you will make a good impression on Miss Bennet. However, you must try your best to overcome your shyness and attempt to make conversation so that you can become well acquainted with her," said Mrs. Annesley kindly.

At that moment, the carriage entered the village of Meryton, and the occupants turned their faces toward the windows in order to see what might be discovered.

"It reminds me a bit of Lambton," Georgiana said.

"I imagine that most small country villages are similar," observed Richard.

"There are certain common things that are needed by estates, no matter their size; consequently, the same businesses would be needed in each village," Mrs. Annesley remarked.

"I never thought about it like that," said Georgiana. "I have never considered what was needed to maintain our estate and lifestyle. Perhaps I have been taking things too much for granted. I hope that I have not been unappreciative to you or William," she said looking at Richard.

"Do not worry, Little One, you have always had a kind heart and grateful attitude," he said with a warm smile.

"Mrs. Annesley, do you think there are things I could do to help our tenants, so they know our family is appreciative of their hard work?"

"That is a very wise question, Miss Darcy. Your family has been very blessed by the hard work and efforts of your ancestors and tenants. Not every family is as fortunate, but all families have the same basic needs. We all need a shelter, food, clothes, and someone to care for us. Most families have enough to get by, but unexpected illness or other unplanned for events, can cause many hardships to most working families. Perhaps this is something you could discuss with Miss Bennet. She may be able to tell you what her family does to help their tenants," suggested Mrs. Annesley.

As the discussion continued, the carriage turned into the gates of Netherfield and approached the house. Looking from the window, Georgiana saw that William was waiting on the porch with Mr. and Miss Bingley to welcome them. The carriage stopped, and Gregson let down the stairs. Richard exited first and turned to assist both Georgiana and Mrs. Annesley to descend. He offered his arm to Georgiana, and they mounted the stairs.

"Welcome to Netherfield, Miss Darcy, Mrs. Annesley, Colonel Fitzwilliam. We are pleased that you came to join us," Bingley enthused.

"Thank you, Mr. Bingley, I am glad to be here," Georgiana replied softly.

Miss Bingley rushed forward and took Georgiana's arm, "My dear Miss Darcy, you must be exhausted from your trip. Let me show you to your room. Perhaps we can visit a bit before time for tea," she said as she towed her toward the entry door.

Georgiana tried to pull away to greet her brother, but Miss Bingley did not release her arm. She cast a disturbed glance at Darcy, who spoke up quickly, "Please wait a moment, Miss Bingley. I have not yet had the opportunity to greet my sister. I will show her to the room that was prepared for her, and you can assist Mrs. Annesley and the Colonel." Darcy stepped up and kissed Georgiana's cheek and offered her his arm. Miss Bingley had no choice but to release her. Darcy had noted the angry look on her face before she schooled her features into a more pleasant one. As he moved towards the door, he looked over his shoulder, offering "It is a pleasure to see you again, Mrs. Annesley. I hope your trip was pleasant." To Richard he said. "Thank you, cousin, for accompanying the ladies. I will stop by your room shortly."

"Colonel, would you care for a drink before you are shown to your room?" Bingley asked as he escorted the Colonel into the house. Caroline did not even acknowledge Mrs. Annesley but turned to follow her brother and the colonel. So, with a shake of her head, Mrs. Annesley quietly followed her into the house. Caroline went directly into the parlor, leaving it to Bingley to instruct Mrs. Dawson to show the Colonel and Mrs. Annesley to their rooms.

Georgiana was in the room across from Darcy's. Her sitting room also connected with Mrs. Annesley's room. They would be able to attend to Georgiana's lesson there as it contained a large table near one of the windows. Georgiana's room was decorated in soft shades of rose while Mrs. Annesley's was in burgundy. The sitting room was in shades of rose, burgundy, and cream. Her maid came in to unpack for Georgiana and help her freshen up from the trip. When she was ready, Georgiana moved into the sitting room to await Mrs. Annesley. Darcy said he would come and collect her in time for luncheon. Gregson took up his position at the end of the hall outside of Georgiana's room.

Richard's room was decorated in dark green with rich gold accents. He was just washing up as he heard a knock on the door from the sitting room. After he was invited to enter, Darcy stepped into the room and took a chair.

"How was the journey?" he asked.

"It was enlightening in many ways," Richard responded.

Lifting his brow questioningly Darcy asked, "Would you care to explain in what ways it was enlightening?"

"Well, for most of the journey your sister was bouncing in her seat. I think she wanted to call to the coachman to hurry. She seems very excited to meet Miss Bennet. As we came into the village, Georgie remarked that the village 'reminded her of Lambton.' This sparked an interesting conversation about estate life, small villages, and the needs of all people. She wanted to know how she might help Pemberley's tenants to show her appreciation for them."

Darcy's face expressed his surprise and pleasure. "She wants to help our tenants?" he asked.

"Mrs. Annesley encouraged her to try to overcome her shyness when in conversation with Miss Bennet and even suggested that she ask her about what they do for Longbourn's tenants."

"Well, I must say I am impressed with Mrs. Annesley's methods. Georgiana seems to have grown even in the few weeks they have been working together."

"Why was Miss Bingley trying to drag Georgie off so quickly? Is she up to something?" Richard asked.

"She was in fine form yesterday at tea. Her questions to Miss Elizabeth and her sister were intended to place the young ladies in a bad light.

When that did not work, she was embarrassed and quite upset. I watched Miss Elizabeth taste her tea when she received it, but she put it down immediately. Later, I pretended to mix up our cups to find out what was wrong with it. Miss Bingley deliberately put spoiled milk in Miss Elizabeth's tea. When I called her on it, she prepared a new one only to spill it in Miss Elizabeth's lap. As for dragging Georgie away, I believe she wanted to discourage Georgie from a friendship with Miss Elizabeth. Miss Bingley has taken a decided dislike towards her."

Darcy's expressions through this explanation had Richard wondering what else might be afoot at Netherfield. Knowing that a frontal assault was not the best way to encourage information from Darcy, Richard asked, "Is there something to be worried about where Miss Elizabeth is concerned? Should we be introducing Georgie to her?"

The slight smile on Darcy's face as he answered raised even more questions in Richard's mind. "There is nothing at all about which to be concerned. Miss Elizabeth is a delightful young lady. She is kind, witty, intelligent, and joyful. I am sure that she and Georgie will be great friends."

"If she is all these things, then why does Miss Bingley dislike her so?"

Trying to look nonchalant, Darcy said, "I think she believes I am attracted to Miss Elizabeth."

Oh ho, Richard thought. "What would give her that idea?"

"Well, I danced with Miss Elizabeth twice at the assembly the other day. I thought she might be the girl who rescued Georgiana. There was something familiar about her, and then I heard her laugh. It was the same laugh from the night at the theater five years ago." Richard's eyebrows rose. *It was the same laugh? He remembered a laugh from five years ago?*

Darcy continued, "During our first dance, I asked a few leading questions and determined she was the same young lady. We spent much of the evening discussing the details of the event since Georgie could never tell us much. As we were still talking, I asked her to dance again when the last set began. It seems I was so absorbed in my conversation; I forgot to request a dance of Miss Bingley, and she has been belittling Miss Elizabeth and her sister ever since. After yesterday's performance, Bingley threatened to have her removed from his home if she could not improve her behavior toward his guests. Miss Bingley's other complaint is her brother's attraction to Miss Bennet. She believes Miss Bennet to be beneath them. Miss Bingley's self-importance never fails to amuse me. She, a tradesman's daughter, believes the daughter of a gentleman beneath her," Darcy concluded with derision in his voice.

"Well, I guess we will have to keep a close eye on her and not allow her to be alone with Georgie. Perhaps it would also help to introduce

Georgie and Miss Elizabeth as soon as possible. Might we call on the family today?"

"I did mention to Miss Elizabeth that we might visit this afternoon if Georgiana felt up to it after the trip. Perhaps we should collect Georgie and make our way down to lunch. We can ask if she is up to visiting on the way."

The gentlemen crossed the hall and knocked at the door to Georgiana's sitting room. Upon her call, they entered.

"Well, Georgie, how do you like your rooms?"

"Everything seems to be very lovely. I was surprised that our rooms were so far from the family rooms, though, is that usual?"

Darcy could not tell her the real reason for his room choice. "I requested my room during a tour of the house because of the lovely views. Naturally, I wished to have you placed near me." Georgie seemed to accept his reply, so he continued. "Little One, are you feeling up to a visit this afternoon? I thought perhaps we might pay a call on Miss Elizabeth and her family."

"Oh, William, I would dearly love to go. I was hoping I would not have to wait too long before meeting her!" Georgie exclaimed with a happy smile.

"Well, let us go down to luncheon, and then perhaps afterward you might like to rest for an hour or so before we pay our call."

As the three entered the parlor, Miss Bingley rushed forward and again took Georgiana's arm. "Dear Miss Darcy, it has been such a long time since we last visited, please do sit with me so we can catch-up with one another." Miss Bingley directed her toward the couch without noting her expression of disquiet.

Darcy and Richard took seats nearby to keep an eye on Georgie and help her if needed. They talked quietly with Bingley and Hurst as Mrs. Hurst joined in the conversation with her sister. Darcy observed that Mrs. Hurst seemed less effusive than usual and noticed the angry glances her sister cast at her. Shortly after taking their seats, the butler arrived to announce lunch. Darcy noted that Georgiana was seated very close to Miss Bingley. She was obviously determined to get her opinion of Miss Elizabeth across to Georgiana. Well, he would just have to keep the conversation away from the Bennets.

"Miss Darcy, I hope that you will not find the company here in the country too dull during your visit," began Miss Bingley. "The society is a far cry from what you are used to in town."

"I have some good friends in the country around Pemberley. I am sure that the people here will prove to be just as pleasant, but I thank you for your concern, Miss Bingley," she replied quietly.

"The entertainments are not what you are used to either. The music at the assembly we attended the other evening was barely tolerable. However, I will be delighted to devote myself to your entertainment," Caroline continued.

"Please do not go to any trouble, Miss Bingley. I will enjoy spending time with my brother and his friends, and I do have to attend to my studies while I am here." After Miss Bingley's comments about the people in the neighborhood, Georgiana did not feel comfortable sharing that one of her reasons for visiting was to meet Miss Elizabeth Bennet.

Both Darcy and the Colonel had attended to their conversation closely. They were pleased with the way in which Georgiana handled herself. She had indeed improved under Mrs. Annesley's tutelage. Mrs. Hurst had also observed Miss Darcy since she had entered the parlor and was surprised to see how uncomfortable she seemed to be with Caroline. *Had she always been this way,* she wondered? *Had giving into Caroline so often in the past blinded her to Miss Darcy's discomfort?* Louisa began to question what else she might have failed to observe in the past.

The meal progressed pleasantly enough, and at its conclusion Georgiana announced that she would like to return to her room and rest for a while. The gentlemen left for the billiards room, and Caroline and Mrs. Hurst went to the blue drawing room. Mrs. Hurst picked up the latest issue of the Ladies Monthly while Caroline paced muttering quietly to herself. Caroline was frustrated that she had not been able to warn Georgiana about Eliza Bennet. She knew they were to be introduced soon, and she must plant her seeds of doubt and dislike immediately. Turning to her sister she said, "I think I will just go and check on Miss Darcy to see if she has everything that she needs."

"You will disturb her rest if you go up now. You can ensure her comfort when she returns downstairs later," suggested Mrs. Hurst. "Caroline, did you notice anything unusual about Miss Darcy's behavior earlier?" Mrs. Hurst asked.

"Not at all, she is still very quiet and dull in conversation. I hope for her sake that she grows out of it, as she will never attract a suitor if she cannot converse with a gentleman. It is necessary to pay her so much attention so that Mr. Darcy will realize what a good example I could be to her. Of course, when we marry, I will convince him to send her off to boarding school."

Unknown to Miss Bingley, Georgiana was in the hall outside of the parlor. She had been too excited to rest and was hoping to find William to see if they could leave immediately to visit Miss Bennet. Georgiana's face first paled at Miss Bingley's unkind remarks, and then she became angry—angrier than she could ever remember being. She determined never to let Miss Bingley intimidate her again. She would also spend as little time with her as she possibly could. Just then, a footman entered the hall and asked if he could be of assistance to her. She asked after her brother and was told he was in the billiard room. Georgiana asked the footman to request her brother come to her sitting room as soon as he could. She then turned and went up the stairs. She did not wish to encounter Miss Bingley in her present state of mind.

Georgiana heard the rapid knocking at her door and her brother's worried voice calling her name. She quickly opened the door to see both her brother and Richard. Darcy took in the unusual look of anger on his sister's face and glanced quickly towards Richard. They entered and shut the door behind him. "Whatever is the matter, Little One?" Darcy asked with concern.

Georgiana took a deep breath to calm herself. "I am sorry if I worried you, there is nothing really the matter."

"Georgiana I have never seen you so angry, what has happened?"

Taking another deep breath, she stopped pacing and turned towards her brother and cousin. "I came downstairs to find you because I was too excited to rest and wanted to leave for our visit earlier. As I reached the bottom of the stairs, I could hear Miss Bingley speaking. I was not trying to eavesdrop, but her voice was quite loud." A brief flash of anger again crossed her face as she continued, "Miss Bingley said I was 'quiet and dull in conversation and would never attract a suitor if I remained so.' She also said it was 'necessary to pay attention to me so that you would think her a good example for me, but that when you marry she will have you send me to boarding school.'"

Darcy and Richard stared at her, dumbfounded. "Georgiana, I am so sorry, my dear, that you were hurt by Miss Bingley's words. I would certainly not wish for your feelings to be injured in such a way. I will speak to her brother about her behavior so that it will not happen again," Darcy said, his anger rising to match hers. Richard placed a hand on his shoulder to keep him from rushing off to find Bingley.

They both looked at Georgiana with surprise as she began speaking again, "No, William, I would not wish for you to distress Mr. Bingley by hearing of his sister's behavior. It is not necessary. I will do one of two things, continue to be boring and dull to avoid conversing with her, or I can improve my verbal skills and leave her out of my conversation. But, dear brother, you must promise me that you will never marry her!" Georgiana exclaimed with feeling.

Darcy and Richard both laughed at this statement. "I can promise you, Georgie, that there are absolutely no circumstances that could ever force or convince me to marry Miss Bingley," Darcy said with a shudder. "As to your original purpose in seeking me out. I will arrange for the carriage to be prepared and will meet you and Richard in the foyer in ten minutes. I will also let Bingley know of our plans, as I am sure he will wish to accompany us. He appears to be quite taken with the eldest Miss Bennet," Darcy said with a smile.

The four of them were soon on their way to Longbourn. Darcy briefly described each of the Bennets to his family. He did not want Georgiana to be overwhelmed meeting so many new people at once.

"You did not tell us about Mr. Bennet, brother," Georgiana noted.

"That is because I have yet to meet him. I understand from Miss Elizabeth that her father spends a great deal of time in his library. Perhaps with so many women in the house, it is the only way he can get any peace and quiet," Darcy said with a smile.

Just then, the carriage turned into the drive at Longbourn. Conversation ceased as everyone's thoughts anticipated what was to come. Both Richard and Georgiana noticed that a smile grew upon Darcy's face as he checked to be sure his clothes were in good order. Gregson quickly had the step down and the door open. Darcy exited the carriage and extended a hand to assist Georgiana. They were immediately followed by Bingley and Richard.

The visitors were announced and admitted to the parlor. Mrs. Bennet again greeted them effusively, and many of her remarks of the previous visit were repeated as she settled the group to her satisfaction. Mrs. Bennet then turned her attention to Miss Darcy and the Colonel. She fussed over Miss Darcy and frequently mentioned how much her gown must have cost. Seeing

Georgiana's embarrassment, Elizabeth tried to turn her mother's attention away from Miss Darcy. Fortunately, her mother was ready to interrogate the Colonel. She nearly called for her smelling salts when she learned that he was the second son of the Earl of Matlock. Kitty and Lydia had dragged chairs from the table to join the group. They began to pelt him with questions, Lydia constantly casting flirtatious looks at the Colonel.

Elizabeth took a deep breath, trying to hide her embarrassment at the behavior her family was exhibiting. Then she turned to Georgiana and softly said, "Miss Darcy, I am so pleased to finally meet you. I do hope that your adventure that day did no real or lasting harm. I was sorry that I could not be of more help to you."

"Oh, Miss Elizabeth, you were so brave. I would never have been able to give chase to a kidnapper," Georgiana said a look of admiration in her eyes.

"What is this about you chasing someone, Lizzy? When will you ever learn to act like a lady?" Mrs. Bennet admonished.

Surprised by Mrs. Bennet's harsh words to her daughter, she hurried to explain. "Oh she was wond—" began Miss Darcy.

"You misheard, Mama," said Elizabeth speaking over her. "Mama, I would like to take Miss Darcy to see the garden; we will return shortly."

"Please allow me to escort you ladies," offered Mr. Darcy quickly. The group moved to the foyer for their outerwear and quickly left the house.

Richard would have loved to escape from the two youngest Misses Bennet by joining the group in the garden. However, he thought it might be more telling to observe his cousin from a distance. He suspected that Darcy might have feelings for Miss Elizabeth though perhaps he did not yet realize it.

As Elizabeth exited the house with Mr. and Miss Darcy, she turned to the girl and said, "Please forgive my poor manners in speaking over you, Miss Darcy. But, you see, I have never told my mother about that particular event. She would have complained of her nerves and admonished me unceasingly about my poor behavior in public."

"Oh, I am sorry!" exclaimed Georgiana. "I did not mean to cause you any trouble," she said worriedly.

"There is no cause for concern," said Elizabeth with a warm smile. "Tell me about yourself, Miss Darcy. What are your interests? Do you care for reading? It is one of my favorite pastimes," Elizabeth encouraged.

"Oh, yes, I do enjoy reading and discussing books with William," she said with a smile at her brother.

"Who are your favorite authors?" prompted Elizabeth.

"I am particularly fond of poetry and Shakespeare," she replied and leaning closer to Elizabeth lowered her voice to add, "I also enjoy Mrs. Radcliffe's novels." She gave a quick glance at her brother to see if he had overheard.

At Elizabeth's warm laugh, Darcy looked towards her, his smile contained until she looked into his eyes. She gathered he was already aware of his sister's penchant for novels.

Elizabeth returned her eyes to the young girl's face. "What other activities do you enjoy?"

"I am particularly fond of music," replied Georgiana her eyes alight with joy. "I am studying the pianoforte with a master in London and am currently learning a piece by Herr Mozart. It is quite complicated, but the music is heavenly. Do you play, Miss Elizabeth?" she asked.

"I do enjoy playing, but fear I play poorly. I just never seem to find the time to practice enough, though I love to sing," Elizabeth answered. "Perhaps while you are visiting we might find a song we could perform together."

Georgiana's face paled slightly, and her grip on her brother's arm tightened. He saw Elizabeth's look of concern at Georgiana's reaction and spoke quickly. "What a lovely idea. I am sure you would enjoy spending some time with Miss Elizabeth practicing. It would be a good experience in performing. You could perform it for just Richard and me if that would make you less uncomfortable. I am sure we could use the music room at Netherfield at a convenient time," he tried to reassure her.

"I would enjoy spending time with Miss Elizabeth, if she would care for it, but performing for a group would be too frightening," stated Georgiana timidly.

"I often wish I was not forced to perform either, but being out in society, I have no choice in the matter. I must perform if I am asked. Your brother is correct, though, performing in front of a small group you know well would be good experience," remarked Elizabeth encouragingly. "I know the perfect place for us to practice where we would be quite alone," said Elizabeth with a smile. "My sister Mary is constantly on the pianoforte in our home, and I would not wish to disturb Miss Bingley with our practice. However, I am very close to our rector. I am sure we could use the pianoforte in the Meryton chapel for our practices. Would that be acceptable?" asked Elizabeth.

Georgiana looked at her brother for his opinion, and he nodded his agreement. "Yes, I believe that would be agreeable, and I am looking forward to knowing you better, Miss Elizabeth," she said with a slightly more confident smile.

Darcy looked over Georgiana's head and smiled gratefully at Elizabeth. The warmth in his eyes sent a shiver up her spine. "Shall we return indoors?" asked Darcy as he turned Georgiana the other direction and offered his other arm to Elizabeth. She did not hesitate to take it. She looked up at Mr. Darcy as she wrapped her hand around his muscular forearm. The shiver she felt earlier returned when she touched him. Darcy was surprised by the tingle that ran from his arm where her hand lay and then throughout his body, but he smiled warmly, down into her upturned face.

The group returned to the parlor just as Hill was bringing in the tea service. As they rejoined the others, Richard noted the looks on the faces of both Miss Elizabeth and his cousin. He would have to question his cousin a little further. During tea, Darcy asked Elizabeth if she would care to ride over on the morrow and then take the Darcy carriage into Meryton for their practice.

"Though I can ride a little, I am afraid I will not be able to do so, as I am sure the horses will be busy on the farm. I do not mind walking over to meet Georgiana," Elizabeth said.

"Please, Miss Elizabeth, do not put yourself to the trouble. I will send Georgiana and her companion, Mrs. Annesley, in my carriage to pick you up. I will also send along a couple of footmen to accompany you."

"That is very kind of you, Mr. Darcy, but unnecessary. I do not mind the walk."

"It is no trouble at all, Miss Elizabeth. I would be honored to be of service. I am sure that I will be fully repaid when I get to hear your performance with Georgiana. What time would be convenient?" he asked.

"I believe that ten in the morning would be perfect if that suits you, Miss Darcy," Elizabeth stated politely. "I will send a note around to Reverend Winthrop to let him know we wish to use the chapel pianoforte at ten in the morning," she said with a confident smile.

"I will look forward to seeing you in the morning, Miss Elizabeth," Georgiana responded with a smile.

Shortly afterward, Darcy and the others left for Netherfield. Other than Elizabeth and Georgiana, they would not meet again until the dinner at Lucas Lodge the day after tomorrow. Being one of the last to leave the room, Bingley took the opportunity to kiss Jane's hand before departing.

After the guests had departed, Mrs. Bennet called Jane to the parlor again. She wished to speak with her about her progress with Mr. Bingley. Elizabeth decided she would visit her father in his library. Upon his call to enter, Elizabeth opened the door saying, "Good afternoon, Papa. How are you today? You should have joined us for tea. We had interesting company. I am sure you would have enjoyed yourself."

"And who was this company?" her father inquired.

"They were several members of the party at Netherfield," she replied. "Mr. Bingley, the young man who has leased the estate, came. He brought with him three guests, his dear friend Mr. Darcy, Mr. Darcy's young sister, and his cousin, Colonel Fitzwilliam."

He noted the slight change to her voice and face as she said Mr. Darcy's name. "And, why would I have found them interesting?" he asked with his eyebrow raised.

"Well, Colonel Fitzwilliam is quite amusing. His tales of life in the army had the whole room laughing, and Mr. Bingley is a pleasant and easy-going man who seems to like everyone he meets. Mr. Darcy is intelligent and well read, and I am sure you could find books in common to discuss. Surprisingly, I have met Mr. Darcy before." Her father raised his eyebrows at this unexpected statement. "Do you remember my little escapade in Hyde Park a few years back?" At Mr. Bennet's nod, Elizabeth continued, "Well, it was Mr. Darcy's younger sister that I attempted to aid. He apparently remembered me, though we had not, in actuality, met. When we encountered one another at the assembly the other night, he asked me a few questions to be certain I was the young lady he thought me to be. He asked if he might have his sister join him here so that they might offer me their thanks."

"Miss Darcy is a delightful young lady, but a bit shy. I believe she is Lydia's age." *If only Lydia and Kitty could be so well mannered,* she muttered under her breath. Her father heard her softly spoken words and wondered at the frustration in her voice.

"Is something bothering you, Lizzy?" her father asked.

"It is nothing, Papa," she replied, not meeting his eyes.

"Elizabeth, tell me what is bothering you," he stated firmly.

She could not meet her father's eyes. "Having such well-mannered visitors in the house provides a glaring contrast between the behaviors of polite society and those of my mother and sisters. It has been somewhat mortifying to be forced to endure the behavior of some members of my family in front of our new acquaintances."

Mr. Bennet was very surprised by Elizabeth's reaction. Usually, she would shake her head and laugh off the poor behavior of her family. What had changed? Perhaps he should attend tea the next time these visitors came. Could Lizzy be interested in one? Could that be the reason she was embarrassed by her family's actions?

"I will promise to attend the next time these visitors are here, and I will even do my best to check your sisters if they misbehave."

She left her father shortly after that, and seeing Jane ascending the stairs, followed her. Elizabeth caught up to her before Jane reached her room, so they entered together.

"How was your visit with Papa?" Jane asked.

"I told him about our visitors and encouraged him to join us the next time they visit. He promised that he would."

"It was a delightful visit," Jane sighed, a dreamy look in her eyes.

Noting her expression, Elizabeth raised her eyebrow venturing, "Just what made it so delightful, Jane?"

With a deep blush gracing her face and her gaze fixed on her lap, Jane replied, "After everyone had left the parlor, Mr. Bingley kissed my hand and said he looked forward to seeing me soon."

"Jane, are you in love with Mr. Bingley?"

"I believe I am on my way to being in love with him, yes. I know that I like him more than any gentleman I have ever met, and I so enjoy spending time with him," she finished with another blush.

"Is there anything I can do to help things along?" Elizabeth asked with a grin.

"Please do not tease, Lizzy," Jane said beseechingly. "How was your visit with Miss Darcy?"

"She is a delightful young lady, but quite shy. She loves to play so we are going to the chapel daily to practice a piece we will perform for her brother and cousin. She was terrified at the thought of performing for a larger group. He will send Miss Darcy and her companion in his carriage to pick me up at ten o'clock tomorrow morning. He is even sending footmen to watch over us while we are in town. Perhaps you might like to walk to Meryton to meet us. I was hoping to stop by the sweet shop to get a treat after we finished our practice. You could wait for us somewhere you could see the church and meet us when we leave. Then you could ride home in the carriage with us."

"That sounds enjoyable. Do you think that Miss Darcy will mind my joining you? I would not wish to make her uncomfortable if she is shy," Jane asked with concern.

"You are so gentle and kind, Jane. I am sure she will enjoy your company. However, I do think we should keep our younger sisters at a distance," Elizabeth answered with a grin.

CHAPTER 8

Promptly at ten o'clock, the Darcy carriage pulled to a halt in front of Longbourn. Elizabeth had seen its approach and was waiting under cover of the porch for it to stop. Gregson let down the steps, handed her into the carriage, and it promptly departed.

"How are you this morning, Miss Darcy," Elizabeth asked pleasantly as she settled into the plush seats of the carriage. She looked around the interior of the elegant vehicle and thought she had never seen its like.

"I am very well, thank you, Miss Elizabeth," Georgiana replied. "Miss Elizabeth, allow me to present my companion, Mrs. Annesley."

"It is very nice to meet you, Mrs. Annesley. I hope you will not be bored as we practice this morning."

"It is a pleasure to meet you as well, Miss Elizabeth. I'm sure that I will enjoy your practice, as it is always a pleasure to listen to Miss Darcy play. She is quite talented."

"Have you thought of a piece we might be able to perform together?" Georgiana asked Elizabeth.

"I brought several with me and thought we could decide together what we will play." Elizabeth pulled out the music, and they settled to a discussion of possible pieces for the duration of the short ride to Meryton.

Having secured his horse in front of the inn, Wickham walked down the main street of Meryton seeing what the village had to offer. As luck had turned against him recently, Wickham was in truly dire straits. Being away from London and finding a source of income was rapidly becoming necessary. When last in London, he had happened upon his old friend, Denny, and during their conversation Wickham discovered Denny had enlisted in the militia a few years ago. He said it kept him busy but the work was easy, the pay was reasonable, and there was plenty of opportunity for socializing. Denny's description of militia life made it sound like a good option--until a better one came along. Wickham also knew that a uniform would make him even more irresistible to young ladies. Denny said that he should come to Meryton if he decided to join the militia and he would introduce Wickham to his commanding officer.

Wickham was just passing an alley when he noted a familiar carriage enter at the other end of town. *What was Darcy doing in this backwater,*

Wickham wondered? He stepped into the shadows of the alley as he watched the carriage. It came to a stop outside of the church. He watched as a footman helped the passengers alight. The first to descend was a petite woman with dark curls. She was laughing when she stepped onto the sidewalk, and there seemed to be something familiar about her though Wickham could not place her. She turned back to look at the other passengers as she descended. The sun glinted off the blonde curls peeking out of the back of the bonnet of the young lady who had just descended. All thought of the first young woman vanished from his mind when he saw the profile of the passenger who had just exited the carriage. It could be none other than Georgiana Darcy! She was entering the church with the other young woman, followed by an older woman whom he did not recognize. Wickham stepped deeper into the dim alley to ensure that he was not seen. *Was Darcy in the area, as well,* he wondered? This changed everything! With Georgiana nearby, he would not have to join the militia. If he could successfully get to Georgiana, his problems would be solved. He no longer intended to hold her for ransom. No, if he could get to her, they would be off to Gretna Green—even if he had to keep her drugged all the way to the Scottish border! After marrying dear little Georgie he would have his way with her, and then abscond with her dowry at the first opportunity. With thirty thousand pounds, he could live like a king anywhere he chose. Wickham knew that the loss of money would not affect Darcy as he had so much of it. However, causing harm to his beloved sister would devastate Darcy and leave him guilt-ridden for the rest of his life. Wickham almost laughed aloud with the pleasure of his thoughts.

He maintained his position in the shadows as he watched the women enter the church. The large footman who had helped them from the carriage took up a position by the entry. He wondered at the man's behavior and eventually reasoned Darcy had employed someone specifically to protect his sister. Obviously getting to Georgiana would not be easy this time. He would have to keep watch on her and look for a weakness that would allow him to get close enough to her to take Georgiana away.

Trying to remain in the shadows, Wickham moved towards the church and eventually found a small window that gave him a view of the interior. Inside Georgiana was seated at the old pianoforte playing while the other young woman sang.

As Elizabeth finished the Scottish ballad they were performing, she turned to Georgiana saying, "Miss Darcy, what a marvelous talent you have. You play with both passion and perfection. It was an honor to hear you."

Blushing at the praise from her new friend, Georgiana demurred and returned the compliment. "Oh no, Miss Elizabeth, it is your performance that was quite remarkable. I do not think I have ever heard better at any of the musical events I have attended in town. Your voice is truly extraordinary."

Wickham could hear the performance and acknowledged to himself the quality of both performers. He observed as the girls looked through some sheets of music and began again with a new piece. They continued to practice for more than an hour. As he saw them gathering their outerwear, he moved towards the front of the church, careful to remain out of sight of the footman, where he could observe and overhear them as they departed.

"Miss Darcy, if you are agreeable, I thought we would walk to the sweet shop for a treat before we return home."

"Oh, that would be so much fun! I do not often have an opportunity to do such things," the girl replied excitedly. Then worrying that her behavior was a little untoward, she glanced quickly at Mrs. Annesley to see her reaction.

Mrs. Annesley smiled pleasantly at the young ladies. "I believe that would be a pleasant way to end our outing," she replied with a slight nod.

They left the church and wandered down the sidewalk past where Wickham had hidden earlier followed by the large footman. They glanced into the shop windows, laughing and talking as they went. At one of their stops, they were joined by another young lady. Her obvious beauty briefly stirred Wickham's lust, but he did not let it distract him and continued to follow from a distance. He needed to know all he could before formulating his plans. He would have to find a way to follow the carriage if he were to learn where the ladies were staying. As they entered the confectionery, Wickham retrieved his horse and mounted. He circled around behind the buildings in the village and positioned himself so that it would appear he was just entering town. This gave him the ability to follow the carriage as it departed to return the ladies to their homes.

Wickham moved from the road to the field beside it, positioning himself behind some tall bushes that bordered the field. He observed as the two young ladies with Georgiana descended from the carriage. They turned and waved to the carriage's remaining occupants before entering the house. As the carriage retreated along the path it had come, Wickham continued watching as it made the turn to return to the village. Moved from his hiding place, Wickham again followed to see where Georgiana might be residing. It went all the way through town and turned to the left at the crossroad. He watched as the carriage turned in at a gate and went up the drive. Finally, it pulled to a stop in front of the house. The footman was assisting Georgiana to exit the carriage when she heard her name called. No one was in sight, but she paused there. It was not long before Darcy came into view followed by his friend, Bingley, and the Colonel. Another man followed, but he was unfamiliar to Wickham.

So Darcy is here as well, Wickham mused with a smirk—though the colonel's presence was a cause for concern. He gleefully realized he could do a little damage to Darcy's reputation while he made plans to get closer to Georgiana. Wickham moved off after everyone had entered the house. He needed to discover the lay of the land to help in his planning. While he was traversing fields around the manor where Darcy was staying, he came upon what looked like a crumbling, unoccupied tenant house. It was located near a fence and he could hear water somewhere close. One room was still intact, and it would provide him with shelter while permitting him to keep his presence in the area unknown.

Wickham made his way back to the village and stopped in at the tavern. It was time to start spreading his tale of woe at the hands of Darcy. As Wickham listened to the conversations around him, he heard Darcy's name. Ambling towards the table where the men who had spoken of Darcy were seated, Wickham sat down at the next table and continued to listen. He was shocked at the content of the discussion. Apparently Darcy had danced twice with the same young lady at a recent assembly. They were speculating about a possible attachment. It was his perfect opening.

"Excuse me gentlemen, but are you speaking of Fitzwilliam Darcy?" he asked.

"Yes," one of the men replied. "He is staying at the estate of Netherfield with some friends. Do you know the gentleman?"

"Yes, I do, but I'd hesitate to call him a gentleman."

"He seems to be pleasant enough, if a bit reserved," the man replied cautiously.

"Yes, but appearances can be deceiving. You see, I grew up with Mr. Darcy on his family's estate in Derbyshire. My father was the steward for the elder Mr. Darcy. He was a very good man and very fond of me. He educated me and intended for me to have a living in his gift. However, he died unexpectedly; so when it came time for me to take orders before receiving the gift he had left for me, the current Mr. Darcy denied it to me. He had always been jealous of his father's affection for me so took his revenge in this way. I am passing through your fair village on my way to accepting a position found for me by a kindly friend. I only spoke up as I heard you mention his attentions to a young lady of your neighborhood. He is not at all what he seems, and the young lady should beware," cautioned Wickham as he turned back to his table. He heard the men discussing what he had said as he quickly finished his pint and departed the tavern, an expression of satisfaction on his face.

Darcy reached the front steps of Netherfield, Richard at his shoulder, and placed a quick kiss on Georgiana's cheek as he offered his arm to escort her inside. "How was your morning with Miss Elizabeth?" Darcy asked with interest.

"Oh, brother, she is so wonderful. It is so easy to talk with her, and her voice is quite beautiful. I cannot recall ever hearing a better one. She made me feel so at ease. It was much easier to play with her than I expected. She was so positive and encouraging," she concluded, her face lit with a large smile. It was an expression he had not seen in a long time.

Darcy glanced at Mrs. Annesley in surprise at Georgiana's rather exuberant speech. "The young ladies practiced together for over an hour. Miss Elizabeth is truly a gifted performer. I believe you and the Colonel will be most pleased with your concert, sir," she said with a smile.

"Yes, brother, and after we had practiced, we walked through the village to the sweet shop for a snack before returning home. The village reminds me very much of Lambton. We passed an interesting looking bookshop, and I saw a beautiful hat as we looked in the store windows. Perhaps we could go shopping and find some gifts for Christmas—perhaps even one for Miss Elizabeth," Georgiana said softly.

Darcy smiled largely in return, sharing a look with the Colonel, thinking of the great good Miss Elizabeth had done for Georgiana in only one morning. "Well, I am very glad you enjoyed yourself. Did you make plans to meet again tomorrow?" he asked. Georgiana nodded in reply, and Darcy continued. "By the way, Mr. Bingley sent word to Sir William of the addition of two to the Netherfield party and he replied that you and Fitzwilliam should join the party for tomorrow night's dinner.

Georgiana looked nervously at her brother. "You want me to attend an event with you?"

"You are now sixteen, Little One; it would be appropriate for you to attend. It will be much less overwhelming than an event in town. Miss Elizabeth and her family will be there," Darcy said encouragingly.

"Well, perhaps it will be alright then," she said with a faltering smile. She took a breath to calm herself and asked William how his shooting had been.

He and Richard shared the news of their morning as they all ascended the staircase to their rooms. After changing, Richard knocked on Darcy's door and entered at his call. "I do not believe I have seen Georgie this animated in almost five years," he commented as he took a chair near the fire and watched Chalmers tying Darcy's clean cravat.

"I agree. I had hoped that Miss Elizabeth might have a good effect on her, but I had no idea that she could work miracles," Darcy said with a smile. "I hope that with Miss Elizabeth's encouragement, we will continue to see positive changes in Georgiana.

Richard and Darcy descended to join the family, offering Georgiana's apologies as she felt she needed to attend to her studies. As the gentlemen departed for the billiards room, Caroline was struck with an idea. She glanced at her sister who was bent over some needlework and quietly left the room. She ascended the stairs and knocked at the door to Georgiana's sitting room. Mrs. Annesley opened the door to see Miss Bingley standing in the hallway. She had been cautioned by Mr. Darcy of his sister's discomfort around Miss Bingley and looked to Miss Darcy for approval to admit the visitor. However, Miss Bingley had no intention of being denied her chance to speak to Miss Darcy, so she stepped around Mrs. Annesley smiling at Georgiana as she said, "My dear Miss Darcy, I have been dying for a chance to visit. I hope you will forgive my interruption, but I was afraid if I did not take the opportunity now, we might not get one, and there is something very important I must discuss with you." She smiled disarmingly as she continued into the room. "You may be excused to have some tea if you like, Mrs. Annesley," Caroline said dismissively.

Had she not already been on her guard because of Mr. Darcy's warning, this condescending comment would have given her cause for concern. With a determined smile on her face Mrs. Annesley said, "Thank you for your thoughtfulness, Miss Bingley, but we have just finished the tea so kindly provided by Mrs. Dawson."

Caroline frowned at Mrs. Annesley but knew there was no polite way to get rid of her. Mrs. Annesley moved to a corner of the room and picked up some needlework. Caroline encouraged Georgiana to join her at the chairs before the fireplace as far from Mrs. Annesley as they could get.

After asking about her time at the seaside—and failing to notice the way Georgiana stiffened at its mention—and her activities in town before she had joined them, Caroline leaned in and said, "It is so good you have come. I have been very concerned for Mr. Darcy."

A look of worry in her face Georgiana asked, "Concerned for William? Has he been ill?"

"No, it is nothing like that," she replied. "It is much worse." She smiled inwardly at Georgiana's look of horror. "Dear Mr. Darcy is being pursued by the worst kind of fortune-hunting female. Miss Elizabeth Bennet has been throwing herself at your brother. If he is not careful, she may catch him in a compromising position, and he would be forced to marry her. He has been hesitant to believe me when I mentioned that she was trying to entrap him with her wiles, but I know that he will listen to his beloved sister."

Georgiana was relieved of any real concern for William but masked her feelings. She knew exactly why Miss Bingley was concerned. She was jealous of Darcy's attentions to Miss Elizabeth. After the unkind remarks she had overheard from Miss Bingley yesterday, she thought carefully before she answered. "Miss Bingley, are you certain there is cause for concern? I met Miss Elizabeth at her home yesterday, and we spent the morning together as well. I have not noticed any partiality from Miss Elizabeth for my brother, but he does seem to show an interest in her that I have never seen him display for another. I do not believe William need be concerned about being compromised by her. Though my brother is the perfect gentleman, Miss Elizabeth may be the one who has cause for concern as he does seem so drawn to her."

During Georgiana's reply, Caroline's face paled, then turned red with anger, and finally paled again at her last remark; Caroline continued trying to convince her there was a reason to worry. As Georgiana refused to believe it, Caroline realized she would have to find another way to separate them. With a forced smile, and through gritted teeth, Caroline excused herself and left Georgiana to her studies.

Mrs. Annesley had heard the entire exchange and was very proud of the way her charge had handled the difficult situation. "Miss Darcy, you were quite poised during your conversation with Miss Bingley. I was very impressed with the way you allayed her concerns with kindness and maintained your position in the face of her attempts to change your mind."

Georgiana smiled her thanks at the compliment. She stood up to Miss Bingley for the first time and had done it well, according to her companion. Secretly, she was thrilled that she had thwarted Miss Bingley's efforts to get her help in discouraging William from Miss Elizabeth. In fact, she was beginning to think Miss Elizabeth was perfect for her brother and would be the perfect sister for her, as well. She was determined to tell William about the conversation and hoped it would make him laugh. She also decided that she would watch his interactions with Miss Elizabeth in the hope that she could help to bring them closer together.

The remainder of the day passed pleasantly. Miss Bingley was surprisingly quiet, which perhaps contributed to the pleasantness. The others would have been more concerned had they been privy to Miss Bingley's thoughts. It frustrated her that the disparaging things she had learned about the Bennet's family did not seem to bother either her brother or Mr. Darcy. Her attempt to make Eliza Bennet ill from the sour milk in her tea had failed. Not only that, but Mr. Darcy had discovered her ploy. Dousing Elizabeth with tea had given her a little satisfaction, but it had not helped her achieve her goal. She was angry and frustrated that she had been unable to convince Georgiana of the danger Eliza Bennet presented to her brother. She had to find a way to separate the couples—even if only temporarily. She was sure with more time she could convince Darcy of her superiority. She set her mind to find another way to separate the two couples.

Before retiring for the night, Georgiana had the opportunity to share her conversation with Miss Bingley with both her brother and Richard. Mrs. Annesley had already informed Darcy of an encounter between the two ladies. She gave no details but said that Miss Darcy had handled herself with poise and confidence. Richard had laughed aloud as she told her tale, and Darcy chuckled as he complimented her on the way she had handled the difficult situation. Darcy also asked if she would like to join them for an early morning ride. Georgiana agreed, and they set a time to meet in the morning.

The household had been quiet for some time as the clock had long passed struck one. Caroline Bingley opened her door and looked carefully into the hallway. There was only one small lamp glowing at the top of the stairs. She stepped into the hallway, closing her door behind her, and gathered the sheer fabric of her burnt orange negligee close around her. She tiptoed down the hallway towards Darcy's room. She had come to the decision she would have to compromise Darcy and force a marriage, thereby gaining what she most wanted—the Darcy name and all that comes with it—and thwarting Eliza Bennet in the process. She paused as she heard a soft sound coming from the Colonel's room. Finally, she came to Darcy's door and gently turned the handle. She was surprised when nothing happened. She tried again, leaning her shoulder into the door to push more firmly. Still nothing happened. She put her ear to the door, but could hear nothing. She moved back up the hallway to his sitting room door. She tried this door, but again met with no success, and her frustration increased. *All the doors seemed to be locked. Why would he do that,* she wondered? Suddenly she heard a sound behind her.

Turning she saw the large footman who had come with Georgiana standing behind her, his arms folded across his chest. His eyes raked over her figure barely concealed by the sheer fabric of the negligee. A smirk on his face, he asked, "May I be of assistance, ma'am? Have you become lost in the hallway due to the darkness? I believe your room is in the *other* wing. May I offer my assistance in escorting you there?"

Caroline's face was red with mortification. She raised her chin, and glaring at the footman, hurried down the corridor to her room. The footman's soft chuckle followed her.

CHAPTER 9

THE NEXT MORNING dawned bright and clear. Wickham, just returning from a night spent in the arms of the tavern maid, heard a voice singing nearby. He had almost reached his hideout, but knew if he continued on he would be seen. Not wishing to be discovered, he quickly ducked behind a large tree to hide himself. Glancing around the tree, he noticed a young woman and recognized her as the one who had been with Georgiana the previous day. She paused as she finished her song, then looking around to ensure she was alone, picked up her skirts and ran towards the fence near his hideout. Something in his memory stirred at the sight of her dark curls trailing in the breeze, but he could not pinpoint the memory. She had stopped near the fence and was fixing her bonnet, which had come loose during her run and was hanging by its ribbons down her back.

Suddenly Wickham heard the sound of horses approaching. He pulled back from the window and pressed himself into the wall in the corner of the shack. Then he heard a voice he would know anywhere.

"Good Morning, Miss Elizabeth. How are you on this lovely day?" Darcy asked a warm smile upon his face. He had observed her run across the field and was warmed by the look of joy that had been upon her face.

Her cheeks, pink from the exertion, blushed darker at the fear she had been observed. "I am quite well this morning, and you Mr. Darcy? Good day, Miss Darcy, Colonel Fitzwilliam," she added.

The four friends visited briefly; Colonel Fitzwilliam's eyes remained on his cousin as he interacted with Miss Elizabeth. Suddenly Richard looked up sharply; he took in the area all around them. His sixth sense, which had often saved him on the battlefield, had alerted him to the fact they were being observed. He did not see anyone, only a tumbled down house a little ways off, but still the feeling persisted. He returned his attention to the conversation as he heard his cousin say to Miss Elizabeth, "I believe we should make our way back to Netherfield if Georgiana is to be ready in time to pick you up for your practice this morning." He smiled widely at her. "Sir William was kind enough to extend tonight's invitation to include Georgiana and the Colonel. We will look forward to seeing you again this evening at Lucas Lodge," Darcy said with a smile, his eyes filled with admiration. "Till this evening, Miss Elizabeth," he called over his shoulder as he turned his horse and rode towards the Netherfield stables. Georgiana and the Colonel bid their farewells and turned to follow Darcy. Each smiled inwardly as they thought of Darcy's reaction to Miss Elizabeth.

Wickham was shocked; he may have even gasped aloud causing the Colonel to look around. The Darcys and Colonel had been talking with the young woman he had seen with Georgiana yesterday. The faint memory had solidified in his mind's eye when Darcy and Georgiana had spoken to the unknown woman. He remembered a small woman with dark hair who had thwarted his first attempt to kidnap Georgiana, so many years before. Could it be the same woman? Well, well, he thought. Fate was being kind. He might have the chance for revenge upon her for ruining his first attempt at kidnapping Georgiana. If Darcy had feelings for the young woman, as it appeared he might, it would make it doubly sweet since he would be hurt yet again. Wickham sat down to give some thought as to how he would accomplish his desires.

As usual, Bingley's party was one of the last to arrive at Lucas Lodge. It seemed to Darcy that Miss Bingley was incapable of being on time. Sir William greeted them in his usual effusive way, with only the slightest hesitation when greeting Darcy. Darcy quietly introduced his sister and cousin to Sir William, all the while trying to find Miss Elizabeth in the crowd. He was able to hear her mother's loud voice and the raucous laughter of her younger sisters but had yet to find her. Suddenly his eyes connected with hers as she had glanced towards the entry. She was standing in conversation with Miss Bennet and Miss Lucas. *Had she been watching for his arrival,* he wondered? He found that though quite pleasant, and he smiled at her. Darcy excused himself and Georgiana and led his sister to Miss Elizabeth. He knew that Richard could handle Sir William's enthusiastic conversation.

He approached the ladies, "Good evening Miss Lucas, Miss Bennet, Miss Elizabeth." Charlotte was startled at the change in Mr. Darcy's voice when he addressed Elizabeth and raised a brow in her friend's direction. The only answer she received was the slight blush that colored Elizabeth's cheeks. Darcy continued, "Miss Lucas, may I present my sister Miss Georgiana Darcy? Georgiana this is Miss Lucas, Sir William's eldest daughter."

"It is very nice to meet you, Miss Lucas," Georgiana replied quietly. "Good evening, Miss Bennet, Miss Elizabeth, how are you this evening?"

Darcy stood quietly as he listened to the young ladies converse. He delighted in watching the play of the candlelight on Elizabeth's hair. The red and gold amongst the dark strands seemed to shimmer and undulate with each move of her head. Then there was the way several small curls escaped her coiffure, dancing along her neck. He wondered how soft those curls would feel if he were to kiss them? And what of the skin of her neck, would it be soft and sweet? He returned to the conversation as he heard Miss Lucas request that Elizabeth perform for them. She tried to demur, but Charlotte would not relent. He added his voice to that of Miss Lucas.

"It would be a pleasure to hear you, Miss Elizabeth. My sister and Mrs. Annesley have been singing your praises since your first practice together."

Elizabeth blushed anew at his words and assented to play and sing. She chose a well-known English love song. As her fingers moved over the keys, she raised her voice in song. Darcy was mesmerized. He had moved to a position along the wall where he could watch her unobserved by others. He stared at Elizabeth as she sang, but his face gave no clue as to his thoughts on her performance unless you looked into his eyes. Those who knew Darcy well, such as his sister and cousin, could easily see his opinion of Miss Elizabeth. William was besotted. He joined in the applause at the end of her song as well as the encouragement for an encore. Her second song was a light and happy air.

Miss Bingley made her way to his side during the second song. She took his masked look to mean that he was unimpressed with the performance and bored by the company. Before the last note had faded away, Miss Bingley leaned towards Darcy saying, "I am sure you noticed the many mistakes Miss Eliza made. I am shocked that she is regarded as accomplished, but perhaps that is the best one can find in this dull village."

Darcy looked at her with a cold hard glare, "I would hate to disagree as your family is hosting me during my visit, but in this case I must. Miss Elizabeth plays with great passion, and I have never heard a voice that can compare with hers—

not even in my travels. She has a voice that would be welcomed by the Heavenly choir." *Perhaps I will have to send her to join them* Miss Bingley thought as she moved from Darcy's side.

Darcy was not seated near enough to Elizabeth to converse with her during dinner. He was able to observe her though and enjoyed watching her ease with her companions and the delightful way in which she kept the conversation flowing. He felt sure that she would be able to hold her own with London society, given the chance. Darcy was so preoccupied with his thoughts of Elizabeth that he had failed to notice the talk swirling around him. Wickham's rumors were making the rounds, but no one was brave enough to address Darcy directly.

After dinner, Mary Bennet advanced to the pianoforte. She began to play a sonata, but whereas she was more technically proficient than her sister, she played woodenly without any emotion. She was just beginning a second piece when Lydia Bennet approached the instrument and whined, "Mary, play a reel, we want to dance!"

Mary's lips compressed into a thin line, and she looked hurt. However, she began to search through the music for another selection. Georgiana had noted the hurt looked and moved to stand next to Mary at the pianoforte. She looked through the music as well, "This one might be suitable, Miss Mary. I would be happy to turn the pages for you," Georgiana said kindly.

"Thank you, Miss Darcy, I would appreciate your assistance," Mary smiled shyly at Georgiana, who returned a shy smile of her own.

As the two sat down at the instrument, Richard glanced at Darcy in amazement. Georgiana had always been kind-hearted, but her shyness usually prevented her taking action when she was not well acquainted with someone. Darcy's look had changed from surprise to pride. He noticed Miss Elizabeth at his side.

"That was very kind of Miss Darcy. Mary tries so hard to improve, but she often seems to be lost among the other members of our family. She hasn't had the opportunities that Jane and I have received, and my mother barely notices her at all, except to correct her behavior. Unfortunately, her reading choices have not endeared her to my father, but she has a sweet temperament. I am at fault, too. I have always been so close to Jane, that perhaps I have neglected my relationship with Mary."

"I am sure that you could never intentionally hurt anyone, Miss Elizabeth," Darcy said warmly. "Would you care to dance?"

"Though I look forward to perhaps dancing again in the future, I am afraid it is a bit crowded to truly enjoy a dance at the moment." She noted Darcy's look of disappointment and felt warm inside. She could not resist a small tease, though, and said, "Come now, Mr. Darcy, I have heard that you rarely dance and can only assume that you dislike the occupation. Admit it, you are relieved at my refusal," she said with a grin and a raised eyebrow, her eyes sparkling.

Darcy took in her teasing look and thought he would try teasing in return. "You have been misinformed, Miss Elizabeth. It is not that I dislike dancing. It is that, until recently, I had yet to find a partner whose company and conversation I truly enjoyed." He noted her blush and smiled with pleasure.

As the evening was winding to a close, Georgiana approached Elizabeth with a request. "Miss Elizabeth, perhaps we could take a break from our practicing and instead ride tomorrow?"

"I am afraid that I do not have a mount as my father's horses will be busy on the farm."

Bingley had been approaching with Jane and heard Elizabeth's remark. "I would be happy to provide you with a mount Miss Elizabeth if it will enable you to ride with Miss Darcy. Would you care to ride as well, Miss Bennet?" he asked. "I have more than one spare mount."

"I thank you for your offer, Mr. Bingley, but I must help my mother in the still room tomorrow."

"I thank you as well, Mr. Bingley, for the use of the mount, but I pray you choose a gentle one for me. Though I can ride, I do not often have the opportunity, and, consequently, I am somewhat out of practice." Turning back to Georgiana she said, "With Mr. Bingley's kind assistance, I would love to ride with you tomorrow, Miss Darcy. What time shall we meet?"

They decided Darcy's carriage would pick up her at 10:30, and Bingley invited her to stay for luncheon after their ride. The two groups said good night to one another and returned to their homes.

As they were ascending the stairs, Bingley told Caroline he had invited Miss Elizabeth to stay for luncheon after her ride with Miss Darcy on the morrow. "She will be using one of my mounts, as well," he added. Caroline lay awake for a long time wondering how she could use this information to her advantage, and finally fell into a sound sleep happy with the plan she devised.

CHAPTER 10

ELIZABETH ARRIVED AT Netherfield ready for her ride with Georgiana, who was waiting for her on the steps. She was wearing a very becoming dark green habit that was a few seasons out of style. A jaunty little dark green hat with a small veil perched upon her curls, she presented a charming picture. As they entered the foyer, Miss Darcy informed her that the men had gone shooting that morning but would be returning in time for luncheon.

Both ladies looked up at a sound from the stairs. There descending was Miss Bingley, dressed to go riding. "I do hope you will not mind if I join you," she said with a smirk. "It is such a pleasant day."

Though neither Georgiana nor Elizabeth was happy at this change in plans, there was nothing they could politely do about the situation. Knowing what Miss Bingley's feelings were about Miss Elizabeth, Georgiana was a little concerned. She vowed to keep a close watch on her friend during their outing. They made their way out to the stables where mounts had been prepared for the ladies and were underway shortly. Miss

Bingley took the lead riding towards the boundary with Longbourn. They rode far afield looking at the grounds, fields, and tenant homes of Netherfield. After a brief respite by a cool stream, the three young women prepared to remount.

"Miss Eliza, your girth seems to have become loose. Let me tighten it for you before we return." Caroline made a pretense of tightening the girth, but before turning away, she placed a thorn under the saddle and blanket. Georgiana watched Miss Bingley suspiciously, but could not find anything untoward in her actions. Miss Bingley then quickly remounted and called a race as she headed for the stables.

A laughing glance passed between the friends, as Elizabeth helped Georgiana to mount. Then she led her horse to a boulder and used it to help herself mount. As soon as she sat in the saddle, the horse felt pain as the thorn was pushed into its skin. He reared once, but Elizabeth managed to retain her seat. However, she was not as lucky when he reared again. Elizabeth was thrown to the ground as the horse bolted. She lay still on the ground; Georgiana looking on in horror.

Gregson had been following the riders at a discrete distance and saw Miss Bingley returning alone with a satisfied smirk on her face. His suspicions aroused, he increased his pace, heading in the direction from which Miss Bingley had come. He reached them just as Miss Elizabeth's horse reared for the second time. Gregson quickly dismounted and rushed to the still figure on the ground. He checked her over quickly, but there did not appear to be any broken bones. Georgiana was surprised by his sudden arrival but was too concerned for her friend to wonder much about it. Just then Elizabeth moaned, and her eyes fluttered open. She raised her hand to her head, immediately closing her eyes against the bright sunshine. She attempted to sit up but quickly lay down again as she was overwhelmed by dizziness. After a few more moments of lying still, Georgiana was able to help her to a sitting position. Elizabeth sat very still waiting for the spinning to stop before the others attempted to help her to her feet.

"I am afraid, Miss Bennet, your horse bolted. Would you permit me to return you to Netherfield seated before me on my horse? I believe we should get back as quickly as possible, or I would lead you mounted upon my horse. I am also concerned that you could become dizzy again and perhaps fall from the mount if I weren't holding onto you. Please forgive my forwardness, but I truly believe it will be for the best."

Darcy had been surprised to see Miss Bingley approaching the house in riding attire as he returned from shooting. He had asked after his sister and Miss Elizabeth, knowing they had intended to ride this morning.

"We were racing back to the house, and as you can see, I won!" she gloated. "I am sure they will be along soon." Then she hurried away to her rooms.

Being suspicious of her behavior, especially after the earlier incident at the tea, he rode out to meet the ladies. He arrived just in time to hear Gregson's suggestions.

"You are correct, Gregson," came Darcy's familiar voice. "However, perhaps you could hand Miss Elizabeth up to me and instead ride for the doctor in the village."

"I am afraid that there is no doctor in Meryton, just Mr. Jones, the apothecary," said Elizabeth quietly. She was terribly embarrassed that Mr. Darcy should discover how poor a horsewoman she was. " I will be fine, there is no need to fuss. I merely had the wind knocked out of me when I hit the ground so forcefully. It is just a slight headache and some other aches from the fall, nothing more," she said her face red with embarrassment.

"Please allow me to convey you to the house, Miss Elizabeth, it would greatly ease my mind," said Darcy with a look of concern.

At Elizabeth's nod, Gregson did as Darcy asked and handed Elizabeth up to him. Darcy held her securely as she found a position that was comfortable. He was surprised at the feelings evoked by holding Elizabeth in his arms. Gregson then moved to helped Miss Darcy to remount, as she had jumped from her horse when Elizabeth fell. At his approach, Georgiana's face paled as she saw the blood on his coat.

Georgiana cried out in concern, "Gregson, there is blood on your coat!" Everyone looked at Gregson, who was looking down at his livery.

Realizing the cause of the blood, everyone looked at Elizabeth as Darcy said, "Miss Elizabeth, I believe your head is bleeding." Elizabeth flushed from the scrutiny as she tentatively reached up and touched the back of her head. When she pulled her hand away, her fingers were coated in blood.

As Darcy turned his mount to head for Netherfield, Gregson spoke. "Sir," he said giving Darcy a significant look, "I will just stop by the stables to be sure that Miss Bennet's horse has returned. If not, I will let the stable hands know the direction I last saw him go so that they can retrieve him."

"Thank you, Gregson, but please hurry into town as quickly as you can," replied Darcy tersely. He was concerned about Elizabeth's well-being, so the trio all started off towards Netherfield. Gregson, kicked his horse into a gallop and rapidly left the others behind. Darcy and Georgiana started quickly, but the motion bothered Elizabeth's head and made her feel nauseous, so they slowed their pace. As they approached the house, Darcy and Georgiana went straight to the front entrance. A stable hand came running to hold the horses, as a footman opened the door. He helped Miss Darcy dismount as Darcy slid down and reached up for Elizabeth. He set her gently on her feet then bent down to sweep her up in his arms. He entered the house calling for Bingley's assistance. Mrs. Dawson arrived quickly with

Bingley and Richard fast on her heels. Darcy started up the stairs turning towards the hallway where his room was located. Mrs. Dawson hurried ahead and opened the door to the room next to Mrs. Annesley. Hearing the commotion, that good lady came out to check on her charge and see if she could be of assistance. Darcy gently placed Elizabeth on the bed and stepped away. He hovered nearby not wishing to leave her. Mrs. Annesley coughed softly to gain his attention.

"Sir, has someone gone for the doctor?" she asked.

It took Darcy a moment to tear his eyes away from Elizabeth before he could answer. "Yes, Gregson has gone to fetch the apothecary as Miss Elizabeth said there was no doctor in Meryton."

"Well, sir, perhaps you would excuse us so we can prepare Miss Elizabeth for his visit.

"Come on, Darcy," said Richard. "Let's go wait in the library, you look like you could use a drink. I am sure the ladies will let us know what the apothecary has to say regarding Miss Elizabeth." With one last look towards Elizabeth, Georgiana sitting beside her on the bed holding her hand, Darcy turned and left the room. Richard clapped him on the shoulder in support as they made their way down the corridor.

Before following his guests, Bingley turned to Mrs. Dawson. "Please be sure that Miss Elizabeth and the apothecary have everything they need."

"Certainly, sir," she replied.

Bingley caught up to the others in the library as Richard was handing Darcy a brandy. Darcy swallowed a large gulp of the fiery liquid as he attempted to calm. He sat down and finished off the drink quickly. However, he could not remain still and began pacing the library floor.

"What happened, Darcy?" Richard asked. Darcy paced a bit longer as he tried to quiet his thoughts. He was preparing to answer when the men heard the knocker. In unison, the three men rose and walked to the library door; they saw Gregson entering with the apothecary, Mr. Jones. As Dawson led Mr. Jones up the stairs, Darcy motioned to Gregson to join them in the library.

When the door was closed, Darcy turned to Gregson and asked, "Can you tell us what happened?"

Gregson related the story to the gentlemen as he knew it. He mentioned passing Miss Bingley, seeing the horse rear twice, and of Miss Elizabeth being unseated. "When I arrived sir, I checked Miss Bennet over. Nothing appeared broken, but she was unconscious. She came around quickly but was dizzy when she tried to move. We had just gotten her to her feet when you joined us, Mr. Darcy." Darcy nodded his thanks and released a deep sigh of relief. *If she had only been unconscious for a short time, her injuries hopefully would not be too serious.* Darcy dismissed Gregson, who stopped at the door and turned once more to the men. "Mr. Darcy," he said, "I did find Miss Bennet's horse in the stables. They were just removing the saddle and blanket when I arrived. The stable hand cried out in surprise, as there was blood on the horse's back. It seemed that a thorn had been wedged under the saddle. When Miss Bennet sat down on the saddle, it drove the thorn into the horse. It is no wonder that it reared. There's just one thing that is odd, sir," he continued. "How could the thorn have gotten there? It could not have been there when they left the stables, or the horse would have reacted to it then."

He turned to leave, and Darcy quickly followed him. "What aren't you saying, Gregson?" he asked shortly.

"Sir, I do not have any proof, but I suspect Miss Bingley's involvement. When I passed her, she had a look of satisfaction on her face and was riding away from the other ladies very quickly. Even in the servants' quarters her opinion of Miss Bennet is well known though she is the only one to hold that opinion. Perhaps she wished to embarrass her or demean her in your eyes, or mayhap she hoped the result would be more serious. Sir, I believe you should ask Miss Darcy about what occurred before Miss Bingley departed. Also, I have not yet had the opportunity to tell you this, but the night before last, I caught Miss Bingley outside of your rooms. She was rather scantily clad and tried to gain entrance through both the sitting room and bedroom doors. She was surprised and quite annoyed to find them locked. I did offer my assistance, sir, to help her find the correct room as she was obviously lost in the dark corridors," Gregson said with a barely suppressed grin. He turned and left his master standing in the hall, staring off absently, deep in thought.

Darcy knew Miss Bingley disliked Elizabeth and that she could be ruthless in pursuit of something she wanted, but her usual weapons were hurtful words and gossip. Could she really be heartless enough to try to seriously injury Elizabeth? Had she felt forced to this behavior? Did she do it because she could not get into his rooms to stage a compromise? Did she feel removing the competition was her only option? Did his failure to make his feelings for Miss Bingley clear by refusing to visit when she was present set these events in motions? Was he somehow responsible for Elizabeth's injuries? His thoughts made him feel quite ill.

Shaking off his dark thoughts, Darcy determined to do whatever was needed to keep her safe. He would need to ensure that Gregson got some rest before going on duty tonight, and he would ask Bingley to station someone near Miss Elizabeth's door in case she needed assistance during the night. He also determined to speak to Georgiana as soon as possible.

Mr. Jones entered the room where Elizabeth had been placed. He looked at his patient and smilingly asked, "Well, Miss Lizzy, what trouble did you get yourself into today?"

"I had help getting in trouble today, Mr. Jones," she replied with a smile of her own. "After a pleasant ride out to the creek, my horse decided he was tired of carrying my great weight and threw me from his back. I am alright; it just knocked the wind out of me."

"Oh, Miss Elizabeth, you know it was more than that. You hit your head on a rock, and it only just stopped bleeding. She was unconscious for a short while, Mr. Jones. She was also dizzy when she regained consciousness," Georgiana told the apothecary.

Mr. Jones looked her over well. He was able to report that she had a knot on the back of her, but the cut was superficial, and she did not need stitches. Nothing is broken, and she should be all right in a day or so. "However," he said, "you are to remain in bed for the rest of the day and all day tomorrow, just to ensure that you are not more seriously injured than it appears. Head injuries can be unpredictable."

"You may have to put that in writing, Mr. Jones. You know how my mother can be. No one is ever so sick they must remain in bed unless it is she with her nerves."

"You will not have to worry about your mother, as you must stay in this very bed. It is not good to move someone who may have a concussion. I believe yours is a very mild one, but we must be cautious," Mr. Jones replied. "Also, I will leave these powders in case your headache becomes too severe."

Elizabeth looked uncomfortable at the thought of remaining in Mr. Bingley's home. "Are you sure I cannot return home, sir? I would hate to inconvenience my host."

"I will inform him that it is my orders that require you to remain. I am sure that Mr. Bingley will not think of it as an imposition. He is far too kindly for that," Mr. Jones remarked.

"Do not you worry, Miss Elizabeth," Mrs. Dawson said soothingly. "Mr. Bingley said that you were to have everything you needed for your care. I am sure that applies to his home as well." She gave Elizabeth a warm smile as she escorted Mr. Jones from the room.

There was a knock on the library door. Bingley called, "Come," and the door opened. Mrs. Dawson appeared with the apothecary. "Mr. Jones would like to speak with you, sir, before he departs."

"Certainly. Please come in," said Bingley cordially. "Tell me, Mr. Jones, how is Miss Elizabeth?"

"She was very fortunate, sir. A fall from a horse can be a dangerous thing, but her injuries are relatively minor. The cut on her head did not need stitching, and nothing is broken. I am sure she will be a bit bruised and stiff, but it will pass quickly. However, because she did lose consciousness, I would like her to remain in bed through tomorrow. She was concerned about her presence being an inconvenience. But, as the one in charge of her care, I must ask that you allow her to remain here during that time."

"Certainly, Mr. Jones. It is not an inconvenience at all. Miss Elizabeth will have everything she needs for her recovery," Mr. Bingley assured him.

"Thank you, sir. I will stop by tomorrow to see how she is feeling. Good day, gentlemen." Mr. Jones turned to leave, and it was not long before they heard the front door close behind him.

"Gentlemen, shall we go and visit Miss Elizabeth?" Bingley asked. Darcy was the first one up and out the door. The other two men smiled and followed behind. Darcy knocked on the door of Elizabeth's room, and Mrs. Annesley opened it. The gentlemen gathered in the doorway. Elizabeth had been propped up on pillows and appeared to be wearing one of Georgiana's nightdresses. Her hair was down, the long braid upon her chest hanging almost to her waist. In spite of the bandage and slight bruise on the side of her forehead, Darcy thought he had never seen a more beautiful sight. He stared at Elizabeth, his feelings clearly visible in his eyes. Seeing his look, Elizabeth's eyes welled with tears even as a wide smile spread across her face. Her tears told him of her feelings as well.

"Miss Elizabeth, I hope you are feeling better," said Bingley. "Is there anything I can get you for your comfort?"

"If it would not be too much of an imposition, might I have some writing materials? I must let my family know what has happened."

"I would be happy to write to them for you. In fact, I shall invite Miss Bennet to come and stay the night with you. I am sure that would give you some comfort." *It will give me pleasure as well,* Bingley thought to himself. The three gentlemen wished her a speedy recovery and departed.

Richard grabbed Darcy's arm and turned him towards their sitting room. Once behind the closed door he remarked, "I am glad Miss Elizabeth was not seriously injured."

"No thanks to Miss Bingley," Darcy said harshly. Richard was shocked at Darcy's words and the look on his face.

"What do you mean, cousin?" he asked.

Darcy related what Gregson had told him—including his suspicions of Caroline—and that Gregson had caught her trying to get into his rooms in the middle of the night. "I need to speak to Georgie before I am sure. Even if we discover that Miss Bingley tampered with Miss Elizabeth's saddle, how will I ever find the words to tell Bingley that his sister intentionally tried to hurt Miss Elizabeth?"

Richard had no answer for him but said, "If you can't find the words, I certainly can. I like Bingley but am not as invested in the relationship as you are. She could have killed Miss Elizabeth," Richard angrily remarked. "In the meantime, we will just have to think of the best way to keep Miss Elizabeth safe."

Darcy and Richard were approaching the top of the stairs when they heard raised voices below. Before they could retreat, Caroline screeched, "What do you mean Miss Eliza is staying the night?"

"I told you, Caroline; she was injured during her ride this morning, and the apothecary says she must remain in bed for a day or two. By the way, I thought you accompanied the ladies on their ride. How did you not know of her injury?"

Caroline stammered trying to come up with a reason. "I . . . I . . . We began a race back, I was in the lead, so I could not see what was occurring behind me. I did not realize what happened. I went straight to my room to freshen up when I returned." Darcy looked to Richard at her words. Both faces wore the same grim expression.

Bingley continued, "I expect Miss Elizabeth will be here two nights. I have also invited Miss Bennet to stay so that she can be with her sister. Please have the room next to Miss Elizabeth's prepared for her." With that Bingley turned and headed for his study.

Caroline still stood in the hall practically shaking with rage and muttering softly, "We had ridden in the direction of the Longbourn border, why did they bring her here to recover? Whatever little aches and bruises she received were supposed to keep her away from Netherfield and Mr. Darcy! He was to be discouraged by her poor horsemanship and see how accomplished a rider I was by comparison." She stamped her foot in frustration. "Now to make matters worse, instead of being rid of Miss Eliza, Miss Bennet is also coming to stay, and I shall have to endure Charles's moon-eyed stares." Stamping her foot again, she turned to go find Mrs. Dawson to have Jane Bennet's room prepared. Caroline never realized her rant had been loud enough for Darcy and Richard to overhear.

When she was gone from view, the gentlemen continued down the stairs and into the library. "Well, it appears Gregson is correct in his suppositions regarding Miss Bingley," Richard said sharply.

"She could have killed Elizabeth!" Darcy cried angrily.

"We can manage to keep an eye on her, Darcy. We can ensure they are not alone together and monitor her interactions with Miss Elizabeth. I will be here to help, as I do not report to my regiment until the day Miss Elizabeth can return home."

"I know you are right, Richard, but I feel dreadful knowing that I am responsible for Miss Elizabeth's difficulties."

"How in Heaven's name are you responsible? All the actions were by the hand of another, and it is Miss Bingley's stubborn delusion and refusal to listen to what others tell her that are responsible," Richard said with a frustrated sigh. "Do you feel guilty for Aunt Catherine's delusions as well?"

Darcy glared at the mention of their aunt but softened and said, "Point taken. Thank you, Richard, for your help and support. I appreciate it more than you know." Darcy's heartfelt tones conveyed his gratitude.

Richard eyed his cousin. "What are your plans for Miss Elizabeth? It is quite obvious you have strong feelings for her."

Darcy paled slightly, "Is it really that obvious?"

"It is to those who know you well," Richard replied.

"If I had nothing else to consider but my own wishes, I would like to make her my wife. When I am with her, I am filled with a joy I have not known since I was young. She is intelligent, witty, and warm. I have never met anyone like her before—and you know that I have had countless single young ladies paraded before me. I believe that she would be perfect for me. I can only imagine the happiness a life with her would offer. Unfortunately, there are other things to consider. What would your parents think? I already know what Aunt Catherine's opinion would be," he said with a grimace. The worry in his voice, he continued, "Would she ever be accepted by the ton? Is it fair to force her to face the difficulties that a marriage to me would bring? I would not wish her to change as I find her perfect as she is, but would she have to change to fit into the first circles of society? Would I be hurting Georgiana's chances to make a good match if I married her? I am not sure what I should do." Darcy was shocked when Richard began to laugh. "I fail to see what is funny about this situation," Darcy stated coldly.

"I am sorry, cousin," Richard answered, attempting to contain his mirth. "It is just rare to see you so indecisive. It makes me feel a little less inferior to realize you are merely human like the rest of us," he said with another chuckle. Darcy's lips lifted in a small smile as well. "We will ignore Aunt Catherine as we usually do," Richard continued, "However, I believe mother and father would be happy for you. There are no glaring faults that need to be corrected before she faces the ton. Her lack of fortune and connections might give them pause, but knowing my mother as I do, I am certain she would find a way to present that information so that it was palatable to the ton. We both know Miss Elizabeth has handled Miss Bingley skillfully, and what is the ton but a large group of Miss Bingleys? I believe she will charm many of them with her wit and intelligence. If she loves you, as I think she may be well on her way to doing, I am sure she would not consider giving you up just because of a few challenges. Lastly, I do not think you could find a better example or sister for Georgiana. Look at the progress she has already made and their acquaintance is of but a few days duration. I think both the Darcy name and Miss Elizabeth would do more than survive. I know they would thrive."

Darcy considered his cousin's words for several minutes before speaking, his smile growing with each passing moment. "I believe you have helped me decide my course. Perhaps she can come to town to stay with her Aunt and Uncle, and I could court her there. It would like to give her a taste of life in my world. It would also give us a chance to become better acquainted. I will speak to Miss Elizabeth soon and procure her father's permission before departing for Christmas," Darcy said decisively.

Richard tried to smother his chuckle. Darcy looked as if the weight of the world had been lifted from his shoulders with the decision.

As the gentlemen sat in the library, Miss Bennet arrived and was escorted to her sister's room. "Oh, Lizzy, are you alright? I have been so worried!" Jane exclaimed.

"I am fine, Jane, truly," said Elizabeth. "I just demonstrated my poor riding skills by allowing my horse to unseat me. I hit my head and was unconscious very briefly. Mr. Jones is just being cautious by forcing me to remain in bed through tomorrow. Other than a slight headache I am perfectly fine," said Elizabeth with a rueful smile.

Jane and Georgiana stayed with Elizabeth all afternoon visiting with and reading to her. When she dozed for a brief time, Jane sat quietly working on her needlework, and Georgiana went to practice her music. When dinner was announced, Elizabeth insisted that Jane join the others and spend time with Mr. Bingley. "At least if I must be stuck at Netherfield, some good can come of it. It will give you the chance to spend extra time with your Mr. Bingley," Elizabeth said with a laugh.

Jane blushed at her sister's reference to Bingley being "hers" but allowed herself to be persuaded to go down to dinner. Bingley jumped up upon Jane's entrance to the parlor before dinner, took her arm to escort her to the table, and seated her beside him. Richard watched Bingley and Miss Bennet as they conversed exclusively with one another. He first caught Hurst's glance. They looked at the two and back to each other rolling their eyes. Richard caught Darcy's eye and nodded toward Bingley and Jane. Darcy and Richard looked at each other and had to cough to cover their amusement.

After dinner, Darcy had an opportunity to ask Georgiana for the details of what had occurred before Elizabeth's accident. Georgiana told him Miss Bingley said the girth appeared loose on Elizabeth's saddle, and she tightened it for her. Then Miss Bingley immediately mounted and hurried off calling over her shoulder to Georgiana and Elizabeth that it was a race.

The friends sat in the music room listening to Mrs. Hurst and Miss Bingley play. Richard had asked Georgiana to play also, but she had declined, a panicked look upon her face. After Miss Bingley had finished playing, she arose and announced her intention to take Miss Eliza a cup of tea and check on her before retiring. She said her good nights and swept from the room. Darcy and Richard looked at one another. They would give her a few minutes to go and get the tea and then excuse themselves to say good night to Miss Elizabeth.

With Miss Bingley's departure, Jane realized she should return to Elizabeth as well. She said her hurried goodnights and quickly ascended the stairs. She checked on her sister, who was reading quietly, and then went to prepare to retire. During Jane's absence, Miss Bingley knocked on Elizabeth's door and entered without waiting for her call to do so.

"Miss Eliza, I came to bring you this special cup of tea. I have added something that always helps me to sleep. So just drink it down, and I will take the cup away and retire."

At that moment, there was another knock at the door. When Elizabeth called enter, the door opened to reveal Georgiana, Darcy, and the Colonel. Elizabeth set the cup on the table beside the bed as they entered.

"I realize it is not quite proper for gentlemen to be in your sickroom, Miss Elizabeth. However I hoped, perhaps, since it was a large group and we were not alone, you might forgive us." Darcy neared the side of the bed where Miss Bingley stood as he spoke. "We will not keep you long but did wish to see if you were feeling better?" Darcy gazed steadily at Elizabeth as he spoke, which provoked Miss Bingley yet again.

"Miss Eliza, please drink your tea, and I will leave you to your visitors," Miss Bingley said harshly.

Elizabeth looked at her, surprised by the harsh tone. "I do apologize, Miss Bingley, but I had just finished some tea Mrs. Dawson brought me before your arrival. I thank you for your thoughtfulness, though," Elizabeth said warily.

"Oh, but, Miss Eliza, it will truly help you to sleep. Please do drink it," Miss Bingley pushed.

Darcy, wondering at Miss Bingley's persistence, said, "I will be happy to drink it, Miss Elizabeth if you do not mind. It would be a shame to allow Miss Bingley's *kindness* to be wasted."

Caroline cast a terrified glance towards Darcy as he reached for the teacup on the table. The Colonel was watching Caroline closely. "I do not think you would care for it, Mr. Darcy," Caroline said reaching to take the cup from him. "It is much sweeter than you take your tea."

"You did say it would help a person sleep though, did you not? I believe I can tolerate the sweet if it brings me a good night's sleep."

"Well, if you insist, be my guest." She swept her arm towards Darcy in acknowledgment, knocking the cup from his hands. Darcy managed to catch it before all of the contents were gone. "Oh, I am terribly sorry. I hope I did not ruin your clothes," she said, relief in her voice. "Well, if you will excuse me, I will send someone to clean up the mess. Good night everyone." She hurried from the room.

"Miss Elizabeth, please accept my sincerest apologies. We only wished to assure ourselves that you were well. I did not mean to cause so much disruption and create a mess in your room." Darcy's gaze was concerned, but very caring, as it rested on her face. It made Elizabeth feel warm all over, and she knew that a blush covered her cheeks.

"Please, Mr. Darcy, do not concern yourself. Accidents do happen, and I believe it was Miss Bingley who made the mess," Elizabeth said with a cheeky grin. "I do want to thank you, Mr. Darcy, for taking the time to visit me this evening." She colored at her slip of the tongue and continued quickly, "It was very thoughtful of all of you."

"Perhaps we might visit again tomorrow?" Darcy asked hopefully.

"I would be happy for any company. I am sure it shall try my patience to have to remain in this bed for another full day," said Elizabeth with a grimace.

"Well then, good night, Miss Elizabeth." Lifting her hand from where it lay on the counterpane, Darcy bestowed a soft, linger kiss on it while gazing intently into her eyes. After returning her hand to its place on the bed, he quickly scooped up the teacup and departed.

Georgiana stepped up beside the bed and kissed Elizabeth's cheek. "I am so sorry your accident ruined the remainder of our day. Perhaps we can try again when you are feeling better?" Georgiana asked tentatively.

"Our day was not ruined. I enjoyed every moment spent with you, and you took such good care of me after the accident. Thank you for your kindness." She gave Georgiana a grateful smile. "I hope you will allow all the bruises and soreness to disappear before we go riding again," said Elizabeth with a rueful grin.

"I promise. In the meantime, we will just have to find other things to do."

Darcy was waiting for Georgiana by the door with Richard beside him. Richard clicked his heels and gave Elizabeth a courtly bow and a wink, which brought a laugh from her. The three departed the room with Darcy the last out. His eyes met Elizabeth's one last time and held until the door was closed between them.

Darcy kissed his sister goodnight at her door and then stepped into the sitting room he shared with Richard. He showed the teacup to Richard. Darcy dipped the end of his little finger into the remaining tea and stuck it in his mouth. His face screwed up in disgust, and he rushed to the fireplace and spit.

Richard looked at him in astonishment both eyebrows raised. "Would you care to explain your behavior?"

"I was concerned by Miss Bingley's insistence that Miss Elizabeth drink the tea. You saw what she did when I when I said I would drink it. She *accidentally* knocked the cup from my hand when she could not dissuade me from drinking it. However, I managed to catch it before all the evidence was gone."

"But why did you make the face?"

"Taste for yourself," Darcy offered holding out the cup to his cousin.

Warily the Colonel mimicked Darcy's earlier actions right down to the face and spitting into the fire. Darcy laughed at his cousin's expression. "What was that?" Fitzwilliam asked looking around the sitting room for a decanter to wash away the terrible taste.

"That was the taste of a horse chestnut," Darcy answered. "I ate one by mistake when I was young. It can be hard to tell them apart, but I quickly learned how after my mistake.

Unfortunately, like with most children, I chewed and swallowed without fully tasting it. As the terrible taste registered, I knew I had not eaten a chestnut. It was not long before I was extremely sick. I had stomach cramps and nausea. My arm and leg muscles twitched, then got very stiff, and when that stopped, I felt weak as a newborn. Dr. Elliott, the physician in Lambton, said they could be deadly in large doses, but, fortunately, because of the foul taste, few people eat enough for that to happen. It took a few days before most of my symptoms were gone, but I was weak for much longer, and it took several days before my energy levels returned to normal. Dr. Elliott said the way to tell them apart is that edible chestnuts look flattened on both sides. Horse chestnuts are only flat on one side."

"Do you think the dose in Miss Bennet's tea could have killed her?" Richard asked.

"I doubt it, but that would not have prevented her from being extremely sick. It would have kept Miss Elizabeth from my company for several days."

"What are you going to do now? Are you going to seek out Bingley or wait for morning?" Richard asked. "I would be happy to accompany you if the moral support would help."

"I think that I must go to Bingley tonight. The longer Miss Bingley is in the house with Elizabeth, the longer she will be in danger. Certainly the fall from her horse could have been much more serious. Miss Bingley might have caused her permanent harm or killed her, even if that was not her intent."

"You go fetch Bingley. I will meet you in the study shortly."

After preparing for bed, Jane returned to Elizabeth's room. They curled up together on the bed to talk.

"How was your evening with Mr. Bingley?" Elizabeth observed as Jane's face suffused with color, and her eyes took on a dreamy look.

"Oh, Lizzy, it was wonderful! He escorted me to dinner and sat me next to him. He conversed exclusively with me, totally ignoring Mr. Darcy, who was on his other side. The gentlemen did not separate after the meal, but Mr. Bingley escorted me to a small sofa in the music room where we continued our talk until I retired. He is such a kind gentleman, Lizzy. He is everything I could want in a husband. I know the relationship is of short duration, but I do believe that I am falling in love with Mr. Bingley."

"I am very glad you had such a lovely evening. Mine was far busier. First, Miss Bingley brought me a cup of tea. She was very insistent that I drink it, but before I could respond to her, Miss Darcy, Mr. Darcy, and the Colonel came to check on me before retiring. I explained to Miss Bingley that I had just finished my tea, and Mr. Darcy offered to drink the tea if I did not want it. Miss Bingley made a big fuss and knocked it from his hand though she said it was an accident. After the spill, she rushed off to her room. It was all very strange," Elizabeth said, a confused look on her face.

"Lizzy! You let Mr. Darcy and the Colonel into your bedroom?" Jane's face expressed her shock.

"Miss Bingley and Miss Darcy were here as well, Jane. It was not like I was entertaining gentlemen alone," Elizabeth said with a laugh as she regarded Jane's shocked expression.

"I am surprised that Mr. Darcy would do something so out of character. Mr. Bingley says he is always very proper."

"Do not be alarmed. He was concerned about propriety as well but assumed with his younger sister and cousin also in attendance, perhaps the breach of propriety could be overlooked," said Elizabeth.

The warm unguarded look on her face caught Jane unawares. "Lizzy, do you have feelings for Mr. Darcy?" she asked.

"I try not to, as I know that I am far below him in importance. He moves in the first circles of society, and I move in Hertfordshire society. We have no exalted connections and no dowry. I do not want to be disappointed if Mr. Darcy cannot offer for me. But, oh, the way he looks at me sometimes. It takes my breath away and makes me feel warm all over."

Jane knew her feelings, and Elizabeth was describing them perfectly. Whether she admitted it to herself or not, Elizabeth was falling in love with Mr. Darcy. Jane hoped for her sister's sake that all would be well. They talked for a few minutes longer, before Jane rose, kissed her sister's forehead, and retired to her room for the night.

Darcy rapped lightly on Bingley's bedchamber door. As Bingley was preparing to retire, he had just removed his coat and cravat. "Darcy, what is it? Is something the matter?" Bingley's face showed concern as he took in Darcy's solemn expression.

"I am sorry to disturb you so late, but there is a matter of extreme importance I must discuss with you. Would you join me in your study where we can speak privately?"

"Certainly, Darcy. Just give me a moment and I will join you there." Darcy turned down the hallway toward the stairs where Richard was waiting. They descended to the study to await Bingley. Richard was in the process of pouring out three brandies when Bingley arrived. He handed one to each man as they seated themselves.

Bingley waited for Darcy to speak, but he remained silent. Finally, the suspense was more than Bingley could take. "For goodness sake, Darcy, what is it? Speak up man!" Bingley cried.

Darcy looked up at Bingley with such an expression of sadness and rage that Bingley was taken aback. "Bingley, there is no easy way to say this. Miss Bingley has twice attempted to harm Miss Elizabeth, and both attempts occurred today."

"Darcy, you cannot be serious!" Bingley cried. "What makes you think this? What proof do you have?"

Darcy recounted what had transpired on the ladies' ride that morning, showing Bingley the thorn that Gregson had given him. Darcy then related the story about the tea. He even explained how he knew what had been put in it.

"Yes, the same thing happened to Caroline once. She was dreadfully sick." It was obvious from his face how difficult it was to hear of his sister's actions. Darcy felt concern for Bingley.

"I am sorry to have to tell you all this Bingley. But the proof is from Miss Bingley's own words." He related what he had overheard her say earlier. "We cannot let this go unchallenged. Miss Bingley, in her misguided efforts to keep me away or turn my interest from Miss Elizabeth, could have killed her," Darcy said more forcefully than intended. "I demand you confront her with the knowledge of her actions, but if you will not, I will," he declared firmly.

Bingley was devastated. He seemed to have aged since entering the study. "Darcy, I do not know what to say. I am sorry seems so inadequate.

What should I do? Is she only behaving this way because of her obsession with you, or is there something inherently wrong with her?"

Richard spoke up. "If I may offer an opinion, Bingley?" he asked. "Perhaps, removing her from the immediate temptation would suffice for now. You should confront her with your knowledge, and then send her from Netherfield as punishment. Perhaps ask your sister and brother-in-law for their opinions before meeting with your sister. From her remarks about aches and bruises, I don't believe she intended to cause serious harm to Elizabeth. I feel, however, you need to let her know that her attempted mischief could have had a much more serious outcome. Had Miss Elizabeth been fatally injured, your sister would be facing charges of murder. That must be impressed upon her."

"Thank you for the suggestion, Colonel. I believe you may be correct about removing her from temptation. She is so determined to be Mrs. Darcy that she will not listen to anything anyone tells her to the contrary. I will send her to London on the morrow, and then explain to Louisa and Hurst what I have done and why. My Aunt and Uncle Bingley are staying at the townhouse while visiting London. I will send them an express immediately so they understand the situation and can keep a proper watch on Caroline. She may go with them to whatever invitations they accept, but I will be sure to let them know she is to have no funds whatsoever."

"Might I suggest that you post a footman outside of her room for the night so that she cannot leave. We would not want to risk her trying again," Richard prompted.

"That is a good suggestion. I will also make sure the footman outside of Miss Elizabeth's door knows not to admit Caroline under any circumstances."

"Darcy, again, please accept my apologies and be sure to pass them on to Miss Elizabeth."

"Bingley, Miss Elizabeth is unaware that the incident with the horse was anything other than an accident. She did not drink the tea, so she is unaware there was a problem with it. I do not think we should mention this to Miss Bennet while she is recovering. Caroline will be gone tomorrow, so she will no longer be in danger. I do not wish to cause her further distress or needless worry."

"As you wish. Is there anything else we need to do, tonight? I really think I need to retire," he said dejectedly.

"I am sorry to have to do this, Bingley, but there is one more thing of which you should be aware. The other evening, Caroline was observed attempting to enter both my bedroom and sitting room. Fortunately for me, I have been keeping the doors locked since her earlier attempt," said Darcy.

"Her what?" Bingley shouted.

Darcy looked sheepish as he told Bingley of finding her with an ear to his door one morning. "I instructed my valet to keep the doors locked at all times and to remain in the rooms as much as possible. He is even sleeping in the dressing room. I am sorry to add to your burdens, but I feel I must reiterate that I will not marry your sister under any circumstances, particularly ones of her making," Darcy said emphatically.

"Please, no more tonight, I do not think I could stand it. Now, I must prepare the express, and I am for bed and pray for a peaceful night to prepare for the battle tomorrow. Again, my sincerest apologies," said Bingley wearily.

"I think that would be best for all of us," Darcy agreed. "I am sorry, Bingley, that I had to lay this burden on you."

"You were right to do so, Darcy. It is long past time that I took charge of my sister. I am sure that giving in to her so often to keep the peace makes me largely responsible for her bad behavior now."

The three gentlemen climbed the stairs their steps measured, their thoughts concerned. They all headed into the wing where the guestrooms were located. Bingley stopped to give orders to the footman about denying Caroline entrance to Miss Elizabeth's room. As he was preparing to depart, Miss Elizabeth's door opened, and Miss Bennet stepped into the hallway.

"Mr. Bingley, I did not expect to see you here," Jane said with a start.

"I am leaving Miss Bennet, do not fear."

"I am sorry, Mr. Bingley, that did not come out as I intended. What I meant was is there something I can help you with?" Jane asked softly. He seemed to be different, much more serious and tired than he had appeared earlier.

"Do not worry, Miss Bennet, I took no offense. I was just checking with the footman stationed by your sister's room before I retire. I wanted to be sure he understood my wishes. Good night, Miss Bennet, sleep well."

Jane watched him walk away before returning to her room. She was disturbed to note how weary and heartsick he appeared.

As soon as the door closed behind them in their shared sitting room, Richard said, "Darcy do you really think it wise to keep information from Miss Elizabeth? After the courage she showed when she tried to help Georgie all those years ago, I do not believe she is the type of lady who would appreciate secrets being kept from her. If she were ever to be in the company of Miss Bingley again, having this knowledge would help her to protect herself."

"Perhaps you are right, Richard. I will try to discuss this with her at the first opportunity that arises for a private conversation. "Good night, cousin." Darcy, deep in thought, entered his bedchamber, closing the door behind him.

CHAPTER 11

Elizabeth was awake early, but there would be no walk this morning. She had a few aches from her fall and a slight headache, but overall she felt very well. Elizabeth knew it would be hard to remain abed as Mr. Jones had ordered. The only good thing about it was that she would see Mr. Darcy again.

Darcy awoke at his usual early hour. He would normally take a ride before breakfast, but he determined to pass the morning in his sitting room where he could be close to Elizabeth if he were needed. She had invaded his dreams last night. That was not unusual, as he had dreamed of her every night since the assembly. But the dreams last night were much more intense. Having decided that he would ask for her hand, he dreamed of having her in his home and his bed. If reality came anywhere close to the dreams, he knew he would have a wonderful life with Elizabeth, one filled with laughter and love. He would have to find a way to make her laugh often, as it had become his favorite sound in the world.

He thought about the unpleasant chore ahead of Bingley and wondered if Caroline could finally be dissuaded if she heard directly from him regarding his lack of interest. He would offer to be with Bingley during the interview, should he be needed.

He picked up the book that he had purchased for Elizabeth. He would have Georgiana give it to Elizabeth today. Perhaps it would help her to pass the time. *Or perhaps she would allow me to read it to her,* he thought. It was not long before he heard noises from Richard's suite indicating that his cousin was awake. He knocked on the door and entered at Richard's call. The gentlemen chatted as Richard finished his preparations for the day. They descended the stairs to the breakfast room where they found Bingley.

"How are you this morning, Bingley?" The concern appeared on Darcy's face as he looked at his friend.

"I am well, Darcy, do not worry."

"Bingley, I wanted to let you know that should you need my assistance in the interview with Miss Bingley, I would be happy to be present. Perhaps hearing from me directly might convince Miss Bingley to drop this obsession."

"I believe that you could be correct, but you must promise to be both direct and blunt if polite subtlety does not reach her."

"If that is your wish, Bingley. What time do you plan to conduct your interview?"

"I have informed Caroline's maid to have her in my study by ten this morning. I hope to get it over with promptly and get her on her way to London. Since she will stay at the townhouse, I have decided to remain at Netherfield for the holidays."

"I wish that I could join you," said Darcy, "but we are already committed to joining the Matlocks in town."

Jane entered the dining room at that moment, and the gentlemen all rose.

"Good morning, Miss Bennet." Bingley spoke quietly, and Jane looked at him surprised by the reserved greeting.

"Good morning, Mr. Bingley," she replied with a smile and a blush. Turning she acknowledged, "Good morning, Mr. Darcy, Colonel Fitzwilliam."

"Miss Bennet," the gentlemen, replied.

"How is Miss Elizabeth this morning?" Darcy asked intently.

"She seems perfectly well and says even her headache is gone. I am sure the challenge of the day will be keeping her entertained and in bed as Mr. Jones ordered," Jane added with a smile.

"I do believe I have something that will help with that endeavor," Darcy offered enigmatically.

"And other than attempting to get your sister to rest as ordered, what are your plans for the day, Miss Bennet?" Bingley asked.

"I have no plans, sir. I am here to attend to Lizzy," Jane replied shyly.

"Well, if Miss Elizabeth can spare you for a few moments, I thought perhaps you would take a stroll through the gardens with me. I have something I wish to discuss with you." His cheeks reddened as he looked at her awaiting an answer.

"I am sure Lizzy will be able to spare me for a time." Her rosy cheeks matched his, and she saw him smile with her answer.

"Perhaps my sister and I could visit with Miss Elizabeth while you are out, Miss Bennet? I know we would enjoy the time with her," Darcy offered hastily.

"I believe that would be acceptable if Mrs. Annesley is also in attendance."

The clock struck three-quarters past the hour. Looking back to Jane, he said, "If you will excuse me, Miss Bennet, I have an appointment at ten and must be ready. Darcy, could you join me for a moment?" he asked.

The gentlemen excused themselves and left the dining room, and Richard turned his attention to entertaining Miss Bennet. They were joined shortly thereafter by Mr. and Mrs. Hurst.

"I wonder what is keeping Caroline this morning?" Louisa asked.

"I believe Mr. Bingley asked to see her this morning before she began her day," Richard said, his eyes meeting Hurst's.

"Is anything wrong, do you know?" asked Louisa her expression worried.

"I believe that he mentioned the need to speak with you when he was through with his discussion with Miss Bingley," Richard replied calmly.

Bingley and Darcy had settled in the library where Bingley reviewed his plan for the interview. Darcy could tell he had given much thought to what he intended to say.

"May I make a suggestion, Bingley?" At Bingley's nod he continued, "From dealing with difficult tenants, I know that confidence and control of the situation can help a great deal. I would suggest that you speak to her from behind your desk and that my chair be pulled off to the side also facing you. Her chair should be the only one in front of the desk placed directly across from you. You show your authority as head of the family from this position. My being to the side, also diminishes my position in the discussion and forces her to face you."

Caroline's knock was heard. They stood quickly and placed the chairs as discussed. Then from his seat behind the desk, Bingley called, "Come."

Caroline entered closing the door behind her, noting some changes as she glanced about the room. The only available chair was directly across from Charles. Caroline began to feel uneasy.

"Please be seated, Caroline."

I have always been able to manage Charles; she reminded herself. *However, to do so, I must maintain control.* She lifted her chin and said, "I prefer to stand, Charles, as I have very little time for you this morning."

"Sit down, Caroline," Charles said firmly. She quickly did as instructed.

However, she was not ready to concede. "Charles, where are your manners? Raising your voice in front of Mr. Darcy is quite rude."

Charles ignored her comment. "Caroline, could you please tell me how a large thorn got under Miss Elizabeth's saddle and blanket yesterday?"

Her eyes showed nervousness. "I am sure I do not know. Perhaps you should ask your incompetent stable hands."

"I have talked to the stable hands, but had it been their fault, Miss Elizabeth would have taken her fall at the time she first mounted. Since that did not happen, I can only assume you placed it there when you pretended to fix Miss Elizabeth's saddle girth."

"Is Miss Eliza trying to blame me for her poor horsemanship? Is that why you are questioning me so rudely?" Caroline asked angrily.

"Miss Elizabeth has said nothing about her accident at all, but from other information I have received, you are the most likely cause of said accident. You could have killed her, Caroline."

"Do not be ridiculous, Charles. A fall to her posterior would hardly kill her—it would just show how unsuitable she is for our society. Now, I refuse to be treated in this manner a minute longer. I am leaving, and I do not wish to speak to you again until you can treat me with the respect I deserve as your sister." Caroline began to rise.

"Sit down, Caroline," Bingley cried, louder than before. "You will sit in that chair until I tell you we are through with this interview!"

Now Caroline was really concerned. All of her usual tricks to control Charles were failing.

"There is another matter to be discussed, Caroline. I remember you offered to take a cup of tea to Miss Elizabeth last evening. You told her it would help her sleep. I was wondering if you had found the effects of horse chestnut helped you sleep when you ate it. As I recall, it just made you very, very sick for a few days. I do not remember you sleeping; I just remember your constant complaints."

She had spilled the tea—how did he know this? "I do not know what you could be talking about, Charles. I took Miss Eliza some tea, but she did not drink it. Mr. Darcy was going to drink it, but I, unfortunately, knocked the cup from his hand. It was just a cup of tea to help her sleep. What is all this nonsense about horse chestnuts?" Caroline stared at him defiantly.

"Caroline, in spite of your denials, I know you have twice attempted to hurt and embarrass Miss Elizabeth. I want to know why." Charles stared at her intently.

"Charles, I have no idea why you are insisting that I did these awful things. Perhaps you are delirious with fever to be making these wild allegations. I shall send for the physician before I attend to my other duties, but now I really must go." She started to rise again, but Bingley jumped up and leaned across the desk toward her.

"Sit down, Caroline!" he shouted a look of fury on his face.

"Now you have exactly five seconds to answer my questions, or so help me . . . "

Caroline was angry now, as well, and resented her brother's treatment of her. Unfortunately for Caroline she was often irrational when she was angry. "All I did," she shouted at him, "was try to get that two-faced little nobody out of our home and away from my fianc . . . our dearest friend. He should not have to be bothered by such unsuitable company. She is nothing but a social climbing fortune hunter! She has been a distraction to our happiness since we first arrived here. I hate her!" Caroline screamed at her brother.

Darcy had reached his limit. "Excuse me, Miss Bingley, but I do not remember engaging myself to you, yet you seem to think me your fiancé? I believe we *should* send for the doctor, Bingley, your sister is delusional," Darcy's calm, cold voice was more frightening than her brother's shouting. He continued to address Caroline, "To be certain there is no misunderstanding, permit me to be as clear as possible. There are absolutely no circumstances that would ever compel me to marry you. You could be seen in my rooms naked by hundreds of witnesses, and I still would not marry you. Do I make myself clear?"

Caroline nodded numbly; her mouth hanging open in shock. "Furthermore, consider yourself fortunate that Miss Elizabeth was not seriously hurt or killed when she fell from her horse, for I would not hesitate to turn you over to the magistrate. I had a suspicion you were involved in her riding accident, and that is why I took the tea. I suspected you were attempting to harm her again."

Caroline's anger returned, "I have known you these last several years; why cannot you see that I am the perfect choice for your wife and the

Mistress of Pemberley? I was educated at the best seminary; she was not. My performance on the pianoforte is far more proficient than hers. She has no sense of style; she cannot speak the modern languages, and she does not draw or paint. Then there is her family! Her mother is without class or manners, and her youngest sisters are hardly less than tarts. Her best relations to speak of are a country solicitor and a gentleman in trade. She is not even pretty!" Caroline screamed.

Darcy stood up and, moving much closer, faced her. "You may be seminary educated, but they cannot teach a person kindness or compassion, both of which you lack. Miss Elizabeth has used her time very well to educate herself. One can carry on an actual conversation with her, as she knows about much more than the weather, fashion, and gossip. She plays with great emotion; that is much more appealing than a perfect piece played without feeling. As for her appearance, she is the most beautiful woman of my acquaintance; she has an understated elegance that is vastly appealing. And lastly, Miss Elizabeth is the daughter of a gentleman while you are the daughter of a tradesman. Bingley, I do believe you should send for the doctor. I question Miss Bingley's mental state. She seems quite unable to determine reality from fantasy. Perhaps she should be institutionalized."

So saying Darcy turned on his heel and left the room. He returned to the dining room and poured another cup of coffee. Georgiana had arrived in the dining room during his absence.

When she finished her meal, Darcy asked her to accompany him upstairs.

At Mr. Darcy's last words, Caroline had slumped into her chair. She was staring disbelievingly at the door through which Darcy had just left. Thinking he now had his sister's attention, Bingley said, "I warned you once before that if you could not conduct yourself in a proper manner as my hostess, you would leave the house. Your maid is currently above, packing your belongings. You will remain in your suite until that time. When your belongings are packed, you will be leaving Netherfield in my coach with your maid and two footmen to accompany you. I have sent an express already. You will stay at the townhouse with our aunt and uncle. You may accompany them to any events they attend if you wish, but you will not receive any more funds until the next quarter, and I will cancel your credit with your modiste. I will no longer be covering your expenses when you overspend your allowance. Lastly, my carriage will be returning, as I will have need of it. You will need to pay for a hack or depend on others for your transportation. When Aunt and Uncle Bingley return to their home, you will be required to remain quietly at home as you will have no chaperone or companion."

"I will be remaining at Netherfield for the holidays, so I will wish you well now. I hope by the time we meet again, Caroline, you will have taken my words to heart, as well as Darcy's. We all tried to tell you he was not interested, but you refused to listen. Since you have now heard directly from him what his feelings are, learn from this. Move on and make a real life for yourself. Now please go to your room," Charles said tiredly. There was a footman awaiting her in the hall. He followed her to her room and remained outside until it was time for her to depart.

Wanting to get all of this over quickly, Bingley rang for a servant and asked for Mr. and Mrs. Hurst to join him in the study. When Louisa and Hurst appeared, Charles told them all that he had learned, beginning with Elizabeth's riding accident up through his interview with Caroline and Darcy's comments to her.

"Good for you, Charles," Hurst said encouragingly. "I think that you made the right decision. Caroline has manipulated you and Louisa since I have known her. Hopefully, this will be the best for all of us. Perhaps Caroline will take your words to heart and find her own life. Louisa, I believe I would like to stay here for the holidays, what think you?" he asked his wife.

"I have seen Caroline through different eyes since we arrived here. I agree with my husband, Charles, you did the correct thing regarding Caroline. As for your question, Gilbert, I would very much like to remain for the holidays," she replied with a smile. "I would be happy to serve as your hostess if you wish Charles."

"I would appreciate that very much. Hopefully, the time between now and the holidays will be more peaceful than the last few weeks have been." Bingley gave a brief chuckle then sobered. "By the way," he said quietly, "I plan to ask Miss

Bennet for a courtship. I know Caroline's feelings on the matter, but what are your feelings, Louisa?"

"I think she is a sweet young lady and just the type who would suit you perfectly," said his sister fondly.

Upstairs in his sitting room, Darcy sat with Georgiana and Richard. "Georgie, I was wondering if you would do something for me. Shortly after my arrival in Meryton, I bumped into Miss Elizabeth at the bookshop. She found a book that she wished to purchase but did not have the funds as she had loaned some to her youngest sister. After she had left, I purchased the book for her. I wanted to make it a thank you gift for the service she did our family five years ago. You know we would have found a way to thank her if we had met her at the time. I know this may not seem like much as compared to your life, but I feel certain it is something she will cherish. Since I cannot give it to her directly, would you present it as being from both of us?"

With a smile at the earnest look on his face, she took the book from her brother. "I will be happy to give it to her, and I am sure she will love it. We have spoken about poetry, and she mentioned hoping to obtain this book."

At that moment, a rap came on the sitting room door. Upon Darcy's call to enter, Bingley asked if they would accompany him to Miss Elizabeth's room. "I thought now that my meetings were done, I might convince Miss Bennet to take a walk with me in the garden."

With the addition of Mrs. Annesley, the group knocked upon Elizabeth's door. "How are you feeling this morning, Miss Elizabeth?" Bingley asked cheerfully.

"I am physically well, but getting tired of sitting in bed. Did Mr. Jones say when he would return?" Elizabeth asked hopefully.

Chuckles were heard from everyone at Elizabeth's comments. "Your sister warned us that you would be restless today," Darcy said with a smile.

"I am afraid I am just not happy when I cannot be active." Her rueful expression brought another chuckle from the others present.

"Well, Miss Elizabeth, perhaps a change of company will improve your spirits. I was hoping to persuade your sister to take a walk in the gardens with me, but the others have offered to keep you entertained during her absence. Would that be acceptable?"

"I am sorry to be such a difficult houseguest, Mr. Bingley," she responded penitently, but the words were belied by the gleam in her eyes.

"I doubt you could ever be difficult, Miss Elizabeth," Bingley said with a wide smile. This comment brought a laugh from Miss Bennet, and soon everyone else had joined in, including Elizabeth.

"You and Jane have a pleasant walk, Mr. Bingley. I know you are leaving me in good hands." Elizabeth's happy smile and glance towards Darcy clearly showed her feelings. Bingley extended his arm for Miss Bennet and led her from the room.

Georgiana moved to sit beside Elizabeth on the bed while the gentlemen found chairs to pull closer. Mrs. Annesley took a chair in the corner and concentrated on her needlework.

"Miss Elizabeth," Georgiana began, "my brother and I have a small gift for you. I am sorry that it is five years late in coming," she continued holding out the book to Elizabeth.

"What do you mean it is five years late in coming?" Elizabeth's expression was confused.

"Miss Elizabeth, we never had an opportunity before to properly thank you for helping Georgiana. Had we known who you were at the time we would most certainly have done so, but I hope you will allow us to thank you now." Darcy's earnest expression warmed Elizabeth's heart.

"Mr. Darcy, you do not need to thank me. I was happy to help Miss Darcy. I hope I would have helped anyone in need."

"Miss Elizabeth, you returned to me a beloved sister—"

"and cousin," inserted the Colonel.

"No gift could every properly compensate for that, but please accept this small token. Your efforts will never be forgotten." The warm, loving look he bestowed on Elizabeth brought a bright blushed to her cheeks as she shyly accepted the book.

Unwrapping the package, she gasped glancing at the title. "Oh, how wonderful! Thank you very much, Miss Darcy, Mr. Darcy. This is the very book I had been wanting." Elizabeth looked at Mr. Darcy as she said this, her eyes warm and teary, a soft smile on her face.

"Miss Elizabeth, I know we have not been acquainted very long, but would it be appropriate for me to call you Elizabeth? I would like very much for you to call me Georgiana or Georgie," the girl said shyly.

"Friendships are not determined by a length of time, but by a feeling of connection. I would be delighted for you to use my Christian name, or you can call me Lizzy as my family does, Georgiana," Elizabeth replied with a wide smile.

The four friends visited for quite some time, and laughter frequently filled the room. The conversation covered a wide variety of topics, and there were no awkward silences. Mrs. Annesley often smiled at the merriment that came from the group. She was deeply impressed by Miss Elizabeth. As the laughter died following one of Colonel Fitzwilliam's stories, the door opened to admit Jane and Bingley. Both had bright eyes, flushed faces, and beaming smiles. Suspicious of what the looks might mean, Elizabeth asked, "Jane, do you have something to tell me?"

Jane and Bingley shared a look, and Bingley answered the question. "Yes, Miss Elizabeth, we do have an announcement. Your sister has given me permission to court her. I will accompany you home tomorrow to ask for your father's blessing." There were congratulations all around. Jane moved to the bed to receive an embrace from her sister while Bingley shook hands and received pats on the back from the gentlemen.

Mr. Jones arrived not long after the announcement of the courtship. He checked Elizabeth thoroughly and pronounced her fit to return home on the following day. He also gave her permission to join the company for dinner if she returned straight back to her room afterward.

As they sat down to dinner that evening, Georgiana realized that Mrs. Hurst was seated at the foot of the table where Miss Bingley usually sat. "Mr. Bingley, is Miss Bingley, unwell? It has been such a busy day I have not seen her. Will she be joining us?"

After a brief pause during which Mr. Bingley, Darcy, and the Hursts exchanged tense glances, Bingley replied calmly, "Miss Darcy, Caroline decided that she wished to return to town. I believe she is to stay with a friend for the holidays."

"Oh," said Georgiana, unaware of the exchange. Richard seemed unsurprised, and Jane and Elizabeth shared a confused glance, each giving a small shrug. The remainder of the meal was a real celebration. The food was excellent, the conversation was merry, and the affection between Jane and Charles unmistakable.

After dinner, Elizabeth spoke in a quiet aside to Georgiana. "I think we should perform one of our songs tonight. Even without much practice we were performing several of them very well. It would be a perfect end to the celebration."

"Oh, Lizzy, I do not know. There are so many people," Georgiana said nervously.

"Yes, but you know everyone well, and it has been such a pleasant evening. You were participating in the conversation—why does playing make you nervous? I think this is the ideal setting for your first public performance."

"Yes, but Mr. Jones said you should return to bed immediately after dinner."

"I promise to leave without comment as soon as we finish our song," Elizabeth said, a pleading look upon her face.

"Oh, very well," Georgiana conceded.

Elizabeth gripped her hand and turned to the company. "If you would all follow us, Georgiana and I have a song we would like to perform. It will be Miss Darcy's debut public performance." Elizabeth and Georgiana led the way down the hall to the music room. Georgiana took her place at the keyboard, with Elizabeth in front of the pianoforte. Georgiana's hands gently touched the keys, and Elizabeth's voice came in a short time later in a beautiful love song.

Their audience sat spellbound. At the conclusion of the piece, there was a momentary silence before the company burst into enthusiastic applause.

Darcy stood and came over to the piano, pulling Georgiana up into a hug. "Little One, you played beautifully. It was a poised and polished performance. You will astound the ton with your talent," said her brother proudly.

He turned to Elizabeth, and taking her hand, raised it to his lips. He lowered it but retained possession of her hand as he gazed into her eyes. "Miss Elizabeth, I have truly never heard anything more beautiful," he leaned a little closer and lowered his voice, "unless it is your laugh," he said warmly. "You have the voice of an angel. I can only be glad that you escaped the heavenly choir to reside here with me . . . us," he corrected quickly. Elizabeth blushed warmly at his slip of the tongue. Their eyes remained locked until Richard approached to offer his congratulations.

True to her word Elizabeth excused herself after the congratulations were over and retired for the night. Jane rose to accompany her, but Georgiana spoke up, "Please do not trouble yourself, Miss Bennet. I would like to go up with Lizzy and visit with her for a while."

"That is very kind of you, Miss Darcy, thank you. Goodnight, Miss Darcy. Goodnight, Lizzy."

The girls left the room arm-in-arm and ascended the stairs. Elizabeth suggested they both prepare to retire and then Georgiana return for a visit. For a girl with no sisters, this sounded like fun to Georgiana, so she hurried through her preparations and returned to Elizabeth's room quickly. The girls sat up against the headboard surrounded by pillows.

"Do sisters do things like this, Lizzy?" Georgiana asked.

"Jane and I do. We spend time each night talking about our day before we go to sleep. When we were little, we would talk about our hopes and dreams. As we got older, we talked about husbands and marriage as most young ladies do," Elizabeth said with a smile.

"What do you want in a husband?" Georgiana asked with a sly smile.

"Most importantly I want a man whom I can love and respect and one who will love and respect me in return."

"That sounds wonderful. William always tells me stories of how much our parents loved one another. I love to listen to those stories. You see, I hardly knew my mother as she died when I was very young. My father has been gone for five years, and I still miss him every day. William is a wonderful brother, but sometimes it gets very lonely."

Elizabeth reached over and put her hand on Georgiana's. "I am sorry for your many losses, but you must have friends your own age."

"There are a few in Derbyshire that I have had all my life. At school, other than one or two girls, most just wanted to be my friend so they could meet William. It has been harder since then to trust people who offered friendship. I always thought Miss Bingley liked me—even though I was not comfortable with her. However, I overheard her the other day saying that I was dull and boring, but she wanted William to think she was a good friend and example for me. She also said she would convince William to send me to boarding school after they married."

"Is your brother going to marry Miss Bingley?" Elizabeth asked in a shaken voice.

"According to him, there is absolutely nothing that could make him marry Miss Bingley. He has never said this to me, but I do not think William is anxious to get married. He only goes to balls or dinners held by my aunt or very close friends. Everyone always seems to want something from William. When we are out together, people are always stopping him. Most want to discuss business or introduce their daughters to him. He barely speaks at these times and looks over the heads of the young ladies who are always batting their eyes at him and have the same tittering laughs. He almost cringes when they laugh."

With a blush Elizabeth recalled what he had said of her laugh, 'I heard a delightful laugh and simply had to find its source . . . I have a confession to make, I knew to whom the charming laugh belonged . . . I first heard it at the theater in London five years ago, and I have never forgotten it . . . Your musical laugh has often been in my thoughts; I have never heard another so warm and sweet.'

Her head slightly tilted, Georgiana watched the emotions crossing Elizabeth's face. "What are you thinking about Lizzy? You look very happy."

Elizabeth started from her musings, a blush upon her cheeks. "I was just thinking about laughter."

Changing the direction of the conversation Elizabeth asked, "What kind of outings do you and your brother enjoy?"

"We often walk in one of the many parks, and he likes concerts, plays, and the opera. He will take me shopping, so long as we also stop in his favorite bookstore. William will take me out for tea or a visit to the sweet shop. But he also has a lot of business meetings that he must deal with, and, of course, there is Pemberley for which he must care. He also has social obligations, though he doesn't really like those. He would rather be at home with family or friends. Sometimes I think he would be happy never to leave Pemberley."

"What is your estate like?"

"I think it is the most beautiful place in the world. The house is large and very lovely. But inside it is warm and cozy. There are formal gardens, and places where nature has designed the landscape. There are several fountains, two lakes, several streams, and the river goes through one corner of the estate. There are forests, meadows, and lots of farmland. In the distance, you can see the peaks."

"It does sound wonderful. I cannot even imagine such a place as it is so different from Hertfordshire."

"Perhaps you could visit me at Pemberley during the summer," suggested Georgiana excitedly.

"That is a long way off; we will have to see."

"Lizzy, would it be alright if I write to you when we return to town?"

"I would be happy to correspond with you. Conversation with someone outside of my family would be a delightful change," Elizabeth said with a laugh.

At that moment, there was a knock at the door, and Mr. Darcy and the Colonel appeared. "I had looked for Georgie in her room to say good night, but she was not there. I thought she might still be visiting with you, and it appears I was correct," Darcy said with a smile.

Georgiana looked at the clock and realized the late hour. "I am so sorry to have kept you up, Lizzy. Please forgive me."

"Do not be silly," Elizabeth said with a laugh. "I have enjoyed our conversation very much. Sleep well, Georgiana, I will see you in the morning."

Georgiana and the Colonel moved to the door with another wish for a good night. Darcy stood at the foot of the bed gazing at Elizabeth. "Thank you for your kindness to my sister, Miss Elizabeth. She doesn't have many friends her own age. Your friendship has had such a positive influence on her. I knew you would be good for her. I have not seen her this happy in a very long while."

"Thank you, Mr. Darcy, for introducing me to your sister. She is a delightful girl, and I enjoy the time we spend together. I have agreed to correspond with her when she returns to town if that is acceptable to you?"

"I think that a splendid idea," he said with a warm smile. "Well, goodnight, Miss Elizabeth, sweet dreams." With a last, lingering look at her he moved to the door where the others waited.

"Oh, by the way, thank you for my gift, Mr. Darcy. I do appreciate your kindness."

"It was my pleasure, Miss Elizabeth."

Elizabeth settled down into her bed, her thoughts on Darcy. It was the first night that he was in her dreams.

CHAPTER 12

ALL OF THE houseguests were gathered around the breakfast table the next morning to bid farewell to the Bennet Sisters and Colonel Fitzwilliam. The Colonel was to depart after luncheon, but the young ladies were to leave mid-morning for the short drive to Longbourn. Bingley was accompanying them so that he might ask Mr. Bennet's permission to formally court Jane. Jane mentioned that their cousin, heir to the estate, was to arrive this afternoon. She told them he was the parson at Hunsford, attached to the estate of Rosings Park in Kent.

At this news, Darcy, Georgiana, and Richard shared a startled look. For Darcy and Richard, it was annoyance and concern. Georgiana, however, looked terrified. Elizabeth noticed the look and wondered at its meaning. Suddenly, Darcy turned to Elizabeth and spoke softly, "Miss Elizabeth while I would dearly like to see you home myself, I feel it might be best to stay away from your guest." Elizabeth gazed at him questioningly. "You see my aunt is Lady Catherine de Bourgh. She is the mistress of Rosings Park. My aunt likes to believe that she can order the lives of all her younger family members. She can make things very unpleasant when she does not get her way. She mistakenly believes that I will marry her daughter, just because she wishes me to do so. My cousin, Anne, and I have told her many times that we do not wish to marry and will not do so. However, this has not stopped her from implying there is an understanding between Anne and me. I wanted you to know the truth, in case my aunt has discussed her wishes with her parson."

"I am sorry to know that my cousin's presence will of necessity curtail our time together. I will miss my new friends," Elizabeth replied sadly gazing directly into Darcy's eyes.

"I do not wish to curtail our time together in any way," he stated emphatically. "Perhaps it can be arranged that you and Miss Bennet visit Netherfield regularly."

They were interrupted by a question from Richard. "Darcy have you met this new parson of Aunt Catherine's?"

"Not yet. I assumed we would meet him during our annual visit at Easter."

"Since I must return to my unit today, I will look forward to your first correspondence detailing your meeting," Richard laughed.

Darcy shook his head with a groan. "Your sense of humor, Richard, is certainly unusual."

Georgiana accompanied Elizabeth upstairs to gather her things before their departure. As she took a last look around, she casually asked, "Georgiana, why are you afraid of your Aunt Catherine?" Georgiana stared at Elizabeth with a dumbfounded expression on her face. She started to stutter out a reply when she was interrupted. "Friends share and keep each other's secrets, Georgie."

"Oh, Lizzy, Aunt Catherine terrifies me. She is overwhelming. She always sits in the largest chair in any room and holds court, like she is a queen. She talks down to everyone. Her opinion is the only one she will allow. And she does not converse—she lectures and only wants you to speak to agree with her. She thinks she is an expert on everything and expects everyone to obey her orders. She keeps telling me that she should have raised me instead of William; that my mother would have wanted it that way. Aunt Catherine is always telling me that I do not practice enough, or to stand up straight, or to speak up. Being around her makes me miserable. My cousin, Anne, is nice, but her health is not the best. She does not say much when around my Aunt, but she is quite funny when we are alone."

"Georgie, listen to me. You are a wonderful young lady, intelligent, poised, and talented. Do not listen to your Aunt because nothing she says about you is true. Remember what you learned from overhearing Miss Bingley. You confidently defended your beliefs, and you stood up to her. You do not argue with what she says—just remember that none of it is true. In some ways, she sounds a bit like my youngest sister Lydia. When she is unhappy, she says mean things about the rest of us—most of which are not true—to make herself feel better. Perhaps your aunt is unhappy and doing the same thing," Elizabeth suggested.

"Can we still go to the church and practice our music in the mornings? I know we performed the other night, but I enjoy having someone with whom to share my music."

"I would love to do that. Shall we start again on Monday?"

"I will be there at ten o'clock, just like before," Georgiana said with a smile.

A knock at the door brought Jane. "Are you ready to go, Lizzy?"

"Well, if we must," Elizabeth replied with a laugh. Jane just shook her head and led the way out into the hall.

The others were waiting in the foyer to say goodbye.

"Miss Bennet, Miss Elizabeth, I have enjoyed getting to know you better. I hope that we will see each other again soon."

"Thank you, Mrs. Hurst," said Jane, "I look forward to seeing you, as well."

"Thank you for your hospitality, Mrs. Hurst. Good Day, Mr. Hurst." Elizabeth said with a curtsey.

The Colonel bowed to each of the ladies. "It has been a delight to make your acquaintance. I do hope to have the pleasure of seeing you again."

Bingley extended his arm to Jane and proceeded out to the waiting carriage.

Darcy extended his arm to Elizabeth and the other to Georgiana, and led them out behind Bingley and Jane.

Bingley and Jane stood aside as Darcy handed Elizabeth up into the carriage. He bent to kiss her hand and gave it a squeeze before he let go. Darcy and Georgiana moved back up the stairs as Bingley handed Jane in the carriage and then entered himself. Darcy and Georgiana waved from the stairs until the carriage turned out of the drive.

They returned to the house and entered the sitting room to see the Colonel sprawled on a sofa. He said the Hursts had gone for a walk in the garden. Darcy and Georgiana sat on the opposite sofa. Richard eyed Darcy and asked seriously, "What are you going to do if Aunt Catherine gets wind of your visit here?"

"Nothing she can do will change my plans. I refuse to worry about what could happen. Instead, I plan to enjoy this time to the fullest."

"Should I mention to my parents your intentions, or do you prefer to do it?"

"Perhaps I should write to them today and lay out my intentions. As you have recently been here, I am sure they will ask for your impressions. I assume I can count on you for a good report."

"I am wounded that you would think otherwise," Richard declared his hand over his heart. Darcy and Richard chuckled and smiled at each other.

Georgiana had been following the conversation with a puzzled look on her face; finally the meaning dawned on her, and she looked at her brother in delight. "William, do you have something you need to tell me?" she asked.

"Georgiana, I do have hopes and plans but have not had an opportunity to act upon them," he said with a smile.

"Do these plans include Miss Elizabeth?" The hopeful look on her face was unmistakable.

"They do," he replied seriously though his face was alight with happiness. A squeal came from Georgiana as she launched herself into her brother's arms. "I take it you approve?"

"I do most heartily approve! When will you ask? I do not know how I will contain my joy if I have to wait for very long."

"I have trusted you with my secret. Was I wrong to do so?" Darcy asked her solemnly.

"No brother, you weren't wrong. I will keep your secret, but you must let me know as soon as I can talk to Lizzy about it."

"All right, Little One. You will be the second to know, right after Elizabeth," he said with a smile.

"Elizabeth will make a wonderful sister. She is so kind. When we went upstairs, she asked me why I am afraid of Aunt Catherine." Georgiana repeated her conversation with Elizabeth. Darcy's heart swelled with love for the care and kindness Elizabeth had offered for his beloved sister. She grew dearer to him with every passing day.

"I agree with everything Miss Elizabeth said, Georgie. She is a very intelligent and compassionate young woman," Richard said. Having noticed the emotion on Darcy's face, he knew it would be difficult for him to speak at present.

The carriage ride from Netherfield to Longbourn passed quickly and pleasantly. Jane could hardly contain her excitement. As the carriage pulled up to the door, her mother came out with her handkerchief fluttering. "Oh, Jane dear, you are back. Mr. Bingley, how wonderful to see you again. Lizzy." She took Jane's arm and led the way into the house. *I am the one who was injured and in bed for a day and half, but she does not even ask how I am doing.* Elizabeth knew she should not be surprised but being ignored still hurt. *Just as Mary must feel,* she reminded herself and promised to devote more time to her next younger sister.

The others had settled in the parlor by the time Elizabeth entered the house. She saw her father coming from his library with his arms open to her and stepped into his embrace as he asked, "How are you doing, my Lizzy? Are you recovered from your accident?"

"I am fine now, Papa. Just this small cut," Elizabeth indicated the bandage on her head, "and a few bruises that make sitting uncomfortable," she said with a small laugh.

Mr. Bennet stepped into the parlor to welcome Jane home. "Ah, Mr. Bingley, nice to see you again."

"Good morning, Mr. Bennet. I was wondering if I might have a moment of your time."

"Certainly, young man. Please join me in my library." Mr. Bennet cast a teasing glance at his wife as he departed.

The door to the library had barely closed behind the gentlemen before Mrs. Bennet screeched. "Oh, Jane, I knew he would be attracted to your beauty. You have saved our family. And, Lizzy, how wonderful that you had an accident at Netherfield so that Jane could spend more time with Mr. Bingley."

"Mama!" cried Jane and Mary together. "Mama, Lizzy was thrown from a horse! She could have been seriously injured or worse," said Jane. "How can you be so inconsiderate to her?"

Ignoring Jane's remarks, Mrs. Bennet said, "Oh, Jane, do not keep me in suspense. What is Mr. Bingley discussing with your father?"

Jane smiled apologetically at Elizabeth, who just shook her head. "Mr. Bingley is asking Papa for permission to court me."

"Oh, Jane, only a courtship." Her daughters were startled by the sad, stricken look on her face. "You must do all you can to get him to propose. We are not saved if you are not married. And that horrible Mr. Collins is arriving today. I know he is just here to look over his inheritance. I am sure he will throw us out into the hedgerows as soon as your father is gone." She began fluttering her handkerchief and complaining of her nerves.

In the study, Mr. Bennet contained his smile as he looked at the nervous young man across the desk from him. "Was there something you wanted to discuss with me, Mr. Bingley?"

"Yes, Mr. Bennet. I would like to ask your permission to court Miss Bennet. I assure you my intentions are honorable, and I hope to someday call her my wife!" Bingley exclaimed in a rush.

"Have you spoken to Jane about this?"

"Yes, I have, sir. She has accepted my request for courtship."

"Well then, you have my permission as well. Mr. Bingley, Jane is a special young lady. I expect that you will treat her as such."

"You are correct, sir, she is special. I will treat her like the angel she is."

"Well, then, shall we share the news with the rest of the family?" Mr. Bennet asked as he opened the library door for the young man to precede him.

Mrs. Bennet was loud and effusive in her congratulations and apologies. "Oh, Mr. Bingley, I am sorry that I cannot invite you to stay for luncheon, but we are expecting a visitor this afternoon. Please say you will forgive me, and that you will come another day."

"There is no need to apologize, Mrs. Bennet. I was aware of your guest from Ja . . . uh, Miss Bennet and would be happy to accept your invitation for another day. I will leave to allow you to prepare for your visitor. Good day to you all."

"Jane, dear, will you please accompany Mr. Bingley to the door?"

"Yes, mama." Bingley offered her his arm, and they exited the house. "Might, I sit with you in church tomorrow, Miss Bennet?"

"I would enjoy that, Mr. Bingley," Jane replied with a shy smile. Bingley kissed her hand and entered the carriage. Jane waved to him as he drove away.

Jane and Elizabeth went upstairs to unpack and freshen up before their cousin arrived. "Jane, I am so pleased for you. How are you feeling now that it is an official courtship?"

"Oh, Lizzy, I am so happy. I do not know how I could have been so fortunate. Mr. Bingley is wonderful. He asked to sit with me in church tomorrow."

"I truly am happy for you. You are the sweetest person I know, and you deserve all this happiness and more." Wistfully her thoughts drifted to Mr. Darcy. "Perhaps someday I will be as fortunate."

Had it been only thirty minutes since Mr. Collins' arrival? It felt so much longer. Never in her life had Elizabeth met such a ridiculous little man. His person was not particularly attractive, and it was quite obvious that personal hygiene was not of concern to him. He had greasy hair and wore strong cologne, mixed was something even less pleasant smelling. Perhaps that could be overlooked, but for the fact that his every utterance was both sycophantic and self-important. He constantly spoke of his patroness and her condescension. Every word confirmed in Elizabeth's mind the things Georgiana had said about her aunt. Dinner seemed unbearably long, and watching Mr. Collins eat was enough to cause Elizabeth and Jane to lose their appetites. Mary listened to all he said with a respectful air while Kitty and Lydia barely concealed their laughter behind their hands. Elizabeth asked her father to be excused as she had a headache, so she was spared Mr. Collins' soliloquy after dinner. Much like his patroness, Mr. Collins did not require any input from others in his conversation.

It had taken just thirty minutes of Mr. Collins' company after dinner before Mr. Bennet escaped to his library. Upon his departure from the room, Mr. Collins approached Mrs. Bennet. "Madam, my patroness, Lady Catherine de Bourgh, has instructed me to marry so that I might set the proper example for my parishioners. With her suggestion in mind, I felt the best place to look for a wife was among my fair cousins. All of your daughters are quite lovely, but it would, of course, be proper to honor the oldest with my attention. As she is the most lovely, it would be my pleasure to ask for her hand in marriage."

"I am sorry, Mr. Collins, but Jane is already being courted. None of the others are yet spoken for, so might I suggest the next eldest, Elizabeth? She is not as lovely as Jane, but she is quite accomplished. She plays and sings and is very well read."

He looked around the room again, "And which one is Miss Elizabeth?" he asked.

Mrs. Bennet looked at all of her daughters and noticed that Elizabeth was not present. "Jane, where is Lizzy?" her mother asked, annoyed.

"She retired immediately after dinner, Mama, due to a headache."

"I am sorry, Mr. Collins, that she is not here. She retired with a headache, but I am sure she will be fine in the morning." *I will make sure she is fine,* her mother thought with determination as she smiled at Mr. Collins.

The next morning, Elizabeth was up early and out of the house for a walk. She had been home for only a few hours and had been insulted and overlooked by her mother on more than one occasion. Without having realized where her feet were taking her, Elizabeth arrived at the fence between Longbourn and Netherfield. She leaned on the fence and let her memories drift to the first morning she had encountered Darcy here. Her memory seemed very realistic, as she thought she heard hoof beats. She was still lost in her thoughts when she heard a deep voice,

"I am very pleased to see you this morning, Miss Elizabeth," said Darcy with a warm smile and a look in his eyes that made Elizabeth tingle from head to toe.

"Good morning, Mr. Darcy." Her eyes were misty as she returned his smile.

"I hope you are fully recovered."

"I was until I returned home, where my headache recurred." Darcy looked at her with concern. "However, the cause was not my fall, but our visitor. Mr. Collins defies description and must be experienced to be understood yet it is an experience I would not wish on anyone. He spoke endlessly of his patroness, and his words confirmed everything that Georgiana told me about your aunt."

"Yes, like your cousin, my aunt must be experienced," Darcy said his expression unreadable. "I understand that Bingley will be sitting with your family this morning. Should that make your pew too crowded, I am sure Georgiana would be happy if you joined us."

Elizabeth liked the way that he always suggested she do it for Georgiana, but let her know that he would also be pleased. "I thank you for the offer, especially as we must accommodate Mr. Collins, as well. I must be getting back so that I can prepare for church. Goodbye, Mr. Darcy."

"Until later, Miss Elizabeth." Again Darcy watched until she was out of sight then turned in the direction of Netherfield.

As they were descending the stairs for breakfast, Jane glanced at Elizabeth. "You seem happy this morning, Lizzy. I hope it is because you are feeling better."

"Yes, thank you, Jane, I do feel better. I had a wonderful walk this morning. It was very refreshing." Jane noted the dreamy look on her face but said nothing.

Mr. Collins was seated next to Elizabeth at breakfast. He was very attentive and tried to engage her in conversation, giving her another unfortunate display of his manners at the table. He stayed close by her side, even brushing against her inappropriately, as they were waiting to enter the carriage.

During the ride to church, her mother kept praising her appearance and accomplishments to Mr. Collins. "Be sure you sit by Mr. Collins, Lizzy, so he can hear you sing."

Elizabeth cast a horrified glance at her mother and looked pleadingly at her father. He just rolled his eyes and smiled at her in return. She shook her head sadly. When they arrived at the church, Elizabeth saw Mr. Bingley, Georgiana and Mr. Darcy standing near the entrance to the church. She and Jane made their way to their friends and exchanged greetings. Mr. Bingley offered his arm to Jane, and they entered the church behind her family.

As Mr. Collins lingered as though waiting for her, Elizabeth linked her arm with Georgiana's. "I am so glad that you asked me to sit with you this morning." Georgiana looked confused, but Darcy smiled warmly. He took his sister's other arm and led the ladies into the church to the pew where Mr. and Mrs. Hurst were already seated. Darcy dropped Georgiana's arm so that she could enter the pew; Elizabeth followed, and Darcy entered last taking the seat next to Elizabeth. He glanced at Elizabeth with a happy smile. Mr. Collins entered the Bennet's pew and took the seat on the aisle. He frequently looked toward Elizabeth, an unhappy expression on his face.

Darcy was enjoying the experience of sitting with Elizabeth in church. He had the pleasure of hearing her sing; he could smell the sweet fragrance of her perfume, and occasionally their arms would brush. He was also aware of the discontented, almost angry, glances being cast in their direction by the funny little man in the Bennet's pew. He wondered if that was his aunt's parson.

As the service came to an end, Elizabeth remained seated with the Darcys discussing the sermon. Suddenly Mr. Collins appeared in the aisle. "Come, Cousin Elizabeth, let me escort you to the carriage."

"Please go on, Mr. Collins. I am still speaking to my friends and will be with the family shortly."

Elizabeth turned back to her interrupted conversation. Mr. Collins glared at her angrily and marched away. Darcy heard her quiet sigh of relief as he left. *Did this silly little man think he had a claim on Elizabeth,* he wondered? He focused his attention back on the conversation as he heard the ladies confirming their plans to practice their music in the morning.

"Might I join you after your practice and treat you to some sweets?" he asked them.

"That would be delightful, brother. Thank you."

"Well then, what time should I meet you at the church?"

She looked at Elizabeth and asked, "Do you think we will be tired of practicing by half past eleven?" Elizabeth nodded her agreement.

"Then, ladies, we have an engagement for the morning. I shall be greatly anticipating our outing." The plans confirmed the party moved down the aisle and out of the church. Elizabeth's family was waiting in their carriage, so Darcy handed her in, and they departed.

CHAPTER 13

It had been a week of ups and downs Elizabeth thought as she laid in her bed watching dawn light the window. All of the ups had occurred when she was with the Darcys. She and Georgiana had practiced every day that week. On Monday, Mr. Darcy had come to escort them for the promised sweets. They had taken seats at one of the small tables in the shop and enjoyed a cup of tea and conversation while consuming their choices. Georgiana had selected a lemon filled tart topped with meringue. Mr. Darcy's choice was a slice of sponge cake layered with custard and topped with sliced strawberries. Elizabeth had her favorite chocolate tart covered with freshly whipped cream. The threesome was having so much pleasure in each other's company that they did not notice the strange looks and whispers directed toward them. Apparently Wickham's stories had made their way throughout the village, but it seemed that those involved were unaware of what was being said.

They met at the fence most mornings, but Darcy was very conscious of propriety. When he was alone, he did not stay long, and if Georgiana were with him, they would dismount and head for the stream Elizabeth had shown him the first time they met. They would talk about anything that came to mind, and laughter was often heard coming from the copse. During one of their talks, they planned an outing to Oakham Mount. Elizabeth suggested Friday, but Mr. Darcy said the men had been invited to a hunt at Mr. Goulding's estate. Consequently, the outing was set for Saturday, and they planned to take a picnic lunch with them. Bingley and Jane were to go as well, and Elizabeth intended to invite Mary to join them. Georgiana and Mary both had a love of music to discuss and had spoken together whenever they encountered one another at a social event. Hopefully, with time, Georgiana's manners would help to soften Mary's.

On another day, Darcy had quietly entered as the girls practiced. He had taken a seat in the back of the church and listened to the beautiful music. The thought occurred to him that he could spend many evenings like this once he and Elizabeth were married. When he could tell the ladies had completed their practice for the day, he came forward to share how much he had enjoyed their performances and how he hoped he would have that pleasure often repeated. Elizabeth thanked him for the compliment and indicated she was looking forward to spending the remainder of the day at Netherfield with Georgiana.

All of the downs had occurred when Mr. Collins was near. He seemed determined to attract her attention and interest. Elizabeth was only free of his attentions when she was away from home, and she found as many excuses to be gone from home as she could. He made frequent comments about the importance of setting a proper example for his parishioners in all things including marriage. He said that any man could be happy with a beautiful, well-mannered, and obedient wife. When he went on in this way, Elizabeth and Jane would just roll their eyes and bend their heads over their embroidery to hide their amusement.

As Mrs. Bennet would praise Elizabeth when Mr. Collins spoke of marriage, she realized her mother wished for her to be Mr. Collins's wife. She could not imagine a more terrible fate and was determined that it would not be hers.

One morning at breakfast, Mr. Collins was even more attentive than usual, but Elizabeth refused to acknowledge him, maintaining a conversation with Jane throughout the meal. As soon as breakfast was over, Elizabeth rushed from the room to prepare for her trip to Netherfield. She hoped to be able to avoid Mr. Collins altogether until it was time to depart. She glanced from her bedroom window and noted the Darcy carriage approaching the house, so she gathered her belongings and headed down the stairs. Unfortunately, Mr. Collins was waiting for her in the foyer.

"Cousin Elizabeth, if I could have a moment of your time this morning, I have something I most particularly wish to ask you."

"I am sorry, Mr. Collins, but I have not time at the moment as I am leaving for an appointment."

Mrs. Bennet, who had been lurking nearby, said, "Lizzy you must give Mr. Collins your attention immediately, I insist upon it."

"I am sorry to be disobliging, mama, but it would be rude to keep the carriage driver waiting." And so saying, she ran out the front door and allowed Gregson to quickly assist her into the carriage.

An angry Mr. Collins turned to glare at Mrs. Bennet. "Madam, I believe you have misled me regarding Cousin Elizabeth's qualities. She does not show me the proper respect. That being the case, how could she ever be a proper wife?"

"Oh, I am sure she would make you a very good wife, Mr. Collins," Mrs. Bennet said. "Perhaps she does not realize the reason for your attentions as she has had no previous suitors. I will speak to her upon her return and prepare her. I am sure you will find her much more agreeable once she understands your intentions."

"If she does not show me the respect I deserve, I will have to rescind my offer, Mrs. Bennet," he declared before stalking off.

As she entered the carriage, Elizabeth sighed in relief at having escaped Mr. Collins. She feared he would make her an offer, and her only answer could be an emphatic "No!" She knew if she refused him her mother would be furious with her and her future days would be very unpleasant.

There were horses standing at the door as the carriage arrived, and Darcy, Georgiana and the other gentlemen of Netherfield were awaiting her arrival on the steps. Darcy helped Elizabeth down from the carriage and escorted her to Georgiana.

"Ladies, I pray you enjoy your morning," Darcy said as he turned to mount his horse. "We should return from the hunt in time for a late luncheon." With a wave, the gentlemen were off down the drive.

"I am so glad that you could come today, Elizabeth. There was something I particularly wanted to discuss with you."

The nervous look on Georgiana's face made Elizabeth wonder. "You know that you can talk to me about anything, Georgie. What is it that concerns you?"

Georgiana linked her arm through Elizabeth's as she recounted to her what she had learned upon her arrival in Meryton about estates and those who make them run. "I was disappointed with myself that I had never thought about it previously. I was hoping you could tell me what you do for the tenants of your estate. I want to do something for the tenants and staff at Pemberley in the future, but I do not know where to start."

Elizabeth was relieved that it was something so easy to address. After the servants had taken her outerwear, she and Georgiana headed to the library, where they spent several hours discussing ways to recognize the tenants and staff of Pemberley and Darcy House.

Wickham was very frustrated. He had been observing the meetings between Darcy and Miss Elizabeth each day. She was an attractive young woman with a ripe figure. He realized from observing their interactions that Darcy had feelings for the woman. He hoped that he could find her alone one day and enjoy her company, leaving her in such a way that Darcy would want nothing more to do with her. Unfortunately, the opportunity had not yet appeared. He was pleased to learn of their upcoming activities, however, and set to work devising a plan to make use of them.

This morning would be his first opportunity. Darcy was joining a hunting party at the Goulding estate. From spending his evenings in a dark corner of the pub, Wickham learned where Mr. Goulding's property was located. He had scouted out the lay of the land and discovered that there was a cluster of trees that would offer good coverage and would let him see things in several directions. He planned to go very early the morning of the hunt and await his opportunity. In all the confusion and shooting that would take place, an accident could easily happen.

Wickham was getting cramped from being huddled in the same position for so long. As he pulled out his watch to check the time, he heard the sounds of the beaters and the dogs as they searched for the coveys. It was not long before he heard the flapping of wings, and the first shots were fired. Creeping from his hiding place, yet still within the concealment of the trees, Wickham looked over the hunters searching for his target. Darcy's tall height helped Wickham to locate him off to the left of the group of hunters. He was the closest of them to the trees where Wickham was hiding. Wickham smiled with glee as he raised his pistol to take aim. The squawking and flapping of birds taking flight was again heard, and he pulled the trigger aiming for Darcy's broad back. Unfortunately for Wickham, the winds had picked up since he had hidden himself in the trees. Not taking that into account, the bullet went wide to the left. It passed through the sleeve of Darcy's greatcoat and into the trunk of a nearby tree without his even being aware of how close he came to a serious injury or death. Wickham was furious to have wasted the shot and hurried to reload, but by the time he had finished, the hunters had moved out of range. He waited for some time, but the hunters never returned near enough to the copse of trees for him to get another chance.

Wickham headed back to his temporary home, thinking of other ways to achieve his goals. Darcy seemed to have the Devil's own luck, so he would have to plan his next attempt against his enemy more carefully, if he hoped to be successful. He wondered if he would have time to check out the area around Oakham Mount to see if it would allow an opportunity for an attack on Darcy or a chance to take Georgiana. Mumbling to himself he continued on his way.

Saturday morning dawned bright and clear. The sky was blue and dotted with puffy white clouds, and the temperature was surprisingly pleasant. The Darcys and Bingley were due to arrive at Longbourn by ten o'clock. Bingley was bringing the picnic basket prepared by the Netherfield cook. Jane, Elizabeth, and Mary readied for the day and were awaiting their visitors in the parlor. Fortunately for everyone, neither Mrs. Bennet nor Mr. Collins was nearby when the visitors knocked at the door. Mr. Bennet heard the knock and came out of his study to wish everyone well as they set off for their walk.

Since the path was wide, Elizabeth took Georgiana's arm and placed her on the path between herself and Mary. Mr. Darcy positioned himself on Elizabeth's other side while Bingley and Jane slowly followed the others. Elizabeth skillfully began a conversation on the music she and Georgiana had been practicing. She suggested that Mary and Georgiana might like to practice a duet to perform along with which Elizabeth could sing. As Mary and Georgiana began to discuss different pieces of music, Elizabeth gently dropped Georgiana's arm and walked a little faster, with Mr. Darcy keeping pace beside her.

"That was a masterful display of conversational skills, Miss Elizabeth!" Darcy said with a small chuckle.

"While talking with Georgiana and discovering how lonely she is, I realized that my sister, Mary, must feel the same. Jane and I have always been very close, and Kitty and Lydia have each other, as well. Poor Mary is left alone without a companion near her age. I promised myself that I would work harder at developing a closer relationship with Mary."

Darcy was worried as she said that Georgiana was lonely. "Is Georgiana unhappy, Miss Elizabeth? I did not realize that she is lonely. I assumed it was just her shyness that kept her from developing many relationships." He trailed off with a frown on his face.

Elizabeth placed her hand on his arm and gave him a reassuring smile. "There is no need to worry so, Mr. Darcy. She is not unhappy. She was enjoying our conversation that night you found her in my room and mentioned that it was lonely when you were away. She said she would love to have a sister to talk to like I had Jane."

Realizing that her remarks about wanting a sister could seem as though she was attempting to entrap him, she blushed and looked down as she began to quickly remove her hand from his arm. Darcy stopped her from doing so by placing his other hand over hers. As they were quite a bit ahead of the others, he ceased walking, forcing her to do so, as well. Still he did not release her hand,

and she finally looked up at him. "Thank you for reassuring me, Miss Elizabeth. I hope that I can soon give Georgiana a sister she will love."

Elizabeth flushed with pleasure but reminded herself not to get her hopes up. They came from two different worlds. Flustered and wishing to change the subject, Elizabeth looked quickly around hoping for inspiration on what to say. It was then that her eyes noticed a hole in his coat.

"Mr. Darcy, what have you done to your greatcoat?"

Still daydreaming of his future life with Elizabeth, he was surprised by her comment.

"I beg your pardon, Miss Elizabeth?"

"It appears that you have a hole in your coat," Elizabeth said as she reached out to place her finger in the hole on his shoulder. She was surprised when her finger found a matching hole and came out the other side. They both looked at her finger poking through a round hole in his coat.

"I have no idea how that came to be there as it certainly was not there when I went on the hunt yesterday."

At his comment, Elizabeth's face paled. "Mr. Darcy this looks suspiciously like a bullet hole."

Taking her elbow to steady her, he said, "I am sure I would have noticed if someone had taken a shot at me, Miss Elizabeth. I will have Chalmers take a look at it later." The others were approaching where they stood, so Darcy took Elizabeth's arm and wrapped it around his, and they again moved up the hill.

After more than an hour of walking, the group reached the summit of Oakham Mount. The visitors who had not yet seen the area from this location were delighted with what they saw. The friends strolled around the peak taking in the view in every direction before settling to enjoy their picnic. The gentlemen spread out the blankets as the ladies opened the basket and began removing the items. They arranged the food on the blankets, and all seated themselves around the edges, maintaining the pairings that had existed as they walked. The conversation was pleasant and the group so comfortable with one another that no topic was ignored, and everyone's opinions were sought and respected. After those present had eaten their fill, some again strolled while others remained seat in quiet conversation. More than another hour passed as they enjoyed the beauties of nature and good company.

As the food was being repacked for their departure, Bingley said, "I would like to give a ball at Netherfield!" There was a small pause as everyone took in what was said, and then all began speaking at once, excitedly expressing approval of the idea. "When do you return to London, Darcy? I would like to hold it before you must depart."

"I believe we should leave for London on December tenth."

"That gives us plenty of time. I will discuss it with Louisa after returning and let you know when we have set the date."

The group started off down the hill with many of them discussing the ball. This time, Darcy and Elizabeth trailed the others. Darcy cleared his throat several times as though he wished to speak. Elizabeth waited patiently, but as many minutes passed she finally asked, "Was there something important you needed to discuss with me, Mr. Darcy? You know that I always enjoy your conversation," she concluded with an encouraging smile.

"That is what makes this difficult to say, Miss Elizabeth, as it will not be a pleasant topic."

Elizabeth flushed and pulled her arm away from him. "Then spare yourself the difficulty Mr. Darcy," she returned coldly. She attempted to increase her pace and join the others, but Darcy reached out and took her arm in a firm grip, forcing her to stop.

Realizing by her actions that his words could have been misinterpreted, he put a finger under her chin and forced her to look at him. "Miss Elizabeth, the unpleasant topic has nothing to do with me but with Miss Bingley."

"Miss Bingley!"

"Yes, were you not surprised at her sudden departure from Netherfield?"

"It did seem a bit sudden, but she obviously disliked the neighborhood and her neighbors. Her desire to return to town was only surprising in its abruptness."

"She did not return to town to spend the holiday with friends. It was necessary for Mr. Bingley to send her away."

Elizabeth looked at him in confusion. "Why was it necessary to send her away?" she asked hesitantly.

Darcy wrapped her hand around his arm again and began to slowly continue their walk. "She attempted to harm you on several occasions, Miss Elizabeth."

"To what are you referring, Mr. Darcy? I know nothing of any attempts to harm me." Elizabeth's confusion and concern were evident on her face.

"The first occasion occurred when she invited you to tea. You cannot have missed her rude behavior. What you don't know is that she purposefully misinformed Bingley and me about your arrival time. I feel sure she planned to use the information she learned during tea to disparage you to us at a later time."

"I suspected as much," said Elizabeth sadly. "It is obvious that she wishes for your attention and would be upset at your paying attention to anyone else. But I do not understand how anyone could find fault with Jane. She is sweetest, kindest, most wonderful person I know!"

Darcy went on to recount the incident with the horse and the tea Miss Bingley brought to her room. He explained how he knew what Miss Bingley dosed the tea with and what its consequences might have been. Though Elizabeth tried to hide her reaction, Darcy noticed how her eyes widened at his words.

"Oh, that poor animal! Was the horse badly injured?"

Darcy could not help laughing aloud, but at Elizabeth's indignant look he explained. "I just told you that someone deliberately tried to harm you more than once, and you are worried about the horse," he said with another chuckle.

"I guess it is easier to be concerned for an innocent animal than to accept that Miss Bingley wished me harm," said Elizabeth sadly. With his free hand, Darcy gripped the hand on his arm giving Elizabeth an encouraging squeeze.

He told of his meeting with Bingley and went on to recount what had occurred during their meeting with Miss Bingley, even repeating his comments regarding marriage to her. Darcy told her of Miss Bingley's desire to separate them so she would have Darcy's undivided attention. Finally, Darcy told of Bingley's decision to send his sister away separating her from Darcy, just as she had tried to do to Elizabeth. By the time he had finished his tale, he had noted tears on Elizabeth's cheeks.

Darcy instantly sobered. "I know that it is all my fault she behaved in such a way. Can you ever forgive me?"

This time it was Elizabeth who stopped. "Why on earth would you think Miss Bingley's behavior your fault?"

Darcy looked deeply into her eyes before saying, "She was jealous of my admiration for you."

"Oh!" was all Elizabeth could say, but Darcy noticed the color that suffused her face and neck, as well as the blissful look in her eyes.

Looking at how far ahead the others were, Darcy quickly walked on, asking Elizabeth's opinion of Bingley's idea to hold a ball and of other inconsequential things. Before long the picnickers arrived back at Longbourn, where the sisters remained on the porch to wave their visitors off.

CHAPTER 14

THE DAYS AND weeks passed with the friends spending much time in each other's company. Jane, Elizabeth, and Mary often visited at Netherfield, or the groups met at various gatherings held by the neighbors. All the while, Elizabeth tried to avoid Mr. Collins whenever possible and to ignore or discourage him when avoidance was not possible. When they met at events to which they were all invited, Mary, Jane, and Mr. Bingley all helped to distract Mr. Collins allowing Elizabeth to spend time with Mr. and Miss Darcy.

One morning in November as Elizabeth arrived alone to visit with Georgiana, she found her friend standing with Mr. Darcy on the steps of Netherfield waiting for her. A groom stood at the foot of the stairs holding the reins of a saddled horse.

Darcy greeted Elizabeth and helped her from the carriage. "I have to go into Meryton to attend to some business, but I look forward to spending some time with you upon my return." With a brief kiss to her hand, Darcy mounted his horse, waved his hat, and set off down the drive at a canter.

After posting his letters, Darcy stopped by the bookshop to see if the book he ordered had arrived. Mr. Stevens was not in sight as he entered, so Darcy called out to him.

"Ah, good morning, Mr. Darcy. How are you today?" Mr. Stevens called from the back of the shop.

"I am very well, thank you, Mr. Stevens. How are you? Has business been good?"

"I am doing well," he said adding with a smile, "and I am glad to say so is business of late, thanks to your patronage."

Smiling in reply Darcy asked, "I was wondering if my order has arrived?"

"Indeed it has. I was just unpacking it." Mr. Stevens slipped into the back and returned with the book. As he was wrapping the book, he continued to chat with Darcy. "You know sir, I do not believe the nonsense that is being said about you."

"To what are you referring, Mr. Stevens?" Darcy asked puzzled.

"There is a story that has been going around town for a while now about you cheating some young man out of a living gifted to him by your father."

Darcy stiffened in anger and fear. "Do you happen to know where this story started, Mr. Stevens?"

"It was Mrs. Long who told me, I believe, sir," he replied.

"But do you know where it really started?" Darcy asked urgently, "It is very important."

"I do not know for sure, sir, but I can do some checking."

"It is also a matter of some urgency, Mr. Stevens. I would prefer not to go into great detail, but I can guarantee that the story is false, and I have the documentation that can prove my assertions."

"I do not doubt that, sir. I can tell from our dealings that you are an honorable and fair man."

"I thank you, Mr. Stevens," Darcy said gratefully. "The man who claims to have been cheated uses his story to damage my family and garner sympathy for himself. He can be quite charming, but it is an act. He runs up debts with local merchants as well as debts of honor but disappears without paying them. He is also not to be trusted with young ladies. If he was just passing through, then Meryton is very fortunate. Thank you, Mr. Stevens, for your support and the information. One thing you can be grateful for is that should George Wickham ever come to Meryton, yours will not be a shop he abuses, as I doubt he has ever opened a book for the sheer pleasure of reading."

"Thank you for the information. If I can discover the source of the story, I will contact you. Well, good day to you, Mr. Darcy, and thank you for your business. I shall see what I can find out for you, sir," said Mr. Stevens as he waved his customer out the door.

Darcy felt an urgent need to return to Netherfield. He had to be sure that Georgiana and Elizabeth were safe. As he cantered his horse in the direction of the estate, he thought again about the hole Elizabeth had found in his coat the morning after the hunt. *Could Wickham have been near? Could he really have taken a shot at me?* Now more concerned than ever, Darcy kicked his horse into a gallop.

So far, the young ladies had enjoyed their morning together. They had visited with Mrs. Hurst for a while in the parlor and had gone on to practice their music in the Netherfield music room. The day was bright and pleasant with just a nip of fall in the air, so they decided to walk through the gardens before luncheon as Darcy had not yet returned.

Fortune smiled on Wickham when he came to Meryton to investigate the militia. He discovered the presence of his most hated enemy.

And, even better than that, Georgiana was in the neighborhood. His good luck had not ended there, for it turned out that the nuisance who had disrupted his first attempted kidnapping of Georgiana lived in the neighborhood. The most unlikely thing of all, though, was that it appeared Darcy had fallen in love with this little country nobody. He could not fault Darcy's taste, as she was quite a luscious little thing. Now he could deliver a double blow to Darcy, one from which Wickham hoped he would never recover. He would kill the woman Darcy loved and take off with his beloved sister. He would only reappear when he was legally married to Georgiana. He was certain that an unfortunate accident would befall Darcy a short while later. Then Wickham would get what he always felt was his due: He would become the Master of Pemberley.

Fortune's last favor was the discovery of his hideout. There had been one room intact, which provided adequate shelter, and since the weather had been somewhat mild, he had been able to survive without a fire. A quick walk from his cottage enabled him to witness the frequent early morning meetings of Darcy and Elizabeth and later follow Elizabeth and Georgiana when they were in Meryton. He knew if he were patient the perfect opportunity for revenge would present itself. That opportunity came yesterday. After observing their morning meeting, he had been able to creep close enough to hear some of their conversation and plans.

"Good morning, Miss Elizabeth. How are you this morning?"

"Mr. Darcy, we must stop meeting this way," Elizabeth said with a laugh and a warm smile.

"I would prefer that we could meet with more frequency, not less, Miss Elizabeth." Darcy's bold reply brought a bright blush to Elizabeth's cheeks.

"I find I must agree with you, sir; but as you reside in London and Pemberley and me in Hertfordshire, I am afraid that may not come to pass."

"You are sometimes in London are you not?"

"I am, sir, but I am afraid those times are infrequent," she said sadly.

"Perhaps you could come for an extended stay in the near future?" he asked hopefully.

"As my relatives from town will soon be visiting Longbourn for the holidays, there would be no one in town for me to visit," she laughed.

"Well, at least we will have a good deal of time tomorrow to visit. There is something that I would particularly like to discuss with you," he said softly his eyes warm, but his expression serious.

Again Elizabeth blushed but managed to reply as she gazed steadily into his warm brown eyes. "I am sure that will be delightful, Mr. Darcy, as all of our conversations are quite enjoyable."

"I have some errands in Meryton to attend to in the morning, but I should return in time for luncheon. Perhaps you would accompany me on a walk in the garden afterward?"

"I shall look forward to it, sir. I shall also pray for good weather that we might be able to enjoy our outing even more. Perhaps if I stroll with Georgiana before luncheon, she will not object to our walking afterward."

He lifted her hand and placed a gentle, lingering kiss upon the back of it. "Until tomorrow, Miss Bennet." He continued to gaze steadily into her eyes and retained her hand for some time.

Elizabeth was mesmerized by the look in Darcy's eyes and the warmth of his hand holding hers. The tingle in her hand created by his kiss had spread to every part of her body. She had tried to remind herself they could never be more than friends because of the difference in their social circles, but it was all to no avail as her heart was lost. She loved Mr. Darcy totally and completely.

Elizabeth was not alone in her feelings. Darcy was lost as well, and he knew it. He loved Elizabeth ardently and could no longer imagine his life without her. He would like to marry her tomorrow, but felt she deserved a proper courtship and engagement period. He would speak with her about it tomorrow while they walked. He could wait no longer.

Eventually, Darcy realized they had been staring at one another for quite some time. He slowly released her hand, watching the blush rise in her cheeks.

"My apologies, Miss Elizabeth—"

"Mr. Darcy, I apologize for my forward—"

They spoke over one another in their rush to apologize for the breach of propriety. They stopped abruptly, still looking at each other, and laughed softly.

"Please, Miss Elizabeth, you were saying. "

"I have never before behaved in such a forward manner. Please forgive me." Her words were quietly spoken, eyes downcast, a deep blush upon her face.

Darcy placed one finger under her chin and lifted her face so she was forced to meet his eyes. "Miss Elizabeth, please do not apologize, for the fault was mine. The beauty of your eyes made me forget myself momentarily. I do apologize if I made you uncomfortable." His voice was soft and wrapped around her like a caress.

"I was not uncomfortable, Mr. Darcy, quite the contrary." Elizabeth's color heightened even more with her bold words. "I believe I should return home or I shall not be ready when

Georgiana sends the carriage. A very good day to you, Mr. Darcy."

"And to you, Miss Elizabeth." She turned abruptly and hurried away from him. With the safety of a little distance between them, she paused and looked back. The sound of her soft sigh was carried to him on the gentle breeze as he stood watching until she was no longer in view. *Elizabeth said she was not uncomfortable with their encounter. Could her feelings be as strong as mine?* He hoped that would be the case and wondered how he could survive the wait until he was with her again.

Wickham could barely contain his amusement at the conversation. No wonder Darcy had not yet married—he had no idea how to talk to a woman. Wickham felt sure that he could have charmed Miss Elizabeth into his bed quite quickly. He truly regretted that he would not be able to enjoy Miss Elizabeth's charms before he disposed of her, as that would further devastate Darcy. Unfortunately, there was not the time for such pleasantries; he would have to settle for the pleasure to be found with Georgiana and sharing all the salacious details with Darcy.

Wickham could not believe his good luck; everything was falling into place. Elizabeth and Georgiana would be alone in the garden sometime before luncheon. He knew the large footman assigned to protect Georgiana would be somewhere nearby, but he usually held well back to give the ladies their privacy while they were on the estate. He followed much closer when they were in society. Wickham returned to his cottage to plan.

Wickham was ready. He had managed to scout the area around Netherfield's formal gardens at various times the day prior. He carefully observed the gardeners' schedules and the areas of the gardens where work was ongoing. He discovered several good spots in which he could conceal himself. Wickham could even move between some of them unseen.

Now he was concealed in the most central of the locations he had selected. His horse was nearby, and his belongings were attached, in preparation for a quick retreat. There were a gag and rope in his pockets to control Georgiana until they were well away. Wickham had stolen a carriage and hidden it away along the route they would traverse. He planned to quickly put Meryton far behind him. They would travel a circuitous route to the carriage. Once he was sure he was not being followed, he would transfer to the closed carriage and head for the border with Georgiana. As it was a journey of several days, he brought some laudanum with him so that he could keep her quiet until it was time for her to speak two important words.

Wickham saw the girls meandering down a nearby path. They were arm-in-arm heads close together talking and laughing and totally unaware of the danger lurking nearby. Wickham noted Gregson, the footman, walking a parallel path, on the opposite side of the garden, his gaze never leaving the young ladies. Wickham moved to a convenient spot, and when the footman passed his position, Wickham soundlessly brought the butt of his pistol down hard on the back of the footman's head. Gregson crumpled to the ground at his feet. As the body could not be seen lying upon the path until one was directly upon it, he left Gregson there. Wickham then hurried to a new hiding place where he could be closer to the girls to overhear their conversation.

Wickham was pleased, as his plan was going perfectly. He would take his revenge on Darcy, leaving nothing but a broken man mourning the loss of his sister and his love. Being Wickham, he was not content to just take his revenge. He wanted to inflict as much pain and damage as he could. He intended to allow the girls to pass him on the path. He would grab Georgiana from behind and silence her with his hand. He would force them further down the path, and then he would tell Elizabeth why she was going to die. He would tell her of Darcy's love for her and of his eventual plan to kill Darcy and take his rightful place at Pemberley.

The girls changed directions and passed behind a tall grouping of boxwoods. *Their path is perfect,* Wickham thought, as he moved closer to meet the girls when they emerged on the other side. Things were going according to plan. Georgiana was trailing slightly behind Elizabeth as they walked through a narrow spot on the garden path. After both young ladies had passed, Wickham stepped out from behind grabbing

Georgiana around the waist and pulling her tightly back against him. He pressed the gun between Elizabeth's shoulder blades as he hissed, "Not a word, ladies. Just continue on down the path. Do not speak and do not look back, for I will not hesitate to shoot you if need be." Georgiana was frozen in fear; she could not have spoken had she wished it.

They moved further away from the heart of the gardens, passing a pathway that lead out of the gardens to the fields beyond when Wickham suddenly stopped. He leaned into Georgiana and kissed her cheek whispering, his voice all charm and politeness, "Hello, dear girl. How I have missed you. What fun we had playing games when you were a little girl. Do you not remember, Georgiana? My, but you have grown into a beautiful young woman since then." Again he placed a wet kiss on her cheek though his eyes and gun were still trained on Elizabeth's back. Georgiana shrank from his kiss and the lewd words he was now whispering in her ear. Her large eyes reflected her terror, and a small whimper escaped her lips.

Though extremely frightened, Elizabeth bravely whispered, "Who are you? What do you want here?"

"I am quite disappointed you do not remember me, Miss Elizabeth. I have often been told I make quite an impression."

"Be that as it may, I do not know you. The impression I have is of a coward who sneaks up behind innocent young women threatening them with a weapon."

"Turn around if you wish, and I will answer your questions. You will not be able to describe me to anyone when our meeting it through, so it matters not if you see me." Elizabeth turned slowly at his words. She was terribly afraid, but knew that Georgiana would need her strength if they were to escape from their captor. When she was facing the man, a brief feeling of familiarity flashed through her mind. "My name is George Wickham, and I am here to get the prize you interrupted me from taking some years ago."

At his words, Georgiana began to tremble in earnest. *Was it Wickham who had tried to kidnap her from the park five years ago? Why would he do that? She had thought him William's friend, and her father had been fond of him.* She could not bring herself to look at the man who held her so tightly, but her fear and confusion were evident to Elizabeth.

"Perhaps I should thank you for interrupting me that day, Miss Elizabeth. Had I succeeded, I would have simply ransomed her back to Darcy." He said the name as though it left a bad taste in his mouth. "I believe I should prefer to marry her and enjoy both a lovely wife on my arm and in my bed as well as her thirty thousand pound dowry. And I am sure it will not take long after that for Darcy to meet with a dreadful accident, putting me in my rightful place as Master of Pemberley."

Was the man insane? Did he think himself the rightful master of Pemberley? Elizabeth was stalling for time, hoping that Gregson would come looking for them. "How could getting away do you any good? Miss Darcy is under age and cannot marry without her brother's consent."

"That may be true, but in Scotland they are not so particular about such matters."

"Perhaps not, but how, exactly, do you plan to get away? What makes you think that I will not try to stop you again?"

"Well, Miss Elizabeth, as no good deed should go unpunished, I do not expect that you will be able to stop me as you did the first time," he said as he waved the gun menacingly in her direction.

Now even more frightened and wondering where Gregson could be, she said determinedly, "You cannot just shoot me, sir, as that will draw unwanted attention to us all. The gardens are full of workers, after all."

"I do not necessarily need to shoot you to silence you, Miss Elizabeth." She wondered what he could mean by that and took a step away from him. She determined to keep her distance so he could not lay his hands upon her. "First, you will help me to contain my prize, and then I shall deal with you." He released Georgiana with a hard push straight into Elizabeth causing both girls to lose their balance. By the time they had righted themselves, Wickham had retrieved some ropes and a rag from his pocket.

He tossed them to Elizabeth. "You will take this gag and place it in Miss Darcy's mouth. When she is silenced, you will tie her hands behind her and her ankles closely together. You will tie her sufficiently tight that she cannot get away. Remember, do as I say, or you will suffer the consequences," he threatened. He kept the gun trained on the two girls.

Murmuring soothing words all the while, Elizabeth did as commanded. She tried to be gentle but knew he would check to see if she had done as he asked. All the time she was tying up Georgiana, Elizabeth was desperately trying to think of something that could help them. Perhaps if she returned Georgiana to Wickham in the same way she received her, Elizabeth could knock the gun from his hand or overset him so they could get away. Consequently, Elizabeth, with a whispered apology, shoved Georgiana back towards Wickham.

It didn't work quite as planned because with her feet tied, Georgiana couldn't stumble forward towards Wickham. He stepped forward to catch her, and then just pushed Georgiana to the side, letting her fall to the ground on the path that would lead him from the garden. Elizabeth winced when she saw the force with which Georgiana hit the rocky path. She looked back in time to see Wickham slowly advancing upon her with a menacing look on his face. Just then, Darcy's voice was heard calling to the ladies. Wickham reached forward and grabbed Elizabeth by the hair, quickly silencing her by bringing his lips down hard on hers. The force of the assault caused her some pain, but she desperately tried to extricate herself. She heard Darcy's voice much closer now as he again called their names. Wickham had the arm holding the gun wrapped tightly around her waist, holding her body to his. Moving his other hand from her hair, he allowed it to roam freely over Elizabeth's curves as he forced her lips to part with his seeking tongue.

Wickham smelled of alcohol and sweat as though he had not bathed in days. Elizabeth was repulsed with him, but no matter how hard she struggled, she could not get free from Wickham's grasp. Suddenly she bit down on Wickham's tongue hard enough she could taste blood in her mouth. He pulled back and swore loudly as he backhanded Elizabeth with the hand holding the gun and ran towards Georgiana. The blow sent Elizabeth reeling back a few steps and caused her to briefly see stars. It also caused blackness to creep along the edges of her vision, but she knew she could not succumb to the pain and blackness. She had to be strong; Georgiana still needed her.

Wickham rushed to where Georgiana lay, lifting her effortlessly, he threw her carelessly over his shoulder. Looking at Elizabeth, Georgiana saw her slight smile and nod of encouragement and found her own courage. She began to kick and struggle, making it hard for Wickham to maintain his hold on her. He tried to make good his escape, but he heard Elizabeth close behind him. He could now hear another set of, much heavier, footsteps behind him as well. Wickham knew he had to make his escape quickly.

Angry at being foiled again, he turned, and without pausing to take aim, pulled the trigger, just as Darcy called out, "Wickham, put her down!"

Elizabeth turned at Darcy's call, just as Wickham pulled the trigger. She felt a searing pain against her side. The pain was overwhelming, and she collapsed to the ground in a faint as Wickham turned and continued down the path. Wickham did not know if the wound were serious or how long it would delay Darcy from following. Darcy reached Elizabeth quickly, catching her before her head could hit the hard stones of the path. He laid her down gently, hoping the wound was not serious, and continued to chase Wickham and Georgiana. When Wickham realized how close Darcy was to catching up, he unceremoniously dropped Georgiana and took off running as if the hounds of hell were on his heels. Wickham reached his horse just as Darcy reached his bound and sobbing sister. Darcy was in a murderous rage. He wanted to give chase to Wickham and knew should he catch him that he would kill Wickham with his bare hands. It was perhaps fortunate that Darcy had to attend to Elizabeth and Georgiana. Otherwise, he may have become a murderer. He began shouting for help as he carried his sister back to where Elizabeth lay. Two young gardeners quickly appeared and Darcy tersely gave them orders. He sent one to fetch Mr. Jones, and the other to alert the house and send for Bingley. He reassured Georgiana that all would be well and promised to untie her as soon as he had Elizabeth's bleeding stopped. He began to check her wound all the while comforting Georgiana with soothing words. Just as Elizabeth stirred, he heard a noise behind him. Gregson, none too steady on his feet and holding his head, appeared. Despite his pain, Gregson took in the situation quickly. He withdrew the knife from his boot, gently cut the ropes binding Georgiana, and removed the gag.

She was still sobbing but moved closer to Elizabeth. "Oh, Lizzy, you saved me again." She looked at her pale face and the blood seeping through her brother's fingers. "Oh, William, what can I do to help?"

Seeing her distress and wanting to calm her he said, "Untie my cravat and fold it up. I can use it to stop the flow of blood from Miss Elizabeth's injury." She did as he bid, but her hands were shaking so that it made untying the knots quite difficult. She pulled the wrong way once or twice nearly strangling Darcy in the process. Had the situation not been so dire, he would have found it amusing.

Georgiana folder the cravat and placed it against Elizabeth's wound. Darcy again clamped his hands down trying to staunch the flow of blood. "I need more padding or something to tie this with!"

Again, retrieving his knife from his boot, Gregson leaned down and lifted the edge of Elizabeth's gown. Making a quick cut, he tore two strips from around the bottom of her petticoat. He waded on up and handed it to Darcy. While Darcy held it firmly in place, Gregson used the other strip to wrap around her body, tying the bandages tight to her. They had just finished, when he heard running behind them.

Bingley rounded the bend in the path and exclaimed, "Good God, Darcy! What has happened?"

"Not now, Bingley. Just help me get them to the house. Darcy rose from the ground with Elizabeth in his arms and strode off quickly down the path towards the house. Bingley followed with Georgiana. He tried to put his arm around her to steady her, but she stepped away from him with a small cry. So with a concerned look, he extended his hand in the direction before them and very gently offered his arm to her as they moved down the path after Darcy.

CHAPTER 15

HAVING HEARD THE gunshot and the cries of the man who had come for help, Mrs. Dawson was waiting to lead Darcy to Miss Elizabeth's room. She ordered the housemaid to fetch hot water, towels, bandages, and her medicine kit so she could clean the wound and try to stop the bleeding. In spite of Darcy's efforts, Elizabeth was losing a lot of blood; they needed to get it under control before Mr. Jones arrived. Mrs. Annesley was waiting at the top of the steps to help. Darcy laid Elizabeth gently on the bed. This time he did not step away but dropped to his knees by the side of the bed taking her small, cold hand between his large, warm ones.

"You are safe now, Elizabeth. Please open your eyes and look at me." She was so pale, and a large bruise was beginning to appear on one cheek; it seemed that Wickham had struck her as well. Darcy felt as if his world was ending. He knew his heart and had planned to speak with Elizabeth this very afternoon. *Would she be well? Would he get a chance to tell her of his feelings?*

Breaking through his thoughts, Mrs. Annesley attempted to move him so that she could attend to Elizabeth. "Sir, you must leave. We must get her undressed and clean the wound and stop the blood loss. Please, sir, you must leave." Though her tone was urgent and firm, it was filled with compassion.

Darcy looked at Mrs. Annesley as though in a daze. Bingley had delivered Miss Darcy into the hands of her maid. He was passing the room and stepped in as he heard Mrs. Annesley's words.

"Come, Darcy, you look like you need some of Chalmers attentions yourself. As soon as there is anything to report, will you please inform us, ladies?"

"Of course, Mr. Bingley," they both answered.

Darcy gave himself a shake and straightened his shoulders. "I will be in my sitting room awaiting any news. Mrs. Annesley, please notify me of any change immediately."

"Certainly, Mr. Darcy."

With a last look at Elizabeth, Darcy left the room with Bingley. Stepping into the hall, Darcy suddenly recalled Georgiana. "Where is my sister, Bingley?" he asked.

"I left her in the competent and comforting hands of her maid."

"If you would like to wait in my sitting room, I will be with you as soon as I have checked on Georgiana and changed." So saying, Darcy made his way to his sister's door.

Bingley was waiting, somewhat impatiently, for Darcy's return. "Now, Darcy, what the devil happened?"

"Until I can speak with Georgiana or Elizabeth, I will not be sure of the details; however, I came into the gardens just as George Wickham was attempting to abduct Georgiana. He shot Elizabeth, and it appears he struck her also as she attempted to protect Georgiana. I believe he attacked Gregson first and then moved on to the young ladies. I am sure he is far away by now, but we need to have the surrounding areas searched. Perhaps we can get a clue as to where he was hiding. I do not wish to involve the authorities, as it may be perceived by some that Georgiana and Miss Elizabeth have been compromised. We must protect them at all costs."

Bingley reached for the bell pull to summon the butler. Almost instantly, Dawson appeared in the sitting room doorway to announce that Mr. Jones had arrived and was examining Miss Elizabeth. Bingley asks Dawson to send Mr. Moore to him immediately. After relaying what he needed, Mr. Moore organized the stable hands and groundskeepers to search all the buildings at Netherfield and to question the tenants about any strangers they may have noticed recently.

Closing the door after the steward, Bingley said, "Now, Darcy, who is this Wickham and why was he trying to kidnap your sister?"

"If you are going to hear this tale, you had better pour us both a drink," said Darcy, anger and frustration evident in his voice. Bingley handed him a glass of brandy, and Darcy took a gulp as he proceeded to tell Bingley about his long history with Wickham.

"Good heavens, Darcy, I had no idea! What the devil is wrong with the man? Why have you never had him arrested?"

"I had the Bow Street Runners looking for him after the first attempt, but he could not be found. It was as though he vanished from the face of the earth, and usually by the time trouble turned up in a new location, he was gone without a trace. Now, Bingley, how could I have him arrested without damaging Georgiana's reputation?"

"She was traumatized by the childhood incident. I could barely get her out of the house for months. I hired Gregson as her bodyguard after the attempt at Ramsgate; fortunately, she does not realize that is his purpose as it would frighten her again. If what happened at Ramsgate ever becomes public, Georgiana will be totally ruined as he was carrying her while she was clad only in her nightdress. Obviously, I cannot mention Wickham's actions today without hurting both Georgiana's and Miss Elizabeth's reputations." Darcy began to pace the room. "Had I not needed to attend to the ladies, I would probably have chased him down and killed him with my bare hands."

"I began to suspect Wickham was nearby just today after speaking to Mr. Stevens in the bookshop. Mr. Stevens told me about the rumor going around. It is said I deprived Wickham, though they did not know his name, of a living left to him by my father. I can assure that the rumor is false. He has the education to make something of himself, but he seems to believe that my family owes him his support."

They were interrupted by a knock at the door. Darcy jerked it open to find Mr. Jones there. "How is Miss Elizabeth? Does she need anything? Should I send for my family physician or a surgeon from town?"

Mr. Jones almost laughed at the expression on Mr. Darcy's face. "I do not believe that will be necessary, Mr. Darcy. Miss Elizabeth has a bruise on her face though I cannot yet tell what caused it or how severe it might be because of the swelling. If there is any ice available, I would recommend its application to her cheek. It will help with both the pain and the swelling.

As for her most serious wound, she was very fortunate that the bullet only grazed her side. I was able to stop the bleeding, but the wound required more than fifteen stitches to close it. She is in a good deal of pain and will likely remain so for several days. Again, Mr. Bingley, I must ask that you allow her to be your guest for the foreseeable future. I expect it could take up to two weeks before she is completely recovered. I will visit daily to check on her and see how she is progressing. She should lie flat for a few days and will require assistance in obtaining a reclining position in order to be fed with an invalid feeder until she is able to fully sit up. Once she can attain a sitting position, she will require nourishing food to help her regain her strength due to the amount of blood she lost. After the first week, we will need to get her to her feet to begin walking for very brief periods each day."

"I will be leaving a recipe for a poultice that should be applied to the wound for thirty minutes each time the bandage has to be changed. Then, the wound should be cleaned and redressed. I will also leave some laudanum for her, in case the pain becomes too severe. The main concern will be to prevent infection. Someone should be with her at all times. We need to ensure that we catch any fever as early as possible. That will give us the best chance of managing any infection and preventing its spread. I will return this evening to check on her. Be sure to notify me of any change to her condition, particularly if a fever occurs."

"Well, I should write to Longbourn with the news, but what should I tell them as to the cause of the injury?" Bingley asked.

"Mr. Jones, would you close the door please," Darcy directed.

He did as requested and turned to the gentlemen, a puzzled look on his face. "I did wonder myself how this happened. Miss Elizabeth would say no more than that there had been an accident," said Mr. Jones.

"Sir, I hope that I can trust your discretion in this matter," Darcy remarked with a stern gaze.

"Certainly, sir. Miss Elizabeth is a favorite of mine and has often been of assistance to me in a severe crisis." Mr. Jones replied.

"I do not yet know all of the details of the events, but my sister and Miss Elizabeth were attacked in the gardens by a man attempting to kidnap my sister. I would not wish word of this to get out because of the harm it could cause to both young ladies' reputations."

"Why would someone attempt to kidnap your sister?" Mr. Jones asked in surprise.

"I would prefer not to go into details, sir, but suffice it to say that it is someone with a grudge against our family, though there is no actual basis for his resentment. However, perhaps you could help with another possible explanation for Miss Elizabeth's injury? I do not want to tell her family something she would not wish them to know, and I am sure she would prefer to explain the situation to her family herself. However, as before, I am sure Miss Elizabeth would be comforted by her sister, Jane's, presence perhaps you can help arrange that as well."

"You might suggest that it was a stray shot from a hunter, or perhaps you could just invite Mr. & Miss Bennet to tea. If Miss Elizabeth were going to tell anyone what happened, it would be the two of them. Mr. Bennet can determine what he wishes to tell his wife to protect her nerves.

"Thank you, Mr. Jones, I believe that is an excellent suggestion. By the way, while you are here, would you please check Miss Darcy and my footman, Gregson? I do not believe that my sister was harmed physically, but she was much shaken by the events. This man has attempted to kidnap her twice, the first time she did not see his face but was so upset she would not go out of doors for quite some time afterward. She was unaware of the second attempt, as he had drugged her. The shock may be more severe this time, as the man has always publicly acted to her as a friend of our family and that is the way Georgiana remembers him. Also, Gregson was knocked unconscious by the intruder."

"I will look in on them immediately, Mr. Darcy. Do you wish me to leave something to help Miss Darcy sleep, if necessary?"

"I believe that may be a good idea. Just review the instructions with both her maid and Mrs. Annesley."

"I might add that you may want to set the time for tea as late as possible. Miss Lizzy is asleep at the moment, but she did not wish to take any laudanum, so she may not sleep very long. She is anxious to talk to you, Mr. Darcy. Perhaps something she has to say will affect the meeting with her family, so you might wish to talk with her first, if possible."

"Again, thank you for your sound advice, Mr. Jones."

The apothecary turned and left the room to check on his other two patients. Darcy crossed the hall to check on Elizabeth. The maid attending her said she was currently sleeping, so Darcy asked to be notified as soon as she was awake. Bingley went to his study to send the note to the Bennets inviting them for tea at four-thirty today; while Darcy penned a letter to the Colonel about the events as he waited for Elizabeth to awaken.

His letter writing was interrupted when Mr. Jones returned to report on his other two patients.

"Mr. Darcy, your sister is indeed very distressed by the events of the day. She was unresponsive to my questions only murmuring 'Why George?' and 'Lizzy must hate me!' over and over again, but she does not appear to have any serious injuries. She has several bruises starting to show, and there is some chaffing on her wrists and ankles. I provided some salve to her maid with instructions on its use. I also gave her some laudanum to help her sleep for the present, but I recommend that someone sit with her until she awakens. I would not be surprised if she were to have nightmares from this experience. As for Mr. Gregson, he has a mild concussion. It appears he was struck from behind, and my guess is that it was the butt of a pistol that hit him. He should rest for a few days, and someone should keep an eye on him, as well. He told me he dealt with a similar injury when he was on the continent. I believe that he will make a full recovery."

"Thank you for your report and assistance, Mr. Jones. We will see you later when you return to check on your patients," said Darcy.

Shortly after the apothecary left, the maid knocked on the open sitting room door to say that Miss Elizabeth wished to speak with him. He asked her to summon Mrs. Annesley to sit with them and waited in the hallway for her to join him before knocking on the door. Hearing Elizabeth's call to enter, Darcy opened the door to find her attempting to sit up. She was grimacing in pain and Darcy rushed to her side placing his hand gently on her shoulder to prevent her from moving.

"You must not attempt to sit up for a few days according to Mr. Jones. He says it could cause your wound to open, and you must be careful to avoid twisting as much as you can." When Elizabeth stilled, he removed his hand but was surprised by his feelings. In spite of the seriousness of the situation, Darcy received a shock throughout his entire body as he touched her through the thin fabric of her nightgown. He looked at Elizabeth and noticed that she seemed as deeply affected as he was. Her face suffused with a soft blush that increased as their eyes met.

Elizabeth was warm all over from the brief touch of his hand. Her body tingled in spite of the pain. She knew that she loved him, and as time had passed she felt that perhaps he might return her feelings.

Lost as they were to their emotions and locked in one another's gaze, they were both startled when Mrs. Annesley cleared her throat. Darcy stepped back from the bed his face turning red.

"Thank you for your words of caution, Mr. Darcy." Her cheeks were still tinged with the blush, and it contrasted sharply with her pale face.

"How are you feeling, Miss Elizabeth? Can I get you anything for your comfort?" he asked sincerely.

"No thank you, Mr. Darcy, but I must speak with you."

"You must allow me to speak first in this instance, Miss Elizabeth. How can I ever thank you for protecting Georgiana today? I am dreadfully sorry that you were caught in this dangerous situation. You, again, put yourself in great peril to assist my sister. I cannot but feel responsible for your injuries and am deeply indebted to you. Georgiana could not have a more caring friend. In fact, as she was a complete stranger to you the first time you came to her aid, I cannot but feel that you are the most courageous and caring young woman of my acquaintance. Are you sure there is nothing that I might get for you to increase your comfort at this time? If it is within my power, it shall be done." His words were accompanied with a look of such earnestness that she could not doubt his sincerity.

"Mr. Darcy, how is Georgiana? I hope she was not hurt too badly when I pushed her? Did Wickham hurt her? Did he take her away?"

"Do not worry. Georgiana has only a few bruises and some marks on her wrists and ankles from the rope; however, she is very frightened again." Darcy repeated to her what Mr. Jones had said. "Perhaps you might know of something I could say that would help assuage her fears? Perhaps your courage could help her to find some of her own."

"She did show some courage; she kept kicking and struggling as he tried to carry her off. Georgiana made it hard for him to keep his hold on her, but I would be happy to talk to her, if you think that would be helpful."

Darcy was surprised but pleased by Elizabeth's description of Georgiana's actions and smiled slightly. "It may be necessary for me to hold you to your offer."

Shyly, but with fervency, Elizabeth spoke. "Mr. Darcy, I must thank you, as well. Had I not turned at your call, Wickham's shot could have been so much worse. I might never have seen you again. The fact that you took the time to catch me when Georgiana needed you so desperately, . . . I have no words . . . I do not know how to thank you enough." Her voice was very soft and tremulous, and her tears began to spill over onto her cheeks.

Startled, Darcy said, "How did you know that I caught you?"

"Well, I only assumed that you did. Had I fallen to the ground unaided, I'm sure I would also have a terrible pain in my head to match the one in my side," said Elizabeth with a lopsided smile. The bruising and swelling of her cheek prevented her mouth from turning up on one side. "Again, I cannot thank you enough for your thoughtfulness."

Darcy was saddened to see the damage to her beautiful face and turned to the maid. "Could you please see that some ice is located for Miss Elizabeth's cheek. Mr. Jones said it would help with the pain and the swelling." The maid bobbed a curtsey and quickly departed to attend to his request.

Darcy had still not acknowledged Elizabeth's words and she began to worry that she had betrayed too much of her feelings. Finally, she looked up and encountered his glittering gaze. The depth of emotion in his dark eyes said what his words could not. "I could have done nothing else, Miss Elizabeth." Elizabeth's mouth opened in a small "o." "I am only sorry I did not arrive sooner. When I visited with Mr. Stevens this morning, I learned about the rumors in town that Wickham had spread. I was worried he was in the area, so I rushed back to check on you and Georgiana. I am so sorry I did not arrive in time to save you from being hurt."

She now saw guilt and pain in his expression and spoke quickly to exonerate him from any perceived responsibility.

"My injuries are not serious, Mr. Darcy, and you did something much more important. You saved me from death."

They were again lost in one another's gaze. This time it was a slight cough from Mrs. Annesley that brought them to awareness of their surroundings.

"Oh, Mr. Darcy, there is something else I must tell you. Wickham thanked me for disrupting his first attempt to take Georgiana. He said things would work out even better now, for now he could marry Georgiana. He said he would have a pretty wife on his arm and all her money, too. He also said you would meet with an accident, allowing him to take his rightful place as the Master of Pemberley. You must be very careful Mr. Darcy, please keep yourself safe," she implored him.

The bullet hole in his coat briefly flashed in his mind, but he would not worry her with his suspicions. Her obvious concern moved him beyond words. He said, "Have no fear, Miss Elizabeth. I promise to be on my guard. I have Georgiana to care for and something else very precious that I hold close to my heart." He stared at her with love shining forth from his eyes.

"Miss Elizabeth, Mr. Bingley and I were concerned about what to tell your family regarding your injury. Not wishing to tell them anything you would not want them to know, Mr. Bingley has invited your father and sister to tea. They are expected at half past four, and Mr. Bingley has arranged for tea to be served here. Mr. Jones suggested you might tell them it was a hunting shot gone astray, if you do not wish for them to know the details. Would you prefer to meet with your family alone, or may Mr. Bingley and I join you?" Darcy asked hopefully.

The pleading look in his eyes let Elizabeth know what he hoped her answer would be. She gave him her half smile. "I should prefer to have your company. I am not very proficient at deceiving my father. Perhaps the presence of others will distract him some. You see my father knows about the events in the park five years ago. I also told him after your first visit with Georgiana, that it was her I had aided that long ago day. I am concerned he will not wish me to continue our friendship if he feels it is a danger to me. I don't know what I will say to Papa yet." Her worried look caused his guilt to return.

"Well, then I shall ensure that Mr. Bingley and Georgiana do not speak of the incident in their presence."

"Do you think that Georgiana will join us for tea? " Elizabeth asked. "I would like to apologize and be sure she is okay," she said with concern.

"Mr. Jones gave her something to make her sleep because she was so upset. She was sleeping when he left her, but I shall check to be sure. Would you like me to have her join us now if she is awake? However, Miss Elizabeth, what could you possibly have to apologize for?" Darcy asked in surprise.

"After he had me gag and bind Georgiana, I shoved her back towards him hoping to knock him off balance or perhaps make him drop the weapon. Unfortunately, he let her fall and advanced on me. He said he could silence me without his weapon before he killed me." Elizabeth's voice had trailed to a whisper by the time she finished her explanation. Darcy looked at her with shock and mounting rage. Elizabeth started at his expression and quickly continued, "I am very sorry, Mr. Darcy, I did not mean to hurt her. I just did not know what else to do to stall for time and perhaps give us a chance to escape him or call for help," she concluded with contrition.

Elizabeth's reaction warned Darcy she thought his anger directed towards her, he quickly schooled his features. "Miss Elizabeth, I am sorry if you thought I was angry with you. I am sure everything you did was for the best. I am angry that he would dare lay hands upon your person. Did he hurt you in any way? Are you truly alright?" he asked his eyes showing the concern and worry that he felt.

Relaxing slightly, and hoping to relax him, Elizabeth replied, "Let us just say, I would have hoped my first kiss might have been a more pleasant experience." Her half grin again made a brief appearance, before she continued. "I do not believe he enjoyed the experience any more than I did as I bit him quite decisively to indicate my displeasure."

Darcy gave a grim chuckle as the image of Wickham kissing her made his blood boil. "Is there any situation you cannot overcome, Miss Elizabeth? Your abilities continue to impress." This time he smiled warmly. Darcy then turned to Mrs. Annesley and asked if she would check on his sister and request Georgiana to join them. "Let her know that Miss Elizabeth is asking after her."

Knowing she would be breaching propriety by leaving Darcy in Miss Elizabeth's bedroom, Mrs. Annesley gave Darcy a significant look and went to fetch Miss Darcy as quickly as she could.

Stepping closer to the bed and speaking softly Darcy said, "Miss Elizabeth, while we have a moment, I would like to ask something of you. I know this is not the most appropriate time, but I had so hoped to speak with you this afternoon during our walk. As we will be unable to take it, I must seize the opportunity offered me." He took a deep breath and continued, "I have come to admire you greatly and would like the opportunity to court you and show you a bit of society as we come to know one another better. Would you accept a courtship with me?"

Elizabeth's heart had begun to beat faster at his request to speak with her and the look in his eyes left no doubt as to his feelings and intentions. She could not believe that he could return her feelings. Their positions in society were so different, would she fit in his world? Her eyes shimmering with tears and a blush upon her cheeks, she softly replied, "I would be very happy and honored to accept your request for courtship, Mr. Darcy."

At her reply, he released the breath he had been holding. "I will speak with your father while he is here this afternoon. Miss Elizabeth, disguise of any kind is my abhorrence, I feel honor bound to be honest with him regarding the events of today, if I am going to obtain his permission for the courtship. I would not wish to present myself inaccurately."

"Mr. Darcy, you are the most honorable man I know, and your desire for complete honesty is admirable," she said with a small smile. He saw concern reflected in her eyes as she continued, "Sir, though a parent should not have a favorite, my father does not hide his preference for me. I would be terribly disappointed should he not grant his approval because of unnecessary concern for my safety. I have complete faith in your ability to protect me," she stated with conviction. "Mr. Darcy, might we discuss telling him about the incidents after you have obtained his permission?" she asked hesitantly, her eyes pleading with him.

Darcy was thrilled with her words as she was stating her faith in and affection for him as directly as she could. Though slightly uncomfortable with her request, he could deny her nothing. "I believe that would be an acceptable compromise," said Darcy with a smile. "It would definitely make it more difficult for him to withdraw his approval once given—especially if your mother knows of our relationship," he said his grin growing wider. "We can discuss it with him together when you are feeling better."

Hearing the sounds of Mrs. Annesley returning, Darcy quickly stepped away from the bed. Mrs. Annesley stopped in the doorway and said, "I am sorry, Mr. Darcy, but Miss Darcy is still sleeping."

"Thank you, Mrs. Annesley," he said. Turning to Elizabeth he continued, "I will leave you to rest now until your family arrives. Please know you have my best wishes and prayers for your speedy recovery. Until later then, Miss Elizabeth," said Darcy with a bow as he exited her room.

He stepped down the hall and knocked softly at Georgiana's door. Her maid opened it and stepped into the hallway. "Miss Darcy is still sleeping sir, but she is very restless. Her sleep is not a peaceful one." At that moment, a scream was heard from the room behind them. Darcy threw open the door and rushed to his sister's bedside. She was sitting up screaming, so he wrapped her in his arms crooning soft, reassuring words.

She calmed eventually and recognized her brother. "Oh, William, why would he do this? I thought he was our friend; Father treated him as if he was part of our family. Why would he betray us in such a way and try to hurt me? What did I do to him?"

"You did not do anything, Georgie. Wickham has spent years trying to harm our family and its reputation. He seems to have the misguided notion that Father should have treated him better. From something Miss Elizabeth said, he expected to be treated more like a son."

"Oh, how is Elizabeth? Will she be all right? How can she ever forgive me?"

"She said the very same thing about you," Darcy said with a smile. Darcy could see that the medication still had a hold on her, so he eased her gently back onto her pillows. "You rest now, Georgie, and you can see Miss Elizabeth in the morning. She will need a great deal of company over the next several days as she will be forced to remain in bed for quite some time."

"Alright, William, I will see you in the morning. Would you stay with me until I fall asleep?"

"Certainly, my dear," he said as he picked up her hand and held it between his own. She returned to her slumbers within moments.

Bingley and Darcy were comfortably seated in Darcy's sitting room talking when Dawson appeared and announced, "Mr. and Miss Bennet."

"Welcome, Mr. Bennet, Miss Bennet," Bingley said warmly.

Jane looked around the room curiously. "Where are Elizabeth and Miss Darcy?" she asked confused.

A flash of disquiet for Jane briefly crossed Bingley's face before he answered. "Please, come with me and I shall take you to Miss Elizabeth."

The gentlemen led the way down the hall. Bingley quietly knocked on the door, which was quickly opened by the maid.

Jane was startled to see they were entering the bedroom Elizabeth had used on their last visit. Her surprise grew as she saw a very pale Elizabeth lying in the bed among the pillows. Jane rushed to take a seat at her side exclaiming, "Lizzy are you well? What has happened?" There was a look of concern on her lovely face.

Before Elizabeth could answer Jane's query, Mr. Bennet said with a small chuckle, "I see you have been getting into mischief again, Lizzy."

Elizabeth took Jane's outstretched hand as she attempted to explain what had occurred. "I was walking with Miss Darcy in the area behind the gardens when I was struck by a hunter's shot gone astray. Fortunately, Mr. Darcy called out to us at the same time. Had I not turned at his call, things could have been much worse." She gave Darcy a warm look as she finished her statement.

Their faces paling at her words, Jane and Mr. Bennet simultaneously cried, "You were shot!"

Fortunately, Jane was seated for she looked as if she might faint. Not looking much more in control, Mr. Bennet dropped into the chair Darcy quickly pulled forward for him.

"Really, there is nothing to worry over," Elizabeth said quickly in an attempt to reassure them. "The bullet only grazed my side and did not cause any internal damage. It is somewhat painful, and Mr. Jones said I must stay in bed for several days to give the wound time to heal, but truly I feel fine. Unfortunately, that means that I will be Mr. Bingley's guest again," she concluded with a smile. Her smile did not fool anyone as her pain was obvious to those who knew her well.

Mr. Bennet shook his head, "Lizzy, had you not already done so, this escapade of yours would have turned my hair white. What am I going to do with you?" he asked with a wry grin.

"It is not as though I did this on purpose, Papa. It could have been much worse had Mr. Darcy not come upon us when he did," said Elizabeth with another glowing look at Darcy who returned her look. Mr. Bennet raised an eyebrow in surprise at the exchange he witnessed between his favorite daughter and the gentleman from Derbyshire.

Jane asked, "Lizzy, is there anything special you wish me to bring from Longbourn for you?"

Bingley quickly spoke up. "I am sure what Miss Elizabeth would most enjoy is your company, Miss Bennet. Will you not consider being my guest while your sister is recovering?" he asked with a hopeful smile.

"Oh, that is very kind of you, Mr. Bingley, but I would not wish to impose."

"You could never be an imposition, Miss Bennet," Bingley said warmly.

Smiling shyly at him, Jane replied, "If you are sure I would not inconvenience anyone," she hesitated and looked at Bingley who shook his head, "then I would be happy to accept so that I might care for Lizzy. Thank you, Mr. Bingley," she finished with a small smile.

The conversation became more general for some time. Eventually, Mr. Bennet said that perhaps they should leave so that Jane would be able to pack the things she and Elizabeth needed for their stay and return in time for the evening meal. Darcy looked to Mr. Bennet and said, "Sir, before you depart, might I have a word with you in private?"

Remembering the look he had observed between the gentleman and his favorite daughter, Mr. Bennet replied, "Why certainly, Mr. Darcy." He smiled to himself, wondering what the gentleman's request would be and knowing he would enjoy teasing him during this interview.

"If you would care to accompany me back to my sitting room?" Darcy asked as he rose and led Elizabeth's father from the room.

As she, Jane, and Bingley were still conversing, only Elizabeth noted their departure. She wondered how long their interview would last and knew that the nervous feeling in her stomach would not go away until she was sure of the outcome. She tried to participate in the conversation as before, but with limited success. Her eyes were constantly shifting to the door as thoughts of the feelings she had experienced when he touched her raced through her head along with curiosity regarding their conversation.

Mr. Darcy closed the door as he followed Mr. Bennet into the room. They took the chairs before the fireplace and sat silently for some moments. Mr. Bennet enjoyed watching the range of emotions that played across Darcy's face as he sought for the right words.

"Was there something you wished to discuss with me, Mr. Darcy?" Mr. Bennet was barely able to conceal his grin.

Darcy stood up and paced before the fireplace as he attempted to calm himself and prepare to speak. Finally, he took a deep breath and stopped in front of Mr. Bennet's chair.

"Mr. Bennet, earlier today I had the opportunity to speak with Miss Elizabeth. I asked her if she would accept a courtship from me, and she consented. I hope you will agree to allow our courtship, sir."

Darcy looked intently into Mr. Bennet's eyes as he awaited his response. Though his face showed nothing, there was merriment in his eyes. *They look just like Elizabeth's;* he thought with a small smile.

"Mr. Darcy, why would you—a gentleman of the highest levels of society—wish to court the daughter of a country gentleman? Are there not plenty of others you could choose?" Mr. Bennet asked seriously.

"That is the very reason I wish to court Miss Elizabeth. She is nothing like the young ladies of the ton."

Mr. Bennet's face showed his indignation. "I beg your pardon, sir," he said coldly.

Darcy's face blanched as he realized the double meaning of his words. He stammered, "Oh, no, I . . . I . . ," Darcy hung his head and took another deep breath. "Mr. Bennet, please let me clarify what I meant. Miss Elizabeth is the finest young woman I have ever met. She is intelligent, kind, witty, and very lovely. My parents are both passed, and as the heir I now have the responsibility for our family estate, Pemberley, our townhouse, my young sister, my tenants, two smaller estates, and many other business ventures. Wherever I go, I hear the whispers of my income and observe the many covetous looks cast in my direction. I feel like livestock at auction. However, with Miss Elizabeth, I have never felt that way. Her looks are all open, and her eyes tell you everything she is thinking and feeling. She does not agree with everything I say, as do most of the debutantes of the ton. She is also very uninterested in my money. I know that our backgrounds are quite different, but I believe we are well matched," Darcy concluded in a rush. "May I also say, sir, that her laugh is the most joyous, unforgettable sound I have ever heard. I know you are aware of the incident in Hyde Park five years ago. The only thing I was able to truly learn about my sister's rescuer was that she had dark curls and that laugh. We never got an opportunity to meet or for me to thank her for her efforts. Mr. Bennet, I have heard that laugh in my memory many times over the last five years. It is what drew my attention to Miss Elizabeth at the Meryton Assembly where we first met. Sir, I want to hear that sound every day for the rest of my life."

Mr. Bennet, touched by the genuineness and intensity of Darcy's remarks, decided he would no longer tease him. Obviously Elizabeth had attracted a truly good gentleman. He could not be more pleased for her. "Mr. Darcy, I appreciate the value you place on Lizzy and hope you will always recognize and show appreciation for the wonderful woman that she is."

"I promise to do just that, Mr. Bennet. I dearly hope to win her heart, sir, and someday ask her to become my wife. I wished to ask for you further assistance, sir. As you pointed out, Elizabeth has little experience with the ton. I was hoping that perhaps Elizabeth could visit town and stay with the Gardiners after Christmas. I would like to have her experience some of the events that would be a regular part of her life should we marry. I have written to my aunt, Lady Matlock, and she is willing to sponsor Elizabeth and introduce her to many of her friends in the ton. Personally, I do not care to participate much in society, but it is required of me since I must maintain good connections, and Georgiana will make her debut in the next year or so. However, I want Miss Elizabeth to experience life in the ton and decide if she will be happy there. I would do anything in my power to make Miss Elizabeth happy."

"As her father, there is nothing I wish to hear more, Mr. Darcy. I believe I can agree with your request, and I am sure the Gardiners will, as well. However, I would ask that you not pressure her for a quick engagement. I do not believe she will find life in the city and high society to her liking. I want her to have the time she needs to understand exactly what life in your world entails. Can you agree with this?"

At Darcy's nod of acceptance, he said, "Now, shall we return to Lizzy's room and share the good news? You are quite fortunate that you will not be present when Mrs. Bennet learns of the courtship; but, on consideration, you may hear her response all the way to Netherfield."

Darcy smiled slightly though his discomfort was evident.

"I trust, Mr. Darcy, that your behavior will be that of an exemplary gentleman during my daughter's stay here," said Mr. Bennet firmly with an unyielding expression in his eyes.

"I would never do anything to compromise or dishonor Miss Elizabeth, sir, you have my word," said Darcy very seriously.

Though she had been watching the door frequently, Elizabeth did not see Mr. Darcy and her father return. At hearing the door close behind them, she turned her head and looked straight into Darcy's eyes. His warm smile and the happiness in his dark eyes gave rest to her concerns as warmth spread through her entire body, and a blush appeared on her cheeks. Darcy walked immediately to the far side of the bed and lifted her hand placing a light kiss on the back of it before returning it to its previous position upon the bed.

Mr. Bennet cleared his throat, and when all eyes looked his way said, "I have the great pleasure to announce the courtship of my Elizabeth and Mr. Darcy."

The noise swelled as everyone began to offer congratulations at once. Jane came to hug Elizabeth as Bingley slapped his friend on the back crying, "Congratulations, Darcy! It looks like we will be brothers someday," he beamed.

"Yes, but not because of your sister," Darcy said with relief. Both men laughed, causing the others to look their way.

Finally, Mr. Bennet was able to offer his congratulations to Elizabeth. "Well, my dear Lizzy, I hope it was my agreement you wished for," he said with a teasing smile.

"Oh yes, Papa, I am so happy. Mr. Darcy is the best man I know."

"I believe that you are right, my girl. My Darcy is a very fine man. He has asked that you return to town after the holidays to stay with your aunt and uncle. He would like you to enjoy part of the small season, and his aunt, Lady Matlock, will sponsor you about town. What do you think of that idea, Lizzy?" he asked with an eyebrow raised and head cocked.

"You know that I always enjoy a visit to town, Papa, and I love staying with the Gardiners. However, I admit the real pleasure of this particular visit will come from getting to spend more time with Mr. Darcy." Mr. Bennet laughed at the small smile and blush that followed her words.

Mrs. Dawson entered the room with fresh tea during the midst of the congratulations. As everyone resumed their seats, Bingley asked, "Jane, would you do the honors as the hostess?" She quietly assented, returning his warm smile with a smile of her own.

"Now we will have two courtships to celebrate at the ball," Bingley interjected into the conversation. He rang for a maid and sent her to see if the Hursts had returned from the village.

After their arrival, Bingley informed his sister about the second courtship. He asked how the plans for the ball were coming, and there was some general discussion among the group. The date of the ball was set for December third, in the hopes that Elizabeth would be sufficiently recovered by then to attend. Conversation and ideas for the event continued for another half an hour before Mr. Bennet and Jane finally rose to depart.

As they made their farewells, Mr. Bingley offered, "I will send my carriage for you within the hour, Miss Bennet. Will that allow enough time to prepare the things you need before you return?"

"Yes, Mr. Bingley, that should allow me sufficient time to prepare."

CHAPTER 16

THE NEXT MORNING, Elizabeth awoke slowly, her mind confused, and she could not immediately recall where she was or why. When she attempted to move, the intense pain in her side quickly reminded her of the events of yesterday. She stilled her movements as the images played over in her mind. She did not wish to think about Wickham and so chose to dwell instead on the fact that she was officially being courted by Mr. Darcy. Her heart soared! She glanced at the window and noticed the bright sunlight around the edges and wondered what time it was. She turned to the clock on the mantle and was surprised to see that it was half past nine. As she was looking for the bell pull, the maid assigned to care for her entered.

"Good morning, Miss Elizabeth," said Annie, "how are you feeling this morning?"

"Good morning, Annie. I feel very well rested, but the pain in my side is certainly making itself known."

Annie helped Elizabeth to refresh herself and prepare for the day. By the time she was finished and back in bed, Jane entered followed by a maid with the breakfast tray. As the maid prepared the tray and poured tea for the ladies, Jane and Annie moved Elizabeth to a reclining position. Annie continued to support her while Jane brought the invalid feeder filled with broth and helped her to drink. When she finished the broth, Jane asked if she wanted to have tea or if she preferred to rest for a bit first.

"If you do not mind, I would rather have the tea now; being moved into this position was a most unpleasant experience, and I would much rather attempt it as infrequently as possible." After she had finished, Jane took a seat beside her and visited while she drank her cup of tea.

They had not been talking very long when there was a knock on the door. At Elizabeth's call to enter, Mr. Darcy and Mr. Bingley entered, remaining near the door.

"Good morning, Miss Elizabeth, how are you today?" asked Mr. Bingley in his usual jovial manner.

"Good morning, Mr. Bingley, Mr. Darcy. I am well, thank you." Elizabeth's attempt at a smile did not quite achieve its purpose as the swelling in her face was more pronounced today.

"I was hoping that I might borrow Miss Bennet to join me for a walk in the gardens. It is a little chilly, but the sun is shining brightly, and I thought we should take advantage of the good weather while we can."

"I would be happy to release her to you, sir. Perhaps Mr. and Miss Darcy might be kind enough to keep me company in your absence?" she asked Darcy, an eyebrow arched in question.

"It would be my pleasure, Miss Elizabeth." Darcy gave her an affectionate smile. Darcy turned to Annie. "Would you please ask Miss Darcy and Mrs. Annesley to join us here?" Annie bobbed a curtsey and left through the dressing room door.

The others chatted briefly as they awaited the arrival of the ladies. It was only a matter of moments before Mrs. Annesley entered the bedroom. She cast a significant look at Darcy as she seated herself in the corner and took up the stitchery she brought with her.

As soon as Jane and Bingley left, Darcy turned to Mrs. Annesley and asked, "How is my sister this morning? She is up, I presume."

"Yes, Mr. Darcy, she is awake and has been for some time, but she is hesitant to see Miss Elizabeth. She feels responsible for her injuries and is afraid to face her," replied Mrs. Annesley softly, shaking her head.

Darcy looked at Elizabeth questioningly, and before he could answer, Elizabeth turned to Mrs. Annesley saying, "Would you please tell Miss Darcy that I must speak with her? Tell her I cannot rest without assuring myself of her wellbeing."

"Of course, Miss Elizabeth," she answered. She gave Darcy a meaningful look before exiting the room to find her charge. It took several minutes before Mrs. Annesley re-entered the room and resumed her seat.

Georgiana stood near the door, hesitant to enter. Darcy and Elizabeth exchanged a look, concern and questions in their respective eyes.

Elizabeth reached out her hand to Georgiana with a smile on her face. Georgiana's tenuous control over her emotions broke as she rushed forward, tears streaming down her face. She sank to her knees beside the bed clutching Elizabeth's outstretched hand. "Oh, Lizzy, I am so sorry. I am a terrible friend, whenever I am near, you get drawn into trouble."

"Georgie, you did nothing wrong," said Elizabeth firmly, "and you certainly had nothing whatsoever to do with my injuries. It is I who must apologize to you. I pray you were not hurt in your fall. I had hoped that by pushing you towards Wickham, we might have a chance to escape by catching him unawares. I forgot that with your feet tied you would not be able to stumble towards him, and I certainly never dreamed that he would let you fall. Please tell me you were not injured." The obvious concern in Elizabeth's voice helped Georgiana to regain control of her tears.

"Oh no, please do not worry. I have only a bruise or two, but they do not bother me. You, however, were shot! Are you in much pain?" she asked in concern.

"Let us just say that it is an experience I hope not to repeat," said Elizabeth with a wry smile. "The pain is not too bad unless I twist my body. Mr. Jones said that I will have to be still for several days. I am sure that I will be more bothered by boredom than discomfort, so I will depend on your company to keep me sane," said Elizabeth smilingly.

The three continued their conversation for quite some time. They were surprised when the clock showed that it was half past twelve.

"I wonder what could be keeping Jane and Mr. Bingley?" Elizabeth asked. "I would have expected them to return before now."

She had barely finished speaking when there was a knock on the door that was quickly followed by Mrs. Bennet bursting into the room.

"I will not have you lazing about here at Netherfield, Lizzy! You need to be home at Longbourn, as Mr. Collins wishes to spend time with you. I demand that you return home with me immediately!" Mrs. Bennet cried crossly.

Elizabeth stared at her mother with her mouth open, her cheeks blushing a deep red in humiliation. Darcy, barely able to keep his temper in check at this thoughtless and uncaring behavior towards his dear Elizabeth, glared at Mrs. Bennet, his lips pressed together firmly and his arms folded over his chest. Georgiana, could not imagine a mother speaking to her child in such a way and moved closer to and slightly behind her brother.

Elizabeth finally managed to find her voice saying, "Mama, perhaps we could discuss this when Mr. and Miss Darcy are not present."

Mrs. Bennet looked around for the first time noticing the others. "Oh, Mr. Darcy, Miss Darcy, please do not feel you must spend time with Lizzy. I am sure she is only pretending to be hurt for the attention." Turning back to Elizabeth she raged, "What can you be thinking entertaining a gentleman in your bedchamber? You will shame our family with your wanton behavior!"

Elizabeth was nearly in tears from the harsh words her mother flung at her. Seeing this, Darcy could remain silent no longer. "Excuse me, Mrs. Bennet, but Miss Elizabeth was seriously injured during a walk through the gardens yesterday morning. Mr. Jones has said it will be at least a week before she can get out of bed, and most likely two weeks before she will be able to return home." Darcy's words were coldly and firmly spoken, and a frown was in evidence upon his face.

Mrs. Bennet turned back to Elizabeth, sneeringly asking, "What were you doing, Lizzy, climbing trees again? Will you never learn to act like a proper young lady? What would Mr. Collins think if he knew of your poor behavior?"

Lizzy wanted to scream, *"What do I care what he thinks of me!"* but was far too tired and too embarrassed to continue to fight with her mother. "I am sorry to have inconvenienced you, Mama; you need not return to check on me. I shall be home as soon as Mr. Jones allows," she said in a defeated voice.

"You may be certain I shall not waste my time in coming to see you. I intend to speak to Mr. Jones and insist that you come home. If you must remain at Netherfield, I will send Mr. Collins to visit with you. If you are well enough to entertain Mr. Darcy in your bedchamber, then you can certainly entertain Mr. Collins and show him the attention that he deserves." The disdain from her mother was obvious, and the words were delivered with a sniff.

Turning to the Darcys she practically simpered. "Miss Darcy, you must not squander your time in visiting Lizzy. I am sure you would much prefer the company of my youngest daughter, Lydia. She is so lively and beautiful. She would be a wonderful friend for you, much better than Lizzy."

Georgiana, who was starting to be angry on her friend's behalf, said, "I do not consider it a misuse of my time, Mrs. Bennet. Lizzy is the best person I know and the dearest friend I have ever had. It is a pleasure to spend as much time with her as I can."

Mrs. Bennet looked a little startled at her response; she could not imagine why anyone would wish to spend time with Elizabeth especially when they could enjoy Lydia's lively company.

"Dear Miss Darcy, you are too good to my Lizzy. She certainly does not deserve such attention."

Mrs. Annesley had drawn closer to the side of the bed during the conversation in concern for Miss Elizabeth's health. She spoke firmly to Mrs. Bennet. "Please allow me to show you to the door, Mrs. Bennet. I believe that Miss Elizabeth needs to rest as the doctor suggested." Darcy gave Mrs. Annesley a grateful smile and nod of appreciation for her words.

Thinking that Mrs. Annesley's comment showed great attention to herself, she said, "How kind of you, madam." Unfortunately, before leaving, she turned back to Elizabeth and said. "I will not be back to see you again, and I expect you home soon, Lizzy. Do not dare ignore my instructions."

"Good day, Mr. Darcy, Miss Darcy." Mrs. Bennet's tone was ingratiating as she flounced out the door after Mrs. Annesley.

Elizabeth had turned her head away from the Darcys so that they would not see the tears streaming down her face. Darcy and Georgiana shared a look as each moved to kneel on a different side of her bed. Georgiana reached for her hand and said, "Oh, Lizzy, I am so sorry to have brought your mother's displeasure upon you. Did your father not explain to her what had happened?"

"I do not know what he told her, but it would appear he made light of my injuries so as to spare himself listening to her wail about her nerves." Annoyance and hurt were evident in Elizabeth's soft voice.

"What was all that about Mr. Collins?" Darcy was confused and decidedly irritated.

Not wishing to tell Darcy about the way her mother was pushing her at Mr. Collins, she evasively replied, "I have no idea. My mother is always going on about one thing or another."

Darcy was certain that she was withholding something from him but decided that it was a conversation better left until they had a moment alone.

At that moment, a maid appeared at the door announcing that lunch was being served. Darcy stood to leave, but Georgiana said, "William would you mind if I stay and have lunch with Miss Elizabeth?"

"Not at all, Georgie. I will see that a tray is sent up to you and Mrs. Annesley with Miss Elizabeth's lunch." He kissed his sister's head and picked up Elizabeth's hand from the bed. He bestowed a soft kiss on the back before returning it to its place. With a smile for the two ladies dearest to his heart, he left the room, closing the door softly.

Georgiana settled into the chair near the bed and began speaking softly with Elizabeth. "Lizzy, I do not know how to thank you for staying with me and trying to protect me from Mr.

Wickham. I wish that I could be as brave as you are."

"I think you are brave in your own way, Georgie. You made it difficult for Mr. Wickham to take you away yesterday, and today you defended me to my mother just now."

"Lizzy, why does your mother treat you so poorly?"

"I wish I knew, Georgie. I know I am not one of her favorites, but it seems as the years go by she dislikes me more and more."

"But, you are such a wonderful person! It is almost as if she does not even know you. Your mother would not behave in such a way if she did." Georgiana's confidently spoken words gave solace to Elizabeth's battered feelings.

"I am just glad I get to recuperate at Netherfield, as it will spare me her daily displeasure," said Elizabeth solemnly.

Mrs. Annesley, who had quietly returned as the girls spoke, said, "Miss Elizabeth, if I might suggest, perhaps your mother is envious of your close relationship with your father. As you said, sometimes, unhappy people take their unhappiness out on others," Mrs. Annesley offered quietly.

"That is correct, Lizzy. When I told you about my Aunt Catherine you said, 'You are a wonderful young lady, intelligent, poised, and talented. Do not listen to your Aunt because nothing she says about you is true.' The same thing could be said regarding what your mother said about you." Elizabeth mustered her best smile in thanks and acknowledgement of Georgiana's encouragement.

The maid entered with lunch for the ladies and the broth and tea for Elizabeth. Mrs. Annesley helped Annie raise Elizabeth again to the reclining position. As Annie supported her, Mrs. Annesley held the invalid feeder for her until she had completed the broth and her tea. Elizabeth lay back among the pillows and chatted with the ladies as they enjoyed their luncheon. They were happily discussing the upcoming ball when Georgiana looked over to ask Elizabeth a question, only to find her fast asleep.

The day after her accident, information was received from Mr. Moore, Netherfield's steward, that it appeared Wickham had been staying in an abandoned cottage near Netherfield's border with Longbourn. While Elizabeth was sleeping, Darcy and Bingley rode out to see the cottage, and there were signs of recent use—scraps of food and trash remained as well as empty liquor bottles. There had been no sightings of Wickham, but Darcy still felt certain he had been there. When he realized how close it was to where he met Elizabeth on her morning walks, he realized Wickham could have easily heard their conversation that morning and known of their plans for the day.

Then the very next day, Darcy heard from Mr. Stevens regarding the rumor of the denied living. He said a stranger in the pub told three gentlemen the story after overhearing them speak of Darcy dancing twice with a young lady at the last assembly. Darcy now knew all he could about the situation to relay to Richard in his next letter. They would have the men they had used after the event in Ramsgate come to Meryton and see if they could find anything to help them locate Wickham. He hoped that Richard might have some new idea about how they could find Wickham as well. Darcy desperately wanted him found and finally punished for his many misdeeds.

It was teatime and a knock on the door aroused Elizabeth from her slumbers. Rising from her chair, Annie answered the knock as Elizabeth stretched and rubbed her eyes. Darcy entered with a tray followed by Mrs. Annesley. "Good afternoon, Miss Elizabeth," Darcy said warmly. He stopped as he got a good look at Elizabeth. She lay back among the pillows, her face flushed, eyes warm and sleepy, and dozens of curls had come loose from her braid and curled around her face. He imagined seeing this every morning for the rest of his life and felt his body react to the well-loved look she presented.

Attempting to control his reaction, he said, "How are you feeling this afternoon? Did you enjoy your rest?"

"I am well thank you, Mr. Darcy," she said with a slight smile that did not reach her eyes.

A concerned look crossed his face as he glanced at Mrs. Annesley. Darcy set the tray down and moved to Elizabeth's side. "Here, allow me to assist you, and Mrs. Annesley will help you with the feeder."

"I am not very hungry." Elizabeth's listlessness caused Darcy to look at Mrs. Annesley in concern.

"Mr. Jones left strict instructions about how often you must eat, Miss Elizabeth," said Mrs. Annesley firmly.

Darcy moved to the edge of the bed and placed his arm under Elizabeth's body lifting her shoulders to allow her to drink the broth. He loved the feel of her in his arms but soon became conscious of the fact that she seemed unusually warm.

"Miss Elizabeth, has Mr. Jones been here to see you yet today?"

"Jane told me there was an emergency, and he said he would be delayed until this afternoon before he could visit."

Darcy looked at Mrs. Annesley and tried to convey his question to her without speaking. She nodded her understanding and reached out to brush some curls from Elizabeth's forehead managing to allow her fingers contact with the skin there. Concern on her face, she nodded to Darcy.

Darcy looked at Annie seated quietly in the corner. "Please have Mrs. Dawson bring some cold water and rags as well as her medicine bag immediately. I believe Miss Elizabeth has developed a fever."

Annie rushed to do as she was bid. Darcy and Mrs. Annesley encouraged Elizabeth to finish the broth and tea and had only just succeeded as Mrs. Dawson, Jane, and Georgiana all arrived in the room.

Darcy laid Elizabeth back onto the bed and was tightly holding her hand in his. Mrs. Dawson and Jane rushed to the other side of the bed where Mrs. Annesley was, and Georgiana stepped up next to her brother putting her hand on his shoulder.

"Mr. Darcy," said Mrs. Dawson, "you must leave the room, sir. I need to remove the bandage and check the wound. Darcy looked at Elizabeth lying so still beside him, her eyes glassy and half closed.

"I will be nearby, Miss Elizabeth. You must fight this infection and recover. I wish to dance with you at Mr. Bingley's ball, and we have an appointment in town after Christmas. Please, Elizabeth, promise me you will fight to get better." Darcy squeezed her hand and was encouraged by the faint pressure he received in return." He moved to the door and, with one last look he exited, closing the door behind him.

Darcy found Bingley in the hall staring at the door. "What is happening, Darcy?"

"Miss Elizabeth has developed a fever," he answered grimly.

Bingley led Darcy next door to the sitting room attached to Elizabeth's room and poured two drinks. He handed one to Darcy as they sat to wait.

Suddenly Darcy asked, "Has someone been sent for Mr. Jones?"

"There was an accident this morning, and he had to attend the emergency at a farm about ten miles from Meryton," answered Bingley. "I sent one footman to his office in case he had returned and another to the farm where the accident occurred this morning. With any luck, he is finished there, and the servant will meet him on his way here."

The gentlemen became silent as they waited for word of Miss Elizabeth's condition.

Next door, Mrs. Dawson removed the bandage covering Elizabeth's wound, and the ladies could all see the redness expanding out from the wounded area. Getting her first look at the wound, Georgiana paled a little and swayed on her feet.

"Sit down, Miss Darcy," said Mrs. Annesley firmly.

Georgiana straightened her spine. "I am fine, Mrs. Annesley. I want to help Lizzy."

"Perhaps you should join your brother for now. There will be much to do to care for Miss Elizabeth. Let us get her settled and you can come back and help in a bit."

Georgiana leaned down and kissed Elizabeth's forehead. "Please get better, Lizzy."

The ladies waited until the door closed before discussing what they should do. Jane and Mrs. Annesley were each wiping Elizabeth's face, neck, and arms with the cool water and rags. They were discussing various poultices that could help to reduce her fever and fight the infection. Into this conversation walked Mr. Jones.

"What is going on, ladies?" Concern for the young lady was clear in his voice.

"Miss Elizabeth has taken a fever, sir, and I do not like the look of her wound," Mrs. Dawson informed the apothecary.

Mr. Jones moved to the bed and examined Elizabeth's side. The skin around the stitches was swollen and red, and there were streaks beginning to appear that radiated out from the wound. "You are correct, Mrs. Dawson; this is not good. You've made a good start by attempting to cool her body down, but we need to make a poultice for the wound." Rummaging through his medical bag he pulled out a card. "I think this would be the best one."

Mrs. Dawson took the card and rushed from the room. She gathered the needed items from the stillroom and took everything to Mrs. Mills, the Netherfield cook. She instructed Mrs. Mills to prepare the poultice per the instructions on Mr. Jones' card and send it up as soon as it was ready. While in the kitchen, she got another bowl of cold water and returned to Elizabeth's suite.

Within twenty minutes, a maid brought the poultice. Mr. Jones applied it to the wound and re-bandaged the area. "This should be changed every two hours until the redness is gone. If it grows any redder, you should change it every hour. Do you think you will have enough of the needed ingredients, or should I send more to you?" asked Mr. Jones.

"I believe we will have enough of everything, but I will send a message if I run low on anything," Mrs. Dawson replied.

"Do you wish me to check back later this evening or would you prefer to call me if something arises?"

"I believe we will be able to manage things, sir," Mrs. Dawson informed him, "but I will not hesitate to send for you if you are needed."

"Well, ladies, I will leave you now to get some rest in case I am needed later," and, so saying, he departed for his office.

Georgiana left the room and went in search of the gentlemen in Darcy's sitting room. When he was not there, she returned to the hall and called, "Brother?" Darcy came from the entrance of the sitting room attached to Elizabeth's chamber where he and Bingley waited and asked, "How is she?"

Making her way towards him, Georgiana replied, "I am not sure; her wound was all red when they removed the bandage, and Mrs. Annesley suggested I join you."

Georgiana took a seat near her brother, and he reached out and patted her hand comfortingly. At that moment, they noticed Mr. Jones passing the door on his way to Elizabeth's room.

Darcy began to pace the carpet as he waited for a report. He was frantic to know what was happening with *his* Elizabeth. He did not know what he would do if something happened to her. He could not imagine facing the rest of his life without her.

After what seemed like an eternity, Mr. Jones exited Elizabeth's room. Seeing him pass the sitting room door without stopping, Darcy called out, "Mr. Jones, how is Elizabeth?" If anyone noticed his familiar use of her name, they said nothing.

"If we can keep her fever from increasing and pull the infection from the wound with the poultice I prescribed, she should be fine.

Unfortunately, Mr. Darcy, fevers can be very unpredictable. We can only wait and see, and I would suggest praying. I will return in the morning, but Mrs. Dawson has promised to send for me if her fever increases."

Darcy looked at the empty doorway as Mr. Jones' footsteps faded away. He moved to the entrance of Elizabeth's room and knocked impatiently. Mrs. Dawson opened the door slightly in answer to his knock, and he gruffly said, "I need to see Miss Elizabeth."

"I am sorry, Mr. Darcy, but admitting you at present would be inappropriate. Miss Elizabeth is asleep, and we are attempting to bring her fever down as quickly as we can." Mrs. Dawson gave him an understanding smile as she closed the door.

Darcy turned and slowly made his way back to the sitting room. The look on his face caused Bingley to pale and tears to spring to Georgiana's eyes. "What is wrong? Is Elizabeth worse?"

"I do not think so, but I was not permitted to see her for myself to be sure." His tone was dejected and his concern obvious. "Georgiana, perhaps you could go to her. I just need to know how she fares—to be sure that she is no worse," he pleaded.

"Of course, brother, I will return as soon as possible." And so saying, she rushed from the room, entering Elizabeth's room without even knocking. "How is she?"

"Her condition is unchanged, but we should know something more when we change the poultice for the first time. I suggest you remain with your brother for he will be in need of comfort. Perhaps you can attend her after dinner until it is time for you to retire," Mrs. Annesley offered to placate Georgiana.

"Very well, but my brother would like to be kept apprised of everything that happens with Miss Elizabeth. I have never seen him so worried before."

Georgiana's return to the sitting room was the beginning of one of the longest days of Darcy's life. He refused to leave the room even to eat. He said he needed to be near Elizabeth in case she needed him. Bingley and Georgiana remained with him there until dinner was announced. Georgiana offered to stay and dine with her brother, but he insisted that she eat in the dining room. He needed some time alone with his worry.

After dinner, Georgiana went to Elizabeth's room to relieve Jane in bathing Elizabeth's skin with the cool water to help bring her fever down. She was able to observe the wound when the poultice was changed. She was thankful that it looked no worse, but she could not see that it had improved either, which was cause for concern. She worked for three hours helping to care for her dearest friend. As night approached a knock at the door revealed Mr. Darcy. "I have come to escort my sister to her room and request that I be allowed to see Miss Elizabeth before retiring."

Annie, who had just returned to care for Elizabeth through the night, looked at the others in the room before answering. Georgiana cast a pleading look at Mrs. Annesley, who had been with Elizabeth throughout the afternoon. She paused in her work and pulled the covers up over Elizabeth's body before nodding her head in approval. Annie opened the door wider, and Darcy rushed to the side of Elizabeth's bed. He knelt there and reached for her hand, holding it between both of his. Her skin was still warm to the touch, but he was relieved to see that it felt no hotter than the last time he had held it. Mrs. Annesley and Georgiana stepped back a bit to allow a moment of privacy between the couple.

"My dearest Elizabeth," he said softly, "you must rest and fight this infection so that you will recover. I need to request my dances for the ball before another can ask. It will be a wonderful evening! You must recover so that we can enjoy it together. Good night, my dear, sleep well. Know that you will remain in my prayers throughout the night." After placing a lingering kiss on her hand, he stood and moved to his sister and Mrs. Annesley offering to escort both of them from the room.

After delivering the ladies to their rooms, Darcy retired to his dressing room and allowed Chalmers to assist him in preparing for the evening. Knowing that he would not find sleep this night, he was washed and shaved and dressed in his shirt, pants, and robe with house slippers on his feet. He took up his book and seated himself in a chair by the fire, a glass of brandy at his side. His book held his attention for quite some time, but eventually his thoughts drifted to Elizabeth. He tried to push his worry aside and think instead about their future life together and the things he would like to show her during the upcoming visit to town. He wished to take her to the theater and an opera, to the British Museum, and his favorite bookshop. He would like to walk with her in the park and take her for ices at Gunter's. He knew it would be more enjoyable for him to view it all anew through her eyes. Eventually, he drifted off to sleep where dreams filled with his Elizabeth waited.

CHAPTER 17

ELIZABETH'S FEVER BROKE around four o'clock in the morning, and Annie fell into an exhausted sleep in the chair by Elizabeth's bed. She had her head resting on the bed and was holding onto Miss Elizabeth's hand to ensure that the fever did not return. She was awakened from her sleep by a weak voice calling her name.

"Annie, will you please get me some water?"

"Oh, yes, miss," she said with a smile. She eased Elizabeth up to give her some of the water. "You sure gave us a fright, Miss Elizabeth, what with your fever and all. Almost everyone was helping to cool you for the last twelve hours or more."

"I am sorry to have been such a bother," Elizabeth said weakly.

"'And poor Mr. Darcy, he was so worried about you, he was."

"Was Mr. Darcy here?"

"Well, Mrs. Annesley would not let him in much because we had you uncovered, but she did let him come and say good night. He would not move further than the sitting room next door all day—not even to eat, poor man."

Despite the early hour, a soft knock was heard at the door, and Annie moved to open it.

"How is Miss Elizabeth this morning, Annie?" came Darcy's soft voice.

She looked back at Elizabeth, who nodded weakly. "She is doing better, sir. Her fever broke early this morning, and she is awake now. Would you like to speak with her, sir?"

"Certainly, if I may."

Annie opened the door wider and admitted Darcy to Elizabeth's room. As they were not properly chaperoned, he remained near the door, but the relief he felt at seeing her beautiful eyes once again open was great.

"Good morning, Miss Elizabeth." He bowed slightly, a relieved smile on his face. "I hope you are feeling much improved this morning."

"I am, thank you, Mr. Darcy, but I did not feel poorly before, in fact, I cannot even remember the last several hours."

"Well, you must promise never to be ill like that again; I do not believe that I could withstand the strain."

"I am sorry to have caused everyone so much worry."

"I will let you return to resting, but hope you will allow me to visit with you later?"

"I would like that, Mr. Darcy." The words were barely out of Elizabeth's mouth before sleep reclaimed her.

With a warm smile and a bow, he left the room, pausing for one last look at the beautiful sleeping woman he left behind.

Later that day, after Elizabeth awakened, and her needs had been attended to, she was able to receive the others at teatime. Again Mr. Darcy held her up as she was given her broth and tea. Then she lay back to enjoy her visitors as the others enjoyed their tea.

Darcy looked at Elizabeth inquiringly. "Miss Elizabeth, I would like to take this opportunity to ask you for a dance at the ball. Might I request your hand for the first, supper, and last sets of the evening?"

Elizabeth was taken aback at his request. "Mr. Darcy, are you sure you know what you are asking? Dancing three times will give rise to talk."

"I am very well aware of what my request implies, Miss Elizabeth. As we are courting, and my intentions are honorable, I believe people already assume there will eventually be a marriage between us. I know it is what I hope for." The intense look he gave her sent a shiver down Elizabeth's spine and made her body flush as though her fever had returned.

"If you are sure it is your wish, Mr. Darcy. I would be very pleased to accept your request and grant you the first, supper, and last sets of the evening at Mr. Bingley's ball." Her uninjured cheek showed a blush and her eyes had a sparkle in them for the first time since her injury. He thought she had never looked more beautiful.

Inspired by his friend's behavior, Mr. Bingley made the same request of Jane before the conversation turned to a discussion of other subjects.

The days of Elizabeth's recovery passed quickly and most pleasantly. The young couples, along with Georgiana, Mrs. Annesley, and occasionally the Hursts, passed many pleasant hours in conversation and word games. Mary visited daily, Charlotte Lucas called to visit several times, and Mr. Jones came to check on Elizabeth each day, announcing that he was very pleased with her progress. Mr. Collins also called daily, but he was always told she was resting and never allowed to see her.

When Elizabeth was finally allowed to sit up in the bed, Mr. Darcy requested permission from Mr. Jones for Elizabeth to be moved to the sitting room connected to her bedchamber on the following day. There was a chaise there on which she could recline, and it would give her a much-needed change of scenery. Receiving Mr. Jones' permission, the others made plans to make Elizabeth's first day out of her room a special one.

The next morning, when Annie helped her prepare for the day, she was given a proper bath, her hair was washed, dried, and attractively styled, and she was dressed in a loose day dress.

Once she was ready, a knock came at the door, and Darcy entered her room accompanied by Jane. Darcy noted that the swelling was gone from her cheek and that the bruises were much faded.

"Lizzy, we have a surprise for you today. Mr. Jones has said you may leave your bed, so Mr. Darcy is to carry you to your surprise."

Darcy stepped up to where Elizabeth was seated on the side of her bed and extending his arms said, "With your permission, Miss Elizabeth." Upon receiving her nod, Darcy placed one arm behind her shoulders and another under her knees and effortlessly lifted her, holding her uninjured side against his chest.

He was overwhelmed by the sweet scent of her hair and deep blush suffusing her face. In her turn, Elizabeth felt surrounded by his clean woodsy smell and the warmth of his body. Their eyes met, and their feelings were clearly displayed for the other to see. They were lost in one another, neither able to look away. Fortunately, Mrs. Annesley, who had entered with Jane, softly cleared her throat recalling them both to the present. Darcy and Elizabeth each released a sigh and Elizabeth a soft giggle. He looked down at her, "Is there something you find amusing about this, Miss Elizabeth?" asked Darcy, trying to control his chuckle.

"I think, sir, that our courtship could be a challenge, a delightful challenge, but a challenge nonetheless," she replied with a smile and a raised brow.

"I find all my encounters with you to be a delightful challenge, Miss Elizabeth, so I will have to be on my guard," Darcy lowered his voice whispering, "and my best behavior," he finished with a roguish smile. He delighted in her renewed blush as he moved out of the room and settled her on the chaise in the sitting room.

Everyone in the house, with the addition of Charlotte Lucas, Mary, and Mr. Bennet were in the sitting room awaiting Elizabeth. The room had been rearranged to include a large table, and luncheon was spread upon it.

"We wanted to celebrate your improving health with you, Miss Elizabeth," said Mrs. Hurst pleasantly. "We are delighted to see you doing so much better."

"Indeed we are," added Mr. Hurst.

"I certainly wanted to celebrate with you, my Lizzy, as this improvement means that your return home cannot be too far off," said her father happily. "There has been no sense in the house with you and Jane gone, and Mr. Collins' addition has made things worse, not better. I swear the man is no more sensible than your mother and youngest sisters," he concluded with a wry grin.

Elizabeth felt tears welling in her eyes at the kindness being shown her, especially since her father had, in fact, bestirred himself from his library to visit with her. She looked around the table at those present, the tears glistening. "I cannot thank you enough for all that you have done to aid me in my recovery. I feel very blessed to have such good friends and family here to celebrate with me."

The group passed a merry time as they enjoyed the meal. Later they played a parlor game or two and then enjoyed tea together. After tea, her father announced that it was time for him to leave and offered to convey Charlotte home on his way. "Well, Lizzy, I hope that I shall see you home very soon, my dear. Until then be sure you rest enough as I am quite sure you will not get much rest once you have returned home. I gather from all the fussing your mother has been doing that there is much to be done to prepare for the ball at Netherfield." With a kiss on her forehead, her father and Charlotte departed, escorted by the Hursts.

The remainder of the group continued their pleasant discussions. However, Darcy noticed that Elizabeth had attempted to hide a yawn or two and suggested he return her to her bed to rest until dinner. Though she would have preferred to remain, she was tired and knew that she should rest if she hoped to be completely recovered in time for the ball.

The remainder of Elizabeth's recuperation passed very pleasantly, with each couple spending as much time together as possible. They knew they would not have another opportunity to be together like this for quite some time. Darcy appeared in the sitting room one afternoon with an armful of flowers from the conservatory.

"Oh how beautiful!" exclaimed Elizabeth. "Thank you so much, Mr. Darcy, they are so lovely."

"I know how you enjoy the outdoors, and since you cannot be in the gardens as you would wish, I thought I would bring some of the gardens to you." The warm smile that accompanied his words made Elizabeth's heart beat a little faster. "I wanted to make a request of you, Miss Elizabeth. Would you be willing to call me by my given name when we are alone?"

Elizabeth blushed and replied shyly, "Would that be proper? We are only courting not engaged?"

"I know it is not entirely proper, but it would only be when we are speaking to one another."

She blushed brightly feeling shy at his request. "I would like that, Mr. . . . Fitzwilliam. Is that the name you wish me to use?"

"Well, I do like it better hearing it from your lips than I ever have in the past, but I thought perhaps you could call me William as my family does." The warmth in his eyes as he said these words made Elizabeth's heart beat faster still.

Just then, a maid entered in answer to his summons and took the flowers to put in a vase and to find Georgiana to join them. They continued to converse quietly as they waited for her. She quickly made her appearance, and they passed the remainder of the afternoon in pleasant conversation.

Finally, the day came that the young couples and Georgiana had been both hoping for and dreading. After Mr. Jones' visit, exactly two weeks from the day of the accident, he reported that Miss Elizabeth would be well enough to return home in two days. He gave her permission to be out of bed for the entire next day and to attempt the stairs. If she could successfully handle those tasks, she would be permitted to return home the day after that.

On the day before her return to Longbourn, Darcy and Elizabeth were sharing the sitting room with Jane and Bingley. The couples had separated after tea to opposite sides of the room for quiet conversation since Mrs. Annesley and Georgiana were working on her studies.

"Elizabeth, after I received your father's permission to court you, I mentioned to him that I would like to have you return to town after the holidays. If you are agreeable, I wish very much for you to have the opportunity to experience the life of the ton. The balls and dinner parties among the ton are not something I particularly enjoy," he said with a grimace. "However, it is a responsibility I bear if I wish for Georgiana to have the best opportunities when she makes her debut. There are events that I must attend, and I wish to have you experience them with me. I would not wish you to regret anything should our relationship progress as I hope." Here he paused and gave her a warm look. "I have written to my aunt, Lady Matlock, about our courtship and she offered her assistance in introducing you into society. She was quite pleased to learn that I am courting someone, as I have shown no interest in any of the long line of debutantes to whom she has introduced me over the years. She would like to extend an invitation to you to attend the family's Twelfth Night ball. She also offered to help with preparing a ball gown for you. I do not wish to offend you; but, no matter how lovely you looked at the assembly, your gown would not be appropriate for a ball among the ton."

Elizabeth's face showed slight embarrassment. "I do not believe there would be time to have a gown prepared if I do not return to town until after the holidays."

"I would be most pleased if you would allow me to gift the gown to you for Christmas, Miss Elizabeth," Darcy said hopefully.

"Now we both know that would be most improper, sir." She smiled at him to soften her words.

"It would not be inappropriate if the gift came from Georgiana," he said persuasively.

Elizabeth laughed warmly at his determination. "Be that as it may, sir, there still would not be time to prepare it after the holidays.

"My aunt suggested that you have your local dressmaker send your measurements to her. Then she will meet with her modiste to prepare a gown for the ball. You can have it fitted upon your arrival to town." He spoke decidedly hoping to encourage Elizabeth to accept.

She knew that her clothes were not of the quality or style to mingle among the ton, but she did not wish Darcy to think her mercenary. Finally, she said, "Perhaps I could contact my aunt to have a dress made by her modiste. Though not well known, the gowns she has previously made for me were quite well done. As my aunt is already familiar with my taste, it would be quite easy for her to select something I would like."

Why was she resisting, he wondered? He did not want to offend her, but he very much wanted to give her this gift. There were many gifts he would like to give her, and hoped to have the opportunity to do so often in the future. For now, he would have to be tactful. "I believe I have the perfect solution. Perhaps your aunt would enjoy accompanying my aunt to make the selection together?" Compromise had worked for them before, and he hoped it would be successful now.

Elizabeth knew she could not continue to argue with him without disclosing the fact that she was concerned about the cost of such a gown, so she acquiesced to his request. She felt she could rely on her aunt's good sense to keep the cost of the gown reasonable. "I will accept that I need a new gown for the ball, Mr. Darcy, but I would prefer that my father pay for it on this occasion, please."

Darcy studied the look on her face trying to determine the cause of her reluctance. She looked a little embarrassed and a little concerned. Finally, it occurred to him that she did not want people to think her mercenary should it be discovered that he bought the gown. Smiling to realize that she loved him and not what he could give her, he said, "I believe that would be perfectly acceptable. Perhaps we could stop in town on the way back to Longbourn to pick up the information. Then I will quickly send it off to my aunt. If you could provide me with your aunt's name and direction, I will include that information, as well. Miss Elizabeth, no matter how beautiful the gown they select for you, it can only enhance your loveliness. I shall be quite the envy of all those in attendance, as I will be escorting the most beautiful woman at the ball."

Dinner that evening was a gay affair with good company, good conversation, and a sumptuous meal as the Bennet sisters were to return home on the morrow.

CHAPTER 18

Darcy and Georgiana accompanied Elizabeth and Jane on their return to Longbourn. William handed out Jane and Georgiana and then gently assisted Elizabeth out of the carriage. He offered her his arm, and the four of them made their way into the house. Once the servant had relieved everyone of their outer clothes, they entered the parlor to find the female members of the Bennet family and Mr. Collins present.

"Well, it is about time you returned, Miss Lizzy. I told you to come home sooner as Mr. Collins wanted to spend time with you. Then when he called upon you at Netherfield, he was always told you were sleeping, and he could not see you. Must you always defy me?" Mrs. Bennet asked in a loud, angry voice.

"Mama!" said Jane and Mary in shocked voices.

Elizabeth felt Mr. Darcy stiffen at her side. She started to remove her hand from his arm as she began to speak, but Darcy quickly covered it with his other hand to prevent her from doing so.

"I was not attempting to defy you, Mama. I came home on the very day that Mr. Jones said I could, even though those at Netherfield encouraged me to stay longer to be sure I was recovered," said Elizabeth quietly, her cheeks suffused with embarrassment and her eyes on the floor.

Mr. Collins looked askance at Elizabeth's hand on Mr. Darcy's arm. He hurried up to her and pulled on her free arm to move her away from Darcy causing her to groan slightly, just as Mr. Bennet entered the room behind them.

With a cold glare, Darcy said to Collins, " Please desist in pulling on Miss Elizabeth's arm, as she is only just recovered from an injury and had the stitches removed from her side."

"She is to be my intended, sir. If she needs an arm for support, it shall be mine." Both men heard Elizabeth gasp sharply at this surprising statement. Mr. Bennet also heard his wife's indrawn breath and saw her face suddenly pale as she looked down at the hands clutched in her lap.

"You, sir, are mistaken," said Mr. Darcy. "Now please desist in pulling on Miss Elizabeth."

"Mr. Collins, please leave my daughter be," said Mr. Bennet angrily.

Mr. Collins removed his hands from Elizabeth's arm, and Darcy helped her to a small loveseat. Georgiana quickly seated herself beside Elizabeth while Darcy took the chair at the end nearest Elizabeth. All the while, Mr. Collins glared at Mr. Darcy angrily.

Mr. Darcy turned to Mr. Bennet and asked for an introduction and an explanation. Mr. Bennet replied, "Mr. Darcy, this is my cousin, and the heir to Longbourn, Mr. William Collins, but as for an explanation of his comments, I am afraid I am as puzzled as you."

Collins trembled slightly at hearing the name. Was this his patroness's esteemed nephew? If it was Mr. Darcy, he was engaged to Miss de Bourgh, so why was he behaving in this manner with his cousin, Elizabeth?

"Excuse me," said Mr. Collins, "did I hear my Cousin Bennet correctly? Your name is Mr. Darcy? Are you the nephew of my most benevolent patroness, Lady Catherine de Bourgh?" Darcy could barely nod in acknowledgment of his words before Collins continued. "Then it is even more necessary to remove her from your side, sir, as I am sure that your fiancé would find this a most displeasing sight."

Darcy's glare grew even more glacial. "We have just been introduced, sir. How dare you presume to speak of my personal affairs, and how dare you imply that I am engaged. I am officially courting Miss Elizabeth Bennet with her father's blessing."

Mrs. Bennet's face paled even more as Mr. Collins began stuttering. "B . . bu . . but . . your aunt, my patroness, Lady Catherine de Bourgh, told me of your long-standing engagement to her daughter, sir. You have been promised since you were in your cradles. You cannot mean to ignore your most esteemed aunt's wishes and impose yourself on my cousin who was to be my intended. Now remove yourself from her side, sir, immediately," said Mr. Collins straightening to his full height, which still left him more than a head shorter than Mr. Darcy.

Darcy glanced up at Collins through hooded eyes. The contempt in his gesture was obvious to all in the room, and Mr. Collins bristled with anger as a deep redness infused his face. Turning to Elizabeth, Darcy solemnly inquired, "Miss Elizabeth, may I ask you when this gentleman asked for your hand and presumed your response as he is calling you his intended?"

"Indeed, Mr. Darcy, we have had no such conversation, and if we had my answer would have been no, as Mr. Collins and I are not at all well-suited to one another. You are the only gentleman who has requested any arrangement with me."

"That is as I presumed. I know you to be the kindest, most honest person I have ever met. You would not have accepted my courtship if you were promised to another," said Darcy as he raised Elizabeth's hand to his lips and placed a gentle kiss on the back of it.

Darcy then stood from his chair and stepped closer to Collins. "It seems, Mr. Collins, that you have been very presumptuous regarding your relationship with Miss Elizabeth. I sincerely hope that you have not been spreading this presumption around the neighborhood as I would then be required to defend her honor if you had."

Collins's face lost all of its color in an instant, as he understood the implication of Mr. Darcy's words. He began to sweat profusely and reached for his handkerchief to mop his forehead. He took a quick step back and again stuttered, "N . . n . . n . . no, I have spoken of it to no one outside of this room, but I was promised by her mother that she would be mine. I must return home engaged at the very least. It was Lady Catherine's advice to me to marry one of my cousins to keep them from being homeless upon the loss of their father." His nervousness was pushed aside as his anger again grew. "I am a parson with an excellent living and the heir to this estate, why should she not wish to marry me? She would be lucky to ever receive such a good offer again, and she would be the recipient of the condescension and advice of Lady Catherine's benevolence."

"That is enough, Mr. Collins," roared Mr. Bennet. "How dare you speak so of my daughter and treat a guest in my home with such disrespect. I believe that you should pack your belongings and return to your home in Kent; you are no longer welcome in my home."

Collins's face was again suffused with color as he said, "I have never been so ill-used in my life! How dare you disrespect me, a parson, in this manner! I can now understand why my father wished to have no contact with your branch of the family, and you can be assured that I shall never contact you again! Your family should expect no consideration from me upon your death. I do not care if they do starve in the hedgerows." With that, Collins left the parlor, slamming the door behind him. They listened as he stomped up the stairs to pack his belongings.

Silence followed his departure as everyone glanced at one another not quite knowing what to say. Finally, giggles could be heard coming from the corner where Lydia and Kitty sat. It was not long before a few more chuckles sounded around the room before turning into outright laughter. Even Mrs. Bennet tittered nervously. Over the laughter could be heard the sound of Mr. Collins's trunk thumping down the stairs. They heard him pause in the foyer, and then the door was slammed loudly behind him as he exited Longbourn.

When everyone began to gain control of themselves, Mr. Bennet rose and said, "I believe I have had all the humor I can take for one afternoon. I shall retire to my library." Just as Mrs. Bennet sighed in relief, he continued, "Mrs. Bennet, please join me." He cast a stern eye in her direction as he rose from his chair.

"That would not be proper, Mr. Bennet, as we have guests," she replied nervously.

"I am sure Mr. and Miss Darcy will be thoroughly entertained by our daughters, madam; your presence will not be necessary."

As Mr. and Mrs. Bennet departed to his library, he asked Mrs. Hill to send tea in for the rest of the family.

Elizabeth turned to look at her guests. "Oh, Georgiana, I am so sorry that you had to witness such unpleasantness. What a terrible scene. You will never wish to set foot in Longbourn again." Elizabeth's face flushed with embarrassment.

"Nonsense, Lizzy," Georgiana said encouragingly. "It is not very different from being in the presence of my aunt, and as long as you live here I will always want to visit you." With that, Georgiana patted Elizabeth's hands, arose from the couch, and moved to sit with Mary and discuss music. Jane joined their conversation and gave Darcy and Elizabeth some privacy.

"Please forgive my cousin's behavior, Mr. Darcy. He is a distant relation that we only recently met when he invited himself for a visit. I am sorry for any embarrassment he caused you. I would understand, Mr. Darcy, if you wished to withdraw your offer of courtship. I would not wish for my ridiculous family to cause you any embarrassment in the future." Elizabeth kept her head down through her speech and twisted her hands nervously in her lap.

Darcy stood from his chair and claimed the space on the loveseat that had recently been vacated by Georgiana. He placed his finger under Elizabeth's chin and tipped her face up, forcing her to look at him. It broke his heart to see the tears shimmering in her eyes. "My dear, Elizabeth," he said softly, "there is nothing that could make me change my mind about our courtship. But I hope that you will be equally as forgiving if you are ever in the presence of my Aunt Catherine. She would have no compunction about creating a scene should she feel it necessary." His expression was equal parts smile and grimace, and the look in his eyes made Elizabeth giggle slightly. "That is much better! I prefer your laughter to your tears. In fact, I prefer it to any other sound I have ever heard. It is sweeter than the most beautiful music in the world."

Upon these words, Mrs. Hill entered with the tea tray. Jane moved over to pour for everyone, and the remainder of the Darcys' visit passed peacefully.

In Mr. Bennet's library, however, Mrs. Bennet was not receiving the same forgiveness. "What were you thinking, Mrs. Bennet, promising that ridiculous man the hand of my dear Lizzy. Even if he had proposed, Elizabeth would have said no, and I would have supported her decision. And, may I remind you that any and all applications for the hands of my daughters will go through me, as that is my responsibility and not yours. Do you understand?" he asked firmly.

"Oh, but Mr. Bennet whatever shall we do? I know you will die, and we now know for certain that Mr. Collins will throw us out into the hedgerows. What is to become of me?" Mrs. Bennet whined.

"Have you no sense at all in that head of yours?" Mr. Bennet's frustration was obvious. "Our two eldest daughters are both being courted by wealthy gentlemen. I am sure that Mr. Bingley and Mr. Darcy will do what is necessary to ensure your care upon my demise. However, I would not expect Mr. Darcy to allow you to visit—much less live with them—after the way you have treated Lizzy. Perhaps you will never need to worry about it, and your flutterings and nerves will carry you off before me." Mrs. Bennet's mouth fell open at this remark, as the idea that she might die first had never even crossed her mind.

"Close your mouth, Mrs. Bennet, and open your ears. I have watched the behavior of our guests—particularly Miss Darcy—and realized the disservice that I have done my family through my negligence. Jane and Lizzy behave in the same manner as Miss Darcy, due more to the influence of the Gardiners than that of their parents. In the future, I expect you to think before you speak and to talk with both Lydia and Kitty about their behavior. They are both silly and ill-mannered. I will be speaking to them about this as well. I expect to see marked improvement in all of you, or I will withhold your pin money and deny you permission to leaving the house or receive visitors. Do I make myself clear?"

Mrs. Bennet could only nod her head in bewilderment. Never before had she seen Mr. Bennet behave so forcefully. Upon being excused, she departed for her bedroom to think about what Mr. Bennet had said. She was very angry at the way he addressed her—and particularly angry that

Elizabeth was going to marry better than her dear Jane. However, she knew that Mr. Bennet meant what he said. Could he be correct? She could believe that Jane's behavior and beauty would make any man fall in love with her, but Elizabeth was always so outspoken and did not behave in the way her mother thought a lady should. How could she ever have gained Mr. Darcy's attentions? She had much about which to think.

CHAPTER 19

THE REMAINING DAYS before the Netherfield ball passed quickly. Much excitement and activity filled the Bennet household each day as the girls readied their gowns for the ball. As usual Lydia and Kitty had listened to their mother and added more and more lace to their dresses. Mary, whose style was very plain, had purchased only a new pearl gray ribbon to tie around the waist of her dress. Jane bought some lace and threaded a narrow, pale blue ribbon through it, which she attached it to her collar, sleeves, and hem. She purchased a wider ribbon in the same color to tie at the empire waist of her gown and had another in the same shade to thread through her hair. As for Elizabeth, she chose accessories in shades of lavender.

Though not yet out, Darcy gave permission for Georgiana to sit and watch the dancing with Mrs. Annesley and to attend dinner so that she could hear the announcement of his courtship before retiring for the night.

Georgiana could not wait to visit Elizabeth and share the good news. She wanted to talk about what they would wear and how they would have their hair done. On a morning call to Longbourn, she was surprised to find all of the Bennet sisters in the parlor working on their dresses. It was a surprise to Georgiana that they had to remake old clothes and not just purchase new ones. It made her aware of how fortunate her family was financially. She realized that perhaps the tenants and their children often had to remake their clothes and thought that when she was back at Pemberley, she could do some sewing for children of the tenant families. She would discuss it with Elizabeth and her brother first, however.

The young ladies all welcomed Georgiana warmly, and she sat with them to converse while they worked. She complimented Mary on the delicacy and evenness of her stitches and Lydia on the delightful design of the bonnet she was trimming to go with her gown. Georgiana admired the rose color that Kitty had selected for her trim. As for Jane, she told her she had found the perfect ribbons as they matched her eyes exactly and intensified the color. When she looked at what Elizabeth was doing to her dress, she knew that William would be delighted by her appearance. Jane, Elizabeth, and Georgiana were going up to Elizabeth's room to discuss hairstyles. Seeing that Kitty and Lydia had gone off on their own, Elizabeth invited Mary to join them. Mary was surprised, but very pleased, to be included.

The four girls passed a pleasant time talking about hairstyles and even convinced Mary to try a less severe style for the ball. When they showed her what they had in mind, Mary was shocked at her reflection. She actually looked pretty. Mary was the forgotten sister and was considered very plain beside the others. It was not necessarily true, but she had never allowed herself to try to look her best because she was certain she would still not get noticed amongst her sisters.

"Miss Mary, you look absolutely lovely!" Georgiana exclaimed.

"Indeed you do, Mary!" Elizabeth added enthusiastically.

"You look very pretty," Jane remarked.

With tears in her eyes, Mary's reflection looked back at them as she softly whispered, "Thank you all so much. I enjoyed being included with you, and I never dreamed that I could look like this."

Elizabeth looked at her sister and said, "I am very sorry, Mary. I have not given you as much time or attention as you deserve. I hope you can forgive me?"

Mary rose from the bench in front of the dressing table and threw her arms around Elizabeth as she replied, "Of course, I forgive you. You have always been good to me, and I so admire your kindness to everyone."

Before long the four young ladies were all in tears with hugs and laughter all around. Georgiana spoke up saying, "Thank you for letting me experience what it is like to have sisters. I so hope that you will truly be my sisters someday!"

The girls laughed and talked until they fell upon the bed in giggling heaps. After they had calmed somewhat, Georgiana and Mary decided to go practice the pianoforte while Elizabeth and Jane returned to the parlor to await the arrival of their gentlemen for tea. They did not have long to wait, and the two couples passed a very pleasant afternoon. Elizabeth and Jane walked out with their guests to say their farewells, unhappy that they would not see the others until tomorrow night at the ball.

The day of the ball dawned bright and clear with a touch of frost upon the ground and a chill in the air. Elizabeth bundled up for her walk, knowing that she would need time away from the house and her mother's screeching directions and nervous flutterings as they prepared for the big event. She walked in the direction of the border with Netherfield soon finding herself at the fence. As she looked out across the field, she could see two horses racing across a far meadow. She immediately knew which was Mr. Darcy, and imagined by the flash of red, that the other was his cousin, Colonel Fitzwilliam, who had been expected to arrive the previous afternoon to attend the ball. She was a little disappointed that William had not ridden towards their usual meeting place this morning, but decided he may not have realized she would walk out on the morning of the ball. Elizabeth had watched them race for some time before she turned her steps back to Longbourn. She joined her family for breakfast where Kitty and Lydia could barely contain their excitement about the evening's activity. Mr. Bennet looked up from his newspaper and gave both of them a stern glance with one eyebrow raised.

"Kitty and Lydia, I hope you will remember our discussion of the other day. If you cannot behave in an appropriate manner at the ball, you will be sent home early.

"But, Papa," Lydia whined, "I want to laugh and dance with all the officers."

"You and Kitty may do those things, Lydia, as long as the two of you keep the tone of your voices moderated and wait for the officers to come to you. I will expect you to stand near your mother in between every set. I also expect you to keep away from the punchbowl. You are to have nothing stronger than lemonade. Do I make myself clear?" he asked them pointedly.

"Yes, Papa," they murmured in unison.

"There will be no second chances or reminders. At the first sign of misbehavior, you will be sent home." Mr. Bennet directed a speaking look at his wife reminding her that the same rules applied to her. Satisfied that he had been understood, Mr. Bennet excused himself from the table and took his paper to the library where he could finish it in peace.

Shortly after luncheon an express arrived for Darcy. He looked at the handwriting upon the letter and let out a groan. He excused himself from the others gathered in the parlor and went to his room to read the message from his Aunt Catherine. Seeing the look on his face and recognizing the handwriting Richard excused himself shortly after Darcy left and made his way to his cousin's chamber.

Pouring himself a brandy Darcy settled into a chair near the window and opened the letter to read the following:

Rosings Park
Kent

Dear Nephew,

Recently a report of a most serious nature has come to my ears. My parson, Mr. Collins, says that he met you while visiting his family in Hertfordshire. He informs me that you are involved in a courtship with his cousin whom he wishes to marry. However, as I realized that this young woman is related to Collins, and consequently so far beneath us, I deduced it could not possibly be true, especially in light of your long-standing engagement with Anne.

After much reflection, I can only assume that you are following the practice of so many young men of this day. As she is supposedly a gentlewoman, I imagine it was necessary to request a courtship to be able to take full advantage of this young person. Though I am somewhat surprised at your behaving in such a manner, I can only hope that it means you are having this last indulgence in preparation of finally marrying Anne. That being the situation, enjoy yourself and do not worry about any consequences. I can always make Mr. Collins marry her after you break it off with this nobody.

I shall expect to see you at Rosings for Easter if not sooner, nephew.

Lady Catherine de Bourgh

With each word he read, Darcy's anger increased. By the time he had finished reading his Aunt's letter, he was absolutely livid. "Damn," Darcy swore loudly, causing two doors to open into his chamber.

"Sir, may I be of assistance?" Chalmers, a worried expression on his face, stood at the dressing room door. He was surprised at the outburst, as it was very unusual for Mr. Darcy to use such language.

"What does the old witch say, Darcy?" Richard had rushed into Darcy's room on hearing the oath and closed the door behind him.

Darcy looked up in surprise from the letter he held crumpled in his hand. "No, Chalmers. There is nothing I need at present."

"Yes, sir, but you need only call if you should change your mind." The valet cast a confused glance at the Colonel and retreated into the dressing room.

Darcy waved Richard further into the room. Taking a large gulp of his brandy, he handed the letter to Richard to read, as he resumed his pacing. Richard poured himself a drink before settling in a chair to read his aunt's letter. By the time he had finished it, Richard's mouth was hanging open in shock.

He looked up at Darcy, an incredulous look on his face. "Do you think she has lost her senses? Can she really believe that you, of all people, would behave in such a manner?"

Darcy cast a glare in Richard's direction as he continued to pace. Richard took a drink of his brandy as he watched Darcy continue to pace.

"How could she accuse me of such foul behavior? Does she really think so little of me as to believe that I would take advantage of any gently-born young woman in such a fashion?"

"It is more likely she is just assuming you would behave as she would. You know that she would not scruple to use anyone if it suited her purposes."

"But her insults of Elizabeth are completely beyond belief! How could she dare to dismiss her so when she has not even met her?"

"Darcy, calm down and think rationally. You know that she would insult anyone you showed an interest in who was not Anne. If I were you, I would be grateful that she does not believe you are truly interested in Elizabeth. It gives you time to secure her as your wife before having to deal with Aunt Catherine further."

Darcy paused in his pacing and looked at Richard. Slowly a small smile—more a grimace than a smile—appeared on his face. "Perhaps you are correct, Richard. I will ignore this letter from Aunt Catherine and work on convincing Elizabeth to be my wife."

"I do not think you will have to work very hard, but you may want to work quickly before Aunt decides to question you further on this subject," Richard said with a grin.

"I should be safe until at least Easter, do you not agree?" Darcy asked hopefully. He took a seat in the chair near Richard and took a deep drink of his brandy. Finally, his shoulders relaxed, and he leaned back into the comfort of the chair. Darcy wadded up the letter and made to toss it into the fire, but Richard stopped him.

"Perhaps you should hang onto that letter Darcy. I am sure that my father would find its contents of interest. Who knows—perhaps it will give you or father some leverage in a future discussion with her on this subject."

Darcy paused for a moment in thought, then handed the letter to Richard. "Here, you keep it if you think it could be useful. I never wish to see that piece of trash again," Darcy stated with finality.

Darcy and Richard were returning to the drawing room when an unexpected, and most unwelcome, voice was heard coming from within. They entered to see Miss Bingley standing there with another young woman. Charles was on his feet facing his sister, and the looks being given to the uninvited visitor by the Hursts were far from welcoming.

"What are you doing here, Caroline. I was under the impression you were spending the holidays in town."

"Why, Charles, where else would I be when my dear brother is hosting a ball. And, I knew you would not mind if I brought my dear friend. You remember Miss Evelyn Pottsfield? We attended seminary together."

"Good afternoon, Miss Pottsfield. It is nice to see you again," Bingley offered politely. "Welcome to Netherfield. I hope your trip was pleasant."

Miss Pottsfield, whose appearance was rather mousey, was a somewhat shy but pleasant young woman of good intelligence. She had always found Mr. Bingley attractive and was surprised, but happy, to accept Caroline's invitation to her brother's ball. However, she had quickly realized that Caroline's presence was not welcomed by her family. Miss Pottsfield blushed and stammered as she tried to respond to Mr. Bingley's greeting. "It was, sir. I hope that our arrival has not caused you any inconvenience."

Speaking up Louisa assured the young woman that she was most welcome. She noted that Mrs. Dawson was standing in the doorway and asked her to show their guest to her room.

Caroline turned to assure her friend she would be up directly and noticed Darcy and the Colonel standing there. Practically knocking Miss Pottsfield aside, Caroline rushed to greet Darcy. "Mr. Darcy, Colonel Fitzwilliam, how lovely to see you both again." Caroline offered her hand to Darcy, who ignored it and gave her only the briefest of bows.

Waving her hand airily, Caroline finally turned to Miss Pottsfield. "I shall have some refreshments sent to my sitting room and we can enjoy them there before we rest and prepare for the ball. Be sure to ask the servants for anything you need."

"This way, Miss," said Mrs. Dawson as she escorted the young woman from the room, making sure to close the doors behind as they departed.

As the sound of the ladies footsteps faded away, Darcy announced that he and the Colonel were off to the billiard room, requesting that Bingley join him at his earliest convenience. Bingley halted his exit, saying Darcy had every right to remain for the conversation with Caroline.

The Colonel moved to the far side of the room and stood looking out the window. Darcy moved to stand near the fireplace, his face an inscrutable mask and his eyes hard. Mr. and Mrs. Hurst were seated on a loveseat together, and Charles was still on his feet facing his sister.

"Why did you return, Caroline? I told you were not welcome here at present."

"I told you, Charles, I am here to attend the ball."

"How did you even find out about it?" Charles's anger was evident in his voice and his stance.

"I am sorry, Charles, but it is my fault," said Louisa. "Caroline had complained about my slow reply to her last letter. I mentioned in passing how busy I was with the plans for the ball as a reason for my delay. I never dreamed she would take it as an invitation to return."

"Since when do I need an invitation to attend a ball hosted by my family?" Caroline cried indignantly.

"You need one when I had strictly forbidden your presence in my home. It was quite creative of you to ask Miss Pottsfield to join you. It gave you free transportation, and you knew I would not be able to send you packing the minute you arrived. I would have done just that had you arrive alone."

"Your behavior in the short time you have been here has proved you learned nothing from our discussion prior to your departure. Here me well, Caroline, for I will say this only once. If you cannot be polite to the members of the Bennet family, it would be best if you remain in your room."

"There is no need to be tedious, Charles. I certainly know how to behave at a ball."

"By the way, I am officially courting Miss Jane Bennet, and I will not have you disparaging any of them. Do I make myself clear?"

Caroline Bingley rose from her chair moving towards the door. "I hope you will be happy, Charles, and not come to regret your choice," she called over her shoulder, as she swept from the room.

All those present stared speechlessly at the doorway, through which she had just departed. Eventually, a great deal of conversation took place as they determined the best way to deal with Caroline. They determined she would not join the family in the receiving line. The Hursts and the Colonel also offered to do their best to keep her occupied and away from the two courting couples. Darcy and Bingley both hoped they would be able to enjoy this special evening without disruption. There was also some discussion regarding Miss Pottsfield as they tried to determine if she would aid Caroline in her mischief. Louisa assured the gentlemen that she was a kind and pleasant young lady.

After partaking of tea, everyone separated to prepare for the ball. No formal dinner was planned before the ball so the residents would be receiving trays in the rooms.

Upon her appearance in the drawing room before the ball began, Mrs. Hurst introduced Miss Pottsfield to the guests in residence. She was a petite young woman with light brown hair and eyes of an unusual light gray color. All those in attendance found her quite pleasant. When asked where Miss Bingley was, Miss Pottsfield replied that she had returned to her room for her forgotten fan.

The Bennet family was one of the first to arrive at Netherfield. They were greeted cordially by Mr. Bingley and Mr. and Mrs. Hurst. Darcy was awaiting Elizabeth near the entrance to the ballroom, and as she moved away from the receiving line and he caught his first glimpse of her, he was stopped in his tracks. Georgiana giggled from her position at his side. Elizabeth had stitched a gauzy pale lavender overskirt to her ball gown. It was drawn up around the hem in a scalloped pattern showing the white underdress with rosettes made of a darker shade of lavender. Small roses in the same dark shade had been stitched around the neckline of her bodice, and there was another rosette on the outside of each of her short sleeves pulling them up into a scallop, as well. In her hair, ribbons of both colors were mixed in with her braids and curls. Elizabeth blushed prettily as she saw the look on Darcy's face and in his eyes and gave him a beautiful smile as she moved in his direction.

"Miss Elizabeth, you look stunning this evening. I do hope that you have penciled my name in for the dances we previously discussed." Darcy gave her one of his dimpled smiles.

"Of course, Mr. Darcy, I look forward to our dances with great anticipation."

Darcy presented an arm to each of his favorite ladies and moved with them into the ballroom. They found the area where Mrs. Annesley was sitting and moved in that direction. After shyly hugging Elizabeth in welcome, Georgiana took her seat with her companion. Darcy had just informed Elizabeth of Miss Bingley's unexpected arrival when they were joined by the Colonel and Miss Pottsfield. She was introduced to Miss Elizabeth and the three young ladies conversed amiably. Charlotte and John Lucas had joined the group and been introduced to Miss Pottsfield. John had asked Miss Pottsfield for the first dance.

Soon the sound of the musicians warming up for the opening set was heard. Guests were moving about looking for their partners for the opening set. Suddenly a flash of color appeared in the ballroom door. Miss Bingley was finally making an appearance. She was dressed in her usual burnt orange and there were several tall feathers adorning her hair. She was also wearing an overabundance of jewelry. Rather than the breathtaking effect she thought she would create, many who viewed her appearance found her gaudy. She had assumed that Mr. Darcy would be so overwhelmed he would rush to her side. Instead, it was necessary to hide her annoyance when only Colonel Fitzwilliam appeared.

A musical flourish let the guests know the first set was about to begin. As the host, Mr. Bingley, and Jane were at the top of the set, next came Mr. and Mrs. Hurst, then Darcy and Elizabeth, Colonel Fitzwilliam and Miss Bingley stood next to them. The Colonel had asked Miss Bingley to dance out of pity for the woman. He also knew it would be a good way to keep an eye on her and keep her from mischief. Caroline was furious that she was not opening the ball with Darcy but knew that she could only appear at an advantage standing next to Eliza. He could not fail to notice how much more attractive and fashionable her dress was and how much more gracefully she danced. She was sure that Mr. Darcy would beg her for the next set.

The dance began, but William had eyes only for his beautiful Elizabeth. They smiled at one another with each pass they made. Darcy always clasped her fingers for a second longer than necessary when their hands would meet giving them a little squeeze before he released them. They did not need words; their eyes spoke for them, and many of the guests thought what a handsome couple they made. As they changed partners and Darcy had Miss Bingley's hand, his eyes remained fixed on Elizabeth, and his hand barely touched hers. Caroline tried to draw him into conversation, but with no success. Her anger grew with each passing minute.

All too soon, the set ended, and Darcy returned Elizabeth to where Georgiana sat waiting. "Oh, Elizabeth, you dance beautifully. You and William make a very handsome couple," she enthused.

"I would have to agree with Miss Darcy. You dance very well together. It was very noticeable to all those observing," added Mrs. Annesley.

Darcy stiffened and his mask slipped into place at the thought others had been staring at them. Elizabeth noticed the tension now radiating from his body and gently placed her hand on his arm.

"It is alright, William," she whispered. "You are not in this alone; I am here to protect you." She gave him a winsome smile and watched as he relaxed enough to return a slight smile of his own. Very quickly, Bingley came to claim Elizabeth, and Darcy danced with Jane. Richard asked Mary Bennet to dance having been surprised by her appearance upon first seeing her arrive. She was much prettier than he recalled. With Richard's attentions upon her, Mary was even seen to smile during her dance. When it was over, he returned her to her mother and asked both of her younger sisters for a dance later in the evening. Then as the third set began, he took up his place near his cousin as Darcy stared at Elizabeth and her partner from the side of the ballroom. He was able to converse slightly with his cousin, but Fitzwilliam never fully gained his attention. When Elizabeth returned to him, he took her hand and placed it on his arm with his other hand on top of hers as if holding her to his side. Elizabeth looked at him with an amused expression but did not tease him. The three of them conversed pleasantly until the next set began, which belonged to Richard. This time when Elizabeth came back to his side, it was again Darcy's turn to dance with her as the supper set had arrived. As they took their places, they laughed and conversed through the entire set.

At its conclusion, Darcy led Elizabeth into the supper room followed by Richard and Georgiana. They sat at a table with Bingley, Jane, the Hursts, and the two eldest Lucas siblings. Mr. and Mrs. Bennet were seated at a nearby table with Sir William and Lady Lucas, Mary, Kitty, and Lydia, as well as Maria Lucas. The gentlemen all left to fill plates for their partners. Once the majority of the people had begun to eat, Mr. Bennet called for everyone's attention. Standing, he began his announcements. "Some of you may have already heard this news, but tonight I would like to officially announce that my daughter, Jane, is being courted by Mr. Bingley. My next eldest, Elizabeth, is being courted by Mr. Darcy." The room filled with applause, as the eldest girls were well liked in the community. However, Miss Bingley was shocked by the news, and her anger was obvious. Miss Pottsfield, who had already pieced together much about the reason behind Miss Bingley's unexpected invitation, noted her reaction. She now realized she had been used as a means of transportation. Caroline had obviously done something to upset her family that resulted in her being sent back to town. Her presence at the ball was neither expected nor wanted.

Following dinner, Mr. Bingley called for some entertainment. Rather than allow guests to display first, Miss Bingley rushed to the pianoforte and began to play and sing an Italian love song, staring at Darcy as she sang. Darcy was oblivious to her efforts as his attention was centered solely on Elizabeth. Miss Bingley's song received polite applause, and she was forced to vacate the instrument for the next young lady. Mr. Bingley asked Elizabeth and Mary to play. Georgiana had been working with Mary on a piece that she and Elizabeth could perform together. Mary sat down to the instrument and began to play an aria by Mozart. Elizabeth then began to sing. At the completion of their song, not a sound could be heard. Then the audience broke out into riotous applause. Darcy stood to meet them. Above the applause, Miss Bingley was heard to remark to her friend, in a louder than necessary voice, that the performance would never be acceptable in the first circles, but what could one expect in such an unremarkable village. Again, Miss Pottsfield shook her head, embarrassed by Miss Bingley's behavior, and she walked away without a word. Several of those nearby cast scathing glances in Miss Bingley's direction.

Darcy raised his voice slightly above normal and remarked, "Miss Mary, I do not think I have ever heard you play better. That was a marvelous performance." Mary blushed at the praise as

Darcy assisted her to her seat. Darcy escorted Elizabeth back to their table holding her chair for her to be seated. Leaning down close to her ear he whispered, "You have the voice of an angel, my dear. I look forward to hearing you sing for me often in the future." The sound of his voice at her ear sent a frisson of heat down her spine and a blush to her cheeks.

Before the next performance could begin, Lydia's loud voice could be heard calling to Lt. Denny reminding him he owed her another dance. Her voice had to compete with that of her mother who was saying that she knew how it would be that Jane would catch a rich man, as she could not be so beautiful for nothing. After another performance or two, the sound of the musicians warming up had everyone returning to the ballroom. Darcy and Elizabeth walked with Georgiana to the bottom of the grand staircase where they said good night to her and watched her walk up to where Mrs. Annesley awaited her.

As they turned to make their way to the ballroom, they noted Mr. Bennet at the door with Mrs. Bennet and Lydia, who could both be heard complaining that they did not wish to go home. Mr. Bennet firmly reminded them of his decree that poor manners would not be tolerated. He asked the footman to call for their carriage. Lydia whined, "I cannot go home, Papa, as I am engaged for every dance."

Seeing Darcy and Elizabeth near the staircase, he said, "Elizabeth, please let everyone know that both Mrs. Bennet and Lydia have come down with headaches. I will escort them home and return for the rest of you."

"Certainly, Papa," Elizabeth replied with confusion. She could hardly believe that her father was standing up to the whining and complaints of her mother and youngest sister.

Once in the ballroom, Darcy again remained on the sidelines, watching Elizabeth dance with others of the neighborhood, friends from her childhood. Completely ignoring Miss Pottsfield, Miss Bingley hovered near Darcy, attempting to draw him into conversation and hoping to manipulate him into asking her to dance. Unfortunately for her, he gave only terse, one-word replies, still angered by her earlier comments about Elizabeth's performance. Frustrated with Darcy for his inability to see her superiority, she stalked away, but only a short distance where she could observe him unseen.

Shortly after Miss Bingley left his side, the colonel sauntered over clapping his hand down hard on his cousin's shoulder. Richard whispered, "If you do not stop glaring at Miss Elizabeth and her partners, you are going to scare her away. I know that she has deep feelings for you, Darcy. You do not have to be jealous. I do not think wild horses could drag her away from you," the Colonel said with a wide smile. "What will you do when she is in London? You know that her beauty will draw the attention of many men. You cannot fight them all off." The Colonel chuckled and even got a small grin out of his cousin with his comments.

Caroline Bingley had heard every word of their conversation and was furious. That nobody, Eliza Bennet, was going to London to be seen with Mr. Darcy! She had to stop it, and, if she could not, she would have to find some way to discredit Eliza so that Darcy would turn away from her. And she, Caroline, would be waiting there for him to come to his senses and see her superior worth. Caroline decided that the best thing she could do to allay suspicion would be to begin enjoying the ball and ignoring Darcy altogether. Unfortunately for Miss Bingley, her unkind words about Elizabeth and Mary Bennet did not endear her to those in the neighborhood who had known the Bennet sisters since childhood. It was humiliating to her that she was not asked to dance, so Miss Bingley slipped from the ballroom and went up to her room for the night. I will ruin Eliza Bennet if it is the last thing I ever do, she vowed.

Finally, the last dance of the evening arrived, and Darcy again had Elizabeth back at his side. He took her hand firmly in his as he led her to the dance floor. Again they danced without words, but their eyes spoke all the words left unsaid. Darcy was ready to propose immediately, but he did not want to be unfair to Elizabeth. He felt she deserved an opportunity to know what her life in the ton would be like . . . what their future together would be. He had also promised Mr. Bennet that he would not pressure Elizabeth. He hoped she would still want to be with him after participating in the season because he did not think that he could live without her. He would do whatever was necessary to make her life happy.

The Bennet family was the last to leave the Netherfield ball, as the sky was just beginning to lighten with the approach of dawn.

CHAPTER 20

ELIZABETH FELL INTO her bed after the ball. It was near dawn, but sleep did not come quickly. Her whole body felt tingly as she remembered the look in William's eye during their last dance. She felt so flustered, she could barely remember the steps of the dance they were doing. How she got through it without tripping or turning the wrong way she would never know. Eventually, she snuggled down deeper into her bedcovers and drifted off to sleep with a soft smile on her lips, her thoughts and dreams all about the man who held her heart.

The morning after the ball, most of the Bennet household was late in rising. Elizabeth slept later than usual, as well, but it had only been five hours earlier that she retired for the night. She woke with the same smile and thoughts that had accompanied her to slumber and filled her dreams.

Knowing that it would be some time before the rest of the house was awake, she dressed for a walk and headed out the door in the direction of the fence. She did not expect to see William this early but wanted to be near him just the same.

When she arrived at the fence, there was no one in sight, so she turned in the direction of the path to Oakham Mount. As she reached the base of the mount, she heard hoof beats behind her. She moved to the side of the path and turned to see who approached. A blinding smile illuminated her face as she saw William coming towards her on his big black horse. He quickly dismounted, tied his horse to a tree just off the path and approached Elizabeth, his dimpled smile upon his face.

"How are you this morning, Elizabeth?" His eyes filled with a warmth that matched his smile. "I had not expected to see a young lady out so early after the ball. Miss Bingley will probably sleep until three this afternoon, which is a blessing for the rest of the household."

"Why, William, that is the most ungallant thing I have ever heard you say," Elizabeth teased, "though I am sure I would agree if I resided at Netherfield. Miss Bingley did not appear to enjoy herself last evening, and I am quite sure she will make her sentiments known to the household."

"I beg your pardon, Elizabeth, but my patience with her behavior has reached its limit. She showed up uninvited to attend the ball and generally made a nuisance of herself last evening. She seems incapable of understanding that I have no interest in her and would prefer that she leave me alone."

"Poor, William, I assume that is just the burden you must bear for being one of the most eligible young gentlemen in the country." Her eyes sparkled as she teased him, but she gently placed her hand on his arm in sympathy as she knew that he did not like to be the center of so much attention. I thought it abominable the way she used Miss Pottsfield to get to Netherfield and practically ignored her the rest of the time. I am surprised that Miss Pottsfield and Miss Bingley are friends. They seem to have nothing in common."

"I must agree with you. I found Miss Pottsfield to be a pleasant young woman when we spoke to her. I wonder what the relationship will be like this morning."

"I believe from talking to her that Miss Pottsfield's family may know my Aunt and Uncle Gardiner. Perhaps I will see her again in London," Elizabeth remarked. "I would not object to becoming better acquainted with her."

They slowly followed the path up Oakham Mount as they talked. Upon reaching the top, they sat upon a large boulder looking out upon the vistas below. They talked of the ball, and it reminded Elizabeth of a question she wished to ask, "William, were you upset about something last evening? Often, while I was dancing, I noticed you scowling as you watched. Was something particular distressing you?"

Darcy looked sheepish, his cheeks grew darker, and his eyes remained fixed upon the landscape as he replied, "It was nothing for you to be concerned about, Elizabeth."

"But I do not like seeing you distressed. I want to help, if I can."

Still Darcy refused to meet her eye. "I am afraid if you knew what it was, you might be angry at me," he mumbled.

"We will not know what I might think if you do not share it with me," she replied teasingly.

"I just found it difficult to watch you in the arms of other men. I want my arms to be the only ones that hold you," he said, turning to give her the penetrating gaze that made her shiver.

Not realizing the cause of her shiver, he spoke quickly, "We must have stayed too long outdoors, for you are shivering from the cold."

Now it was Elizabeth's turn to blush as she daringly replied, "I did not shiver because I am cold." The words came out in a whisper, and she would not look at him as she answered. If she had, she would have seen his smug expression as he took her meaning.

"Elizabeth, I wish I could see you later today, but I would not wish to impose on your family when I know everyone was out late last evening. I know Bingley would not mind my inviting you to Netherfield, but I cannot in good conscience subject you to the behavior I expect from Miss Bingley. May I call on you tomorrow morning? Perhaps Georgiana and I could accompany you into Meryton. I would enjoy another visit to Mr. Stevens' shop, and we could visit the tea shop before we return home."

"That sounds like a delightful plan, William. I will be looking forward to your arrival, but now I must return home. My father, at least will be awake, and I do not wish for him to worry."

Darcy rose from the boulder and extended a hand to help Elizabeth up. He then tucked her hand into the crook of his arm, and they made their way back down the path to where Darcy's horse was tethered. Darcy untied the horse and continued to walk with Elizabeth to the fence line between the properties where, after a lingering kiss to the back of her hand, they went their separate ways. He watched until Elizabeth was out of sight before mounting his horse and heading for the Netherfield stables. Upon returning he met Richard just heading out on a morning ride and decided to accompany him as his mount had not yet had a good run this morning.

When Elizabeth returned to the house, she heard her father moving about in his library. She knocked on the door and upon hearing his call entered with a cheery, "Good morning, Papa."

"Good morning, Lizzy," he replied with his eyebrows raised. "Where have you been so early this morning?"

"I wanted to walk and think, so I have been up on Oakham Mount."

"And what did you think about this bright morning?" he asked archly.

Elizabeth blushed as she replied, "Just going over the events of the ball. It was a wonderful evening."

Mr. Bennet chuckled as he noted the faraway look in her eyes. "Yes, it was a very interesting evening," he replied. "I believe that Mrs. Hill has put out breakfast in the dining room. Would you care to join me?" At her nod, Mr. Bennet extended his arm to Elizabeth and led her to the dining room. Father and daughter shared a quiet conversation as they broke their fast. Jane joined them halfway through the meal, and Mr. Bennet watched from behind his newspaper as Elizabeth and Jane discussed the ball. With them both being courted, moments like this will soon be gone, thought Mr. Bennet, as he felt his chest tighten.

The remainder of the day passed quietly—except when Lydia, Kitty, and Mrs. Bennet were discussing the ball. When the noise became intolerable, Mr. Bennet retired to his library, and Elizabeth to the window seat in her room. She held a book in her hands, but her eyes looked out the window towards Netherfield instead of at the pages. Realizing that her attention was elsewhere, Elizabeth decided to put all the details of the ball in a letter to her Aunt Gardiner. She closed it by telling her aunt how much she was looking forward to their visit for Christmas and to returning to town with them afterward.

At Netherfield, things did not go quite as Darcy had expected. He spent some time with Georgiana listening to her delighted recounting of her first ball and asking William endless questions about what happened after she retired. Colonel Fitzwilliam joined the siblings for this conversation, and the room rang with laughter.

During a light luncheon, Miss Pottsfield apologized for bringing Caroline into Hertfordshire. She said it had been immediately clear to her that she had not been expected. "Consequently, I have asked my coachman to prepare for departure and notified your sister of my plans. I thank you for the hospitality you extended to me, and I did enjoy the ball very much. You have chosen a delightful neighborhood in which to live, Mr. Bingley."

"Thank you. We do enjoy the area and were pleased to have you visit, even if only briefly."

Louisa added her thoughts on the matter. "Indeed, Miss Pottsfield, it is our family who should apologizing to you for Caroline's abominable behavior. It has been far too long since we were in company, however, and I truly enjoyed the chance to renew our acquaintance. Perhaps we will see each other while we are in town."

"I would enjoy that Mrs. Hurst. I also hope to see the Misses Bennet again as my family is acquainted with their London relations. Well, if you will excuse me, please. I will finish my preparations for departure. I look forward to seeing you in London."

When Miss Pottsfield next descended the stairs, Miss Bingley made her only appearance on the day. Her anger and frustration were obvious to all those present. She obviously did not wish to leave. However, she ignored Darcy completely, not even glancing in his direction, Had she done so should would have noted his delight with that fact. At this surprising behavior, Richard and William shared a confused look. She explained that Miss Pottsfield had to return to town immediately on a family matter, and she would be leaving with her. She asked Charles when he would be returning to town, but did not receive a satisfactory answer. His plans were to spend as much time with his "dear Jane" as possible. He promised to write Caroline if his plans changed. She told Louisa that she had arranged a lovely ball far nice that could be expected in such an unsophisticated village. "I am sure the locals had never seen anything quite like it and probably never would again," Miss Bingley remarked as she swept from the house.

Miss Pottsfield again offered her thanks and good wishes for the coming holiday season. Bingley walked out with Miss Pottsfield and helped her into the carriage.

As a result of Caroline's sudden exodus, the residents of Netherfield enjoyed a much more pleasant day than expected.

The time remaining before Darcy and Georgiana returned to town passed much too quickly for Elizabeth and William. Neither looked forward to their separation although they both knew it would be of short duration. They spent as much time together as possible, even doing a little Christmas shopping in Meryton.

Elizabeth talked much about her Aunt and Uncle Gardiner, and from her words, Darcy could tell how important they were to her. He noticed the hesitation in her voice as she gave him the Gardiners address in Cheapside. He also heard her small sigh when he took no notice of the information, except to confirm when Elizabeth would be arriving in London so that he could greet her at the Gardiners.

Darcy suggested that Jane join Elizabeth during her visit with the Gardiners. He thought Elizabeth might find the experience of participating in the ton more pleasant if her dear sister was with her. Jane and Elizabeth were indeed pleased with the prospect of sharing their first *season* together. Bingley was delighted with the idea. He and the Hursts decided to return to town in company with the Gardiners and Bennet sisters, and Bingley would stay briefly at Darcy House before moving on to his townhouse.

In a letter to her aunt, Elizabeth told her of the invitation Darcy extended for the Gardiners and their nieces to join them for dinner at Darcy House on New Year's Eve. Mrs. Gardiner gratefully accepted by return post. It was also arranged that Lady Matlock would join the Bennet sisters and their aunt for a trip to the dressmakers prior to dinner that same day. Elizabeth needed to have a fitting for the gown she would be wearing to the Twelfth Night ball.

The day of the Darcys' departure arrived much too quickly for Darcy and Elizabeth. Darcy recognized that this had been one of the nicest visits he had had with Bingley's family—especially after Miss Bingley's departure. Though he always enjoyed his time with Bingley, he realized he had actually enjoyed the company of Mr. and Mrs. Hurst, as well. They took a grateful leave of the hosts and talked of future plans when they all arrived in town. From there, the siblings made their way to Longbourn for additional farewells. There were a great many hugs exchanged between the young women as Darcy took a formal leave of Mr. and Mrs. Bennet.

Mr. Bennet eyed Darcy sternly, holding the hand he gripped tightly, saying, "I expect you to take the utmost care of my Lizzy while she is in London. I am entrusting you with my most precious of daughters and will be extremely put out if she is returned to me in less than perfect condition or unhappy in any way. Do I make myself clear, young man?"

Looking Mr. Bennet directly in the eye, William responded, "Sir, it will be my honor and pleasure to watch over her while she is away from you. I promise that my greatest desire is to ensure

Eliz . . . Miss Elizabeth's happiness and well-being."

"See that you do," was Mr. Bennet's only reply.

Darcy called to Georgiana that it was time to depart and assisted her into the carriage. Hearing her soft sniffles, Darcy sympathized; he felt as if his heart were being torn in two having to leave Elizabeth—even for this brief time. Georgiana placed herself next to the door so that she could see from the window of the carriage.

Darcy moved to where Elizabeth stood near the rear wheels of the carriage. With his back to her family, he whispered, "I do not wish to leave you. You do know I would not do so if it were not unavoidable." Elizabeth nodded, not raising her eyes. "May I write to you while we are apart?" he asked softly.

"You know that is not acceptable for a couple that is just courting," she said sadly.

"Perhaps I could include a page for you with Georgiana's letters. Would you allow me that?"

Elizabeth looked up at him, her eyes swimming with tears and nodded, a small smile turning up the corners of her mouth. "I would like that for I shall miss you so!"

Darcy could not bear to see her tears. "Come, my sweet Elizabeth. I cannot depart with tears as a remembrance, I must hear your delightful laugh." Still Elizabeth managed only a small smile for him. "What can I do to earn one of your sweet laughs before I depart?" He stood looking at her, a puzzled expression on his face. He tapped his chin as a myriad of thoughts raced through his mind.

"Perhaps this will earn me a smile and a laugh." Darcy looked deeply into her eyes and brought the hand he had been holding to his lips. "Goodbye my dearest," he placing a lingering kiss on the back of her hand, "loveliest," he turned her hand over and placed another kiss in her palm, "Elizabeth" he kissed the inside of her wrist. Her eyes had grown wider with each kiss she received. Finally, he turned her hand once again and bowed over it a final time. "Until we meet again, my sweet." He gave her a last brief kiss, glancing up at her and roguishly waggled his eyebrows as he gave her his devastating, dimpled smile.

At the sight of his waggling brows, Elizabeth's heart burst with happiness, and her unforgettable laugh bubbled forth.

"Now I shall have the memory of your wonderous laugh to keep with me until you are once again by my side. I will miss you," he whispered.

He quickly boarded the carriage, and it began to move down the drive. Darcy turned to stare at Elizabeth, his love shining forth in his eyes and his smile. Georgiana waved to everyone from the carriage window until it turned from the drive onto the road that would take the siblings to London.

Elizabeth remained in the drive long after the carriage disappeared from view. She had felt the tug at her heart at Darcy's departure. It was the piece of her he was taking with him. She knew her heart would not be whole again until they were reunited. Sighing, Elizabeth realized the three weeks before her arrival in London would seem much longer. *How could he have become so essential to my daily life so quickly* she wondered? She did not really care how it happened, but she was joyously happy it had!

Look for their continuing story in

Laughter through Trials,

which tells of Darcy and Elizabeth's courtship in London.

Available June, 2015

You can learn more about my books—current or new releases—by following my blog:

https://lindathompsonbooks.wordpress.com

You can contact the author at:

lindathompson.author@gmail.com

Made in the USA
Las Vegas, NV
30 July 2025

25604801R00239